THE ASYLUM

THE ASYLUM

Karen Coles

WELBECK

Published in 2021 by Welbeck Fiction Limited, part of Welbeck Publishing Group
20 Mortimer Street London W1T 3JW

A CIP catalogue record for this book is available from the British Library

Paperback ISBN: 978-1-78739-515-2
E-book ISBN: 978-1-78739-516-9

Printed and bound by CPI Group (UK) Ltd, Croydon, CR0 4YY

10 9 8 7 6 5 4 3 2 1

For my parents

PROLOGUE

Ashton House stands like an old lunatic, all sagging and bowed. How could I have known, that first day, that its occupants would be as warped as those deformed beams, as bent and twisted and sick in mind and spirit? Perhaps they infected me, the others. Or perhaps the madness emanated from the marsh itself, festered in its miasma, in the very air we breathed, for not one of us escaped. Not one.

CHAPTER 1

Crouched here among the hawthorns, shielded by their vicious spines, I should be safe while darkness lasts. It's a cloudy night with no stars and I'm surrounded by the marsh, with its hidden ditches and rivulets, its standing water, its ravenous, flesh-hungry mud.

The marsh could take me, of course. I am sick and faint with hunger, and it's cold, so cold, but perhaps it will be merciful. We are old friends, after all. It knows me well. The night air chills my bones. Waves of shivers run through me again and again. I long to be home, but home no longer exists, not for me.

A figure slips between the trees like a ghost, coming closer. It's a man come to kill me, or worse. Breathe. I must breathe. He can't see me here, not if I keep still and quiet, and hold my mouth open so as to silence my chattering teeth.

He looks about him, peering left and right. And straight ahead – straight at me.

He smiles.

I jump to my feet and turn to run. All is water, water and darkness.

He's almost here, slipping and sliding on the marshy ground, arms spread out like a scarecrow. Fall, please fall. Let the marsh take you; pull you under, cover your face. Let the marsh take you and save me.

Feet splash. The marsh tries, it sucks at his shoes, at his legs, but it's not enough. Dirty white hands reach for me, fingers clawing at my dress.

The water, it's in my ears, in my mouth.

I can't breathe, and the water . . .

Loud voices and blinding light, and the marsh is gone. A shadow looms over me. Before I can scream, she flips me over on to my stomach as if I were a dead fish on a slab and jabs me with a needle. After that there's no point in screaming because I know where I am: in the asylum, with no marsh anywhere about me and no man wishing to kill me.

My racing heart slows. Sounds grow muffled and blessed sleep draws me down into nothingness.

It's morning. On tiptoes, with my face pressed against the cold metal grille, I spy a distant copse of trees – hawthorns perhaps, with dark, shadowy marshland beyond, and lovers with limbs entwined, and dead bodies festering under the surface.

Sometimes, if I stare hard enough, I can imagine myself free of this place, out there in the fresh air with the grass under my feet and the cool wind blowing against my skin. Not today, though. It's impossible to concentrate on anything with the lunatics banging about in the ward next door. I turn my head and shout at the wall.

'Shut up!' I shout. 'Shut up!'

By the time I look back, the trees have vanished, blotted out by mist rolling in from the sea. I lower my heels to the floor and the countryside disappears, leaving an oblong of sky. I like sky as much as anyone, but I wish the window were lower, so I could see the world outside from my bed. What a luxury that would be. Perhaps there's another room I could have, with a bigger window and more light. I could ask, although they wouldn't give it to me even if they had one. They'd give it to someone well behaved, someone nice.

The metal grille is there to stop me escaping, although I don't know why they bother. The window's far too narrow to squeeze through, even for a thin girl like me, and it only opens a tiny bit, trapped by a metal catch. As if anyone would jump from here, anyway. It's a long way down. You'd land in the airing court below and break all your bones on the stone. It makes my knees go weak to think of it.

High-pitched screeching comes from next door, then a crash.

I wish the attendants would take the grille off *their* window. It's bigger than mine and they're all mad enough to jump out, one after the other, to land on the ground in a heap of broken bodies.

Then I'd have some peace.

Watery sunlight filters through the grille and makes a diamond pattern on the floor. For a fleeting moment it looks almost pretty, then it's gone. Light never stays near me for long – repulsed by the darkness within, no doubt.

The attendants say I've been mad for five whole years. They say it as if it's a long time. 'Only five years?' I say. 'Where have the other twenty-two gone, then?' They shrug. They don't know and neither do I. Twenty-two years vanished, as if they had never been. If it weren't for the memory of the marsh, I'd believe myself born here, mad from birth, but there *was* a marsh and the loss of it is like a hollow pain in my chest. It sits there and never moves.

CHAPTER 2

The sky turns white and overcast before I hear a key in the lock. An attendant in a blue dress and starched white apron opens the door. It's the one with the square face and double chin. Her neck's as broad as her head, with the kind of skin usually seen on boiled bacon. 'Doctor's here to see you,' she says.

It's not the usual doctor. My insides twist and tighten. Not that I like Doctor Womack. I wouldn't have tried to kill him if I did, would never have crushed his throat like that.

Where Womack is slick and slimy, with a drooping waxed moustache, this new doctor is clean-shaven and younger. He has kind eyes that crinkle when he smiles.

'Hello, Mary,' he says.

I should tell him my name's not Mary but Maud. It says Mary on my notes, though, and that's what they all call me, so perhaps I've got it wrong. I should know that, for goodness' sake. I should be certain about my own name.

He pulls up a chair. 'My name's Doctor Dimmond,' he says. 'Do you remember why you're in here, Mary?'

It annoys me, him calling me by the wrong name.

'Do you remember how you became ill, what caused it?'

'No.'

He looks at my notes, turns over one page, then another, frowning. His eyes move from side to side as he reads. He turns to Chins. 'Is this usual here – this level of sedation?'

'For this patient, yes.' She says it with a sniff. She doesn't like me. None of them do because I tried to kill Womack, or perhaps because I didn't succeed.

'Then I'm surprised the patient can stand up, let alone remember anything.'

'Her has nightmares, doctor, if we don't give her enough.'

'I see.' The doctor turns to me. 'Well. We'll reduce that and see how we get on.' He takes a book from his pocket, and hands it to me. It's a notebook with flowers on the cover. It's new and clean and no one has written in it.

'I'd like you to write down anything you remember about your past – anything at all. Any small detail will help.'

He doesn't know how things fly out of my head in an instant, but I nod anyway.

'Keep the notebook with you, so you always have it to hand should you recall anything.' He hands me a pencil with a pointed end. I wonder at that since I'm not allowed anything sharp. My eyes flash to Chins. She's spotted it but says nothing, afraid to go against the doctor. I slip it behind the book, out of sight. Perhaps she'll forget.

The doctor frowns. 'Can you write?'

'My father was a teacher.'

'You remember your father?' he says, quick as you like.

'No.' I don't know why I said it, where the words came from. 'It's probably not true.'

He purses his lips. 'Nevertheless, I should like to see what you remember of your past, true or otherwise.'

'I can't remember anything.'

He looks about him, smiles a wan smile. 'You may be surprised.' Another glance around the room and the smile fades. 'Perhaps if you were to lie down and close your eyes?'

I do as he says. These doctors are always trying to trick me into confessing my crimes – all those crimes I can't remember. Whatever I've done is gone now. The past has been snuffed out by the rotting secrets in my head, extinguished by their darkness. They will find nothing in there, no matter how hard they try. Not even the best of doctors can find what no longer exists.

'Relax, Mary, and unclench your hands.'

'It's Maud,' I say. 'My name is Maud.'

There's the sound of a pen scratching on paper. 'Well, that's a good start,' he says, and I think, It's like shelling peas, this. Easy.

'Breathe deeply,' he says. 'Let your muscles relax.'

My fingers are stiff and unyielding, slow to straighten.

'Imagine you are somewhere safe, somewhere beautiful, and try to picture it in your mind's eye.'

Hawthorns. Hawthorns and dank water at the dead of night.

'Imagine yourself walking in this safe place,' he says.

Walking? In that marsh? At night?

'All is peaceful,' he says. 'Nothing can harm you here.'

Someone shouts in the corridor. Footsteps pound on the floor. The vibration reaches my bed.

'Where are you now?' the doctor says.

'In my room.' I open my eyes.

He nods, writes something on my notes. 'Interesting. You didn't remember anything – anything at all?'

'No.'

'Did you see a place where you felt safe?'

'No.'

He nods, scribbles more notes. 'No matter. Hypnosis will reveal more.'

'Hypnosis?'

'You may know it as mesmerism.'

I sit up at that. 'Mesmerism? Like in the music halls?' He means to make a fool of me, a spectacle. 'And have you all laughing at me? No.'

He holds up a hand. 'No one will laugh. You will remain still at all times, and simply drift back in time.' He smiles. 'Hypnosis will allow us to reach your subconscious mind, find memories you've long forgotten.' He's looking away, closing his notebook. 'I am going to unlock your past.'

'But what if I don't want it unlocked?'

'You have nothing to fear.' His eyes are open and honest and warm. It's foolish, perhaps, to be swayed by beautiful eyes. They've betrayed me before, after all.

'Doctors in France have had excellent results in cases of hysteria,' he says. 'I believe it could also treat your sickness.'

'My sickness?'

'Traumatic amnesia.' He leans forward and a diamond of light falls on the middle of his forehead, like a jewel, or a third eye. 'Sometimes after a catastrophe . . .' His voice softens. 'After a frightening or upsetting event –' he thinks I don't understand the word *catastrophe* '– our minds choose to forget. They hide whatever it is away. It's how we protect ourselves – a survival strategy. After all, no one wants to be frightened all the time, do they?'

I don't tell him I'm always frightened, have been frightened for as long as I can remember.

'I've always been ill,' I say, instead.

'No.' His smile makes me want to cry. 'No, you haven't. Once you were well.'

There was a time before the madness, then, and this Diamond doctor wants to bring it back.

I'm not sure that's a good idea. Not sure at all.

The notebook is mine to keep. I can scarcely believe it. Everything else belongs to the asylum, even the clothes I wear, but this pencil and notebook are mine. I open the cover and stroke the pages. It smells clean and new, uninfected by the stink of the asylum. I look about me for somewhere safe to hide it. There are plenty of gaps in this room. Behind the table, there's a good-sized space between the floorboards and the wall. The flowery notebook slips in neatly.

Chins brings my medication after supper. It's half the amount I usually have.

'I'll be watching you.' She shoves her face close to mine. 'Any nonsense, and Doctor Womack will sort you out.'

I stare into her eyes until she looks away.

Once the lights are doused, I curl up in bed and wonder about my father. A teacher, I said. Where did that come from? There's nothing in my head about a teacher, or even a father. No picture, no face, body, voice, or smell. There is not even an empty space where a father should be. Is he dark-haired like me? Do I have his eyes, his nose? Perhaps he has a moustache like Womack, or crinkly eyes like Diamond. How can I have forgotten him so completely, my own father? And yet he must have forgotten me, too, or else he would surely come and free me from this place. He would come and take me home.

I drift into sleep, my mind reaching for this man, this man who perhaps loved me, cared for me, but he's not there. There is only the marsh, the same as ever.

CHAPTER 3

It's a week since I saw the new doctor. I'm waiting to feel different, clear-headed, awake, but I'm as weary as ever, my head filled with a low buzzing sound. Flies, perhaps, clustered over putrefying flesh crawling with maggots. A dead body dragged out of the marsh.

How threadbare my dress has become at the elbows and cuffs, and grubby, too. I pull it on and slip the pencil up my sleeve. It's cool and hard and the sharp point scratches my skin when I move. It's a comfort, knowing it's there, protecting me.

Someone's running up and down the stairs, laughing. You'd think the attendants would stop her, but no. They must all be deaf. If my door weren't locked, I would put a stop to that nonsense. 'Shut up!' I shout. She can't hear me, of course, not while she's making that racket.

The chapel bell is ringing now, too. An ominous bong, bong, bong. That's all I need. It's hard enough to think as it is, without that din. I wait for it to stop, but it doesn't. It goes on and on all morning.

Perhaps someone's escaped. Lucky them. Oh, lucky them. How I wish it were me out there in the crisp, clear air, running for my life – running and running. How I wish it were me.

An attendant with a face like a prune brings my dinner – a bowl of something green, a lump of bread and a cup of water. The bowl and cup are made of tin. No sharp edges for us, no shards of china. She places them on the table near the door. The table wobbles. Water slops over the side of the cup and makes a mess. She pretends not to notice and backs away, closing the door behind her.

The table always wobbles when something's placed on it because one leg is shorter than the other three, its foot gnawed by mice or rats or, perhaps, lunatics.

I wander over and check the door but it's shut fast. No escape today, then. It's probably just as well. I wouldn't get very far with my head all mushy like this. I peer into the bowl. It's celery – the something green – stalks and leaves, stewed and stringy.

Darkness shifts across my room like a veil. A sudden draught hits the back of my neck, cold and sharp. It smells of the marsh. It smells of him, stinking and rotten.

Someone's breathing, breathing behind me. Those jagged breaths are not mine. A shiver runs across my skin, raises the hairs.

The floor turns to mud beneath my feet – mud and grass and foetid water.

And suddenly I'm there in the marsh, running in the dark. My shoes slip and slide on mud and wet leaves. He's coming. His feet splash through the water, close behind me now, too close.

He catches at my hair. I reach out but there's nothing to hold on to, nothing to save me. I fall back. Pain fills my head, sharp and stinging.

Trees rush past, banks and ditches. He's dragging me by the hair, tearing it from my scalp.

My screams are silent, swallowed by the marsh.

There is only him, his laboured breathing, and his rage.

The bowl slips from my fingers, falls, crashes to the floor. I stare at it, at the mess, and a wave of trembling takes over my body. Where's the marsh? The pondweed? I can smell it – the mud, the still water.

No, no, it's the slop I can smell. It's everywhere: spattered over the wall, the floor, the table legs. Bits of onion, celery and potato lie strewn about me. I scoop up the slime in shaking hands and tip it into the bowl, then put it back on the table, wiping my palms clean on the rim. Perhaps no one will notice. Most of the liquid has seeped between the floorboards already. It smells, but my room always smells. I doubt the attendants will notice the difference.

I eat the lump of bread.

The lunatics are on the move next door. Their feet make a shuffling sound on the floor. The maniac's still laughing, pounding up and down the stairs, and there goes the bell. Bong, bong, bong.

'Can you tell them to stop ringing that bell?' I say, when Chins and Prune come that afternoon.

Chins frowns. 'What bell?'

'What *bell*? Are you deaf?'

'Course we'll tell them.' Prune clutches my arm. 'Come on. The new doctor wants to see you.'

'But I'm not ready.' I'm eager to leave my room, but wary of this new doctor and his kind eyes. What if the hypnosis leads to the truth, to the poison at the heart of my madness?

They're talking to each other, so perhaps they don't hear me.

'He's going ahead with it, then, this new treatment?' Prune says, as they lead me into the corridor.

Chins grunts. 'His nibs is none too happy about it, by all accounts.'

'Well, it's nonsense, isn't it?' Prune's eyes slide to me and away. 'Hypnosis, I ask you.'

'Are you talking about Doctor Diamond?' I say.

Chins bends towards me. Her hot breath hits my cheek. 'It's Dimmond. Doctor Dimmond.' She says it slowly, enunciating every syllable. 'Dim – mond.'

'Leave 'er be,' Prune says.

Chins backs away.

I don't care if Dimmond *is* his real name. I'm going to call him Diamond anyway because of his third eye, which must be a sign. Besides, a diamond is something bright and clear and pure, and I'm hoping he's all of those things.

The attendants lead me to the ground floor, but we turn left instead of right, down a corridor forbidden to us lunatics.

'Why *her*, of all people?' Chins says, and I wonder that myself. Why has Diamond chosen me? Why not one of the others, the really mad people, like the laughing maniac, or the ones who think they're on fire, or friends with the king? Why not them?

'He's picking the ones what can't remember,' Prune says. 'Or so I've heard.'

I'm glad it's me, glad to escape my prison room, but I'm not having any of that hypnosis lark. I can do without that on top of everything else.

We stop in front of a door which has Diamond's name written on it in gold lettering, newly painted and shiny.

'Ah, Maud,' he says. 'Here you are.' It's been so long since someone called me by my true name. 'Come in.'

I've forgotten what he looked like. His eyes are brown, not blue, and he's older than I first thought, a grown man. Perhaps it's the lack of moustache that made him seem younger.

Prune leaves but Chins sits on a chair by the wall, hands folded in her lap. I expect she's staying to protect Diamond.

His room is cosy. A warm fire burns in the grate, the coals glowing red and orange. There's a grille on the window just like mine, but the window's much larger, with a view of the gardens, the beautiful trees and the chapel. How I wish I had this room, this window, this view.

Curios sit on shelves and in cabinets – strange-shaped bottles and fossils, lots of them.

He points to the corner of the room where a shabby, beige curtain hangs on the wall. A chair stands in front of it, and a camera on tall legs. 'I'm going to take your photograph.' He leads me to the chair. 'Look into the camera,' he says, and disappears under a black cloth. A light flashes and the camera explodes. I'm expecting it, but I still jump.

My heart clatters as Diamond appears from under the cloth, hair sticking up at the back.

After the photograph, I sit in the chair across the desk from him. It's a good chair, with a curved back and arms. I run my hands over the polished wood, smooth from years of use.

There's tea on a tray sitting on top of the cabinet – a pot decorated with yellow roses, matching china cups and saucers, and small silver teaspoons.

Diamond pours the tea. He drops two lumps of sugar into each cup and stirs, then hands a cup and saucer to me, and one to Chins.

Her eyes widen as if she's never seen a cup of tea before. 'Thank you, doctor.'

Sitting here like this, holding a bone china cup and saucer, reminds me of something or someone. It reminds me of me – the 'before' me, drinking tea from a cup and saucer like an ordinary, sane person. A different me. A different life, long, long before it happened, the thing I can't remember.

I drink every drop. It's been months, maybe years since I had tea. They always give me water these days, or tepid milk on the turn. A punishment of sorts, I suppose.

Diamond looks across the desk. 'This photograph will show how you are before hypnosis. Once the treatment is complete, we'll take another and see what a difference it makes.' He seems very confident there *will* be a difference. 'I've been thinking,' he continues, 'there's no reason . . .'

Chins is perched on the edge of her seat. She can't be comfortable, sitting right on the edge of a wooden chair like that. I shuffle forward and try it. No, it's definitely not comfortable. I shuffle back again.

Diamond's been talking but I've missed it.

'Would you like that?' he says.

'Like what?'

Chins tuts.

'To have company and perhaps make some friends.'

Friends? In this place?

Diamond writes something in his notes, looks up. 'Have you chosen to be segregated from the other patients, Maud?'

While I'm thinking of a response, Chins pipes up. 'Prone to violence, this one. Attacked Doctor Womack, she did.' She pulls her chin back, smug, pleased with herself.

Diamond raises his eyebrows. 'And she's attacked other patients?'

Chins frowns. 'No, but . . .'

'So why is she not on the ward?'

'She's a private patient.' She sends me a sly look out of the corner of her eye. 'They said she was to have her own room.'

'Did they now?' Diamond frowns as he leafs through my notes again. 'And who pays for that? Maud's family?'

'Her employer.' Chins sniffs. 'Must be a forgiving sort, if you ask me. She's a very lucky girl.'

Oh yes, lucky me. I bet she'd like to be shut up in here without ever being in the fresh air, never feeling the wind on her face, the grass under her feet, or the rain, the blessed rain.

Diamond's frown deepens. 'And she's had no visitors, no letters?'

Chins shakes her head.

'Not one? In five years?'

'No.' She sighs. 'Her sort don't.'

'Do you happen to know the employer's name?' Diamond sounds uninterested, but his pen is poised over his notebook.

Chins folds her arms across her chest. 'You'd have to ask Doctor Womack about that,' she says. 'He's the one who brought her here.'

'Ah!' Diamond says. 'Is that so?'

CHAPTER 4

My hypnosis sessions are to take place once a week, on a Thursday, unless 'unforeseen circumstances intervene'. Perhaps they will rid me of my nightmare, banish the man in the marsh, although I doubt it.

With each day I grow less weary. The sickness has lessened too, so that my tiny room seems more of a prison than ever. If I were free, how glad I should be to be alert, with a clear mind, but as it is, it only makes my life worse. They used to give me enough to make me nauseous and sleepy, too tired to cause trouble, easier for them to manage. When you think you're going to vomit at any moment, you have to lie still, just to keep your breakfast, dinner, supper where it should be. Nevertheless, in a strange way, it made my life easier, my captivity more bearable.

If only I had Diamond's room. How wonderful it must be to have cabinets and objects, treasures to look at and to hold, instead of bare walls and empty hands. Always, always empty.

The bell rings – bong, bong, bong – and the clock, the clock never stops. I pace the room, my steps matching its rhythm. Tick, tock. Tick, tock, day after day after day.

Someone's singing in a shrill, tremulous voice. It's not coming from the lunatic side, but the other side.

'She's only a bird in a gilded cage,' she warbles. 'A beautiful sight to see. You may think she's happy la-la-la . . .'

Is that a piano? I hold my breath. Yes, a piano, played badly. She has a piano in her room?

'La-la-la-la-la . . .' The singer takes a deep breath, only for more la-la-ing to follow.

'Shut up!' I shout. She must have been moved from the ward to a private room like mine. A private room with a piano.

'Her beauty was sold,' she trills, 'for an old man's gold.' The high note is beyond her.

'Shut up!' I bang on the wall. 'You don't even know all the words.'

'She's only a bird . . .'

'Stop it.' I hammer the wall with my fists, but the singing goes on just the same, so I sing 'Oranges and Lemons' to drown it out. I sing louder than her and shout the last bit.

'Here comes a candle to light you to bed. Here comes a chopper to chop off your head. Chop, chop, chop.'

There's silence for a moment, then weeping. She's completely mad.

'What are you shouting at?'

I spin around. Prune. Prune standing in my room and the door's closed behind her and I didn't hear a thing. How my hands tremble with it, the horror of not knowing she was there.

'The lunatic in the room next door was singing,' I say.

'Next door?'

'In that room.' I point at the wall. 'In there.'

She stares for a moment, frowns. 'That's the broom cupboard, that is.'

'Then she's in the broom cupboard, isn't she?'

Prune nods, half smiles and hums 'Oranges and Lemons'. 'Used to sing that one as a kiddie.' She places my cup and biscuit on the table. 'I owe you five farthings, say the bells of St Martin's . . .'

It's only my breakfast. Nothing to tremble about, nothing at all.

She's up to 'the bells of Stepney-ee' by the time she leaves. There she goes, wittering away all along the corridor.

I press my ear to the wall. Is that the lunatic breathing? Someone is breathing. Perhaps her ear is pressed to the wall just like mine. I jump back at the thought of it, of her ear so close to mine.

'I know you're in the broom cupboard,' I shout. 'I've told them where you are.'

She starts weeping again, crying as if her heart will break, on and on and on. I hate the sound of it. Hate it.

Chins comes when I'm not expecting her, when I'm busy watching the copse outside.

'Time for your hypnosis,' she says. Perhaps I stare, because she adds, 'It's Thursday.'

I sit in the same chair as before, the curved one with the arms. Chins stands right behind me. She could put her hands down, clasp them around my neck and strangle me. She's thinking that, I bet. I can feel it, coming off her in waves.

Diamond points at a chair by the wall. 'Please, take a seat.' Perhaps he senses her thoughts like I do. We're attuned, Diamond and me. We both understand these things.

Diamond writes something on his notes, turns to a new page. 'I suggest we try a little hypnosis today.'

The thought of it sets me trembling. Whatever happened in the past was terrible enough to destroy my mind. Perhaps it was something I did, something so wicked it sent me mad.

'Relax, Maud.'

I grip my skirts, rub my fingers over the rough wool. He can't see inside my head. No one can, not even me. There's no need for my heart to race like this, so that the blood pounds in my ears.

'It will be very brief, very light,' he says. 'You should feel quite your usual self.'

I'm sick with dread. What if I remember? What if I do?

He pulls up a chair and sits in front of me. 'You may remain seated,' he says, 'as long as you're comfortable.'

I'm not comfortable, not with this doctor trying to prise open my mind, peer into its darkest corners with those curious eyes of his.

'As you drift into the past,' he says, 'you will tell me what you see, and how it makes you feel.'

I will tell him nothing. Oh, please don't let me remember. Let my secrets stay where they belong, buried and forgotten.

Out of the corner of my eye, I see a nurse, standing with her back to us. She's throwing things into a bucket.

Diamond takes a silver ring from his waistcoat pocket and slips it on to the top of his index finger.

I turn to look at the nurse, but there's no one there. It must have been shadows thrown by the trees outside, by their waving branches. Diamond wouldn't ignore a nurse throwing bloodstained instruments into a bucket like that, splashing water all over the floor.

'After the hypnosis, you will wake feeling refreshed and calm,' he says, and waves his finger in front of my face like a metronome. The ring shines, glitters. 'Watch the ring,' he says.

The nurse is there again but I know she can't be real now. That water on the floor, that bloodied water: that's not real, either.

'Maud.' Diamond clicks his fingers. 'Concentrate on the ring, please.'

I can barely see it now, the bloodied water, not now it's seeped into the floor. You'd never know it was there.

'The ring,' Diamond says. Back and forth it goes. Back and forth, sparkling in the light. It's a shooting star, a diamond.

'There's nothing else, nothing else in the world,' he says. 'There is only this ring.' Back and forth it goes, over and over. I try to look away but find I can't. His voice is clear and normal and calm, and I'm wide awake. The hypnosis hasn't worked. Relief makes me want to laugh and yet no sound comes from my mouth, and still my eyes follow that star – left, right, left, right – as if attached to it by an invisible thread.

'When I begin counting,' he says, 'your eyelids will become heavy, so heavy you must close your eyes.'

I won't. I will not close them.

'By the time I count to ten, you will feel completely relaxed. 'One.'

My eyes are heavy, but I hold them open.

'Two.'

They ache, my eyes. I'm so tired, so . . .

'Three.'

Blessed relief as my eyes close.

'Tell me about your childhood,' he says. 'Were you happy then?'

My lips open of their own accord. 'For a while, yes.'

'Go back to that time . . . Can you see a safe place?'

'No,' I say, because it's not safe, the marsh at night. And there he is, the man, rising from the muddy waters, grinning, grinning with those blackened teeth.

'Tell me what you see,' Diamond says.

'Nothing.'

'Think of your childhood, your family.'

And I'm slipping back, and it's not dark there, nor frightening, but bright and sunny. Someone is holding my hand, someone very tall. His skin is warm and rough against mine, and I'm happy. I am safe.

Grass tickles my arms. This man, this tall man I love, cradles a lilac-blue flower in the palm of his hand. 'Field scabious,' he says.

I stroke it, feel the softness under my fingertip. 'Scabious.'

*'And this here.' He points at a low, buttery-yellow flower.
'Bird's-foot trefoil. Trefoil because it has three leaves. Do
you see?'*

*I see them. I see the leaves and the flowers and the but-
terflies rising into the air with a flurry of wings, of colour,
of red and orange, blue and white, and the sky, so blue, so,
so blue.*

*'You're like your mother,' my father says. 'She was clever –
as clever as any man – but the world wasn't ready for her. It
will be different for you. You'll study, go to university. I only
wish your brothers had your aptitude.' And here they come,
the three boys, racing each other across the field, shouting and
laughing.*

*'I despair,' my father says, but he says it with a smile, and
how could he not, with those three strapping lads so joyful and
full of life?*

*The world grows cold and colourless and suddenly they are
gone – my father, my brothers. I turn and turn about. 'Daddy,
where are you? Where have you gone?'*

*I find myself standing in a narrow lane. Icy wind cuts
through my coat, stings my ears. A bird sings close by – a
robin, singing with all his heart while a bell tolls a warning.
One sombre note, slow and deep, over and over again.*

'I don't like it here.' My voice sounds tinny and distant, so
I shout. 'I don't *like* it.'

*Dread, fathomless dread fills my heart. I must turn, must face
it, but I can't. No, I cannot.*

'Come back, Maud. Come back.'

A face looms in front of me – Diamond, his brown eyes filled with alarm. For a moment, I think he's in the narrow lane with me, but we're not there any more. We're in his room with the fire and the large window and Chins.

Diamond's crouched in front of me. 'What frightened you?'

He's too close. I sit up straight, my head spinning. 'Nothing.'

Chins smirks. 'I'll call Doctor Womack, shall I?'

'No, no.' Diamond's flustered. 'This is to be expected. The patient is quite well.'

Chins raises her eyebrows, but keeps her mouth shut.

Diamond returns to his chair and opens his notebook.

'You seemed happy initially.' His sharp, inquisitive eyes probe mine. 'But something crushed that happiness. Do you remember what it was?'

'No,' I say.

He sits forward, hands together as if he's praying. I hope he's not praying for me, because God's long since left me.

'You called for your father.'

My stomach twists into a knot.

'You called for him, Maud. What happened?'

Oh, those pitying eyes. My eyes flinch from them. They flit to the floor, the window, the fire.

'Nothing,' I say, and stare at the ceiling until my eyes stop stinging.

What's wrong with me now? I have survived the hypnosis, for goodness' sake. There was no nightmare, no man in the marsh, no horror. All was sunshine and beauty and, even after that, only a robin on a cold day. So why this melancholy?

CHAPTER 5

Diamond insists I mix with other patients. He says it will 'facilitate my recovery'. Prune and Chins don't approve, if their alarmed expressions are anything to go by, but they take me all the same, to a long room they call 'the gallery'. It has tall windows on one side – with grilles, of course – and pictures on the walls and lots of women milling about. Artificial flowers adorn the light fittings. It's prettier than I expected, as if they're trying to fool us into thinking we're in some kind of hotel rather than a madhouse. Still, I quite like it.

We're all wearing the same dresses, we lunatics – grey, scratchy wool – and on everyone's back, the same three words are embroidered: Angelton Lunatic Asylum.

The chaplain sits at a table laden with books. He's a slight man, all bones and skin. His spectacles slide down his nose. He pushes them up. They slide down again. He pushes them up. His sallow skin droops with boredom. Now and again, he stifles a yawn. He jumps a little when I stand in front of him. I have that effect on some people.

'Do you have *Great Expectations*?' I know he does. I can see it next to his right elbow.

'Um, I think, er . . .' His eyes dart hither and thither.

I point to it. 'There.'

He picks it up, strokes the cover. 'The thing is . . .' He looks up with wary eyes, and blinks. 'It's a very big book; challenging, in the language and so on. Perhaps something less demanding?' His hand hovers over picture books with covers depicting Bible stories or childish characters. 'How about one of these?' He picks up the worst of the lot, a garishly coloured one with a picture of a simpering girl holding a parasol.

I stroke the pencil in my sleeve. 'I'd like *Great Expectations*, please.' Give it to me, I think. Give it to me or it'll be the worse for you.

Perhaps he sees something in my eyes because he hands it over, reluctantly, his fingertips clinging to it even as I take it.

I sit with my back to the wall so I can keep an eye on the lunatics. No one can get to me without my seeing them first, so I can relax. There must be twelve or more women in here, but no one else bothers the chaplain, no one else has a book in their hand. Perhaps they can't read, or have already had their medication, because no one can read after that, not even me.

The woman sitting opposite stares straight ahead without blinking. A dribble of saliva forms at the corner of her mouth, trickles down to form a glistening droplet at her chin. It swells and falls, attached by a silvery thread. It's just as well she doesn't have a book on her lap, I suppose. No one wants to read a story with someone else's dribble all over it – certainly not me. My book is clean, though, as if I'm the very first to open it. *Great Expectations* is my favourite. I've read it many times – many, many times. I stare at the page where Pip and Joe are talking by the fire.

"'Here comes the mare," said Joe, "ringing like a peal of bells!"'

And there it is, the asylum bell, going on and on. Dong, dong, dong, dong. That mournful tolling. If only it would stop, I'd be able to think.

I stare at the page and wait for the time to go.

Tick, tock. Tick, tock.

Blood drips on to the page, on to the word 'bells'. It's my blood. My nails have cut into my palms. I wipe the drop with my sleeve, but it spreads and now it's all over 'quite' and 'musical' as well. Another drop lands on 'marshes', and another on 'froze'. Sweat prickles my scalp. My heart jumps about. I hold my breath and look up. The chaplain's not looking. He's rearranging his books. I breathe, turn the pages with trembling hands, then clasp my hands together until they tingle. On and on I sit there, praying it will stop.

After a while, I unclasp them and watch the pink half-moon dents, four on each palm. No new blood appears. I close the book and fold my hands on top of it.

Will the chaplain check the book when I take it back? Will he see those smudges, those red bloodstains? Every time I think of it, my heart lurches.

Womack's arrived and is loitering near the door. He pulls a fob watch from his waistcoat pocket and frowns. An attendant sidles up to him and says something. How she simpers, the silly woman. They adore him, the attendants – the patients, too, for the most part. They dote on him. Their eyes follow him as he struts about the place. Then again, men are a rarity here. He has little competition.

He's striking, perhaps, in a superficial way, with that immaculate moustache, the dark hair, the oddly pale eyes. I can't abide him. I'll not forgive that shower bath. Fifteen minutes he left me there, trapped in that wooden box with freezing cold water hitting me from above. Fifteen minutes like fifteen years, and then the light-coloured mixture and them pouring it down my throat to make me vomit. I thought I would die, and nearly did.

The door swings open. 'Doctor Dimmond,' Womack booms, striding towards him, hand outstretched. 'How nice to see you again.'

Womack pats Diamond's shoulder as if they're old friends, as indeed they seem to be. They circle the room, Womack pointing out each patient and Diamond leaning forward to speak to them.

Womack rubs his hands together. 'We'll work together well, sir. I can see that.'

Here they come, Womack's shiny brown shoes leading the way. He points at me. 'Here we have one of our most disturbed patients.'

'We've already met.' Diamond smiles. 'How are you today, Maud?'

I open my mouth. 'I . . .'

'Ah!' Womack takes Diamond's elbow and lowers his voice. 'Mary suffers from delusions.' Does he think I can't hear him? He is but a pace away. 'She has many names.'

Many names? I can think of none except my own and the one they've given me.

'One might say legion,' Womack says.

'I see.' Diamond's mouth turns down. He believes Womack, and really, why wouldn't he? Even I don't know if I'm telling the truth.

'One day her name is Patience,' Womack says, 'the next Gladys . . .'

Gladys? Surely not. No matter how mad I am, I could never have been a Gladys.

'She cannot tell truth from fiction,' Womack says, 'so would be of no use to you, I'm afraid. Any so-called recollection would be a fabrication, an invention.'

'Ah!' Diamond says.

Womack's step is jaunty as he moves on to the next person. I can't see it, but there's a smug grin hiding somewhere under that drooping moustache, I just know it. For some reason I feel I have lost a battle, a battle I didn't even know I was fighting.

'I've never been Gladys,' I say under my breath.

Diamond turns back and smiles. 'No, I don't suppose you have.'

On they go, heads bowed in conversation. I didn't want the hypnosis anyway. I have no desire to remember my past, none at all. They will get no secrets from me.

The bell rings for dinner. I close the book and take it back to the chaplain, holding my breath.

He takes it, places it in a box with all the unread books and closes the lid.

And I can breathe. My legs are weak on the way to dinner, wobbly.

It's a long time since I was last in this dining hall. They must think I'm getting better. It's lucky they can't see inside my head, can't see all the silt and grime and broken glass, and shadows hiding God knows what.

Dinner is boiled meat and potatoes. It could be mutton. It has that smell about it, of damp wool, of dresses dragging in the marsh and pondweed.

They soak up the water from the marsh, these dresses. It travels up and makes the skirts heavy so that they cling to your legs, dragging you down, pulling you under. No one comes to save you. No one came to save me. I saved myself.

'She's crying.' An old woman with white hair and staring eyes stands in front of me, pointing. 'It's making the table wet,' she yells. 'Look. She's spoiling it.'

No one listens. I stare at her until her face pales and she walks away, looking back over her shoulder every few steps. I keep staring until she's right down the other end of the room. Then I stare at anyone else who's looking. They turn away, every one.

CHAPTER 6

I stand at the window, on my toes. I shan't look at that copse of trees today. No, I turn my gaze to the right, where the river hides beyond the reed beds. Sometimes, when the sun is in the right place, the water sparkles, as if millions of stars are scattered in a narrow, wavy arc across the landscape.

I reached it once in the early days when they let me wander. A dull day it was, and the river grey and sullen, with no sense of urgency about it, and yet still magical as only rivers can be. That water, so deep and cold and clean as it meandered, wending its dozy way to the sea. How I would love to go there now and feel that icy water over my toes once more, feel the chill numb my feet, the aching cold rise up my legs.

Diamond will not trouble himself with me now, not when he has other patients more willing, more trusting, more truthful. Others happy to spill their secrets for the sake of a warm fire and tea in a china cup, and not a Gladys among them.

'I'm sick of this tiny room,' I tell Chins when she comes the following Thursday. 'I need fresh air or I will die like a plant left in the dark.'

'Think yerself lucky,' she says. 'In the olden days, you'd have been chained to your bed.'

I catch my breath. 'Chained? Chained to the bed?'

She nods. 'I seen pictures – drawings and the like.' She leans close. Her breath smells of cabbage and onions. 'Wrapped in great heavy chains, they was,' she says, eyes wide. 'Metal rings round their necks, some of 'em. Round their necks. Imagine that.'

I try not to imagine it.

'Bet you're glad to be a lunatic now and not then, eh?' She nods.

I can feel them. Heavy iron chains, cold and hard. Manacles cutting into my wrists, ankles and neck, too tight, cutting off the air, and the smell of rusted metal.

I clutch at my throat, but there's nothing there, nothing but warm skin and bones beneath, and sinews and arteries.

She frowns. 'Stop that nonsense.'

Nonsense it is. There are no chains binding me, no manacles, yet I am chained to this place as securely as if there were indeed something around my neck. I'm chained here by my madness.

'Hurry up, now,' she says. 'The new doctor wants to see you.'

The new doctor? He is to continue then, despite my many names. There is to be tea, after all. I am glad of it. Diamond's room reminds me of another kind of life, one filled with warmth and light and hope.

There are no chains in his room, nor anything unpleasant. It is bathed in blazing sunlight and my eyes water at the unexpected brightness after the dark, gloomy corridor. Oh, lucky Diamond to have this room. It's easy to forget we're in the asylum. Even the grille looks softer here, as if it's made from something gentler than hard iron.

I stare into his cabinet, at all the treasures inside, and wish they were mine. Lumps of golden glass sit on a shelf, speckled with darker bits. I look closer and see the speckles are tiny leaves, creatures, flying insects.

'How long have they been in there?'

'In the amber?' he says.

Of course, it's amber. Stupid me. It's far too rich and waxy to be glass. 'Yes – how long?'

'Thousands of years.'

'Thousands?' Some are caught in flight, wings outstretched. 'All that time, trapped in a yellow prison.'

'Well, they . . .'

'Worse than being in here,' I say.

He thinks I'm joking, and laughs, but I can't stop gazing at those creatures – forever flying and never getting anywhere. It reminds me of something, of other creatures trapped in yellow, trying to escape, trying to breathe.

My chest tightens. I catch at the back of the chair, light-headed.

'Maud?'

I look away from the amber, see Diamond's worried face, and the tightness in my chest eases. It's the madness, just the madness. If I don't look at the trapped creatures, it will go away.

Diamond stands. 'Would you like to see anything from the cabinet?'

'I would, I would love that.' I don't look at the amber. It's merely a smudge of yellow at the periphery of my vision.

He takes a small key from his waistcoat pocket and unlocks the glass door. I can scarcely believe it, and yet he seems to think it quite normal, nothing out of the ordinary, to allow a lunatic such a liberty. He picks up an ammonite and hands it to me. Chins sits up at that. I see her out of the corner of my eye, sense her beady eyes on me, feel her muscles tense ready to pounce or run away. I don't blame her. It's a heavy fossil that covers my palm, and it would be a powerful weapon. My fingers close around it. I feel the ridges, the beauty of that long-dead creature, and my heart hurts.

I hand it back to Diamond, then sit heavily on the wooden chair and scrape my side on the arm. I run my fingertips over the grain of the wood. It was living once, until someone chopped it down. It's trapped indoors now, never to be free, just like me.

Diamond locks the cabinet, pulls up a chair and sits in front of me. 'How do you feel now that your medication has been reduced?'

'I remembered something about these dresses.' I rub the coarse wool between my fingers. 'When I was awake, about how they soak up water from the marsh.'

'That's good. How did it make you feel – when you remembered?'

I try to think of an answer but there isn't one.

'Did it make you happy? Sad? Angry?'

'I cried yesterday.' I'm not sure it was yesterday, but it sounds better than saying, 'I cried one day.'

'As your medication is decreased, you may find that your dreams become more vivid, that you can retain some details when you wake.' A small smile. 'You may even remember happy events, but alas this will not cure you. The events that made you ill, those we can only reach through hypnosis.'

He must dredge through the horrors in my head, then. I wonder if he's prepared for what he will find in there. It's like the marsh in my head, a festering, seething broth. Even I don't know what's in there. I don't want to know.

'Distressing memories left buried can poison the mind.'

He knows. He knows what's inside my head.

'Once uncovered and revealed, the past will cease to haunt you, and you will be well.' He sounds so confident, so convinced this will work that I almost believe him. 'Did you write it down,' he says, 'your memory?'

I should have done. Instead, the book is in its hiding place, pristine and unmarked.

'About the dresses?' he says.

Perhaps he'll take it away.

'You haven't.' He's disappointed. It makes his voice lower, quieter.

'I didn't want to spoil the book.'

'That's what it's for – to write in.'

Well, I know that, so I keep my mouth shut.

He rummages around in his desk and brings out a dog-eared notebook. It's smaller than mine, and brown and bent at the corners. He passes it to me. 'Would you prefer to write in this one?'

I take it. 'Do I have to give the other one back?'

'No. You can keep them both.' He smiles, stands. 'Now, let us see what we can uncover.'

There is a price to pay then, for the notebooks.

'After the hypnosis,' he says, 'you will wake feeling refreshed and calm.'

He told me that last time. It wasn't true then, so . . .

His finger waves in front of my face, and there's the spark. Back and forth, back and forth it goes as Diamond counts. A nightmare flashes into my head, of being dragged from the marsh, hauled along its banks by my hair.

'As before, Maud,' Diamond says. 'Think of a time when you were happy, a safe place.'

I concentrate hard on the clock, on that tick-tock. My mind will not wander into danger that way. I can do without any new nightmares.

'I would like you to think about your past, about a time when you were happy.' He pauses, as if expecting me to say something. My lips are pressed together. Not a word will I utter, not a word.

'Go there – to that happy time.'

*

Sunshine warms the back of my head. Something bright and shiny tickles the palm of my hand – a beetle, vibrant green and beautiful.

A shadow falls across me – my father, and there behind him, my brothers.

'We thought you lost, Maudie,' my father says. 'You are hidden by the grass. Did you not hear us calling?'

'No,' I say. I have been entranced by the flowers, by the smell of crushed green grass where I sit, by the bees and hoverflies and ladybirds surrounding me.

Hands clasp me around the waist and up, up, up I go into the air, to sit on my brother Jonathan's shoulders. My hands grip his hair, and all around us, flying around us, as if they too are glad I am found, are butterflies – so many of them, so many.

They are come for me after all this time, my father and brothers. They are come to take me home.

'Are you in a safe place?' Diamond says.

I clutch at Jon's hair, hold it fast.

'Tell me what you see.'

His hair slips through my fingers, slips away.

I can't hold on.

'Where are you now?' Diamond says.

They are gone, my father, my brothers. There is no meadow, no sunshine. There's just the crackling of the fire.

'In this madhouse.'

There's silence for a moment, then a long sigh. 'Very well,' he says. 'We will leave it for now.'

Relief makes my fingers tingle.

'I will count from ten to one,' Diamond says, 'and you will open your eyes.'

And he does, and I do.

How disappointed he looks. A twinge of guilt makes me wish I had said something – just something to make him feel he had succeeded. Why I should care how he feels I can't imagine. It's those eyes, I expect, and that gentle voice, lulling me into revealing my secrets.

'You're most resistant, Maud,' he says.

'Am I?'

'It's not my intention to make you unhappy, you know.' He holds my gaze. 'I seek only to make you well.'

It would be so easy to believe him, so easy, and so foolish.

'Tea, then,' he says, in a cheerful voice. This is followed by much pouring and stirring, and clinking of silver spoons on china – all overly loud and jarring. Throughout, he chatters about the benefits of hypnosis.

Chins responds with, 'Yes, doctor,' and, 'Indeed, doctor,' but I can say nothing at all. Once the tea is done and handed to each of us, Diamond walks behind his desk and sits.

'You smiled, Maud,' he says, 'during the hypnosis.'

My face has betrayed me.

'It seems you did find a place and time when you were happy,' he says. 'Can you remember what you saw?'

'No.' I stir my tea. The golden liquid swirls.

'And yet the memory was happy, was it not?'

How glossy is this tea, steaming and sweet.

'Maud?'

I won't answer, no matter how his brown eyes plead.

'What are you afraid of?'

'Nothing frightens me.'

The door opens and the cup leaps in my hand. Scalding tea splashes into the saucer, spatters my lap.

'Doctor Dimmond,' Womack booms. 'I have a post-mortem you may find of interest. Perhaps you would . . .' His gaze slides to me and his smile turns to a frown. 'You plan to try hypnosis on this patient?'

'I do.' Diamond's eyes are on me, on the spilt tea in my saucer, on my trembling hands. 'She fits the criteria perfectly.'

'Splendid.' Womack's smile is rigid, as stiff as his waxed moustache.

'In fact, we have just finished our second session,' Diamond says.

'Already?' Womack's glassy eyes alight on me for a long moment. 'And have you discovered anything of interest?'

'Not yet, no.'

Womack pulls at his moustache. He's staring into my eyes – staring, staring, as if he's forgotten where he is. At last, he transfers that cold gaze to Diamond. 'It's a great personal disappointment to me, Doctor Dimmond, that Mary continues to confuse fantasy with reality. A failure on my part, I feel.' He pauses, perhaps expecting Diamond to protest.

He does not.

Womack blinks twice. 'You believe your treatment will succeed where the rest of us have failed?' His smile is warm, but his eyes, those colourless eyes, are as cold as the grave.

'I have reason to hope so,' Diamond says.

Womack's eyes narrow. 'I imagine there must be other, more suitable patients?'

Diamond tilts his head to one side. 'I have several patients of interest, yes. More than enough for my study.'

Womack nods. 'Good. Good. Then I suggest you concentrate your efforts on them.'

'Perhaps.' Diamond looks at his notes, scribbles something in the margins.

Womack clears his throat. 'I expect you to keep me informed of your progress.'

'Of course,' Diamond says. 'I shall be happy to.'

Womack turns to the door.

'The post-mortem?' Diamond says.

'I shan't disturb your work now. Next time, perhaps.' And Womack is gone, leaving the door open behind him.

A sudden draught blows through the room, making the fire flare up with long, yellow flames.

Diamond takes my cup and its swimming saucer with a small frown. 'Are you quite well, Maud?'

'Oh, yes,' I say brightly.

His eyes narrow. I was right to keep my mouth shut. Diamond would share my past with Womack, and I cannot have that happen. No, not for all the tea in the world.

Even so, I cannot bear the thought of never leaving my room again, and that will surely happen if I don't tell him something soon. I can think of nothing I would have Womack know. Nothing at all, so I must make the most of Diamond while I can.

'I think if I were able to go outside,' I say, 'I would be able to remember.'

Diamond frowns. 'Surely you go outside now.'

'Her's not allowed outside,' Chins says. 'Doctor Womack's orders.'

Diamond's eyes widen. 'Well, *my* orders are that she be escorted outside to take the air.'

I'm to feel the wind on my face again at last, the grass under my feet. I can hardly believe it.

Diamond waves a hand at the window. 'Why do you think we have these beautiful grounds?' Still his eyes are wide. Still they stare at Chins. 'Fresh air and exercise are known to be good for our health, both mental and physical. These grounds were designed for that very reason.'

Chins pulls her head back, so that her chin disappears into her neck.

'She will need two attendants to accompany her, of course,' Diamond says. 'I'm certain that will satisfy any safety requirements.' His smile is brief, there one moment, gone the next.

'Very well, doctor.' Chins is not happy. Her lips are so tightly pressed together that her mouth has all but disappeared. She grips my arm even harder than usual on the way back to my room. There will be bruises there later, red and purple, fingertip-shaped, to join the others, the yellow, brown and green ones, the old, faded ones.

'When will I go out?' I say, once I'm back in my room.

She doesn't answer. Her mouth is a thin, angry line as she walks into the corridor, shuts the door and locks me in.

There's no room for the brown notebook behind the table, but there, under the window, where the plaster has chipped and crumbled, is a space. It slips in neatly.

All afternoon, I stare out of the window, and wait. The sun sinks into the horizon, painting the trees and hedgerows in gold. Mist hovers over the fields where the river hides. They won't let me go now, not so late, not when the shadows are long and deep – deep enough to hide me.

Prune comes with my supper.

'When am I to go outside?' I say.

'Outside?' She frowns.

'Out there.' I point at the window, where dusk has already settled, rendering the world colourless and grey. 'Out there in the grounds. I am to go for a walk.'

'Not today, you're not,' she says. 'Nor any day as far as I'm aware.'

'I am. I am to go. Diamond said.'

'Ah!' Now she's pitying me. I see it in her eyes, in the way her eyebrows form a triangle. She pities me and I can't bear it. I turn to the window.

''Tis Doctor Womack who decides these things.' She pats my arm, her touch light, hesitant.

Disappointment sits like a boulder in my chest. Diamond lied. I shouldn't be surprised, and yet I am. I thought better of him, fool that I am. Everyone lies in here, everyone but me.

CHAPTER 7

The bell's still ringing. Anyone who's escaped would be many miles away by now, so there must be another reason for that din.

'Has someone died?' I ask Prune when she brings my supper.

'Not as far as I know.'

'Then why are they ringing that bell?'

She frowns. 'What bell?'

'What *bell*? What bell do you think?' There it is, louder now, bonging away – bong, bong, bong, reverberating around my head. 'That one.' I point in the direction I think it's coming from, but now it's coming from everywhere, from all around me. My finger's shaking so I take it back in case she notices. 'It's been ringing since Saturday week.' It's longer than that, I'm sure, a lot longer, but it's better to be specific with these people, even if it's made up. Her stupid expression makes me want to slap her. 'The bell.' My teeth clamp together. 'That. Bloody. Bell. That bell that's ringing now.'

She looks up at the ceiling. 'No.' She shakes her head. 'I can't hear no bell.'

'Yes, you can.' She's lying to make me seem mad. 'The whole flaming asylum must be able to hear it.'

'There's no call for that ripe language.' Her mouth pinches. 'I'll tell doctor.' She backs away to the door.

'Good,' I say, 'because you're deaf.'

She shuts the door behind her. The key turns in the lock.

'You're bloody deaf,' I shout, as her footsteps fade away. 'You're all bloody deaf.'

The bell's so loud now that even with my hands clamped tightly over my ears I can still hear it. No wonder everyone's mad in here. No wonder.

I get into bed and cover my head with the blanket, but it doesn't stop. If anything, it grows louder, slower, deeper. It's like the bell I heard during hypnosis, when I stood in that lane in the cold wind and heard the robin. He's singing now, that same robin, singing his mournful song, here among the gravestones.

How cold it is in the bitter wind. I shiver and pull my coat about me. On and on the bell tolls, each mournful note reverberating around the windswept churchyard. So few of us here, so few of us left. The village is dying little by little, those young and fit enough to work drawn to the wealth of the cities, to their vast mills and factories and their choking, black chimneys.

Down they go, the three coffins, one by one, into that hard, unforgiving earth. The priest drones on, for the most part unheard, the words snatched from his mouth, taken far up to the purpled moors. Perhaps God is up there, because he's not down here with us, that much is certain.

'Man that is born of woman . . .'

The gravediggers fidget. They want us gone so they can fill the graves and get home for their tea.

'. . . blessed are the dead which die in the Lord . . . for they rest from their labours.'

Handfuls of dirt clatter on to the coffins.

'And what of you now, young Maud?' Philemon's weather-worn face is creased with worry.

'Oh, I shall be fine.' His pity irks me. 'I am to live with a distant relative of my father's – in Taunton.'

It's not true. There's no such relative. I shan't tell Philemon that. I won't have people feeling sorry for me. I couldn't abide that.

Tom stands by the church doorway, brooding. His eyes meet mine.

He wanders over, stands close behind me at the graveside. 'Your father has no relatives,' he murmurs, 'so where are you going?'

I turn, stare at him, but he's not afraid, not Tom. He knows me of old, since we were children.

'I know somewhere, if you're interested.'

'I'm not.' Perhaps he means to be kind, but I doubt it.

I walk home alone to our empty house. How cold it looks in the twilight; as dead as my brothers, every bit as cold and lifeless and done with.

'They need an assistant,' Tom shouts from across the lane.

I stop walking but don't turn. He stops, too. Yes, he knows me well.

'He's a scientist, the man – plants and so on. You like all that, don't you?'

I hate that he knows me so well. I hate that anyone knows anything about me. Still, I say nothing.

'Locals won't go there,' he says. 'They think the house is cursed. You know what village folk are like.'

'And is it?' I turn to face him. 'Is it cursed?'

He nods, purses his lips. 'Probably. Are you afraid, then?'

'Of course not.'

'No.' He smiles. 'Thought not.' He follows me down the path, stops halfway. 'Let me know – if you want to go. I have the address.'

I open the front door, step inside and slam it shut behind me. Then I lean back, slide to the floor and breathe the death smell. I can't stay here. I can't. I can't live with that stench, with their ghosts always haunting me.

If only I could go back, just a week. One week, that's all. I raise my head and howl because my beloved brothers are gone, and by my hand – my cursed hand. I howl and curse God, and howl while my desolate heart fractures, splintering into pieces.

A cry from the ward next door startles me awake. Someone's screaming in there. Screaming and wailing.

No, it's me. I'm the one sobbing and wailing. Hush, hush, or the attendants will come.

My brothers are dead. I can scarcely breathe for the pain, so sudden, sharp and deep – a whetted knife in my soul. They are dead. All dead.

I climb out of bed and stand at the window. Out there is the night sky with its crescent moon and stars – so many stars, so beautiful in the heavens, as they have been since time began, through many a life and death, many a grief. I stand until the chill goes through to my bones and the pain fades, until all that remains of the dream is birdsong.

Another nightmare, that's all it was, set off by Diamond and his hypnosis. It felt real, but then they always do. It's probably the change in my medication. I'll soon get used to it, just like the man in the marsh.

The clock ticks. With every swing of the pendulum, a sense of gloom builds, as if something invisible sits on top of me. It's trying to push me to my knees.

I shan't let it.

CHAPTER 8

A new day dawns dull and grey. Despite Prune's words, I still hope Diamond will keep his word. Perhaps today I will go outside and the fresh air will blow this sadness away. They may let me remove my shoes so my feet can sink into the soft earth. I can smell the crushed grass already, that sweet, sharp perfume. Yes, today will be the day.

Footsteps, one set heavier than the other. Chins and Prune, perhaps. I stand as the key grates in the lock and the door opens, and there they are, the very two I'm expecting.

'You're all ready?' Prune smiles.

'Yes.'

Chins scowls.

'I shan't try to escape,' I say.

'Escape?' she says. 'From the gallery? I should think not.'

'The gallery? But I'm to go outside. Out. Out there.' I point at the window. 'Outside in the grounds. That's what Diamond said.'

Prune looks away.

'Out there is not for the likes of you.' Chins grabs my arm. ''Tis the gallery or nothing.'

Prune stares at the floor. She knows how I long to go outside.

Chins gives me a shake. 'Don't dawdle. We have other patients, you know.'

There's to be no fresh air, then, nothing to rid me of the sorrow that makes my heart so heavy.

The gallery does nothing to lift my spirits. No sunshine filters through those windows, no chaplain sits at the table. There's no box of books, no music. The piano is bereft, abandoned. What am I to do? Sit here like the others, dribbling into my lap?

An attendant walks past, one I haven't seen before. She's homely and jolly with red cheeks and bright eyes. She sits at the piano, stretches her fingers, looks over her shoulder and smiles a toothy smile – not at anyone in particular, and certainly not at me, but her smile is a real one, as if she's pleased to be here. She plays 'Greensleeves' and 'London Bridge' and other old songs that everyone knows. Some people sing along. I don't, but at least it drowns out the tolling of the bell and the tick-tocking of the clock.

Someone's weeping. A woman. She's far from me. I can't see her and yet it's all I can hear. On and on she cries. The jolly attendant keeps playing, the lunatics sing. Can no one hear her? She's inconsolable, this woman – inconsolable.

Oh, that sorrow, that terrible lamentation, that bitter weeping. There is no sound like it – the sound of unfathomable loss.

I can't bear it. I can't. I shut my eyes and cover my ears and hum a tuneless dirge. Back and forth I rock, back and forth, and draw breath, and there it is – there it is, that weeping. If she doesn't stop, I will have to . . .

Hands, red and rough and calloused, grip my arms. Chins and Prune half carry me to the door, and out of the gallery, and up the stairs and still I can hear it. Even in my room, even there – weeping, weeping, as loud as ever.

'Calm yourself,' Prune says, dabbing my face with a handkerchief.

'Why did no one comfort her?' My voice is raw, ragged. 'She was breaking her heart.'

'That was you, Mary,' Prune says softly. 'The only one crying was you.'

I wake to find Diamond sitting on the chair, watching me. Seconds tick by.

'Now do you see,' he says, at last, 'what these buried memories are doing to you?'

I sit up, swing my legs out of bed. I should stand, really, but I'm too weary, and something tells me Diamond is not a threat – not in that way, anyway. 'I cannot remember my past.'

'You cannot, or you will not?'

My mouth dries at the anger in his voice. I would like some water, but it's on the table by the door and I would have to walk past him to reach it.

'I can't.' I gaze at my hands.

'What are you afraid of?' His voice is soft now, gentle and coaxing.

I look up and meet his gaze. 'You would tell Womack.'

'Ah!' He nods. 'I thought as much. Your expression when you look at him betrays you.'

My expression, betraying me again.

'He's the medical superintendent,' Diamond says. 'I'm therefore obliged to tell him of your progress. However, I will not divulge the details.' He holds my gaze for a long moment. 'What you recall will not necessarily be true, anyway. We all see things differently. The colour of the sky out there, for instance.'

It's grey, the sky.

'What colour would you say it was?'

'Grey,' I say.

'Whilst I would say it was beige.'

'Beige? No. It's slate grey and nothing like beige.'

He smiles. 'Neither of us is lying. We're both telling the truth as we see it. The past is like that. Memories are our interpretation of events. What we recall is the truth – as we see it. That's all. Sometimes we're wrong. This does not concern me. I'm not a detective.' He sits back. 'No one is trying to trap you.'

I take a breath. 'I have nightmares.' A spasm of irritation jerks my hands. Irritation at myself, or at Diamond, I don't know.

He nods. 'Nightmares are rarely memories. They're the manifestations of a troubled mind.'

I've told him. I've told him about my nightmares and they mean nothing. He wants more. 'I don't want to remember what happened.' There, I've said it. It's done.

'No, of course you don't.' His voice grows sharp with impatience. He's tired, then – tired of talking and talking and getting nowhere. 'That is precisely why you've buried it.' His jaw tightens. 'Can you not see how holding on to these horrors is destroying your mind? These buried memories will destroy you utterly if you let them.'

Destroy me? So what little there is left of me will disappear? It would be no bad thing, surely, no great loss to the world.

'I've treated patients with traumatic amnesia before,' he says.

'And hypnosis cured them?'

'No.' He takes a deep breath. 'No, it didn't, because I hadn't heard of hypnosis then – or not as a treatment. I thought it a music hall act, as you did. Now I know better.'

He won't let me stop the hypnosis. I see it now. He must save me, even if I don't wish to be saved. He must save me to prove himself.

'I understand your reluctance, truly I do,' he says, 'but you must trust me. This treatment can and will cure you if you let it.'

'Trust you?' My hands tremble. I grip my skirts to keep them still. 'Why should I trust you when you lied?'

'Lied?'

'You're no different to Womack, no different to any of them.'

He frowns, taps his pen on his notebook.

'You said I could go outside. You promised.'

'And you haven't been?'

I shake my head.

A muscle twitches in his jaw. 'Then you will go out tomorrow, come rain or shine,' he says, 'even if I have to take you myself. You have my word.'

He stands. He's leaving.

'I had brothers.' The words burst from my mouth in a rush. 'Three brothers and they're all gone.'

'Gone?'

'Dead.'

He frowns, steps back towards me. 'Are you sure?'

I shrug. 'I thought it a nightmare, but . . .' I shake my head. 'I think it was real.'

He sits back on the chair, arms folded across his chest. 'Tell me.'

'I remembered – I remembered birdsong.' It sounds stupid. My face grows hot and the wool of the dress pricks against my underarms. 'It was cold and – and the bell was tolling.'

He leans forward. 'Bell, you say?'

'Yes, it's always ringing.' Is it? I can't hear it now and don't want him to think me mad or I'll never get out of this place. 'I mean there was a bell, at the church, that's all.'

Diamond nods. 'They died together, your brothers?'

'Yes.' I see them. I see them, all three, laid out, their skin cold and hard and clammy when I kiss their foreheads.

'Can you recall how they died?'

So cold, those boys; like ice, so white and still.

'Maud?'

'I can't remember.'

His face pales. He thinks I killed them. I hope he's not right.

'Am I cured now?' My fingers clutch at my skirt, at the fabric, so rough and hard and comforting against my fingertips.

'Do you *feel* cured?' He watches me with sharp, curious eyes.

'Yes.' I hold his gaze and remember not to look away, not to fidget.

'It's unlikely that the cause of such a severe illness would come back to you so easily. Such memories are usually buried far too deeply to be recalled just like that.'

'So there is more?'

'I fear so, yes.'

There is more to come, then, something worse than the death of my brothers. Something far worse.

'Tell me about your father,' he says.

'I don't . . .' Oh, but I do. I *do* remember. 'He's dead, like my mother.' I try to laugh but it catches in my throat and makes my eyes sting. 'He died of influenza when I was twelve. My mother died giving birth to me. I took her life before I had even drawn breath.'

He leans forward, lowers his voice. 'That was not your fault, Maud. You didn't choose to be born.' He means well with his soft voice, but his words can't change the truth.

'Death follows me,' I say. 'It has followed me ever since. I'm cursed, Diamond, and not even your hypnosis can save me.'

He shakes his head. 'No. You're not cursed. I don't believe anyone is.'

'I *am*!' How harsh my voice sounds, as if it's Diamond's fault they are gone and not mine. The memory of the funeral, with all its hollow emptiness and crushing guilt, swamps me. Does he really think he can rid me of this horror with that shiny ring?

His pen is poised over his notes. 'What can you tell me about your brothers?'

'About my brothers?' Three coffins disappearing into the ground, the peaty smell of black earth rising up with each one. 'That they're dead. That without them, I had nothing.'

Diamond nods, and waits, and waits until I can't stand the silence any longer.

'They were older than me.' I knit my hands together, press until they hurt. 'I was never meant to be born. A mistake.' The words come out too quickly, stumbling over each other. 'A mistake that cost my mother her life.'

'Your brothers, Maud,' he says. 'Do you remember their names?'

'Of course. Sam. Sam was the eldest, then . . . then . . .' I know their names. I must do.

'Sam and . . . ?'

Gone. They are gone. I search for them, for these brothers of mine, for their names, their faces, but they're nowhere to be found. I stare at my lap, at the folded hands that lie within it, like someone else's hands, so pale and sickly and not connected to me.

'The memory will come back,' Diamond says, in that gentle voice of his. 'It is not lost, Maud. Nothing is lost.'

Oh, but he's wrong, for I am lost. I have been lost for a long time, such a long time.

CHAPTER 9

My sleep is full of visions of my brothers, cold and clammy. I wake again and again, sweating and trembling and sick with guilt.

It must have been some pestilence, I tell myself, something so virulent that it struck them down as one. And yet here I am, alive and unharmed.

Nausea makes me light-headed. Please don't let me have killed them, not my own beloved brothers.

The sky lightens. The asylum awakes. Nothing will change the past, nothing will raise my brothers from their cold graves, and yet somehow I must survive the day. Outside there are trees and grass, sky and freedom. I will feel better out there, much better.

The clock ticks, the bell tolls. Why didn't I ask what time I should be going out? There's a big difference between early morning and late afternoon. The longer I sit, the harder it is to fight off the gloom.

Prune brings my breakfast, clouds cross the sky, dinner comes and goes, and still I wait. At every sound in the corridor, I jump to my feet and stare intently at the door, and wait, and wait, but they go past, whoever they are. Footsteps go back and forth – heavy ones, light ones, some quick, some slow, some lame. Is it always this busy, that corridor? Why have I never noticed it before?

Finally, my door opens. I stand, brush down my skirts. I'll show Diamond how well I am, how fit to be allowed this freedom.

It's Chins. 'Come on.' Her eyes bulge. 'I haven't got all day.'

'Neither have I,' I say, even though I have, of course. I have all day, all year, all life.

Her lower jaw juts forward. She reaches out. Her fingers close around my upper arm, dig into the flesh as she drags me out through the door. There's no need to drag me when I want to go, but I'm so excited to be going out that I don't care.

Prune's waiting at the bottom of the stairs. She takes my other arm, and they walk me towards the main door. They're holding me so firmly that my feet barely touch the ground. The door opens, daylight streams in, and there – grass, trees, fresh air. We walk, the three of us, arm in arm around the flower beds. Already my head is clearing, the sorrow is lifting. It's the stale air in the asylum, the warmth, the damp, that muddles my brain. If I were outside all day, I should be as sane as can be. We walk almost as far as the reeds, almost close enough to see the river, but not quite. The air smells of clear, cool water and pondweed.

But we are turning back, back to the grey dankness.

'Can't we go a little further?' I say. 'I would like to sit a while.'

'Not now,' Prune says.

'Can I at least see the river?'

They exchange a glance. 'We're not to go to the river.'

'Why not?'

They quicken their pace.

'Why can't I go to the river?'

'You're not allowed,' Prune says, 'not after last time.'

'Not *ever*?'

Chins tightens her grip. 'No.' Her mouth snaps shut as she says it. No, just that. No, not ever.

I could fight them, perhaps, make a dash for it, but it's unlikely I would make it to the water, not now we're almost at the door. Besides, I should never be allowed out again if I did that. No, I must bide my time, be docile and obedient until they become complacent, until they think me subdued.

Oh, to feel cool water rushing through my hair, over my scalp. That would empty my head of all its rubbish once and for all. I could float downstream, away from here, float out to the coast and start a new life where no one knows me, where I can be a different person, a new one, a better one. I will wait. I have all the time in the world, after all.

Back in my room, I pull out the notebook, retrieve the pencil from my sleeve, and draw. I draw a stormy sky – dark, ominous clouds, hurtling across the heavens, and beneath, the river, with frothing waves, and roiling depths. It's nothing like the river I saw those years ago, that slow, muddy, sluggish thing. This river is turbulent, angry. It takes up the whole page.

The next page is every bit as dark. The marsh this time, at night, with tangled branches blocking out the sky, and the water in pools, shimmering in the moonlight. I lost something in that marsh, a long time ago. Something important. One day, I'll go back there and find it. I will be free of this place and I will go back to that marsh.

A clean sheet. I shall draw something pleasing, something innocuous and pretty, in case they think me disturbed by my outing. Something safe, with no marsh, no river, no ominous, grey skies. The pencil sits poised in my hand.

There must be something I can draw.

Nothing. Nothing safe and pleasant lives in my head. Only horrors reside there, roaring in the shadows.

After supper, I sit in bed and wait for them to douse the lights. My eyelids grow heavy. I'm sliding into a dream when the door creaks open.

Womack. My heart skitters as he shuts the door behind him. For once he is on his own. How brave. He doesn't stray far from the door, though. No doubt Chins is just outside, ready to run in and rescue him.

He smiles a weak smile, rubs his hands together. 'I understand you've been outside today, Mary.'

I dig my nails into my palms and try to calm my breathing. He's only a doctor, after all, only a man, and I've done nothing to deserve punishment, not today.

'I imagine you are well aware that your violent nature makes you utterly unsuitable for such a privilege.'

It's years since I apparently tried to kill him. I can't even remember doing so, and yet how he loves to remind me.

'You continue to be wilful, using foul language.' Perhaps he sees the scorn in my eyes, because his jaw tightens. 'Until you learn to be demure and pleasant in manner, you will go nowhere. Do you understand?'

I stare into his washed-out eyes.

He pulls at his waistcoat, discomfited perhaps by my stare, or my silence. 'Doctor Dimmond seems to think you a suitable subject for his study.' He waits, knits his hands together, flexes them. 'He is mistaken,' he says. 'Excitement stimulates the brain, a major cause of sickness in women.'

His eyes flit to the window, the floor, and finally alight on me. 'You're to tell him that you do not wish to take part in his experiment. Do you hear?'

It's fairly evident that I hear, since he knows I'm not deaf. I assume he has nothing more to say, so I turn to the window and wait for the door to click shut. For a long moment, there is no sound. Then finally, the door closes.

Womack means to crush me, to keep me trapped in my madness, imprisoned in this room for ever.

Diamond trusted me to go outside, to hold a treasure in my hand. He trusted me. Perhaps I should trust him, too.

'I need to see Diamond,' I tell Prune the following morning.

She bustles around me, moving this and that, straightening the bedcover. 'Happen you'll see him on Thursday, as usual,' she says.

Thursday. Almost a whole week to wait. 'But I'll remember nothing by then.'

She frowns, chews her lip.

'Will you just tell him?' I say. 'Please?'

She stops at the door, looks back. 'We'll see.'

I go to the window, stare out at the sky. All is a dull, uniform grey. A raven leaves the copse and flies towards me, its long, slow, elegant flight punctured with that deep, resonating call. It veers west and away. I watch it until it's a tiny speck in the sky, and watch still, even after the speck is gone.

There were ravens there, at the marsh – ravens and jays, blackbirds and wood pigeons and nuthatches, and blue tits, great tits, song thrushes. And bats, and toads, and newts. I run to my notebook and make a list of the animals there, of the plants and trees. I see it clearly, hear the trickle of water, the breeze shaking the leaves, the rustling of tiny creatures in the undergrowth – wood mice, shrews and voles, and even tinier ones underfoot – woodlice, earwigs, beetles, worms, centipedes. I cover two pages with my list. Afterwards, I stare at it and realise it will be of no interest to Diamond. It says nothing about my past. It's just a list.

The rain arrives. It patters against the window, tiny drops at first, speckling the glass, then large, fat ones that swallow the small ones that get in their way. They slide down the glass and pool at the grille, swelling and swelling until they can cling on no longer, then spill over the edge to fall on to the next pane.

A key turns in the lock. It's Prune. Just Prune. I turn back to the rain.

'Well?' she says. 'Do you want to see the doctor or not?'

'Yes.' I spin around so quickly, my brain gets left behind, only to catch up with a bump that gives me a headache. Never mind. The joy of getting out of my room soon banishes it. I dash down the stairs, so that Prune has trouble holding on to me.

Diamond's door opens, and there he is – bathed in orange firelight, like an angel or some kind of spectral being. A shiver runs over my skin.

'You wished to see me?' He moves out of the firelight, and he's just a man – flesh and blood and bone and sinew and hair and nail and teeth and all things human and ordinary.

'I'm ready to be hypnotised,' I say.

He studies me with narrowed eyes, as if weighing up my worth, my usefulness, the likelihood of success. 'May I ask what has occasioned this change of heart?'

I stand perfectly still and smile. He's waiting, waiting. I can't say it's that I want to go back to the marsh, because who but a madwoman would want to go back to the place of their nightmares? I can't say it's Womack, that he has forbidden me to do it. No, that would not do at all. I could say it's the tea, the fire, the fact that Diamond lets me speak and doesn't interrupt, that he treats me like a normal person, as it is all of those things.

'I want to be free,' I say instead.

He nods, eyebrows raised.

'But I'm afraid of my past.'

He nods again. 'You've remembered how your brothers died?'

'No.' I wince at a sudden, stabbing pain in my chest.

He sees it, of course, with his sharp eyes. 'The loss of your brothers will never go,' he says, 'but it will become easier in time, Maud, once you know what happened.'

'But what if I killed them?' I look up at the ceiling and blink until the stinging stops. 'I would not wish to know that.'

'And if you *don't* know, will you ever stop wondering, ever stop dreading the truth?'

I shake my head. 'So, if I am to recover, I must know what happened, why the madness came?'

'Precisely.' He walks to his desk, moves papers, pens, pencils, as if looking for something. Then he looks up, his face alight like an excited child's. 'We will continue apace.'

He's in front of me before I have sat down, and there it is, that ring, in front of my face. The fear comes back in a rush, a wave of trembling, but he's counting and I slip away, slide into the past before he reaches three.

'Tell me about your brothers,' he says.

'I'm travelling, in a stagecoach.'

'With your brothers?'

'No. No, alone. It's dark, and I'm weary.'

'Tell me how your brothers died,' he says, but his voice is quiet now and I have no time to listen.

The coach slows, stops. All outside is dark and still. In truth it's scarcely darker than the day has been, with its lowering, blue-grey clouds and relentless rain. Before I can thank the driver, the coach sets off, faster now, relieved of its burden and keen to be home. I watch until it's out of sight. A square church tower looms to my left. I peer at the sign outside. 'Saint Michael and All Angels'. I hold the scrap of paper up to the streetlight and peer at Tom's untidy writing. The paper is damp and fragile, and some of the letters have faded to nothing, but yes, it's the right church, and there, in the gloom, on the other side of the road, stand tall gates. Beyond them, all is pitch black like the mouth of hell. With sinking heart, I retrace the letters with my fingertip. There is no mistake. I must go through those tall, unwelcoming gates.

Beyond the gates stands a yard with outbuildings. Dead crows hang from trees on either side, and there in front of me stands Ashton House, cold and forbidding in the meagre light, and silent – so silent.

I climb the steps to the front door, drop my bags and pull on the bell. It rings in the distance. No flicker of light appears in the window, no friendly face. Nothing. I shiver. Tremors judder through me, one after another. My teeth chatter.

'Hello?' I shout. The wind whips the word away. I hammer on the door with my fists.

The fine rain turns to sleet, which stings my face like pinpricks. I have to get inside somehow, otherwise I will die of cold. Leaving my trunk and bag in the shelter of the doorway, I stand back and survey what I can see of the building. It's more a large farmhouse than the stately home of my imagination. Ivy and some other climber, wisteria perhaps, all but smother the grey, ugly limestone. Perhaps no one lives here after all. Perhaps they're all dead and lying in their beds waiting to be discovered.

I'm about to take a run at the door when it opens. A man of middle age stands there, carrying a flickering candle. He's neither tall nor short, fat nor thin; an ordinary man with nothing particular about him, wearing working clothes of a nondescript muddy brown that matches his hair. He licks his chapped and peeling lips.

'Hello,' I say. 'I'm Mr Banville's new assistant.'

He watches me through narrowed eyes while icy wind whirls around me and cuts through my wet clothes. His tongue flicks out like a snake tasting the air. 'You're a woman.'

'Yes – yes, I am.' Wind tears at my hair, and whips it across my face, half-blinding me. 'Maud Lovell. And you are?'

'You call me Mr Price.'

I want to laugh. Hysteria, probably, or weariness because there's nothing funny about him at all. He's shifty, yes, possibly malign, but not remotely amusing.

'Not expecting a woman,' he says. 'Letter said . . .'

'My letter was signed M. Lovell, and that's my name. I'm pleased to meet you.' I force my mouth into as much of a smile as I can muster with my face frozen.

'You're late.' He turns his back and walks away, leaving me to heave my belongings inside and kick the door shut.

I find myself in a cluttered vestibule. Damp old leaves and twigs have blown in after me. Muddy boots and shotguns stand against the wall. Coats hang on hooks – raincoats and furs, and rich velvet cloaks – so many of them that we have to squeeze past to reach the hall.

An ornate staircase stands ahead. It curves around and ends in a balcony that runs in a semicircle above, like something from a music hall or theatre. Tapestries hang on the walls, red and gold and green – four of them, placed seemingly at random, depicting hunting scenes.

I spin around to take it all in – this, my new home. My arms ache from the heavy bags. For a moment I consider asking Price to help but when he turns his cold gaze on me, I change my mind.

Dogs. You'd think there would be dogs in a place like this, a large, isolated country house, but I've not seen or even heard one. It's too quiet altogether, abandoned, empty. A sense of death pervades the air, or perhaps that's my imagination.

'Come on.' Price heads towards the back of the house, leads me down a small flight of steps to a large kitchen where a glowing fire awaits. I warm my numb hands in front of it.

'You comin' or what?' he says.

I can't bear to leave the heat. 'I've had no food since midday.'

His lip curls in a snarl as he looks me up and down, his gaze lingering on my bodice. 'Plenty o' meat on you. No doubt you'll survive till daybreak.'

I drag myself away from the warmth and follow him up a steep, narrow flight of stairs. Walls hem us in on either side, so close there's barely room for me and my bags. A draught sends the candle flame flickering wildly so that I fully expect it to blow out at any moment. These stairs are treacherous enough as it is. In the dark, they'd be deadly.

By some miracle, the candle stays alight, and we reach a tiny landing, scarcely big enough for one person, let alone two plus bags. We jostle around, Price tutting and sighing all the while.

He opens a door on the right. 'This be your'n.'

I bow my head to enter. My shadow looms huge on the ceiling and opposite wall. There's a bed pushed up against the window. The mattress is bare, bedding folded at one end. That much I see, but the rest of the room is cloaked in shadow.

I turn to ask Price where I might wash, but he's gone and the door is closed. At least he's left the candle, what's left of it. It burns too brightly, the flame long and pale and leaning to one side in the draught. Before I reach the bed, it dies, plunging the room into the thickest, blackest darkness I have ever encountered.

I lie on the mattress and pull the blankets over me, curling my knees up to my chest to keep warm.

Joists creak and argue as the house settles for the night. Wind whistles under the doors, around the window. It howls in the roof space, as if a madman lives up there, one moment whistling a jaunty tune, the next roaring with fury. Cursed? Haunted? I listen to the groans of that poor, wretched house and smile at those who are stupid enough to believe it.

CHAPTER 10

I wake to howling wind and rain and my window rattling under the onslaught. The house itself shudders. I have been dreaming of my brothers, laughing and running and full of joy, full of life. Their deaths hit me anew, as they do at the dawn of every day. Will this never end? Will I never be able to forget, even for one day?

I kneel on my bed and peer out of the grimy window. All is dismal and grey out there – the sky, the rain, the puddles, the wet stones, the road, the grass, the bare trees, all grey and dull in the half-light before dawn. I slide the catch across and push up the window. Cold, damp air hits my face with a violence that takes my breath away. I slam the window back down, turn my head and see the room anew.

There, at the far end, in the deepest shadow, stands a chest of drawers and, at its feet, my luggage. An ache reaches up my calves as my feet touch the freezing cold floorboards. Shivers run through me. I wrap myself in the blanket and shuffle over to it.

Everything I own, everything salvaged from home, my whole life up to now is in this trunk.

I kneel, unfasten the latches and push open the lid before I can change my mind. Oh, that smell! Sweet woodruff and wood smoke. Homesickness, sharp and deep, pierces my heart. It's not just a longing for the house, for the village; it's a longing for the past, for everything that is done to be undone.

This will pass. It will. This smell will fade and die and I will forget. I hold my shift to my face and breathe, just this once. Then I stand and straighten my back. There is no going back. There is only forward into the future, and I must go there whether I will it or not.

New shoes pinch my feet as I tread the dust-laden stairs. They are suede with buttons and laces. My frock of green silk is also new. I purchased them with my last pennies to make an impression on my employer. Oh yes, for I am employed now.

Hunger gnaws at my stomach, but the kitchen is as empty as the night before. A brace of pheasants hangs in the larder, crawling with maggots. The smell of them makes me retch. I turn away.

The man Price stands in the doorway, flexing his white fingers. 'The master's been asking for you.'

'Then perhaps you will show me to him.'

He grunts and disappears through the back door, strides out along an ash path, calling over his shoulder. 'Eyesight's going.'

Is he making an excuse for his rudeness? 'I'm sorry,' I say.

His head snaps around. 'Not mine. The master's.' Then he's off again, even faster than before. 'The Lord punishes sinners.'

I snort. 'I'm certain the Lord has nothing to do with it.'

He stops, turns, his eyes blazing with a rage so intense the hairs on the back of my neck rise.

'I mean,' I stutter, 'perhaps there is a scientific explanation for it.'

He is furious. His face rigid with it, tendons standing out on his neck. 'Their eyes shall consume away in their holes.' He stares, eyes glittering with menace, then turns on his heel and leads the way up an exterior staircase to a half-glazed door.

The man is mad. No sooner have I reached the top than his footsteps clatter down the steps and away. I knock on the door. There's no reply, so I push it open on to a strange room, long and narrow, lined with dust-laden shelves and cabinets, the whole festooned with cobwebs. Papers lie strewn about. Woodlice crunch underfoot as I step inside.

'Mr Banville?'

The smell is of dust and death, and indeed all is death about me – plants, insects, mammals – pinned to cards, or pickled in yellow fluid, or cut into sections and trapped under glass. The only living creatures here are spiders. Black, short-legged hunters scurrying here and there. Thin, spindly-legged patient ones, hanging on intricate webs, waiting and watching for prey. Great, hairy ones, as big as the palm of my hand, wandering in search of mates, or squashed flat by a careless person's shoe – mine, perhaps – or on their backs, dried up with legs curled. There are flies, of course. They are inextricably linked with death. Tiny fruit flies wafting hither and thither, bluebottles buzzing, hurling themselves against the glass in a bid to escape.

A microscope, a real one. How I have longed to see one of these in real life. Glass slides sit upon a narrow shelf. I pick one up between my fingers.

'Don't touch!'

The slide slips from my fingers, shatters on the floor, joining all the other debris. 'I'm sorry,' I say. 'I'm not usually so clumsy.'

A man, whether alive or dead I can barely tell, so cavernous and skull-like is his head, has appeared from nowhere.

'Who let you in here?'

My mouth dries. 'Mr – Mr Price.' I point at the door, even though Price is long gone. 'I'm your new assistant.'

'You're a woman.' His eyes bulge. A blue vein pulses in his temple.

'Yes, yes, I am.' I try, but a smile is beyond me. 'Maud Lovell.' If he dismisses me, I have nothing – no home, no livelihood. 'Where would you like me to begin?' I say, as if eager to work. 'I could tidy this er . . .' I wave a hand at the chaos.

'A woman won't do – won't do at all.'

'But . . .'

'How can a woman go wandering the county searching for specimens? It would not be proper.'

'I'm perfectly capable of . . .'

'I'm sure you are, but the fact remains that it would not be safe for you to do so.'

'I am quite able to look after myself,' I say, growing hot. 'I grew up with three brothers and no mother.'

He purses his lips.

'I have ever wandered the countryside alone. There is nothing I like to do more.'

His eyes narrow. 'You're not afraid, then?'

'Of course not.'

'And what of the curse on this house?' His lip twitches. He could be teasing, or it could be a tic. 'I assume you know of it?'

'It's nonsense,' I say, while my heart jumps about in my chest.

'Ah, the misplaced confidence of youth.' He picks up a large, dusty jar from the shelf and holds it out to me. 'What think you of this?'

I take it, brush the thick, brown dust from the glass, and there, floating in yellow fluid is a monstrous creature with two heads. The jar slips through my hands, but I catch it – just.

'Not so brave, then,' he says.

'What is it?'

He snorts. 'According to Price, it's a captured soul.'

Four cloudy eyes watch me. 'And really?'

'An abnormality – a malformed monkey foetus.'

He replaces it on the shelf. Now I see there are many jars, some much larger than the one I held, all filled with monsters in yellow fluid. I turn my gaze to the microscope, to safety, to plants.

Mr Banville chuckles. 'Price believes I keep demons in these jars.'

I want to laugh, too, to scoff and say how silly the idea is, but the laughter won't come. Instead, I keep staring at the microscope and breathing and trying not to think about those souls in jars.

The chair creaks as he sits. Behind him, the shelf of yellow horrors is almost hidden in shadow. If I'm careful, I will be able to forget they're there. Yes, yes. I can do that.

'You speak Latin, of course,' *he says.*

My heart stutters. 'I . . . I don't speak it, but . . .'

He groans, rubs his forehead.

'. . . but I know the Latin names of plants and their classifications.' *Please don't test me. Please, please don't test me.* 'I've studied Darwin and Linnaeus.' *I must have been mad to think myself capable of this. I know nothing of Darwin or Linnaeus except their names. I know only what my father taught me on our walks – the names of various flowers and insects and birds.*

He shakes his head. 'I did specify . . .'

Tom's words come back to me. 'Locals won't go there. They think the house is cursed.'

I straighten my back, step towards the door. 'Of course, you must have other applicants.' *I reach for the door.* 'I should never have come.' *My heart flutters as my fingers touch the handle.* 'Good day to you.'

He clicks his tongue, and sighs. 'Very well, you will have to do.'

A small earthquake takes place in my innards.

'It frustrates me that I'm unable to manage alone,' *he says,* 'but so it is. I can no longer see well enough to find anything smaller than an oak. And this –' *he holds out a shaking hand* '– this foul palsy prevents me from leaving the house.'

He needs me, then, as much as I need him, and I am saved. I'm not stupid. I can surely learn all I need to know and make myself indispensable to Mr Banville.

'*You've met my wife Imogen, I take it?*'

'*No, Mr Banville. Not yet.*'

'*Ah!*' He breathes in through his teeth. '*I fear you will have little in common.*'

'*I'm sure we will get on splendidly,*' I say.

I am less sure when following Price back to the house for dinner.

'*Won't take mistress long to d'vest you of them high and mighty ways a yourn,*' he says.

'*High and mighty?*'

He quickens his pace, whistling. My God, he's pleased with himself. My God, I'd like to wipe that smirk from his face, knock the jauntiness from his step. He opens the kitchen door and steps inside.

'*This be the new 'un.*' He nods his head towards me.

'*Oh, aye?*' A stout woman stands in front of the stove, stirring some foul-smelling concoction. She emerges from the steam, red-faced with greasy hair, sniffs, and wipes her nose with the back of her hand.

I try a smile. '*Mrs Price?*' I say.

'*That's m'name.*' Her eyes narrow.

'*I'm Maud Lovell, Mr Banville's new assistant.*' The smile is beginning to hurt but I keep it there and look for some sign of friendliness. I find none.

She turns back to her task.

Price sits at the table, so I do the same, only to have a plate put in front of me. On it are thick, grey, slabs of meat and a pile of lumpy mashed potato speckled with grey. The foul-smelling concoction turns out to be a gravy of sorts. The beef is tough and unyielding and exhausting to cut and chew, but I'm famished and cold and this is warming at least, and seems unlikely to be poisonous.

The Prices don't speak, and I can think of nothing I want to say to them, and so the whole meal is passed in silence, except for the sound of slurping, chewing and swallowing, together with an occasional belch from one or the other of my companions.

Price finishes his meal, picks up the plate and licks it all over. A trail of 'gravy' dribbles down his chin. He sighs with satisfaction, puts his plate back on the table and wipes his face on his sleeve.

A bell rings somewhere.

'Mistress wants you,' Mrs Price says, gazing at something over my head.

'Aye.' Price stands, belches, turns on his heel, takes one step, two, before turning back. 'You.' His finger points at my face. 'She wants you.'

'Oh!' I stand, smooth down my skirts and traipse after him through the house.

He stops in front of the last door on the left, and says, 'This is it,' then lumbers off, back where he came from.

I'm not sure what to expect of Imogen Banville – a frail, sickly woman, perhaps, neurotic and unable to control her useless servants. With a stab of pity in expectation, I knock at the door.

'Come.' The terse tone, the strident voice, doesn't sound like a fragile, delicate lady. I push the door open. She's lying across *a chaise, long auburn hair spread like a halo around her pale face. She's younger than I expected, no more than late thirties, a good two decades younger than her husband, with slanting eyes and startling black lashes. There's nothing frail about her – quite the opposite.*

She props herself up on one elbow, and frowns. 'Yes?'

'I'm Maud Lovell,' I say. 'Your husband's new assistant.'

'Oh.' She yawns, picks at her teeth with a small stick.

'I was told you wanted to see me.'

'Did I?' She frowns, then laughs. 'Oh, yes.' She stands in one sinuous movement, then walks around me, looking me up and down as if I were a heifer at market. Once she has completed full circle, she stands back, lips pursed, head cocked.

'When I heard he'd employed a female assistant, I assumed it was a euphemism for whore.'

I can't think of a word to say in response.

'I thought at last he'd found some energy, but I can see that's not the case.' She wanders back to the chaise and falls on to it with a sigh, stretching her long limbs. She yawns. 'My husband has excellent taste,' she says, 'and you, my dear, are not nearly pretty enough.'

I force a smile. 'Then it's just as well I have no intention of pursuing that particular kind of employment.' I turn for the door.

'Girl.'

I take a deep breath. 'My name is Maud.'

'Price tells me you have ideas above your station.'

'No, not at all. I just . . .'

'You think highly of yourself, he tells me.'

'No. No, I merely . . .'

'Then you won't mind cleaning this floor.' She points at the filthy rug, stained and covered with spills of one sort or another.

'You mistake me for the housemaid, madam.'

She snorts. 'I make no mistake. You either scrub the floor, or you pack your miserable little bags and hurry off to the workhouse.' She knows I'm desperate, that I have nothing. I can see it in her eyes.

'Yes, madam.'

And, on my knees, I wash and brush the rug. But it's not enough for her. After that, it's the wooden floor. I scrub the boards, while soapy water stains my frock, and splinters of wood snag the fabric. My dreams lie scattered about me. A scientist? What a fool to imagine such a thing. What a fool. Tears of self-pity fall on to the back of my hands as I work, crawling about the floor in front of her. I won't let her see, not her, not any of them. None of them will ever see me cry.

I open my eyes to see Diamond, scribbling furiously in his notebook. He looks up. 'You're a scientist, Maud.' His voice is strained with forced jollity.

Am I? Perhaps I was once – a scientist of sorts, playing the part, at least.

'And a resourceful one, too,' Diamond says.

I smile and pretend to be pleased, although what use it will be to me now, this fact, I can't imagine. 'Did I tell you that?'

'Yes. You describe very well what you are experiencing.' He turns to his notes. 'But we are yet to find out what happened to your brothers.'

Pain jolts through me.

'It could well be the key to your sickness. Once we have overcome that, I warrant you will be quite sane and ready to be released.' He closes his notebook with a flourish, a finality, as if all is done with.

'And what then?' I say. 'What am I to do then?'

'Well, I see no reason why you shouldn't continue in your chosen profession and resume your scientific studies.'

'Resume my studies?' My eyes are drawn to the window, to afternoon sunlight kissing autumn leaves. How bright the world is all of a sudden, how full of colour and light and promise. All is not lost, then. There is hope yet, of a new future, a better one.

CHAPTER 11

Me, a scientist. Can it be true? I wonder what knowledge I had, what experiments I performed. There must have been many. They must be in my head, somewhere. I slide the pencil from my sleeve, pull the notebook from under the window and turn to a clean page. There were plants, and a microscope, and . . .

Nothing. My head is full of noise, of mutterings and moans, of bells and clocks, with no room for plants or Latin names, or anything else of any use.

An hour or so passes and I have written two words: hawthorn and water.

Tick. Tock. The clock marks the seconds. I would stop that pendulum if I could, but they won't tell me where it is. They pretend they can't hear it, just like the bell. 'What clock?' they say. 'What bell?' They do it to drive me mad. I'll find that clock one day and stop it dead.

Little by little, the glimmer of hope is fading. I must not let it die. No, I must cosset it like the last hot coal in a grate. I must coax it back to life. All I need is a book or two, something to remind me.

I'm impatient to go to the gallery but am careful to hide it from the attendants. Any sign of excitement and I'll be reduced to dribbling on any books the chaplain might give me.

Chins is playing the piano. Her fingers are too big, so she ends up playing two notes instead of one. It wouldn't matter much if she wasn't so heavy-handed, pounding at the keys as if she hates them.

Ah, there is the chaplain, sitting at his table. He sees me rushing towards him and cowers, the poor man. Am I so terrifying, then? I slow my steps and try a smile. It seems to confuse him. He dithers, his eyes flitting here and there, hands picking up one book, then another. At last he seizes on *Great Expectations* and holds it out at arm's length, to ward me off, perhaps.

'Not today, thank you,' I say.

His face crumples.

'I should like a book on science, if you have one,' I say.

He peers at me through his glasses.

'Botany, if possible.' He seems unfamiliar with the word. 'Plants? Any sort of science will do. Biology? Chemistry?' He surely must know. 'Nature – the world out there.' I point to the windows.

He swallows, licks his lips. 'I feel compelled to urge you to turn to the scriptures.'

'Scriptures?'

'Science cannot hope to understand the infinite complexity of God's creation.'

'Nevertheless . . .'

He disappears beneath the table, where another box must be hidden, and reappears with a great, leather-bound tome. It sends out a cloud of dust as he drops it on the table. 'Genesis.' His eyes burn with holy fire – or a fever – or perhaps it's the spectacles that make them bulge like that. 'Genesis explains all one needs to know, about creatures, both land and sea, trees and plants, the stars in the heavens.' He says it with eagerness, and a hopeful smile that withers and dies at my stare. 'Someone with a . . .' He laughs, nervously. 'With a sickness of mind, ladies such as yourself, would do well to trust in the Lord rather than mankind.'

'So, do you have any scientific books at all?'

He clears his throat. 'No.'

'Then I shall have *Great Expectations*.' I snatch it up from the table. No studying for me, then, not today, and I doubt I'll even be able to read because I'm too busy grinding my teeth.

I sit in the same place as last time. A woman is running back and forth across the other end of the room, running from wall to wall, red hair streaming out behind her. Back and forth, back and forth she goes, as if bouncing from one side to the other. She must be the one who runs up and down the stairs.

I sit right back in my chair. That way I can barely see her. She's just an irritating movement in the corner of my eye. At least she's not laughing. I couldn't stand that. I'd have to do something about it. As long as she stays away from me, it'll be fine. As long as she keeps to the other end of the gallery.

The hands on the clock turn. The gallery is noisier than ever. Too many women clustered together. What a din they make with their shouts and cackling laughter. How many of them go to Diamond's room? Do they all have notebooks? Do they all have pencils up their sleeves? My blood chills at the thought.

Great Expectations sits unopened on my lap. I can't hear myself think. I concentrate on the book cover and on not listening to the red-haired maniac's feet tap-tapping on the floor, and her ragged breathing, and the piano, and the singing. It takes a lot of concentration not to listen to things that go on and on and on like that.

The piano continues. Bang, bang, bang go Chins's fingers on the keys. She turns her head when she sings, mouthing the words, eyebrows raised expectantly. 'Daisy, Daisy, give me your answer, do . . .'

If only she'd shut that mouth, that gaping hole with those blackened teeth and the stench – the stench. The water's going in my ears and all I can see is his mouth.

No. No. That's wrong. I have her confused with someone else. Her teeth are yellowish, but not rotten, not black.

A girl stands in front of me and smiles. She's slight, with tightly curled black hair and limpid brown eyes. Her jaw is soft, her skin smooth and still childish. She can't be more than thirteen. 'That's my favourite book.' She points at *Great Expectations*.

I hold it to my chest. She'll find the blood and tell someone. 'I don't want it,' she says. 'I've read it already.'

'So have I.' It's a competition. 'Lots of times.'

'Why don't you read something else, then?' She points at the chaplain. 'He has lots of books.'

'I don't want to.' She must be new and no one's told her to keep away. They should have told her. They should have.

'You should keep away from me,' I say.

She sits down next to me, folds her hands in her lap. 'Why?'

'Because I'm dangerous.'

Her brown eyes stare into mine. 'I'm not scared.'

'You don't know me.'

'We could be friends.' She looks around the room. 'You like reading and so do I. Everyone else in here is mad.'

'I don't want a friend.' I have to look away, angry because my eyes are watering. 'Besides,' I say, 'you're mad, too, and I don't like lunatics.'

She stands and walks away.

I stare at *Great Expectations*. I don't look up for ages, but when I do, she's sitting at the other end of the room, reading a book and her mouth is turned down at the corners.

Why can't I be friendly, nice, normal? It's not in my nature, that's what Womack says. Evil runs through my veins, he says, and perhaps he's right.

The bell goes for the dining hall. I squeeze on to the end of a bench. Dinner is a slimy, greasy soup of ham and pea. The meat is stringy, and most of the peas are still beige and hard, just as they must have come out of the box, except that they're warm and wet.

Everyone else is eating them. Crunch, crunch, crunch, chomp, chomp.

Chins prods me in the back. 'Eat up.'

'They're not cooked, the peas.'

She scoffs. 'Hark at you, Miss High and Mighty.'

The lunatics laugh, open-mouthed, their food sloshing about, dribbling down their chins. There's a strange man in the corner, a man with hate-filled eyes, words spewing from his mouth. 'High and mighty ways. High and mighty. High and mighty.'

The woman next to me has no teeth. She slaps her gums together. Slap, slap. Pink gums. Bright, piercing eyes. Slap, slap. I hum a tune to block out the din, a melody I must have heard somewhere: 'She's only a bird in a gilded cage.'

I push my bowl away, my appetite quite gone, and stand. The floor tilts away from me.

'What ails her now?' Prune says from far away.

'She come over all peculiar at dinner.'

I try to open my eyes, but they're too heavy. Prune says something else, but I'm too weary to listen and, anyway, I have somewhere to be, for I am in employment now and cannot dilly-dally here.

'This ridiculous experiment has set Mary back years,' Womack says.

'Yes, doctor,' Chins says, her voice fat with satisfaction. I can almost see the gleam in her eyes, the smug grin.

No matter. It's nothing to me now, all this. No, it's nothing to me, for I am elsewhere, dressed in a fine frock of palest green, and I must clean the grate and light a fire, tidy books, dust shelves and polish woodwork.

These test tubes are dusty, these flasks, too, and beakers and pipettes, and skillets and pewter pans, and I must wash them. Oh, and there, that shelf with the yellow jars, festooned with cobwebs. They too need cleaning. My chest grows tight, as if it's me in that yellow fluid, trapped in a jar with no air, with no escape. It's the eyes, those desperate eyes. I will turn them all away, so they look towards the wall. Yes – yes. They could be pickled vegetables like that, or strange plants from foreign lands, some hairy, with tails.

My eyes open to darkness, and snores and moans from the ward next door. A vixen's unearthly scream filters through the window. She's hunting, prowling the fields. I close my eyes and imagine I'm that vixen, free to roam, to go wherever I please. I dream of running, of leaping over hedgerows, of freedom.

CHAPTER 12

Today is a blustery day of bright sunshine and sudden, violent hail showers that pepper the window like gunshots. Trees sway back and forth, beaten, and beaten, and beaten again into submission. I push the window open as far as it will go, press my face to the narrow gap and breathe the clean, sharp smell. If only I could be out there, searching for plants as I used to. I close my eyes and imagine the smell of damp woods in winter, of leaf litter and fungi. I breathe it in, that smell, and I'm there.

Mr Banville hands me a slip of paper that shakes and trembles. 'You should be able to find most of these,' he says, 'if not all, within a mile or so of this house. Think of it as a test of your ingenuity.'

It's a test, a challenge. It has rained all night and a steady downpour continues, but if he thinks the inclement weather will stop me, he is mistaken. Rain is not a problem, but this list is, with the writing so tiny and jagged and the plant names all in Latin – Viscum album, Ranunculus ficaria, Mercurialis perennis. Not one is familiar to me. No matter. A book is all I need and any house of this standing must surely have a library.

I catch Price on his way to the kitchen.

'Could you show me to the library please?' I say it in my nicest tone, adding a smile. Either I'm invisible or he's deaf. I hurry after him. 'The library,' I say. 'Where is it?'

He sits at the kitchen table where six knives lie next to a whetstone. He picks up the most murderous of them and proceeds to strike it across the stone in regular, even swipes.

'Would you please tell me where the library is?'

He touches the blade with the tip of his finger, holds the knife up to the light. 'Only one book your sort needs.' He strokes the blade.

'My sort?' Despite my best intentions, my voice quivers.

'Read them scriptures,' Price says. 'Then mebbe you'll save your rotten soul, though I doubt it.' He proceeds to swipe the other side of the blade, over and over.

'Mr Price.' I lean on the table, look into his flat eyes. 'You have known me for less than a week. You cannot possibly know the state of my soul.'

'I know.' He points the knife at my face. 'I always know.' Swish goes the blade.

'I will find Latin names for plants in your precious scriptures, will I?' I say.

Swipe. Swipe. 'Ye shall die in your sins.'

My heart's thumping so hard it hurts. 'You're mad.'

Swish. Swish. The sound of blade against whetstone follows me out of the kitchen.

I find the library without his help, next to the morning room. Every wall is lined with bookshelves, excepting the window, which lets in little light, covered as it is, like every other here, by growth. It's for ever twilight in this place, a green tinge suffusing the whole house. The comforting smell of leather and dusty old books takes me back to my childhood, but I must not think of that now.

It takes less than a minute to find the right book and the common names: mistletoe, lesser celandine and dog's mercury. I pull on my coat, and escape through the front door into the rain. A test: and if I fail? No, I cannot fail. I must not.

By the time I find all three of the plants on my list, the rain has returned and I'm drenched to my underclothes. I hurry back, teeth chattering, and hand the plants to Mr Banville. Why does he look at them like that, with that frown? Why turn them about in his hands this way and that, holding them up to the light? I know they are the correct species, or thought I did when I found them, shouting out in excitement. Now, standing here before him, I'm less certain.

'Excellent,' he says at last.

I have done it. I have passed the test. 'And now?' I say.

'Tomorrow –' Mr Banville rubs his hands together '– tomorrow, we will get to work.'

I am to be a scientist, after all.

Each morning, Mr Banville teaches me how to make decoctions, juleps and syrups from his chosen plants. The air fills with unfamiliar smells, with steam and smoke, and it's the most exciting thing I've ever done, holding those flasks over a flame, watching them bubble and thicken and transform from a simple plant to a medicine. I label each bottle and place them in the cabinet. Whatever he does with these, he does when I'm not there, but the levels go down, so he is using them for something.

Day by day, my understanding grows, both of herbs and of Mr Banville. He's still gruff, but sometimes his eyes crinkle as if he's teasing me. It seems to please him when I laugh. He trusts me to cut plant sections so thin they're almost transparent, and to prepare slides, and I'm happy – as happy as I can be, living with Price and Imogen. The laboratory is an escape – for Mr Banville and, now, for me.

This morning, I'm preparing a section of kidneywort leaf. I place it under the microscope and step back to allow Mr Banville to examine it.

He grunts, turns to me and frowns. 'You are a most capable young lady,' he says. 'I have almost forgiven you for tricking me.'

'Tricking?'

'Your reference,' he says, 'written by your own fair hand, if I am not mistaken, and your letter of application which, if I remember rightly, suggested you were a man.'

I am found out and have no defence. 'I needed a position, Mr Banville, and a home. I was destitute.'

He nods. 'I suspected as much.'

I can't look at him. I stare at my shoes instead.

He coughs. 'I expect you to work hard. I want no complaints, no whining about that hideous creature Price, nor my – charming – wife.'

Tears sting my eyes. I take a huge breath. 'Thank you, Mr Banville.' I am safe. I am saved from the workhouse by one man's kindness. I will not forget it – not ever.

There's no time to write my memory because Prune appears with my breakfast. 'Doctor says you're to go to the airing court later.'

The airing court? That dark and gloomy place? Worse than staying in here. 'I don't want to go,' I say.

She tuts. 'Spot o' fresh air will do you good. Blow some of them cobwebs away.'

Cobwebs? There's more than cobwebs filling my head, and it will take a lot more than a spot of damp air to clear them. 'All the lunatics hate me.'

She sniffs. 'Well, no one's going to like you if you scowl like that, are they?'

I'm not aware I am scowling until she says it.

'If you smile at people,' she says, 'they will likely smile back.'

I'm not convinced about that. She doesn't know them as I do. She sees only the outer lunatic. I know what goes on inside their heads.

The airing court is every bit as small and dank as I remember, with high walls surrounding it on all sides so the sun can never reach it. No escape from here, unless one can fly.

Women stand about, for the most part staring at their own feet. Some of them cluster together in groups, talking. They stop and turn to stare as I come in. I smile. It's an effort to stretch my mouth, but I do it. No one smiles back. They just stare or look away, or make grotesque faces, poking their tongues out. I don't know why I listen to the attendants. They know nothing of madness, nothing at all.

I stand with my back against the wall, look up at the square patch of grey sky and breathe the damp air. Is there a heaven up there somewhere? Do my brothers see me, standing here with all these lunatics? I hope not. How disappointed they would be, and my father, too. They thought me destined for great things, but here I am with nothing, not even my sanity.

A bee buzzes near my leg. A bee. Here, of all places, in this barren courtyard. But now I see, close by my feet, yellow hawkweed pushing between the stone slabs, its flower bright and sunny in this grey, lifeless cavern. Hawkweed and brambles grew there, too, on the terrace at the back of the house.

The door opens behind me. 'Come along,' the attendant shouts. 'Back to the ward.'

I hold the terrace in my mind while Prune takes me back to my room, but by the time I get there, it's faded and vague. I take out my notebook and try to describe it. Hawkweed, I write. Brambles. With each moment, the terrace is disappearing, slipping away. Perhaps if I draw, instead. Yes, if I draw the flower in the airing court. This dull grey pencil cannot hope to capture that bright, sunny yellow, and yet as I draw its stem, its leaves, I see it, see the terrace, and the cracked paving stones.

A wide flight of steps leads down to the garden. Hawkweed and bramble, bejewelled with raindrops, sprout between the stones. Ivy trails at will. Rich green moss clings to the walls. From here, I can see right to the edge of the Banville lands, and beyond, to hills and, yet further, to the sparkling sea. As air fills my lungs, so hope fills my heart. Anything seems possible standing up here, with the world below me. Freedom, that's what I see. If I could only lift my arms and fly, soar over those trees, those hills, that distant sea, anything would be possible. Anything.

A forlorn pool stands ahead, a fountain of cherubs in its centre, and next to it, a summerhouse, roofless and sad. It's as if this side of the house has been forgotten, abandoned, when once it must have been so beautiful. Past the pool lies a clearing, a flat sward of grass, where tennis nets hang tattered and drooping. People played here once, had parties and picnics. They're all gone now, the land left to nature, the territory of crows and foxes.

Trees lie ahead, and a path of sorts, muddy, overgrown and littered with fallen branches. I have barely set foot on it when a sharp cry makes me jump. How my brothers would laugh to see me so timid. But there, the cry again – an animal in pain, or a person. There could be gin traps laid in this garden. Price has plenty of them hanging in the stable, after all. Picking my way with care, I draw closer to the sound. I can't leave it in pain, whatever it is, but I would not fall victim to one of Price's snares. They would hardly come looking for me, the occupants of that house. I would rot out here.

Ahead stands a building. A chapel, perhaps. No, not a chapel. It's too small, little larger than the summerhouse, and there's no tower or steeple. Only its arched windows resemble a church's, and those are glassless now, the grey stone walls crumbling around them. The door – for there is a door of dark wood, rotten and eaten away – stands open. Inside is dark with shadows and corners.

Charred beams lie scattered about, and stone plinths or altars stand here and there, some of them broken. A man is kneeling on the floor, his back to me. He is in a torn, dirty brown coat and dusty shoes, with black hair, shiny and unkempt. He's crying. No, more than crying, he's sobbing, there in that crumbling ruin with no roof.

Perhaps he has fallen victim to one of Price's traps. 'Are you hurt?' I say.

He turns his head, stares at me with dark, red-rimmed eyes. 'Who are you?' He staggers to his feet. He's tall – taller than I thought, towering there in the crumbling ruin. Something glints in his hand – a blade, long and narrow. He points it at me and smiles, a wolf smile, a madman's smile.

'Run.' He takes one long stride towards me. 'Go on, run.' One more stride.

I turn and trip, then stumble and trip again, and lift my skirts and run and run, through trees, so many trees. He's right behind me, right there, feet pounding the earth. Ragged breathing comes over my shoulder, so close behind.

The woods go on for ever. I fly across the lawn, past daisy-strewn tennis courts and the pool, surrounded by cherubs, their mouths round in shock, staring as I sprint up the steps to the terrace, two at a time.

I turn to face him.

There's no one there. My chest aches. I breathe in short gasps and laugh at myself. I'm safe. I've cheated death. Nothing moves in that still, abandoned garden.

'I'm not afraid,' I shout into the trees. 'I'm not afraid of you.'

Deafening bells ring out. They're so loud it's as if I were standing in the bell tower itself. I cover my ears and close my eyes. On and on they peal, echoing, vibrating.

The air grows dry and dusty, and still I keep my eyes tightly shut. Only when the clamour stops do I open them to find myself in a church, dark and gloomy.

The air smells of old books and lilies gone over, sickly sweet. Dust and silence, coughs and sniffs and shuffling feet. Footsteps click on the stones of the aisle, stones carved with names and dates and verses from the Bible.

Price looks over. 'There are people buried beneath.' He jabs a finger at the floor of the aisle. 'Down there, under them stones.'

I suppose he thinks it'll frighten me.

Mrs Price sits between us, all red, puffy face and piggy eyes. She nods. 'Aye.'

'Behold, the day of the Lord cometh,' Price goes on, his voice booming, 'cruel both with wrath and fierce anger.'

He's mad as a hatter.

A mouse or rat scurries under the pew. It's too dark to tell which, and the creature too quick. Poor thing, whatever it is, living in this draughty old church, listening to dry sermons day after day.

Imogen settles herself in the family pew. Her cheeks are flushed. Around her shoulders trails her long, auburn hair, worn loose like a girl's. A man sits next to her. He turns his head. It's him, the knife-wielding man, the crying man. No ragged clothes this time. With combed hair and face clean-shaven, he looks younger, but it's definitely him.

He sits with his legs outstretched and yawns. He's looking around the church with eyelids half closed, mouth curled in contempt. He thinks himself too good to be here, in amongst us common folk.

'Harry's back then,' Mrs Price says, not to me, but to her husband.

'Aye.'

I don't ask who this Harry is or what he's doing there with Imogen. They'd tell me to mind my own business. I'll prop a chair under my door handle tonight, though, just in case. For all I know he could be following me, could have that knife secreted somewhere about his person, waiting for the right moment.

The sermon's about hell and damnation, as it has been every week since I arrived. We'll be sent there for all manner of things, according to the vicar. Even thinking something displeasing to God will be enough to ensure we spend eternity roasting on coals. I wonder how I'm meant to stop myself thinking. What about dreams? When I'm asleep my mind wanders into dark places. Am I damned, then, for my dreams? A shiver runs over my skin.

The music swells and everyone sings. I close my eyes and try to find God, or Jesus, or some kind of holiness. I search in the dark, but there's nothing.

'*Glory be to thee, O Lord most high.*'

Price's voice booms out. He thinks he's going to heaven. He's certain of it. I think he's going to hell.

'*Blessed is he who comes in the Name of the Lord.*'

I open my eyes and Harry is staring at me. I stare back. He doesn't look away, as a gentleman would, but holds my gaze, boldly. His eyes are a muddy green, the colour of a wild river in spate. I can see right inside him, see what he's thinking, and what I see there, in those dark eyes, is not holy. Not holy at all.

Shouts come from the ward next door, a scream and a crash.

'Stop! Please stop it.' I keep my eyes tightly closed, clinging desperately to the church, but it's slithering away. 'No. No, stay. Please stay.'

The noise is too loud, the asylum too real. I could cry. 'Shut up!' I scream. It achieves nothing except to give me a sore throat.

I sit on my bed and write everything in the notebook with a shaking hand. It's not much, more about how I felt than what the church or Harry looked like, but now I won't forget it, now it's there and real.

CHAPTER 13

I cling to the thought of the man and the look in his eye for days. It sends shivers through me, makes my legs clamp together and a bubble of excitement form at the back of my throat. I long to remember more about him, but no matter how many times I try to draw him, I can't see him. Each night, I stare at the patch of sky, willing it to lighten, willing it to be Thursday, so Diamond can take me back there to see those unholy eyes again.

'I've remembered something,' I tell him, when Thursday finally comes. I pass him my notebook and sit in my usual chair.

'Excellent.' He opens it, reads, frowns. 'This man had a knife?' He turns the page, glances up at me, eyes wide. 'He chased you?'

'Yes.' I laugh.

'You find it amusing?'

'Exciting.' It's the wrong thing to say, of course. That's why he's scribbling so furiously on his notes, turning to a clean sheet, and writing and writing. Any normal person would be afraid – any sane, normal person.

Diamond sits back, his frown deeper now. 'This man is a danger to you. Do you not sense it?'

'No.'

'You feel no fear when you think of him?'

'Fear? No.' I can't tell him what I *do* feel when I think of him. No, I can't tell him that.

He purses his lips. 'Well, you should. Let us find out why you don't.'

Yes. Yes. Take me back there. I'm so eager that my hands tremble. Those eyes, I shall see them in just a moment.

'Watch the ring, Maud.' And there it is, that spark, arcing in front of me.

Tick, tock, the pendulum swings.

'The ring, Maud.'

Tick, tock. Back and forth it swings, back and forth.

'Forget this room,' Diamond says. 'Forget the asylum, Ashton House, even yourself. There is nothing – nothing but this ring, remember.'

'And the clock,' I say.

'Clock?' A vertical line appears between his brows.

'The clock – the ticking – the pendulum.'

He rubs his chin.

'It's stopped now,' I say. It hasn't.

'Once more, then.' There's uncertainty in his voice. Why did I mention the clock? Why? I shan't do that again, no matter how loudly it ticks.

'One . . . two . . .'

The ring waves in front of me. 'Go back to that church, Maud, if you can.'

As I drift back there, it's not the church I see, or the knife-man, but the kitchen. 'It's dinner time,' I say.

'Tell me,' Diamond says. 'Tell me what you see.'

Mrs Price places a gravy boat on the table, and plates of sliced pork and potatoes in front of us. I have grown used to her cooking now, and sometimes it's not so bad.

'Thank you,' I say.

She grunts, as she always does, avoiding my gaze. Would she be different if her husband were not here? Would she speak to me, smile, perhaps?

A bell rings, high up in the corner.

Price's cold gaze fixes on me. 'Her be needing a fire.'

'I'm Mr Banville's assistant, not a skivvy,' I say, though he knows it well by now. 'Why don't you do it?'

'Because –' he leans across and pinches my elbow, hard '– I'm tellin' you to do it, that's why.'

I open my mouth to argue, but something in his dead eyes stops me. Besides, there it is again – the bell. On and on and on. It's driving me mad. That noise is not going to stop until Imogen gets what she wants. The pork is grey, the gravy thin and no doubt tasteless anyway. It's no great loss.

I hurry to the drawing room and push the door open without knocking. Imogen's playing the piano – some dreadful dirge. 'She's only a bird in a gilded cage . . .' Her fingers miss the keys, because she's not looking at the music, or even at the piano.

She is looking over her shoulder, smiling and singing, 'You may think she's happy and free from care . . .' Oh, those clashing, clanging notes. They are all wrong. No tune can possibly be meant to sound so. 'She's not though she seems to . . .' I step forward and meet her gaze. She stops playing, slams the lid down.

'You wanted a fire?' I say.

Something moves near the window. It's him, Harry, collar unbuttoned. He leans against the wall and stares, just as he did in the church – bold, challenging. He takes a cigarette from a silver case, places it between his lips.

I kneel at the fireplace and sweep the grate.

'Darling,' Imogen drawls, 'I forgot to tell you I have a new maid.' She claps her hands. 'Imagine!'

'Imagine.'

'I'm a scientific assistant, actually.' I turn to face them. 'Not a maid.'

Harry chuckles. Blue smoke curls in front of his face. It shakes – the cigarette. Smoke rises into the air, zigzagging its way to the ceiling.

'Dull little mouse.' Imogen stretches like a cat, yawning. 'Don't you think?'

He bows low with a mocking smile. 'No one could sparkle like you, Mother.'

Mother? I drop the tongs. They clatter on to the grate.

'Clumsy,' Imogen says. 'You've made my head ring.'

I'm glad of it. Let her head ring as mine does, but worse, much worse. I twist paper, lay kindling, criss-crossed over it, and place coals on top.

'Really, Harry,' Imogen says, 'I can't imagine where your father found such a specimen. Can you?'

I turn my head and meet Harry's gaze. There is something in his eyes – something vulnerable and sad, something I'm not meant to see.

He looks away. 'Damn,' he mutters. 'Damn it.'

Imogen sighs. 'Does she think this fire will light itself?'

I turn back to the grate. I need this job. There's no alternative save the workhouse. I need this job, and to light a fire is such an easy task. I've done it many times. Indeed, I have done it only this morning in the laboratory, and yet something about this grate makes me uneasy.

Those sooty black nuggets of coal. Their smell, earthy and damp, reminds me of home. My pulse quickens, my breathing with it. I hold a light to the ends of the paper – left, middle, right. Flimsy, pale yellow flames lick at the kindling. So weak, so deadly.

I'm back home, watching the flames catch at the twisted paper, flicker over the coals. The wood hisses and crackles. It's too green for kindling, but it's all that's left.

Tick, tock. The steady, comforting rhythm of the old clock marks the seconds, just as it has all my life. Tick, tock. Tick, tock.

Smoke billows, blows back, sickly sweet. My brothers smile, glad of the warmth. How weary and quiet they are after a long day's work. Already their eyelids droop. We say our goodnights and, before I close the door, I know they're asleep. I hurry to my

*cold little room at the back of the house, and I sleep all night
like a babe. I wake the next morning, ready for a new day.*

*How silent is the house that morning, despite the sunshine,
the bright dawn, the birdsong. Silent with a deathly stillness
that clutches at my innards and chills my bones. My feet slap on
the icy cold flagstones as I hurry between my room and theirs,
my heart stuttering with dread, with an unearthly terror,
already knowing somewhere deep in my soul what I will find.*

Tick, tock. Slow, ponderous, the pendulum swings.

*And there they are, my beloved brothers, all three, sitting
where I left them, sleeping still, sleeping for ever.*

My eyes open and look straight into Diamond's.

'I killed them.'

'No.' He shakes his head. 'No, no you didn't.'

I turn away. 'I lit the fire.' My throat closes.

'It was an accident. You could not have known – none of
us would have.' He's trying so hard, and yet he can't change
the truth.

'I knew. I knew something was wrong. I almost went back
to douse the fire.' Tears spring from my eyes. 'But I didn't. I
didn't, and now . . .'

Diamond hands me a clean handkerchief but says nothing.

'I told myself I had lit that fire as I always did, every night,
that they would sit in front of it after their long day, and
drink ale and talk.'

Oh, I can't speak for the horror of it. I told myself they
would be laughing, that they wouldn't thank me for going

back, for putting out that fire. They would say I was fussing, becoming an old maid.

'I wish I'd gone back. I wish I had with all my heart.' I'm shouting, the words ragged. 'But I didn't.' I hold Diamond's gaze. 'Why didn't I go back? Why?'

He shakes his head.

'Why did I survive, when they were so much better, so much kinder than I?'

'I'm sure that's not . . .'

'Because I'm cursed.'

'No. No, Maud.'

'Everyone I love dies – everyone.' I bite my lip until it bleeds, until the metallic taste fills my mouth. 'I'm the one who doesn't deserve to be here, and yet still I live.'

All is silent save for the crackling of the fire.

Diamond's voice, when he speaks, is quiet, gentle. 'It was an accident,' he says. 'Chimneys become blocked – usually a bird's nest. You couldn't possibly have known.'

'I loved them.' I swallow the ache in my throat. 'They were all to me. Brothers, yes, but also fathers, mothers, friends, protectors – and I killed them.' I stare at these hands of mine, these treacherous hands. 'How am I to live with it?'

Diamond clears his throat. 'I shall ask the attendants to give you a sleeping draught.'

Good. Oblivion will be mine.

'For tonight only,' he says. 'This memory is intensely painful, I know.'

Oh, he can't know. He cannot. No one except those who have killed their loved ones can possibly imagine.

'Despite this,' he says, 'I do not believe it's the cause of your illness.'

I catch my breath. 'But surely . . .'

'No.' A sad smile. 'It's distressing, but all this occurred before you went to Ashton House.'

'Yes.'

'And you were perfectly sane there.'

Was I? Was I really?

'You were grieving – are still grieving – but grief is not an illness, it's the price of love.'

He has loved someone, then. He knows grief and failure and perhaps guilt, just as I do. Perhaps I always knew we had that in common.

CHAPTER 14

Nightmares fracture my sleep despite the sleeping draught, waking me with a jolt over and over again.

By morning, I'm dizzy with tiredness – a tiredness that persists for days. It's the grief, Diamond says, and will ease in time. He insists there is more to uncover, but I'm to have a break from the hypnosis. 'I'm wary of tiring you,' he says. 'You must have time to recover from such a harrowing session before we can go further.'

For weeks, I don't see him. Every night, I dream of the marsh, of the man rising from the water, of being dragged by my hair over rough ground, or of three coffins being swallowed up by the earth, over and over, only stopping when I wake, trembling and fearful. They stay with me all day, the nightmares, so that I'm afraid to close my eyes, almost afraid to blink.

Today I'm to go to the gallery. Perhaps *Great Expectations* will banish the nightmares for a while.

Sunshine streams through the windows, and yet a strange mist pervades the air, making it harder to see. If only the attendants would open the windows. They don't seem to notice the fog, but stand about in pairs, gossiping.

The red-haired maniac is running back and forth again at the far end of the room, her feet tap-tapping on the floor.

Sunlight throws shadows. A man stands in the corner, where the light can't reach him. The hazy air makes it hard to see, but he's definitely watching me and laughing in that way some people do, implying they know something that I do not. I turn my head away, but he must have moved, too, for I still see him. Even with my head lowered over *Great Expectations* until the print is too close for me to read, he is there. I hear him breathing, smell his putrid breath.

Ah, the piano at last. Sitting at it is a woman with long red hair, worn loose. Her red dress is garish, too bright and opulent for this roomful of lunatics. The attendants appear not to see these strangers, the man lurking in the shadows, the woman at the piano.

Her fingers press the keys. She sings in a thin, reedy voice, 'She's only a bird in a gilded cage . . .'

I turn away, hum 'Oranges and Lemons', but I can't block out her voice.

'For youth cannot mate with age,' she sings.

No one sings along, although they must know it. We all know it. I cover my ears.

'And her beauty was sold for an old man's gold.' The high note is beyond her.

It's the woman from the broom cupboard. I stand. I'll confront her. I'll . . .

The man has seen me. He steps forward, frowns and shakes his head, waggles a finger as if I were a naughty child.

I sit again and look about me. Where are the lunatics? Gone – every one of them, and the attendants, too. I must have missed the dinner bell, and they've left me, left me here alone with these two, of all people. That red-haired woman, that man. Well, I shan't stay, not with them.

My room – all will be well in my room, familiar and safe, and they won't dare follow me there. I stand. The piano stops with a jarring note. They turn their heads and stare, even as I reach the door, and reach out and pull, and pull.

A strong hand grips my wrist.

I scream.

''Tis only me, Mary.' Prune. Prune has come back for me. No, everyone is back – the lunatics, the attendants, all back in their places.

'I have missed dinner,' I say.

She shakes her head. 'Bell is yet to go. Sit quietly now and it will ring in a moment.'

I look over my shoulder. The man is gone; the woman, too. No one sits at the piano. Perhaps the attendants frightened them off. There are only the usual patients, and the maniac, red hair flying behind her. It must have been her then, playing the piano. I was confused, mistook her for someone else in the mist. It's easily done, after all.

Back in my room, I draw the man from the gallery. I draw his crumpled clothes, his hair. All that's missing is his face, and then I see it. I see him, Price, in the stable, brushing the mare. I try to stop myself slipping back, but it's too late.

He stops his work and watches me, watches as I cross the yard. My legs grow stiff and awkward under his gaze. No wonder locals keep away.

The day is dry, although puddles remain, reflecting white clouds. I walk past the church, past graves with mouldering bones and unquiet souls and on to the copse of trees. It's April, only three months since I came here and yet that old life of mine is gone, as if it belonged to someone else, someone luckier, someone loved and happy, in a warm, sunny world that no longer exists.

Rooks swoop and swirl, settle on black, spidery trees and rise up again in a flurry of black wings, feathers and squawking. The path is narrow and muddy and edged by spiky hawthorns that catch at my clothes. The copse is smaller than it looks from the road and suddenly all is dank, watery marshland – ditches and mounds, tangled with growth beneath twisted hawthorns and willows and ivy, ivy everywhere, blocking out the world.

It's dark here, cloistered like a cathedral where everyone whispers. Even the birds are silent. It smells of death, of stagnant water, mouldering leaves and rotting wood.

A pair of ravens croak, circle above, watching me with black eyes. Water trickles, a meandering stream. Not so stagnant after all, then. I wander beside it, keeping close to the trees, dodging the vicious thorns that try to stop me. There are few flowers this early, it being such a cold April, but soon they will come. Marshmallow will be here somewhere, hidden, buried in the soft, black earth, waiting, and perhaps other medicinal plants. They'll come when they're ready, push their way out of their winter graves and into the light.

The air chills. How long have I been walking? Too long. I must turn back, but oh, the earth is damp now, slippery. A gust of wind ruffles the surface of the puddles, breaks up the reflection of the trees. What dark magic is this? It's already twilight. The afternoon has been and gone and I have not noticed. Birds sing their goodnights as thunder rumbles in ominous purple clouds. The marsh is wetter than before. It's a quagmire. There is barely a dry patch to be seen.

On I stumble towards the trees, my hair adrift, and sticking to my face, and fat raindrops plopping all around. The ground sinks under my feet and my shoes, my poor shoes, are covered in mud, pondweed tangled in their laces. Every patch that looks like dry land turns to marsh under my feet. The water is so cold, halfway up my calves, and the trees still so far away.

There's a noise ahead I don't recognise. I raise my eyes from my feet and catch my breath. He's leaning back against a tree. Harry, the knifeman, but with no knife this time. He stands, arms folded across his chest, looking as if he belongs there amongst the trees, as wild as the marsh.

'This isn't a safe place,' he says with a smirk. 'You were foolish to come here.'

'I'm quite capable of looking after myself, thank you.'

'So you chose to be caught by the rising river.' He nods, lips pursed. *'I see.'*

River? Darkness is closing in and I can see little.

'This is a flood plain. On a full moon . . .' He waves a hand at the waterlogged marsh.

He makes no attempt to help me – not that I'd let him. I stumble onwards to dry land. He's blocking the path.

'Excuse me,' I say.

He moves aside, just a little, so that I have to brush against him to get past.

I do not run, but walk in sopping, mud-spattered frock and soggy shoes, with his low chuckle following, and my face burning despite the cold. I dare not go in at the front door in such a state. I must go through the kitchen.

Price and his wife are halfway through their supper. They stare at my shoes, my muddy skirts, chewing in unison. Perhaps they will say nothing. Perhaps . . .

'Marsh nearly had you, then,' Price says.

I shan't turn back.

'You want to watch your step, missy,' he says. *'Many a godless heathen been drowned there.'*

'Oh, for pity's sake.' I squelch down the hallway, furious that I've pleased them, and yet a bubble of excitement forms at the back of my throat.

He followed me. He followed me. I should be afraid, and yet I'm not. No, I wish myself back there, brushing against him. I wish myself back there.

*

I wake, dribbling, the notebook beside me, the pencil missing.

'Sleeping at this time?' Prune's eyes flash to the notebook discarded on the bedcover. The pencil has rolled on to the floor. 'You haven't had supper yet.' And there it is, on the table. How long has she been there, watching me?

'I was dreaming,' I say.

'What's this, then?' She reaches for the notebook.

I snatch it from her. 'Drawings, that's all.'

'I like a nice drawing.' She holds a hand out. 'Can I see?'

'No,' I say, too harshly. 'They're childish. I should be embarrassed to show you.'

She nods, bites her lip. She won't forget. She will search for that notebook as soon as she gets a chance, but she won't think of that gap beneath the window. She won't see it, unless she should lie on my bed, and why would she do that? No, I'm safe, but I must have a care and keep alert during the day. If it had been Chins who came, she would have snatched up the notebook and taken it straight to Womack.

I write all I remember of the dream. Perhaps the past is not done with just yet. The grief is still there, but there is excitement too – excitement and danger. There is Harry.

CHAPTER 15

Today we are to resume the hypnosis at last. How I've missed Diamond's room, with its large window and cabinet of treasures, and fire and tea. There's no need to look at the amber. No need to see that yellow smudge. No, I shall look at the fossils. Perhaps, when I'm recovered, I can show him how I know about ammonites and devil's toenails, and how they're formed. Perhaps, when all this is over, Diamond and I will be friends. Perhaps he'll let me help him with his collection.

I sit in my chair, keep still and smile.

Wind howls, and rattles the window. Something flies by – a paper bag or some such thing, blown by the gale. How I wish I were in the midst of that storm, being tossed about. It's wild out there, untamed, ferocious. Trees that only yesterday glowed orange, red and yellow are skeletal today, stripped of their colours, which now litter the ground like brightly coloured snow. Autumn already and another winter to come – another winter trapped inside these four walls.

'There's a patient,' I say, 'with red hair.'

He nods. So she is real then, the maniac.

'Would such a patient be permitted to play the piano?'

'No.' He taps his notebook with a pen, frowns. 'Why do you ask?'

'I thought I saw—' I stop at the look in his eye.

'You thought you saw Imogen?'

'It must have been an attendant . . .'

His frown deepens. 'With red hair?'

'No.' I laugh, as if the idea is ridiculous. There is no attendant with red hair, and even if there were, she wouldn't be allowed to wear a dress so rich and luxurious, not in this place. A visitor, then, perhaps. I open my mouth to suggest it but shut it again. He will think it a vision, and so it must have been. A vision, and not real, and he will stop the hypnosis.

'The attendant playing the piano had *brown* hair,' I say. 'I remember now.'

His eyes narrow.

'Her hair. It was brown, not red.'

Still he stares.

'I had her confused with the patient who runs back and forth – the one who runs up and down the stairs.'

'Ah.' He nods, seemingly satisfied. 'That would be Bess.'

'Yes. Yes, that's her. Bess.' I hold his gaze, keeping a half smile on my face, until he turns to his notes with a small sigh. It's probably best not to mention the fog in case that wasn't real, either.

'Your employer intrigues me,' he murmurs.

My employer? No, it's Harry I want to see.

'What does he mean to discover from these plants and so on that you collect?'

'We make concoctions – syrups and juleps, powders, and so on. Nothing of interest.' Please just wave that ring so I can see Harry. 'I think it would be better to go back to that church,' I say. 'Didn't you want to find out about the knifeman?'

Diamond ignores me. 'Medicines, then, of some sort?'

'Yes. Yes, new medicines.'

A man is standing next to Diamond's cabinet, reaching for the amber with a trembling hand.

'Do you remember any of them?' Diamond says. 'Any recipes, or experiments you performed?'

It's Mr Banville at the cabinet. Mr Banville, after all this time.

'What is it, Maud?'

'Nothing.' I blink and there's no one standing by the cabinet. Of course there isn't. It must have been a reflection in the glass, someone passing by the window, or another paper bag, or shadows playing tricks, as shadows are wont to do.

'Are you quite well?' Diamond frowns. 'You seem distracted.'

'Very well,' I say, rather too loudly, so that Prune jumps. 'I am very much improved with the . . . the hypnosis and the dreams. Especially the dreams.'

Diamond nods, scribbles on his notes, frowns. 'Perhaps it's too soon to resume our sessions.'

'No, not too soon. Not at all.' I want to see Harry, would give anything to see him. I hold myself very still and ignore the clock, ignore the bell. 'I should like to go. I should like to go back there *now*.'

Diamond watches me for a long moment. 'You're not experiencing any hallucinations? Any visions, disturbances?'

'No.' I snort. 'Nothing of that sort.' There's no need to mention the strangers in the gallery, or indeed Mr Banville, who is there again at this very moment, reaching for the amber.

Diamond's frown remains, but there's a gleam in his eyes, a hunger. He will do it. He can't resist. Sure enough, he stands, and here he comes, and sits in front of me, and there flies the ring, the spark, the key to it all.

'Tell me of your employer,' he says.

Mr Banville, reaching for the yellow . . . not the amber, no, but yellow jars, filled with monsters.

He picks up the largest of them, his hands steady, as if there were nothing wrong with him. What a strange sickness this is, that comes and goes for no apparent reason, one moment rendering him paralysed, unable to move, the next setting him trembling like the leaves of an aspen.

'You are well today,' I say.

He frowns. I shouldn't have mentioned it. He likes to pretend, on the good days, that he's not sick at all. He likes to forget about it, and who can blame him?

Syrup of mistletoe is the task for the morning. The plants are half-dead already. I mash them to slime in the mortar, leaves, stems and berries, strain the juice through muslin cloth into a pan and set it over the fire, stirring until it bubbles. A revolting sickly-sweet smell fills the laboratory. It seethes and bubbles like a witch's brew.

'Why does no one come here?' I say.

There have been no visitors in the months I have been here, not even a postman. The world outside could have vanished, for all I know.

'Price keeps them away. He doesn't like strangers, nor anyone very much, save for my present wife. I fear he thinks her the blessed virgin, which is very far from the truth.'

I laugh. It's no surprise. There is something shameless about her.

'He tells anyone he meets that the house is cursed, godless, that I keep the heads of my victims in these jars.' He holds a particularly grotesque creature up to the light. 'The man is deranged, of course.'

'Of course,' I say, wondering which of them is the maddest.

'He thinks that when I'm gone, he and my wife will have everything. He is mistaken, but I shan't tell him so.'

'Is that why you keep away from the house?'

He raises his eyebrows. 'You are curious, an excellent quality in a scientist, but likely to lead you into danger elsewhere.'

'Are you trying to frighten me?'

He is. His lip twitches.

'The house has seen too many tragedies,' Mr Banville says. 'Deaths, cholera, plague, suicide.' He turns back to the shelf of jars.

'Suicide?'

He is still, a statue. 'My first wife.' He clears his throat. 'She suffered with her nerves.'

'I'm so sorry.' I've intruded, hurt him with my questions and my curiosity.

'It was a long time ago now.' One jar crashes against another as he slides them into place. 'This was a very different house when she was here – very different. You wouldn't recognise it.'

So, this was Harry's mother then, this poor, troubled woman. Imogen is far too young after all, and they are not alike, she and Harry, nor are they easy in each other's company as I imagine a mother and son should be. There is a tension between them. Old rivalry perhaps, for Mr Banville's love.

The syrup is sticking. I take the pan off the fire.

'Be careful not to anger Price.' He slides the jar safely back on to its shelf. 'His temper is unpredictable.'

The eyes, the yellow eyes are looking at me. I turn to the window, to the sky and trees and normality. 'Price doesn't frighten me.'

Mr Banville grunts. 'The man is a tinderbox. It would be foolish to provoke him.'

I have provoked Price by my very presence, but it's not his rage that bothers me. It's the way he stares, his eyes roaming my body. If I venture into the kitchen garden, he is there, tilling the soil, planting seeds, his oiled shotgun propped against the shed door. If I go to the yard, he is there in the stable, *grooming the horse, or polishing the cart, or cleaning tools, or sweeping the barn. Whatever he's doing, he stops when he sees me, and stares until I'm out of sight. He does it to unnerve me, no doubt, but it will take more than a deranged steward to unsettle me.*

Harry's voice drifts through the window. He's going out, perhaps to the marsh. I cross the room on the pretext of getting more slides. He's below, smoking, pacing back and forth, his head bowed.

He looks up and our eyes meet. I step back, trembling. Perhaps he didn't see me. It's darker in here, after all. I clasp my hands together and calm myself. It's perfectly normal for someone to stand at a window and admire the view. I should have smiled, or waved, or pretended I hadn't seen him and opened the window. How foolish of me to step back as if I were hiding something or spying on him. My face flames at the thought of it.

'Is that boy still here?' Mr Banville says.

'It's Harry.'

He huffs. 'Be careful. He too is unpredictable.'

'I thought he was your son.'

'He is, to my shame. Have you finished those slides?'

'Just one more.' I hurry back to my bench, and attempt to cut a cross-section of stem, but my hands are shaking almost as much as Mr Banville's. What on earth is wrong with me? Perhaps it's this house. Perhaps it is cursed, after all.

I stare at the wilting leaves and withering stems that surround me. They are dying, these plants, murdered by my hand,

and suddenly I'm sickened by it, by their deaths, and I long for life, for the living, for the marsh.

As soon as Price appears with Mr Banville's dinner, I hurry down the steps, through the house and into the hall. I pull on my coat and hat and hurry over the road before I can change my mind. I must study my plants. Harry doesn't own the marsh. I have every right to be there.

A brisk wind sends clouds tumbling across a slate-grey sky, but it's sheltered here, in amongst the hawthorns. It should be a relief that he's not here, and yet it isn't. How ridiculous to be disappointed. After all, I've been warned that he's not to be trusted. No doubt I should be afraid, but it's excitement I feel, not fear.

I sit beside the stream and take my sketchbook and pencil from my bag. Water trickles, wings flutter in the trees, but otherwise all is still and quiet. A sweet perfume fills the air. Violets. I've crushed them but there are more nearby, their shy flowers delicate and beautiful. I uproot one, lay it on my lap, and take the scalpel from my bag.

The snap of a twig breaks the silence. He's careful, light-footed. Had I been drawing, perhaps I wouldn't have heard him. I know it's him. I'm sure it is.

'What are you doing?' No doubt he expects me to be startled.

'Sitting,' I say. 'Breathing, listening.'

'To what?'

'To the silence.'

His face is expressionless. After a long pause, he says, 'Is that all?'

'Yes. Why?'

He pulls the silver cigarette case from his pocket, points. 'You have a knife.'

'It's a scalpel – for dissecting plants.'

He nods. 'I expect to find you painting pretty pictures like a normal girl. Instead I find you murdering plants.'

I laugh.

He looks away, opens the silver case. With shaking hands, he pulls out a cigarette. 'You're not afraid?'

'Of you?'

He nods.

'Should I be?'

'I threatened you with a knife, so . . .' He raises his eyebrows.

'You could have caught me if you'd wanted.'

'Oh, I wanted to,' he says. 'Believe me, I wanted to.' His hand trembles as he places the cigarette between his lips. He lights it. His nails are bitten to the quick, the fingertips raw.

'To kill me?' I say.

'Maybe.' Blue smoke curls up, veiling his face. 'Maybe. I don't know.'

'You took me by surprise,' I say. 'Should you try it now, I wouldn't run, but would knock the knife from your hand.'

His gaze fixes on my scalpel. 'I believe you would, too.'

'Then we understand each other.'

'Indeed.' He bows a mocking bow. 'A pact, then. I don't threaten you with a knife, and you don't dissect me with that fiendish implement.'

'We'll see.'

He snorts. 'Good God, my mother has you all wrong, hasn't she? Dull little mouse?' He watches me, so that I grow hot and have to look away.

'May I sit with you?' he says.

I should say no. I should, but I don't.

He sits close but not touching. 'Are you ever afraid?' he says.

'Not really. The worst things I can imagine have already happened.'

I am afraid, though, of the turbulent emotions that rage inside me. I must concentrate on something else or I will make a fool of myself. There, that tree will do, that bark, at first glance merely dull brown, but on closer inspection, full of colour – fawn, ebony, burgundy, and mustard yellow, too.

He's breathing. I hear it, feel his warmth, the lifeblood coursing through his veins. Even from here, I sense his heartbeat, racing like my own.

I shuffle a little to move away from him. He's taller than I am, and the muscles under his sleeve tell me he's stronger, too.

'And what about them?' He points towards the church.

'Ghosts, you mean?' I say. 'Surely you don't believe . . .'

'Not them,' he snaps. 'My parents, the house, the whole vile . . .' He waves a hand, irritated.

'No, of course I don't fear them.'

'And Price?' He looks away, as if peering through the trees, looking for him. How perfect his ear is, with its curves and

*hollows, and the soft, shadowed skin below. He glances at me.
'Do you not fear him?'*

*His eyes transfix me, scatter my thoughts. 'I . . .' Price; we
are talking of Price. 'I've known many like him, spouting
scripture with no understanding, seeing faults in everyone but
themselves.'*

'He makes me shudder.'

*'Price is a sad, bitter old man, but he's harmless.' I think of
Price's cold eyes and wonder if I'm right.*

*Harry looks up at the circling rooks. 'He accuses my father
of being a murderer, but it is he who is the evil one.'*

*'Then have him dismissed. Surely if you tell your father
how you feel . . .' I stop, remembering Mr Banville's
dislike.*

*'My father believes nothing I say.' He glances at me and
away. 'I told him a truth once that he did not wish to hear.
It cost me dear, that mistake. Besides, my mother would not
allow the Prices to be dismissed. They are hers – her familiars,
you might say.'*

*I should laugh, but a sliver of dread runs through me,
and I can't speak. The silence goes on until it becomes
unbearable.*

*'It's about to rain.' I collect my belongings together and
stand. Come with me, I want to say. Talk to me – talk and
talk, and I will listen. 'Goodbye, then,' I say, instead.*

He makes a sound – a huff, perhaps, or a laugh of sorts.

*Mist rises from the river as I walk through the churchyard.
It cloaks the gravestones. A dark shape sweeps past the church*

and is gone. Someone more fanciful would think it a ghost. It's easy to imagine them here when fog renders the world hidden and silent.

'So they are estranged, Harry and his father?' Diamond says, once I'm back to myself.

'Yes.'

He writes something on his notes, looks up. 'Would you say your employer was a good man?'

'I liked him, yes. He was . . . interesting. A little strange, perhaps, but he was kind.'

Diamond nods. 'Then perhaps the fault lies with Harry. He did after all chase you with a knife.'

'No.' How I'm so sure, I don't know. 'No, absolutely not. Harry is . . . He was . . .' My mind is empty. 'Oh, I don't know.' My eyes fill with tears. I dash them away, glance at Prune in case she's noticed, but she's staring blankly out of the window as if she's fallen asleep with her eyes open. Good. I can't afford to let them see weakness. Any sign of weakness and I'm done for.

Diamond pours tea, his back to me. There's comfort in the ritual – hot, golden liquid splashing into cups, chink of spoon against china.

Is it Harry, then, who drags me from the marsh, tearing my hair out at the roots, while the back of my head hits stones and branches? Dread, horror, comes from nowhere, clutches at my innards, draws me down until I think I will fall to the floor.

Diamond turns and here is tea, hot and sweet, and I feel better – not right, but better. The dread is manageable now, pushed to one side, so that I can almost forget it's there. Almost.

That man in my nightmares can't be Harry. Harry's eyes threaten danger, yes, but of a different kind, a very different kind.

CHAPTER 16

That afternoon, I write about Harry, about his eyes and the danger they hold, about his hands and their bitten nails. Diamond is wrong about him, I'm sure, but not sure enough. I must remember.

I describe him in detail – his wild hair, his long limbs, those dark eyes, black lashes on ivory skin. I describe the look in his eyes, how it sets my body on fire, how it makes me want something sinful, something no decent girl should want. With each word, each letter, his image blurs. He becomes an outline rather than a man. Words are not enough to bring him back, so I draw. I draw his eyes from memory, but they're diagrams rather than a real person's eyes, and nothing like his. His hands then, his fingers. But no, they're either short and stubby, or long and thin with dirty fingernails like Price's.

It's no use. My hand aches from clutching the pencil so hard. There must be some way. I close my eyes and see my hand, and in it a sheet of paper, a list of living things – plants and lichen and mosses. I see myself hurrying through the churchyard and through the trees.

*

There's the marsh, and there he is, Harry, standing among the hawthorns. He watches me, eyes narrowed, with that unholy look. Slowly, oh so slowly, he places a cigarette between those lips. Between those perfect lips, those . . .

Gone. The marsh, the trees, Harry – all gone.

Lichen and moss, I write. I can see the note, in Mr Banville's tiny, cramped hand, see it as clearly as if it were before me, but there's nothing else – nothing. I draw the window, but it's simply my window with its hated catch and it takes me nowhere. The grille, then, or the chair. I draw them and yet the past only grows more distant. The beetle that lies dead on its back, perhaps that will do it. It could easily be one of Mr Banville's specimens, after all, and will surely take me back to the laboratory, and I can find Harry from there. I can find him then.

Nothing. There is only this room, this stale air. The past is a dull, flat, lifeless thing, as if it's someone else's past – pale and insignificant and ordinary and of no interest to me.

My drawings grow jagged and dark. The pencil tears through the paper. Still the memories slip from my mind. With every stroke of the pencil, another image vanishes. Where is he? Where can he have gone?

'Harry,' I whisper. 'Harry, come back.'

He's nowhere to be found. I must make him come back somehow. I will draw him again in these last precious pages and get it right this time. I will draw that face, those lips. I will force him to come to me.

I press on the paper. Crack. The lead has snapped. A black, empty hole stares back at me.

My chest flutters. I shan't be able to draw. I'll be stuck here for ever. No, if I find the lead, I can draw with that. My trembling fingertips run over the blanket, over the bed. Nothing. My skirts then, caught up in the folds. Please be there. Please. Nothing.

What was that? That tap? The sound of lead on wood, hitting the floorboards.

I jump off the bed. It's here. It must be. The light is so dim, and fading with each moment. I get on my hands and knees and crawl. Every bump, every splinter sends a jolt through me. I must find it. Splinters dig into my fingers, into my knees.

No lead.

I sit back, trying to calm my racing heart. There must be more lead in the pencil. It can't all have gone. I pick at the jagged wood with my fingernail, pick at it until my fingers bleed.

The door opens. It's Chins with my supper. She lays it on the table, her back to me. She's writing something on my notes.

'My pencil has broken,' I say.

She's humming.

'The lead. It's broken.'

Perhaps she's gone deaf. I cross the floor until I'm right behind her, so close I can see the fine hairs on the back of her neck.

She jumps, dropping the notes, but she recovers quickly. She picks them up and fixes me with a stare. She's much bigger than me, after all, and is quite used to throwing me about when she feels like it. Even so, her right eye twitches.

'I need a knife,' I say.

'A knife?'

'Yes. You know, one of those sharp things.' I hold up the pencil to show her the broken end, but she's stepping away, back to the door. Her face is pale – deathly so – and beaded with sweat.

'Are you unwell, Chins?' I step towards her, reach out a hand.

She pulls the door open, all the while staring at me with a peculiar expression, as if I were a ghost.

'You look sick,' I shout as she slams the door.

Her footsteps pound down the corridor. She must be very ill, or perhaps she has run to get me a knife.

I sit and wait. Someone's singing outside. I peer down into the airing court, but it's empty. Someone in the fields then, perhaps. I press my ear to the window. Piano, and a trembling voice. 'She's only a bird . . .'

That song again. I climb into bed, cover my ears with my hands and hum loudly. It's not real and it won't last for ever. She'll grow tired, the singer, then her lover will come, and she will lead him to her bed, and . . .

Ah, someone's coming. Chins, perhaps, with my knife. I jump out of bed as the door opens, but it's not her. These two attendants are unknown to me. They're bigger than the others, bigger than the doctors, with huge hands and spiteful eyes.

'Have you brought my knife?' I say it with a smile for each of them in turn – the grey-haired one first, then the mousy one.

Why do they come towards me like that? Why don't they speak?

I ease the pencil down towards my wrist.

Oh, they're coming too close. My fingers tear at my cuff but the pencil is stuck, the splintered wood caught in the fabric. I push it back up my sleeve. Yes, yes, it's free.

Huge hands reach out.

'I haven't done anything.' The jagged tip of the pencil's there – there, there, tickling the palm of my hand. I can almost grip it – almost.

The grey-haired one yanks my arms behind my back.

'I haven't . . .'

She drags me away from the bed.

'I haven't done . . .' I kick back, hard. 'I haven't done anything.' I kick and kick at her shins. She's senseless – too big, too strong.

I cease struggling. They may be strong, but perhaps they're stupid. If she lets go for one moment – just one – I will have the pencil in my hand and then they'd better watch out. 'I apologise for kicking,' I say. 'I mistook you for lunatics.'

My arms will surely pop out of their sockets, she pulls them so. I catch her shin again with my heel and scrape it down but other than her sharp intake of breath, it has no effect. She's invincible.

'Look,' I say, 'just let me go for a moment and I'll explain.' The pencil is there, its jagged end in my hand. If I can just grip it.

The mousy one has something in her hand. A beaker. A beaker full of . . . Oh, it's the light-coloured mixture, that foul, noxious-smelling stuff. The very mixture I had after that shower bath. This is Womack, trying to poison me. I see it now.

She lifts my chin.

I won't swallow it. I won't. The beaker cuts into my gums.

'Open your mouth.' She yanks my hair back. 'Open it.'

She'll break my neck, or the other will push my teeth out, push them in and down my throat. I can't win. The light brown liquor pours down my throat so I can't breathe. So much of it. Never-ending. I'm going to die. At last the beaker is gone. Air rushes into my lungs, liquid with it. I cough and cough, and still she will not loosen my arms.

Once I can get my breath, I spit to get rid of the taste. 'What vile creatures are you?' I say. 'I'll tell Diamond what you've done.' That face. That face with those close-set eyes, that grey hair reminds me of someone back there, back in that house. No, no, not there, but somewhere else, somewhere dark.

They're laughing, the pair of them, so pleased with themselves. If I could get my arms free, I would stop their laughter. If I could only . . .

The heel of a hand presses between my shoulders. 'On your knees.'

'No.' My legs are straight. They will not bend – not for these monsters.

'On your knees.' Yes, I know that voice, that accent. I know it from somewhere . . . somewhere long ago, before . . . The mousy one pushes, pushes. She's too strong for me. My knees hit the floor with a crack, and there's the stinking slop bucket, right in front of my face. I turn my head, but it's coming, and there's nothing I can do to stop it. My stomach tightens. My mouth fills with sweet saliva and up it comes – my supper, my dinner. They hold me over the bucket, pushing down on the back of my neck, pulling my arms back. I heave over and over until my insides sting and hurt and there's nothing left to come out except bitter yellow slime.

They let me go at last. My shoulders ache. Pins and needles prickle at my fingers. I don't have the energy to attack them now. I can't even move from the floor, so the pencil's no use, no use at all.

I flex my hands to get the blood back, and see other fingers, white as newly churned milk, flexing, flexing in the kitchen doorway.

'Come on.' The attendants heave me up and on to the bed. 'Let's have no more talk of knives.'

'No,' I say. 'Sorry,' I say.

They exchange smug smiles. No doubt they think they've done a good job, but I'm alive, and I bet Womack's furious about that. He's probably watching now, livid that his plan hasn't worked.

Even once the attendants have gone, I can tell he's still watching. I have an instinct for these things. If I look closely at the holes in the walls, I'll see his eye looking back at me. A shudder runs through me. I tear two pages from my notebook. It hurts to do it, but it's important, and Diamond won't mind. I check the walls for gaps. There are some between the window and the wall, and some where the pipes come through. I push bits of paper into every one, without looking, just in case I see it – his eye, the yellowy-white and the washed-out blue circle, and that black hole in the centre staring back at me.

I lie back on the bed, close my eyes, and try to imagine myself at the river, wading into the deep and floating away. I drift into sleep and open my eyes to a strange light coming through the window.

The night sky is an unearthly, shimmery purple. My feet slap on the cold floor. I push the window open. The catch gives way, falls into the airing court with a clatter of metal on stone. Now I can breathe, breathe this purple air, so sweet and still. I pull myself up and lean out of the window.

What moves there in the airing court? There, far below my window? It's Womack – Womack climbing up the drainpipe. He looks up and sees me, sees me with his pale, bloodshot eyes. Hand over hand, up and up he comes, like a spider, scuttling. Too fast. Too fast.

I open my mouth to scream, but no sound comes out. His fingers grip the sill, and there is his face, those cold, empty eyes. 'You'll never get out of here,' he says. 'I won't let you.'

I run to the door, pull at the handle, pull and pull.

He laughs.

It's locked. Of course it is. No one will come to save me. I should know that by now. No one ever does. I must save myself.

His head is through the window now, then his neck and shoulders and arms, and soon the rest of him will follow.

I push on his head, push it out of the gap. He grips my arm with those fingers, those stubby fingers.

He's pulling, dragging me out, but I shan't go. The window ledge presses into my middle. I'm not going with him. I won't, not with him. I prise his fingers off, one by one, digging my nails into his flesh.

One by one they are gone, and he falls – falls backwards, arms and legs outstretched like a star. On and on and on he falls.

The stairs are dark as I run downwards. The staircase turns, round and round and round, and down, down, and then corridors with paint peeling from the walls, and the ceiling falling down, and then out into the airing court and there he is, lying on the flagstones, limbs twisted and broken, tongue lolling from his mouth, swollen and purple.

Dead. He's dead, and I'm free. I step over his broken body, and there before me are fields and hills, and trees and all life. I am free.

I turn to see him once more, but he's gone. The airing court is empty, save for one lone hawkweed, and a bee.

CHAPTER 17

My stomach is sore and hurts when I move, waking me time and again. It's a relief when the sky lightens. The nightmare feels so real, and yet it can't be because the window is shut, and there is the clasp, in its place, as annoying as ever. I inch myself to a sitting position, climb out of bed, and step gingerly across the room. I push at the window. The clasp only allows it to open a tiny bit, just as it always has. It was a bad dream, then – hardly a new thing for me – and yet it feels like a portent. Perhaps Womack has indeed died overnight. How much better my life would be without him.

'Is Doctor Womack quite well?' I say, when Prune brings my breakfast.

She frowns.

'I thought he might be dead.'

'He's as alive as you and me.' She's watching me with that look they get when they think I need an injection.

'Good,' I say, loudly. 'That's very good. I needn't fret, then.'

Chins appears at the door. 'Doctors want to see her.' She raises her eyebrows.

'They must wait,' Prune says. 'She's had no breakfast.'

'Does Diamond know I've been poisoned?' I say.

Chins scoffs. 'Poisoned? You get what you deserve in this place, my girl. No more, no less.' She nods – two chins, then three, then two.

Prune's mouth pinches tight. 'Get dressed quickly, Mary, and eat your biscuit. Hurry, now.'

If they would keep still, I would be much quicker, but they fidget and tut, which makes me clumsy, and my hands awkward. I have scarcely pulled my dress over my head before we are out of the door. I leave the biscuit on the bed.

They're taking me downstairs. Doctors, Chins said. More than one. Perhaps they're scared I'll attack them. Safety in numbers. Two by two, like the ark. As if I'd ever attack Diamond. Besides, I can't move quickly enough to hurt anyone, even if I wanted to. The doctors have nothing to fear from me this morning. I can barely lift a hand, and it takes energy to attack someone. I should know.

We go downstairs to the ground floor again, and for a while, I think we're just going to Diamond's office, that the plural was a slip of the tongue, but we go past his door, on further into the dark corridor. My pulse quickens. I've been in this place before. My vision blurs, sounds grow muffled. I bend forward, clutching my knees.

'What's the matter with her now?' Chins snaps.

'Shush.' Prune rubs my back. 'Come on now, Mary. It's only the doctors.'

Only the doctors. Yes, only the doctors.

Diamond's raised voice comes from behind a nearby door.

'. . . little more than a vegetable when I came here. She was in a permanent stupor, for pity's sake.'

Diamond's there. All will be well. I raise my head, take a deep breath.

'There,' Prune says. 'That's my girl.'

The attendants exchange a glance, then turn to the door. Chins knocks. There's silence for a moment, then, 'Come.'

The door swings open. My heart lurches. I know this room, that window without a grille looking out on to the shrubbery, the thick rug that feels like marshland under my feet.

'Is something bad going to happen?' My voice sounds different, shaky.

'No.' Diamond is standing with his back to a glowing fire, fists clenched at his sides like a boy about to fight. 'All is well.'

I don't believe him. A white line traces his mouth, and his nostrils too are white at the edges. If all is well, why the livid, red spot on each cheek? And why are Chins and Prune gone?

Womack sits sprawled in an armchair, his face veiled in a haze of tobacco smoke.

There's a stain on this rug, right by my foot. It's faded now. You'd never notice it if you didn't know it was there. It's blood. My blood. Something bad happened in this room with the grille-less window, something painful and sad, and it's still here, in the air, the walls, the rug.

Tick, tock. A huge grandfather clock stands to the right. Tick, tock. The pendulum swings from side to side. It reminds me of Diamond's finger.

Diamond steps towards me, holds my elbow. 'Sit down, Maud.'

Womack says, 'Good God, man, you don't even know her name. It's Mary.'

Tick, tock.

Diamond's jaw tightens. 'Doctor Womack thinks your treatment – the hypnosis – is making your condition worse. What do *you* think?'

Womack snorts. 'What does it matter what *she*—?'

Diamond talks over him. 'Do you want to continue with the hypnosis?'

He wants me to say yes but Womack is glaring at me and I remember the shower bath he gave me before and I'm frightened.

Tick, tock.

If I say yes, maybe Diamond will protect me. I think he'll protect me.

Tick, tock.

I open my mouth and the word's nearly there, about to burst out between my lips.

Tick, tock.

'You see?' Womack cries. 'She's an imbecile.'

Diamond's jaw clenches and he spins around. 'She is slow due to the purge you ordered last night. Was there really any need for that?'

Womack's lip curls. 'It's the practice here to use emetics to calm agitated patients, as you very well know.'

Diamond nods. 'Yes, yes, it is, and one I disagree with.'

Womack shrugs. 'Disagree all you like. I'm the medical superintendent here, not you. Your treatment has caused my patient to have a psychotic relapse. She threatened an attendant last night.'

Diamond frowns, turns to me. 'Is that true?'

'She demanded a knife. A knife, man.' Womack's pipe has gone out. He taps it into the fire, pulls a pouch of tobacco out of his pocket and commences filling it.

Diamond scratches his chin. 'It's possible that this upset might have been a reaction to the hypnosis. I wouldn't insult you by pretending otherwise.'

Womack watches him, sucks on the pipe, which has gone out again.

'As Maud . . .' Diamond says.

'Mary.' Womack holds yet another flame to his pipe.

'As the memories come back, these . . . unfortunate effects will lessen until they cease to exist at all, until she is completely healed.'

Womack frowns. 'So which particular memory caused this outbreak of violence, in your opinion? Tell me how Mary has benefited so far from this treatment. What has she remembered, for instance? Anything of any meaning whatsoever?'

Diamond turns to me. 'Tell Doctor Womack what you have remembered, Maud.'

I can't tell him of Harry – I would not have him know anything of that, but I must say something, or Diamond will have to, and how can he know what I would hide and what I am happy to reveal? 'I was a scientist,' I say, at last.

Womack's eyebrows shoot up. 'Is that so?' His gaze alights on Diamond. 'And you believe this?'

Diamond shrugs. 'I see no reason to disbelieve it. Maud certainly seems to have a good knowledge of herbs and herbal medicine.'

Womack stares, wide-eyed. 'You know as well as I do, sir, that women's brains are not capable of scientific study. They're too soft, prone to overexcitement.'

'I disagree.'

'Astonishing.' Womack shakes his head. 'How can you imagine these memories, these so-called recollections, are accurate? She's a fantasist, a liar, a woman so unreliable she doesn't even know her own name.'

Diamond shrugs. 'I do not claim to know if everything a patient recalls is true. Some memories will be based in reality, others will be dreams, nightmares and so on that nevertheless seem real to the patient.'

'So, these so-called memories could be nothing but figments of the imagination?'

'Well,' Diamond says. 'It's possible.'

'Lies, in other words.' Womack sneers. 'And you call this medicine?'

Diamond flushes. 'The purpose of my study,' he says, 'is to determine whether the very act of remembering forgotten events, be they real or imagined, can effect a cure.'

Womack turns his scathing gaze on me. 'I hear the patient killed her brothers.'

The colour drains from Diamond's face. 'That was an accident.'

Chins has betrayed me.

Womack's jaw tightens. 'Mary has suffered a psychotic episode due to this foolhardy experiment of yours.'

'Study,' Diamond says.

Womack fixes him with pale eyes.

'It's a study, not an experiment.'

Womack blinks. 'Whatever you call it,' he snaps. 'I insist you confine your efforts to other patients.'

Diamond raises a hand. 'Please, I do not for a second forget your exalted status. However, I believe the Commissioners for Lunacy are not only my superiors, but also yours?'

Womack stares.

'It is they who have asked me to undertake this research.'

'You have plenty of other suitable patients,' Womack says. 'You told me so yourself. More than enough for your study.'

'But Maud is by far the best example of traumatic amnesia.' Diamond's eyes spark with anger. 'Even if that were not the case, to begin afresh with a new patient would set my study back by weeks, months.'

Womack leans towards him, eyes bulging. 'One more chance, *sir*. Should Mary show any further sign of violence, this will come to an end, commissioners or no commissioners. The welfare of my patients takes precedence over any so-called scientific *study*.' He strides to the door and opens it with a flourish. 'I expect you to put the health of my patient ahead of your own ambition, sir.' He waves us out.

Diamond opens his mouth, shuts it again, and we are out in the corridor, cloaked in an aura of pipe smoke.

'Is it true?' he says, once Womack's room is behind us. 'Is the hypnosis making you ill?'

'No, not at all.' I lift my chin and quicken my pace to illustrate how well I am, how perfectly normal and healthy and sane.

'No nightmares, visions, nothing of that sort?'

My laugh is too loud. It echoes from the walls. 'Good heavens, no. Those days are far behind me.'

'Good. Good.' Silence save for our footsteps. Chins and Prune are ahead, waiting at the bottom of the stairs.

Diamond stops. 'Did you truly demand a knife?'

'I wanted to sharpen the pencil.' I look into his troubled eyes. 'The lead snapped, and I needed to draw.'

He laughs. 'Well, why didn't you say so?'

'Womack would never allow me a pencil. He thinks me too dangerous.'

He nods. 'And are you?'

I can't lie to him, not when he's looking into my eyes. 'I don't know.'

'Then perhaps we can find out by looking at your drawings.' He strides towards the stairs. 'They can be very revealing, drawings.'

He wants to see those torn pages, those dark, jagged lines, that meaningless chaos? And what will they tell him of me? Nothing good, of that I'm certain. And what of my writing? All I wrote about Harry?

I hurry to catch up with him. 'I'll bring the book on Thursday.' It will give me time to tear out the worst of the pages and cram them into the gaps between the floorboards.

'I shall see them now.' He starts up the stairs before me. I must stop him, but Chins and Prune have noticed something in me, my expression perhaps, my traitorous face. They take my arms. There is to be no escape.

Diamond sends them away once we get into my room. 'You may attend to your duties.'

Prune leaves, but Chins doesn't move. 'Doctor Womack said . . .'

Diamond holds up a hand. 'I shall be perfectly safe.'

Chins is unhappy, her mouth a tight line of disapproval, and yet she has no choice. Go she must, shutting the door behind her.

'It was Chins who betrayed me,' I say.

'Chins?'

'That attendant.' I point at the door. 'The one with the chins.'

Diamond's lip twitches. 'Are you certain it was her?'

'She was the one there, when I remembered about – about my brothers.'

He walks to the window, stands there for a moment. 'Then we must make sure she can't do that again.' He turns back, smiles, settles himself on the chair. 'Now, I should like to see the notebook.'

If I say no, he'll think I have something to hide and will search for it, and perhaps call the attendants to help, and perhaps take both notebooks and my pencil away. Perhaps I should ask him to close his eyes or turn his back, but he is a doctor, and I, after all, am mad, so he surely will not. Also, he would be very stupid to do so, and I do not think Diamond is stupid.

I walk to the window, pull the brown notebook from its hiding place and hand it to him. He turns each page with painful slowness, leafs through those first, neatly written thoughts and memories, through sketches poorly drawn but recognisable as depictions of some kind of reality. I see them through his eyes, see each drawing darker than the last, messier than the last. My heart quickens as he nears the last few pages.

'I remember the past when I draw,' I say, loudly. 'That house, and the people there. I remember many things.'

He will surely want to hear these memories. He will put the book aside.

'For instance,' I say, 'I remembered making . . .'

He turns one page, then another, and back again, and on to the final, crumpled pages. He runs his finger over the dents and tears where the pencil has dug in, where I have pressed too hard. He will find no sense in that jagged writing, nothing recognisable.

Sweat is slicking my skin. 'This room is too hot,' I say.

He's not listening. No, he is getting his own notebook from his pocket and writing, and writing, and frowning.

I stand. 'I must go outside, or I shall faint.'

'Sit down, please,' he says. So I sit and sweat and curse myself for not destroying that notebook as soon as I awoke. I could have torn those pages into pieces and thrown them out of the window. Too late now. Diamond has finished and is watching me.

'I must draw,' I say. 'If I can't draw, I will go mad – more mad.'

'I agree,' he says.

'So I will need a new pencil.'

He nods.

I'm not expecting it to be so easy. 'And a new notebook.'

'I believe you still have one.'

The flowery one. Of course. 'Yes – yes, I had forgotten.'

He hasn't actually said yes to the pencil. A nod could mean anything. I could have misinterpreted it. Perhaps he wasn't really listening.

'So I may have a new pencil?'

Another nod. He looks up. 'I can't tell what you have recalled from these last pages.' He turns the book this way and that. 'Can you tell me what you remembered?'

'It all vanished as I wrote, as I tried to draw – slipped away, bit by bit.'

Once again, he turns the crumpled pages this way and that. 'I feel it must have been important for you to have exerted such pressure.' Sharp eyes watch me. 'You were desperate to remember?'

I nod, for I was, desperate to see Harry – and still am. Diamond's taking the ring from his waistcoat pocket, slipping it on to his finger, and there's the spark, and no one can stop me now, not Womack, not anyone, because I am there at the marsh.

This is wrong. It's night-time, and dark, too dark to see.

'Diamond?'

Leaves rustle, twigs snap. Someone is coming through the trees. 'Is that you, Diamond?' *It's so dark I can't see.*

'All is well, Maud,' Diamond says from far away.

No – no, all is not well. He's come to kill me. He's come to . . .

'Harry,' Diamond says. 'Tell me about Harry.'

Harry? Yes – yes, Harry, and the marsh, and daylight.

An orange sun hangs low in the sky. The first truly hot day of the year is almost over. The air is still, and filled with the lazy buzzing of insects. In the marsh, though, all is green and cool. Harry's lying next to me, pretending to be asleep. He comes often now to sit and watch me work. He says it relaxes him. We sit on the same bank each time, where the air is still scented by the last, fading violets. Today, I'm attempting to draw the flowers and herbs of the marsh, but my eyes are constantly drawn to him, to the rise and fall of his chest, his long limbs, his face.

'Tell me about the flowers,' he says.

'You'll have to look.'

'Pretend I'm blind and you have to describe them to me.'

I point, even though he can't see me, at white flower spikes rising from the water. 'Bogbean.' I ignore his snort. 'It has pale pink and white flowers and is good for scurvy and for purifying the blood.'

'Latin name?' he says, lip twitching.

He thinks I don't know it, but he's wrong. 'Menyanthes trifoliata.'

He squints up at me. 'Are you making that up?'

'No.'

Because he's laughing, I laugh too. I can't stop smiling. We smile for a long time, holding each other's gaze.

'I prefer bogbean anyway,' he says, glancing around then closing his eyes again. 'What of that white carpet between the trees?'

'Sweet woodruff.'

'And those tall, purple ones lurking beside the stream?'

'Monkshood. Aconitum napellus.'

He opens his eyes, frowns. 'You remember them all?' In this light, his eyes are blue and green and as beautiful as the marsh.

'They interest me.'

'And do I? Interest you?'

I look away, back at my drawing. 'I enjoy your company.'

'And I yours,' he says. 'So we're friends?'

'Yes.'

'Good.' He settles himself, closes his eyes.

My heart is beating too fast. My hand shakes as I pretend to continue with my flower sketch. Instead I draw his face: the curve of his jaw, his shadowed eyes, his mouth.

His mouth.

Something comes over me, some madness. I bend my head and kiss his soft, pale pink lips.

His eyes fly open. There's that unholy look in them, the one from church, the one that makes my body quiver.

'I'm sorry.' Why did I do it? Why?

He places a finger over my mouth. 'Shush.' His hand is on the back of my head, pulling me to him. He presses his mouth to mine, opens my lips with his tongue. It's a mistake. I'm making a mistake, but there's a hunger inside me, a raging fire, a leaping, joyful wanting that overwhelms all reason, so when he pulls away and looks back at the house, I turn his face back to mine and kiss him, and kiss him, and kiss him.

He's lifting my skirts. His hands, his hands, and the hardness of him. I cry out, but he covers my mouth with his. When he pulls his head back and looks into my eyes, it's there again, that look, and my limbs tremble.

He moves inside me, whispers in my ear. 'You're beautiful.'

I've made a mistake.

'You're so . . . you're so . . . you're so beautiful.'

Perhaps I make a sound because, 'Shush,' he says. 'Someone will hear.'

His eyes are half closed, his mouth half open. He moves, faster, harder. He's forgotten me, forgotten I'm there. He's shut inside his own head, in his own pleasure.

I've made a terrible mistake.

He shudders, cries out, and buries his head in my neck.

He's still – a dead weight on top of me. The marsh seeps into the back of my frock, into my hair. It trickles into my ears.

The water. The water. I can't breathe.

He moves, lifts himself from me.

Air rushes into my starved lungs. My hands sink into the mud as I lift myself from the water and sit up.

He lights a cigarette. 'You must go back alone,' he says, smoke curling from his lips. 'Our secret.' His mouth twists. It looks like disgust. At me? At himself? I can't tell.

I'm afraid to see it, so I get to my feet, even though my body trembles throughout, and my legs are weak. I run back. The front door makes barely a squeak as I push it open and slip inside. My heart beats with painful thumps against my ribs in case Price should appear and shout biblical curses at me. But there are only murmurs from the kitchen and the sound of a piano being played, badly, from the drawing room.

Out of breath from taking the stairs two at a time, I close the door behind me, safe in my own room. Rust lines the edge of the mirror, and pops up here and there all over the glass, but I can see enough to know I look different. How wide and dark my eyes are, how flushed my cheeks, my lips purple and swollen – as if he's brought me to life where before I was half-dead.

I peel the wet clothes from my body, peel them away from scratched and reddened skin, from breasts sore and blotchy. His seed runs down the insides of my thighs and a great, swelling joy bursts inside me.

I hope it wasn't a mistake. I so hope it wasn't.

My room vanishes and there is Diamond, scribbling in his notebook, his face crimson.

'I'm sorry,' I say. 'I didn't know it would be so . . .'

'It's perfectly fine.' He coughs, dabs at his face with a clean, white handkerchief. 'Perfectly fine. We must get to the truth, somehow.' Another cough. 'We will continue this at the next session.' Oh, he's all of a dither, the poor man. He thinks me immoral, a harlot.

'I did love him,' I say.

His eyes meet mine. 'I know you did, Maud. I know.'

CHAPTER 18

The thought of Harry sends shivers through me, wave after wave. I can think of nothing else. As soon as I have a pencil, I will go back there and kiss him again – and again, and again, and I will never stop.

Day turns to night, but no one brings my pencil. Tomorrow, then, surely tomorrow. I can't even read my old notebook because Diamond has taken it to aid his research. He will keep it safe, he says, away from prying eyes, and I have no choice but to believe him. Perhaps in my dreams, then, I will find Harry. I close my eyes and search for that lost summer when he loved me, but the marsh I find is dark with stinging frost in the air, and there is no Harry there.

Another day passes with no pencil. There is only Prune and medication and food and drink and sky and endless, endless seconds. Tick, tock, tick, tock, the relentless passing of time. I hate the sound of it, the sound of my life ebbing away.

How many days now since I last saw Diamond? Five, perhaps six, and there has been no gallery, no dining hall, no drawing or writing or even dreaming. The flowery notebook is as pristine as ever, and of no use to me, none at all.

I pace the floor. The clock is louder than ever. Back, forth. Back, forth, the pendulum swings.

'She's only a bird.'

'She's only a bird.'

'She's only a bird.'

'She's only a bird.'

'Shut up!' I shout at the wall. 'Shut up!'

This is what it was like, before Diamond. Me pacing the floor with empty hands, empty sleeves, empty head. This is what it was like before.

Thursday comes and Chins is to take me. Diamond will certainly have my new pencil. He is keen for me to write and draw, after all. He said so himself. And I'll be able to see Harry.

'Ah, Maud.' Diamond's cheeks are flushed, feverish.

I sit in my usual chair and smile, although he is busy writing and can't see the smile. No matter. I smile at the window, instead, at the trees and flower beds and the chapel, and there, a smile for the yellow rose teapot, and cups and saucers and sugar bowl and milk jug and silver teaspoons.

'How have you been since we last met?' He's still not looking at me.

'Very well, thank you.' I clasp my hands in my lap, the fingers entwined, and concentrate on keeping them still. I'm determined to seem like a normal person, a sane one, for I must have a pencil, must draw again, must go outside. 'And how are you, Diamond?' I say.

He hides his surprise well, but not quickly enough. 'I am also very well.' He smiles. 'Very well indeed.'

'That's splendid news.'

Chins snorts.

I shoot her a look, wishing her gone to the grave. She smiles in return. I turn back to Diamond, but my composure has gone. My hands pluck at my skirt and won't cease. Diamond studies my notes. He hasn't seen. I must forget Chins for now.

'May I go for a walk again?' I say. 'In the grounds?'

Why doesn't he look me in the eye? Instead, his gaze is focused on my forehead, as if it is me who has the third eye. 'I'm afraid not.'

Afraid not? Surely I have misheard.

'I was not aware,' he says, 'of your attempted suicide.'

'Suicide? I have never . . .'

'The river?' Diamond says. 'You attempted to drown yourself.'

'In the river?' That day – the day I ran and made it to the sluggish brown water, and jumped from the bank into the cold, deep. 'I didn't intend to do myself harm.'

'Then what exactly *did* you intend?' How those words snap out of his mouth.

'To feel the cool water through my hair, of course.'

A curt nod, eyebrows raised. 'You are able to swim, then?' This is a different Diamond, one whose eyes spark with anger.

'I can't swim but I can float,' I say. 'I lay on my back and looked at the sky and the river ran through my hair.' Oh, that cool water, washing away the dirt and silt.

'You do realise you would have drowned,' he says, 'if those brave attendants hadn't jumped in after you?'

'They disturbed the water. I was perfectly safe until they dragged me under.'

Diamond sighs. 'The river is unpredictable, dangerous.' He moves papers about on his desk.

'Can I at least have my new pencil?'

He has moved those same papers several times, now. Whatever he's looking for can't be there. He looks up, swallows. 'Doctor Womack feels . . .'

'He would stop me drawing?'

'He feels it's too dangerous – that you may do yourself harm, or harm another.' No wonder Diamond can't look at me. 'I cannot go against my superior,' he says. 'I'm sorry.'

'So, I am not to go out, nor to draw.' My words sound calm, but inside, a fire rages.

Diamond holds his hands out, palms upwards. 'Doctor Womack . . .'

'Perhaps Doctor Womack doesn't want me to remember. Have you considered that?'

Diamond stares.

'After all,' I say, 'he would have you cease the hypnosis.'

'Well, he's . . .'

'With no hypnosis, no drawing, no fresh air, the past will stay buried. Did you not say that very circumstance would destroy me?'

Ah, he can't answer. No, he can't because he knows I'm right.

'Did you not say it would kill me?'

I have him. He's flustered, his eyes flitting from me, to the window, to me again. He takes a deep breath. 'Perhaps you're right.' He glances at Chins, who is staring fixedly at the ceiling. 'Nevertheless,' he says. 'I must obey my superior in all things.'

'Of course you must.' I stand. He won't meet my gaze, and no wonder, for he knows what he will see there and he is ashamed.

'Take Maud back to her room,' he says, once more moving those papers.

Chins smirks. 'Yes, doctor.'

Does he have any idea what he's done, how it feels to have something precious given to you only to have it taken away? No, he cannot, for that would never happen to him. He winces at my bitter laugh.

Chins pulls at my arm. 'Quick, now.'

'Goodbye, Diamond,' I say, loudly.

His mouth turns down, as well it might. I am glad to be gone from there. Glad.

'Thought you'd have him do your bidding, didn't you?' Chins says as we climb the stairs. 'We're all wise to your tricks, Mary.'

She will never see me cry – not ever, no matter how she goads.

'You're not as clever as you think,' she says.

And here we are, back in my room. I am back to the beginning, as if Diamond had never been, except that now I know what I've lost, that Harry is out there somewhere, and that I will never find him again.

The sun sinks low in the sky, its golden rays like fire on the tree tops, and there is the river, glistening, gold dust sprinkled across the landscape. I could draw it if I had a pencil, for I will never go there again, to that river. I will never leave this prison now, not ever. I thought I had a friend in Diamond, an ally against Womack, but I was wrong, as I am so often wrong about people. What a fool I was for thinking he would be different.

Night falls and still I stand there, though I can see nothing now but my own fractured reflection, broken into pieces, just like my mind.

The door opens behind me. Chins or Prune, no doubt, come to douse the lights. But no. I see him in the reflection – Diamond.

I turn to face him. He doesn't come near. Wise doctor.

He delves in his pocket and brings out a pencil – a pencil with a sharp point. He places it on the table. A trick, perhaps. I won't fall for it.

'If you should happen to find a pencil,' he says, 'you would do well to hide it, for you are not permitted such things.'

Can he be a true friend after all?

'I cannot give you such things,' he says.

'No, Diamond.'

'On Thursday, I do not expect to see you carrying a notebook.'

'I have no notebook,' I say, 'nor any pencil.'

He nods, turns, opens the door, and is gone.

Is this one of my visions? Is that pencil a figment of my imagination? Perhaps it will disappear as I draw near. Vanish. But here I am at the table and still it sits there, as real as the hand that reaches out for it, the fingers that close about it.

I draw my hand, my thumb, my fingers, their nails and knuckles, and I forget the asylum and Womack and even Diamond. The world disappears. It's like hypnosis, where there is only Diamond's ring. It comes back to me, a passion so intense that the breath flies from my lungs.

How bright the world looks this morning, how pristine and new and full of life. My life is changed. I am changed. Everything is different. I can't imagine ever sleeping again. I'm up before sunrise, and dress carefully, my fingers trembling at what I've done.

The pendulum swings downstairs. Tick, tock echoes in the hallway. The clock spring wheezes and strikes seven.

I'm dismayed that the day is not further advanced. It's too early for him to be there, and yet I must go, I must.

He's there, pacing up and down with that long, loping stride. My heart leaps at the sight of him, at his smile.

'I've missed you,' he says.

'It was only yesterday . . .'

'Too long.' His warm, strong hand folds around mine. 'Did you sleep?'

I shake my head.

'Nor I,' he says, and half laughs.

He feels the same. He feels as I do. Everything is as it should be.

He kisses me, slips one hand around the back of my neck, the other around my waist, presses himself against me.

'Somewhere dry this time,' he says.

A delicious shiver runs through my body.

He takes my hand and leads me across the patchwork of ditches and banks. 'It's treacherous this way,' he says. 'You have to know where to tread, or the marsh will have you.'

He's heading towards a willow further downstream. I've never been that far. It's darker there, and full of shadows.

We stand beneath the trailing branches. The trunk is rough and bumpy against my back. He unbuttons my bodice, rushing with fumbling fingers. He doesn't look at me. He's concentrating on the buttons. They're small and round and awkward. His hands tear at the fabric. Buttons fly off, and his hot mouth is on my neck, my shoulder, my breasts, sucking, kissing, biting.

My knees fold, but I don't fall. He's pressed against me, holding me upright. His hands scratch at my skin, under my skirts. It's as if he's fighting me. I want to slow down, want him to kiss me gently, but he's already inside me. His eyes close and he's gone, somewhere else, somewhere I can't go.

Another day, before sunrise, when the morning light is cold and colourless. I'm searching the marsh for buttons torn from my dresses by him. At the base of the willow lie fragments of lace, and there, along the bank of the stream, buttons, ribbons.

I collect them and hurry back to my room to sew them back in place. Day after day, week after week, I repair torn seams, tears in the fabric until scarcely one dress still has its original buttons. The green silk frock is so patched and darned and altered that it no longer resembles itself at all.

The days grow shorter. No matter how I try, my mind wanders from my work these days, my eyes stray to the window. Each second away from Harry is a small torture. The thought of him makes me swoon with desire.

Mr Banville clicks his tongue. My samples are too thick. Yesterday they were too thin, or had air bubbles trapped inside. 'Are you ill?' he says, irritated.

'I think perhaps I have a slight fever.' My face grows hot at the lie, and yet it is a fever of sorts, a sickness that is beyond my control.

'You may as well go,' he says. 'I would not have you waste any more of my precious samples.'

I hurry from the laboratory before he can change his mind. It's only mid-morning, but Harry will be there, despite the first chill in the air. I sense it, sense him calling me.

Imogen appears in the hallway. 'This room needs cleaning,' she says.

This room, this morning room that I cleaned only yesterday, that has not had time to become dirty. I must clean it all again, and lay the fire, and brush the curtains. It's as if she knows, as if she keeps me from him deliberately.

It's a full hour before I escape and hurry across the road, by which time I'm hot, sweaty and dirty. What does God think as

I pick up my skirts and run past the church? Run through the sleeping dead? Perhaps he is looking the other way. He must be busy elsewhere. Please be busy elsewhere.

Harry's pacing the bank, an unlit cigarette dangling from his right hand.

'I'm sorry,' I say. 'Your mother, she . . .'

He pulls me into his arms, stares into my eyes. 'I can't bear to be apart from you.' Perhaps he means it, perhaps not. His smile is tentative, wary. 'I once thought you a dalliance, a trifle to appease my boredom. Now I can't imagine my life without you.'

'Me? A dull little mouse?'

He looks away, back towards the house. 'Don't speak of her.' A shudder runs through him.

'What's wrong?'

He kisses me. 'Shush.' Another kiss. 'Don't ever speak of her.' Another kiss, and another and I'm lost, and forget about Imogen, forget everything but his mouth, his body.

He pulls away. How dark his eyes are – almost black.

'Tell me what's wrong?' I say.

He shakes his head, and kisses me, but these kisses are different, not heated and frantic, but tender and sweet so that tears spring into my eyes. Oh, let this love never end. May it last for ever. May he never tire of me, never turn to another, never lose this insatiable hunger.

'You're the only good thing in my life,' he says, later. 'Everything else is poisoned.'

I don't ask what he means, but at the back of my mind, I wonder.

Mist rises from the marsh, haunting and beautiful. This golden summer is nearing its end. We lie exhausted in each other's arms. A shadow moves among the trees. I catch my breath. A man, not far from us – not nearly far enough.

'There's someone there.' I button my bodice with clumsy fingers, pull down my skirts.

'Where?'

My heart stutters. 'It was Price. I think it was Price.' I point to a tangle of hawthorns and brambles. 'Right there.'

'There's no one,' Harry says. 'It's just the trees moving. Look.'

He points, and it's true that the branches dip and sway, throwing shadows here and there. 'He'd be torn to shreds there, anyway.'

He's right. Of course he is. It was nothing but branches swaying in the breeze. He pulls me to him and kisses the top of my head. His heart beats a chaotic rhythm against my cheek.

'Have you known many women?' I say.

His heartbeat quickens. 'Yes,' he says, 'but none like you.' He slips his hand into mine. How it trembles. He squeezes my hand, trembling still. 'With you, I feel that I might not be damned, after all.'

'Why should you be damned?'

He turns his face away, draws his hand back to himself, and half laughs – a bitter, harsh sound.

I watch the side of his face and wait, but no words spill from those perfect lips.

'It's the cold.' I shiver as if to illustrate the point. 'It addles your brain.'

'Yes.' He smiles a tepid smile, and I have to look away. His eyes are brimming with dread and despair and fear, and I can't bear to see it.

'It's the cold,' I say again. 'That's all. Just the cold.'

CHAPTER 19

Now I have my pencil, sleep eludes me. My nights are filled with Harry; my days, too. The attendants coming and going, the medication, even the noise from the lunatics next door can't distract me. My thoughts are all of him, all of him and nothing else.

Thursday dawns. A leaden sky blocks out the daylight so it's almost like night-time, but Diamond's room is warm and bright and comforting.

Prune brushes down her apron, turns to her usual chair.

'Perhaps you would come back in an hour or so,' Diamond says, 'to take Maud to her room.'

'Come back?' Her mouth hangs open.

'There's no need for an attendant to be present, and I'm quite sure you have enough work to keep you busy.'

She casts a longing look at the warm fire as she leaves.

'Have you recalled anything new?' Diamond says, once she has gone.

'Yes. Yes, things are much the same as before. I'm working in the laboratory and making syrups and so on.'

'And Harry?'

I stare hard at the window. 'The same as before.' Heat pulses from my face.

'No aggression? No violence?'

'No.' I must look him in the eye, or he won't believe me. 'No, he is gentle.'

He holds my gaze for a long moment.

'I think Price saw us,' I say, to break the silence. 'Harry said there was no one there, but . . .'

'Your instinct told you otherwise?'

I nod, and there he is in the corner, Price, and here am I with grass and pondweed in my hair, on my clothes, and the smell of Harry all about me.

Oh, I'm in disarray. I pull down my skirts. Too late. Far too late.

'Maud?' Diamond says.

My fingers fumble with the buttons of my bodice, and I must pull it together. He's watching, watching with those black eyes.

'What is it?'

Price's stinking breath warms my face. 'They are altogether become filthy,' he says. 'The day of thy watchmen cometh.'

'Maud?'

'Nothing.' I can still smell him, smell that stench, and yet there is only Diamond here, no one else. 'Nothing at all.' I hold my hands still. 'I was remembering something, that's all.'

He nods, frowns. 'Remembering Price?'

A shudder runs through me.

Diamond's eyes narrow. He comes to sit before me, slipping that ring on to his finger.

I don't want to go back there, not with Price lurking, but before I can say so, the spark glitters in front of my eyes, left, right, left, right.

It's nearing the end of a long day. I would rather be at the marsh with Harry than tramping these fields searching for shaggy ink caps and giant puffballs, but his mother has need of him today, he says.

All is pandemonium when I get back to the house – Mr Banville bursting forth from the morning room and her, Imogen, shouting after him, 'Edward, don't be ridiculous. Your eyesight . . .'

He turns, Mr Banville, and his face crumples. 'I believed you.' He is crying. 'I believed you over my own son.'

Imogen takes a step towards him, reaches out a hand.

He shakes his head, lip curled. 'You've been clever, you and your vile servants.' His voice is calm now, cold. 'But not clever enough.'

'Edward.'

'You've taken me for a fool, but you will find I'm not as stupid as you think.'

'Darling.' Her voice trembles. 'You're overwrought.'

'You took my son,' he says, 'my flesh and blood. You took him and made him yours. Well, no more. No more.' He turns and strides away, his movements stilted, rigid.

She doesn't follow this time, but shouts, 'Price. To my room.'

She sweeps past me as if I'm invisible, and up the stairs. I turn to see Harry looking like a small boy, like a small lost boy.

'What happened?' I say.

He turns away, to the front door and pulls it open. The marsh. Of course, we will go there.

The door slams in my face.

A mistake, that's all. The wind blew it shut – a sudden gust on such a still day – and any moment, it will open. Any moment now.

I wait, and wait. The door doesn't open.

Well, I have much to do. The library. I must go and study.

I lay my books on the desk before me but, try as I might, not a single word I read reaches my brain. All I can think of is Harry, the way he flinched, the way he turned his back, shut me out. Have I misjudged his affection? Has it all been a lie?

As I step outside the library, a shadowy figure comes towards me. My heart jumps. He loves me, then.

But it's not Harry; it's his father, striding out as if he were a much younger man.

'Where is she?' This is a new Mr Banville, this man bristling with fury, a man I don't recognise.

I point at the stairs.

One curt nod. 'With my son?'

I clear my throat. 'With Price.'

His laugh is bitter. 'Then it will save me repeating myself.'

He takes two steps towards the stairs, pauses and turns to me. 'Have a care, Maud. They're far more dangerous than you realise.' He stumbles, reaches for the wall.

'Mr Banville?'

His gaze is fixed, unfocused.

'Are you unwell?'

He falls, flat on his face. Crack, on to the tiles, a crack that echoes through the hallway.

I run, crouch beside him, my heart racing. Please don't be dead. I hold the back of my hand to his mouth. There is breath – faint, but there.

'Price!' I shout. 'Fetch a doctor.'

Notes from the piano filter down the stairs. She's singing again. 'She's only a bird in a gilded cage . . .'

The clock ticks, the piano plays, wind whistles under the door.

'Price!' It's a ragged screech.

The piano falters, stops. Imogen peers over the stair rail. 'Price?'

He appears behind her shoulder, as if by magic.

'I believe my husband has fainted.'

'It certainly looks that way, madam.' He saunters down the stairs, looks up at Imogen. They hold each other's gaze.

'Would you take him to his room, please?' she says.

'Aye.' Price bends and throws Mr Banville over his shoulder like a sack of coal.

I follow them up the stairs and around the circular landing. How easy it would be to fall to one's death from here – or be pushed. I hurry into Mr Banville's room. Price dumps him on top of the covers, and is gone without a word, without a glance. Poor Mr Banville.

An hour passes, perhaps two, before footsteps clatter up the stairs and around the landing, the sound jarring in the still house. The door bursts open. Imogen and a red-faced man, out of breath and laughing. Laughing. Her with her red hair unpinned and wild, clinging on to his arm like a leech.

This is the doctor then, this vision in frock coat and waistcoat, and starched, upstanding collar. This man with a full, drooping moustache.

I stand back to allow him to examine his patient. He takes my place beside the bed, so that I find myself staring at his back. It seems the abundance of hair on his face is at the expense of that on his head, which is sparse and wispy, revealing patches of pink, wrinkled skin. Stubby fingers hold Mr Banville's wrist – Mr Banville, clean now that I have washed the blood from his face, and as comfortable as I can make him in this lumpy bed.

'There's nothing to be done for him,' the doctor says.

'Nonsense,' I say, for there is plenty to be done and he is not dead yet, not just yet. 'His colour is good, his heartbeat strong.'

The doctor is not impressed with me. 'Good God!' He throws his hands up in the air. 'Why did no one tell me we had a medical genius in our midst?' He says it to Imogen, not me. 'And there was I, thinking myself the only doctor here.'

Imogen looks at me as if I were a cockroach, or something equally revolting. 'You are no longer required here, Lovell.'

'No longer required?'

'I shouldn't expect you to go tonight, not so late. The morning will do.' She smiles with cold eyes.

Go? Leave Harry? Leave Mr Banville to their tender mercies?

'Your husband will need a nurse,' I say, blood punching in my ears.

'He's unlikely to require one.' Again, the doctor addresses Imogen, not me.

Imogen frowns.

'I have experience of nursing.' I press my case while she hesitates. 'And it will save you all that tiresome advertising and interviewing.'

Please, please, please say yes.

'Perhaps,' the doctor says. 'It would be as well to save yourself any unnecessary strain, my dear.'

She sighs. 'Very well, but just until I find someone better.'

'Of course.' I even manage a smile.

And they are gone, Imogen and the doctor, gone together, clattering down the stairs.

A choking sob comes from the shadows. Harry, white-faced and hollow-eyed.

'He will recover,' I say, 'with care. And I will care for him, Harry. I will care for him as if he were my own father.'

Muddy eyes stare into mine. How lost he is. How utterly lost. He makes a noise, half laugh, half snort, and covers his face with his hands.

'Oh, Harry.' I step towards him.

'No.' He shakes his head, holds out a hand to stop me. He doesn't want me.

'Your father may be able to hear,' I say.

He nods, swallows, waves at the door, and I must go but I fail to close the door fully. It's wrong. I know it's wrong of me and yet I cannot stop myself pressing my ear to the gap.

Oh, he's distraught, my poor love, his words muffled, high-pitched, punctuated by sobs.

The clock ticks in the hallway below, chimes the quarter-hour. The pendulum swings. Tick, tock. Tick, tock, on and on, and chimes the half-hour, and there he is, Harry, eyes puffy and red-rimmed.

I hold out my arms, but he shakes his head, steps back, a look of horror on his face. 'Look after him, will you?' He says it as if he hardly knows me.

'Of course.'

He nods and is gone without a backward glance. I'm a servant to him now, nothing more.

Never have the stairs to my room been so dark, nor so steep. My life, too, has grown dark, altered in only a few hours. All that was secure this morning is now gone, even Harry's love, and without that, what is to become of me? It's as if these last months have never been. All those caresses, whispers, promises are meaningless. And I? I am nothing to him.

I fall into bed fully clothed, too weary to cry. Sleep creeps upon me, creeps over me like a shroud. Moments later, my door creaks open and there he is. There he is, a silhouette framed in that narrow doorway.

He closes the door, treads lightly across the room. His skin is ice cold against mine as he climbs into my bed. He smells of the

*clear night air, of pondweed and hawthorns and everything
I love.*

'Have you been to the marsh?' I whisper.

*He nods, and I kiss him, kiss his forehead, his eyelids, his
mouth. He wraps his arms around me, lays his head on my
chest, and cries. He cries while I stroke his head. He cries until
we both sleep. I haven't lost him, after all. I must never lose
him, never let him go, never. I must hold him like this for the
rest of my life.*

A voice counts in my ear. 'Ten. Nine . . .'

I don't want to leave that bed, leave him all alone.

'. . . Two. One. Come back. Maud, come back.'

I open my eyes, still half there, in that house. 'I wasn't
ready to come back.'

Diamond's writing.

'Did Mr Banville recover, Maud?'

'I can't see so far,' I say. 'I can only see him there, in that
bed. Is that not enough?' I have forgotten myself, have let my
voice grow loud, strident, and Diamond is frowning, writing
on his notes.

'That doctor would have let him die,' I say.

Brown eyes look into mine. 'So, what did you do?'

'I don't remember.'

'Close your eyes and think, Maud. What did you do?'

With my eyes closed, I see it, the laboratory, dull and
lifeless without him, and there his desk and, in my hand,
the key.

All is chaos in the drawer; papers, ink and tiny, cramped writing. Beneath lies a book, and inside the cover, row after row of plant names, of juleps and syrups, infusions and tablets, and their effects. Every medicine I have made is there.

Hope and despair cover these pages, and each ends in misery, each one, for not one medicine has cured his palsy, not one.

But apoplexy is different. There will be medicines of use here, there must be. I turn to Culpeper and search for apoplexy. He lists two remedies only: walnuts, and lily of the valley. There are walnuts in the kitchen, and didn't I distil those scented white lily of the valley blooms in May? I'm certain I did. I will treat Mr Banville myself, he will recover and all will be as it was. All will be right again.

'You made him medicines?' Diamond says. It feels like an accusation.

'I didn't kill him.' I hold his gaze and dare not look away, and yet, as I stare, I wonder. Did I? Did I kill him? How am I to know?

Prune takes me back to my room, keys jangling at her hip.

'I was a scientist,' I say.

'A scientist?' she says. 'That's nice.'

'And a nurse.'

'A nurse, eh? Well, well.' She pushes the key into the lock, turns it and opens the door.

There's someone in my bed – a man – and a doctor standing beside him, holding his wrist. Prune has brought me to the wrong room. I turn to leave and bump into her.

'What now?' she says.

'Nothing,' I say, because there is the table with the chewed leg, and Prune would surely notice if these people were real.

She steps into the corridor and locks me in. They're not real, I tell myself as I turn to face them, but there they are, as clear as day.

'There is nothing to be done for him,' the doctor says. 'Nothing to be done.' He lets go of the man's wrist. It drops to the covers with a small thud.

'There's been some improvement,' I say, because it is Mr Banville in the bed, after all this time, and I remember how he loves Great Expectations. *How we both do. 'I read to him and he responds.'*

The doctor puffs his chest out like an irate cockerel, and glares at me with the palest blue, washed-out eyes.

'He smiles when I do,' I say, 'laughs when I read something funny.'

The doctor packs up his bag, snaps it shut. 'He's deaf and dumb.'

'It's true that only half his mouth moves,' I say, 'but he can certainly hear.'

The doctor leans towards me, eyes bulging. 'He's deaf. And dumb. Deaf and dumb. Deaf and . . .'

'He's not deaf!' I shout. 'He is not!'

That shut him up. Oh, yes, that stopped his nonsense. And Mr Banville, so sleepy now after the doctor's visit. I brush his hair back, tuck in the covers. 'Sleep now.' Sometimes he looks so like Harry – that same beautiful face.

Oh, but there is that doctor again. Is there no getting away from him? And Imogen, too, sitting there by the fire, and the doctor standing behind her. Standing behind her and kissing her neck. '. . . selfless, my darling, utterly selfless', and his hand sliding into her bodice. 'How is that gentle heart of yours? How is it? How is that gentle . . . ?'

'He's not deaf!' I shout.

He will never save Mr Banville like that, not with his hand in Imogen's bodice, fondling her breasts. No, he will not save Mr Banville, so I must.

'He's not deaf!' I shout. My teeth clench together. 'He. Is. Not . . .'

'Lordy, you'll wake the whole asylum.' Prune's shadow moves on the wall, elongated and spindly. 'Could hear you all down the corridor.'

My bed is empty – empty, and the doctor gone. I must get into it, claim it as my own before another vision decides to inhabit this room. Why they would want to is beyond me, it being so small and dull and drab.

I climb into bed, close my eyes, and see them again. Mr Banville, so poorly, and that doctor, so familiar, with those pale eyes and drooping moustache. I sit up, catch my breath and cough. Womack. The doctor is Womack. I am so convinced that I write in my notebook, 'The doctor at Ashton House is Doctor Womack,' only to doubt myself a second

later, and add, 'or looks very like him'. After all, I see many
things and not all of them are real. I wouldn't want Diamond
knowing about my visions. He would be sure to give me that
searching look, and perhaps stop the hypnosis. And then
what? Then Womack would once again be my doctor. He
would steal Harry from me, steal my past, and trap me in my
madness for ever.

CHAPTER 20

My dreams are of the garden at Ashton House, the garden at dusk on a sweet summer evening.

I am wandering through the shrubbery, breathing the clear air, when something, a noise, makes me glance back at the house, at the terrace. I turn, look back and wake with a start. All night, I dream the same dream, each time waking at the same point, until my head aches with it.

For days, days and nights, I'm unable to move from that spot in the garden. No matter how I try, how I write or draw, there is no going forward from there. Oh, I can move back, can see the kitchen and the Prices, but why would I want to do that? Again and again, I stand in that shrubbery and turn, and look. Did the world end then? Did sudden madness overtake me, there amongst the fading blooms, the seed heads? Mr Banville, the doctor, the Prices are all as real as they ever were, but with each day it becomes harder to find Harry. With each day, he fades, until he is a mere reflection, a ghost.

'Something's happened,' I say, when I'm next in Diamond's room, sitting in my chair, my safe chair, embraced by its arms. 'I can no longer see the past, even when I draw.'

His eyes widen, flash to Chins who is yet to leave, right hand lingering on the door handle. She steps through the door, pulls it shut behind her.

'Go on,' Diamond says.

'I was standing in the garden at dusk, and everything stopped. I can't move forward from there.'

He leans forward, eyes bright and eager. 'Were you with Harry?'

'No, I was alone.'

He's disappointed. He wants Harry to be the cause of my sickness.

'I turned to look at the house,' I say, 'turned at some sound, perhaps, and it's as if someone knocked me on the head with a mallet.'

'Perhaps someone did.' Diamond's eyes are troubled. 'I would suggest this might be the moment your sickness began.'

'Yes, so can you take me back there?'

He frowns, purses his lips. 'I fear this could be distressing for you. An attendant should be present.'

'No,' I say. Have them listening? Gossiping? 'They've heard too many of my secrets already – far too many.' I clench my teeth together, smile until my face hurts, and finally there it is, the spark, arcing in front of me.

'You must tell me if you wish to stop,' Diamond says.

'Yes, yes.' Just count and let me go there.

'If you wish to come back . . .'

'Yes. I will tell you.'

'Very well.' Diamond's voice is uncertain, but he counts all the same. 'One. Two . . .'

The numbers fade, grow quieter.

'Can you see the garden?' Diamond says.

'Yes, I see it.'

The sky is pink and purple, the air sweet and heady with stock and hay.

Voices come from the terrace. It's Imogen. She steps through the French windows, laughing, throwing her head back so that her loose auburn hair shimmers down her back. I step into the shade of the shrubbery. There's someone with her. I expect it to be the slimy doctor, but it's not him. It's Harry. He's holding a cigarette. He cradles it in his long fingers, places it between his lips.

They speak in low voices, the pair of them, their heads close together. Every time she laughs, she flings her head back, exposing her white throat. Why do they stand so close together? Why does he look at her throat that way, that same hungry way he looks at me?

I should go to the marsh and watch the bats swooping over the water. I should go.

Her hand touches his shoulder, slides down his arm. That's nothing, is it? That's normal – that's perfectly proper.

He steps back, away from her.

Yes, my love, step away. Step away.

She catches his arm. She's pulling him close, closer, too close. She slips her hand around the back of his head.

Step away, my love.

She's kissing him, as I do, on the lips. And on, and on, and now his arms are around her and his eyes are closed. No – no, I must be mistaken. This light is so dim, and he could not kiss her, not her, not like that. No, it's my eyes playing tricks.

Ah, she's walking back to the house. She's going inside, away from him. He will come to the marsh now, and perhaps we'll laugh about it, about my mistake.

She stops, flashes a coquettish smile over her shoulder. She cocks her head towards the house. It's unmistakable, her meaning. She's calling him in, like a dog on a lead.

He's not going. He holds his half-smoked cigarette up in the air.

He won't go, surely. He loves me, I know, even though he doesn't say it. He doesn't even like her, will not let me speak of her.

I've made a mistake. After all, it's almost dark and they're quite far from me. It's my eyes playing tricks, or my mind, or the devil leading my thoughts where he will.

Harry's staring after her. He looks suddenly helpless, like a small boy, standing there as if paralysed.

His cigarette falls to the ground unnoticed and rolls away. He turns towards the house.

I must stop him. I step forward. 'Harry.' It's nothing but a whisper.

He's gone, through the French windows. After her.

I walk back around the house, through the front door, and stand in the hallway. Grey light seeps through an upstairs window. Small creatures scurry in the darkness. Imogen's playing the piano. 'Her beauty was sold for an old man's gold,' she sings. 'She's a bird in a . . .'

The piano falters, then stops with a bang as if the lid has been slammed down. Chill air clings to my skin, clammy and damp.

Is he there now, in her room? I imagine her taking his hand, leading him to her bed. Does he go willingly? Does he think of me at all as his beautiful limbs tangle with hers? Does he kiss her as he kisses me? Does his hot mouth fasten to her breasts, her stomach, her thighs? Does he tell her she's beautiful as he moves inside her? Does he cry out as he spends himself?

No. No, he can't. Not with her.

I hold my breath, listening, listening for it, that cry I know so well.

The pendulum swings back, forth, back, forth. Tick, tock. Tick, tock.

And there. There it is. That cry.

But it's me who cries.

'Calm yourself, Maud,' Diamond says. 'It's all in the past now.'

All in the past – so why this aching loss?

'It seems we have found the cause of your illness,' he says. 'As is so often the case, it was a broken heart – a betrayal – of the worst kind.'

'Yes.'

'Harry broke your heart, that's the nub of it.'

'I see.' I swallow, breathe deeply and blink hard. 'Yes . . . yes, he did. And there is nothing more?'

He shakes his head. 'It was most distressing for you.'

'Yes.' A broken love affair. Infidelity. How dull, how boring and predictable and normal. How weak I must have been to have fallen apart so at such an everyday occurrence.

Diamond's as disappointed as I am. His jaw sags with it. 'I see little point in delving further,' he says, as we settle ourselves by the fire. 'Over the next few weeks, I will lead you through the events you have recalled, reminding you of what happened, until all is restored.'

So there will be other meetings, and tea, and warmth, and I am not to be banished, discarded just yet. It's some small relief.

His sharp eyes hold mine. 'Do you feel unburdened?'

I should say yes. It would be kinder, and we would both be happier. It can surely be no great sin to lie in order to make someone happy, and yet I cannot.

'No,' I say. 'I'm sorry.'

He sits back in his chair and twiddles his pen. 'Not relieved at all? Not in any way?'

'No.'

He frowns, leafs through the pamphlet on his desk. 'That's most disappointing – disheartening, in fact. It says here . . .' He turns another page, then another, tracing a line of writing with his fingertip. 'It says that there should be a distinct lightening of mood, if not a sense of elation?' He looks up, eyebrows raised.

Perhaps I should say yes, I am unburdened. I am joyful, free of madness and happy, yes, happy, but I'm not. 'Nothing,' I say instead, and it's true. It's as if the loss has drained me. I should at least feel sadness or anger, but there's nothing now. I am an empty shell.

'Perhaps it will take time – a week or two,' Diamond says. 'Let's see if your spirits will have lifted by then.'

'Yes,' I say. 'I'm certain they will.'

CHAPTER 21

'Doctor Womack will allow you to go to the gallery,' Prune says a few days later, 'since you've been so well behaved.'

Well behaved makes me sound like a dog.

The nice attendant who never comes to me – the pretty one with fair hair – is sitting at the piano. Her fingers are long and slender and as pretty as the rest of her. I imagine the other attendants are jealous. I imagine they make her life a misery.

She doesn't play the usual music hall songs. There's no 'Daisy Bell', no sing-along ditties. She plays proper music, sad and beautiful. It makes me long for something, although I don't know what. I like it, and soon the other patients stop moaning and listen. Some of them cry, but I don't, not with all these lunatics about and the attendants watching.

Even the maniac is quieter, dancing and twirling like a ballerina instead of running back and forth.

The young girl with curly hair is sitting at the far end, her head lowered – the one who wanted to be my friend.

I glance at the chaplain's table and catch him watching me. He looks away and busies himself with arranging the books, taking more from the box, and moving them hither and thither. His fear is palpable, his eagerness to be gone from here, his dread of the madness, as if we might infect him with it. As I approach the table, his movements quicken, grow jerky.

'May I have *Great Expectations*?'

He jumps. He must have known I was there, and yet he jumps, the poor man. He picks up the book and hands it to me with a wan smile.

I hold the book close, and walk across the room, to the far end, a place I've never dared go before. With each step, my heart beats faster, my chest feels tighter, as if I'm diving under-water, deeper and deeper with less and less hope of return.

By the time I get there, she's talking to a girl next to her, someone nearer her age than I.

She looks up and sees me. Her eyes are flat and brown and cold.

I hold the book out. 'I've brought *Great Expectations* for you.'

'I've read it.' She doesn't blink, not at all.

My heart beats so vigorously that I can scarcely hear the noise of the gallery. 'You could read it again.'

'Why would I do that?'

'I don't know.' I clutch it to my chest. Stupid. Stupid of me to try being nice. It doesn't suit me and makes my eyes smart and my throat ache, and now I'm at the wrong end of the room, and so far from my place, from where I should be and I'm standing there, just standing and staring, and I don't know how to get back to my seat.

'Turn,' I murmur to myself. 'Turn around.' And I do, and it's easier than I thought. One step follows another and I'm halfway there, in the open, for everyone to see. My legs are stiff and awkward. If I focus on my destination, just focus on that and forget the others, I shall be fine, and I'm almost there, I'm so nearly there, when an enormous woman sits there – sits in my place.

'That's my chair,' I say.

She looks up. Piggy eyes that remind me of someone.

'I need my chair.' How the room swoons about, sways this way and that, tilting and shifting.

Someone catches my elbow. 'Come now. Sit here. Sit down.' It's the chaplain. His grip is stronger than I'd expect for so slight a man, but then they are strong, men, when they want to be, when they want to make you do something.

I sit, not because he's told me to, but because I think I may fall if I don't, fall and make a spectacle of myself, and perhaps the book will open on *that* page.

'There,' the chaplain says. 'That's better, isn't it?'

Is it? Better than what? Better than lying sprawled across the floor, I suppose. Yes, definitely better than that.

It's just as well I didn't make a friend. It was stupid of me to try. I can't afford to like anyone, to care about anyone. It's hard enough looking after myself.

The door opens and in comes Womack. He looks about him, scanning the faces. I stare at my lap and wait, wait for those brown shoes. Sure enough, they come straight to me.

'I hear your behaviour is much improved, Mary,' he says. 'You are calmer now, I see.'

'I should be calmer yet if I were able to go outside,' I say. 'It's unhealthy to be so confined.'

He sits beside me. He shouldn't sit so close, close enough for me to smell him, feel his warmth.

He clears his throat. 'There's nothing I would like more than to allow all my patients the freedom of the grounds.' It's the sympathetic voice, the one that makes my scalp crawl. 'However, I think we both know what you would do if given such an opportunity.'

'I would breathe freely, enjoy the fresh air, the smell of grass and trees and water.'

'And therein lies the danger,' he says. 'I will not risk the lives of my patients, nor the lives of the attendants who have to dive in after them.' The mask of concern is slipping, his words bitten off.

His hands sit on his knees. They're small hands for a man, with short, stubby fingers. 'So,' he says, in a new, breezy tone, 'how much have you remembered about your past?' His fingernails are grubby and too long. 'What, exactly, have you recalled?' His index finger taps on his knee, fast, irritated.

I shrug. 'Nothing.'

He grunts like a pig. 'These recollections of yours cannot be true,' he says. 'Someone like you could never be a scientist.'

Someone like me? Someone mad? Ugly? Dangerous? He doesn't elaborate.

'It's common for girls such as yourself to imagine themselves intelligent and attractive when, frankly, they are neither.'

I meet his gaze and hold it until he looks away.

'There is no shame in having dreams, Mary. We all have them. The problems arise when we convince ourselves they are true.' He stands. 'I fear you will never be fit to be released. You would do well to accept your lot and be grateful.'

Grateful? For this? My mind races for some clever response, but he's already moving away and the best I can manage is a laugh. He hears it, though, because his step falters.

A lunatic calls him from across the room. 'Doctor, doctor,' she cries, her arms reaching out, imploring him. 'Doctor, please.'

Oh, the relief when he is gone. My head swims for it.

CHAPTER 22

The lights are out. I sit on my bed and stare at the night sky. Womack's words go round and round in my head. Perhaps I am truly deluded, my 'memories' merely stories I've invented. And yet Diamond believes me, and Diamond is surely a better doctor than Womack. Besides, if I were going to invent a lover, he wouldn't have fingernails bitten to the quick, nor would he tremble and be so fearful, nor would he betray me. No, he would be strong and brave and true and nothing like Harry.

It will do me no good to think of him. I must forget, put it behind me, but what am I to do now? How am I to escape this place without the past to go to? I'm afraid to draw in case it takes me back there, in case I see them together, but this nothingness is unbearable. Diamond says it is simply a left-over, a remnant of that long-ago grief. It will go soon, he says, taking my madness with it, but it has not gone, not lessened one tiny bit.

Perhaps if I face it, my memory, write it all, feel again the fury, the hurt, the betrayal, then this soft, sick dread that infects my every waking, every sleeping moment will finally go.

I put my pencil to the paper, and see myself there, at the bottom of those stairs. Someone's retching, retching over and over. It's me, there in that house. It's me retching.

I clutch at my middle to stop myself crying out. He's loving her now, just as he loved me, whispering sweet words, kissing her neck. It is all I can see, their two bodies entwined. I shall go mad with the thought of it. All is spinning around me – the house, the world, my life. I stumble through the hall to the kitchen, and up the stairs to my room. I would not have them see me like this, would not have them know my weakness, see my pain. I thought myself loved, fool that I am. Those tender words he spoke to me meant nothing. Those tears he cried on my shoulder, they too must have been a pretence. I thought I knew him, but this Harry is a stranger to me.

I push my bedroom door open. I must leave, pack my things. I pace the floor. Where will I go? I can't live in this house with them. Oh, but Mr Banville. What will become of him if I go? Who will care for him? None of them, that is certain.

I pace up and down, up and down. What am I to do? Will he dare to come here, to pretend all is as it was? Hatred and hurt churn within me. Hours pass and he doesn't come. It's for the best. I couldn't bear to see him now, to watch lies spill from that perfect mouth.

My door is locked, the chair wedged against it, for he always comes to me late at night. How many times has he come to my bed from hers, from the very act of . . . ? The thought makes me feel sick. I climb into bed and pull the covers over my head and wish the world gone, but it goes nowhere. No, for there are footsteps on the stair. My heart punches at my ribs.

'Maud?' The door handle turns. How many times has he done this? How many? And, each time, I have opened my arms to him, welcomed him into my bed.

'Are you unwell?' He raps on the door with his knuckles. 'Maud.'

That voice I once loved is hateful to me now. 'Go away.'

'Why?' The door handle rattles. 'Let me in. I can help.'

I laugh, silently, my mouth as wide open as it can go – laugh and laugh and laugh until all the air is gone from my lungs, while he hammers on the door until it shakes fit to burst.

'Maud, for God's sake.' Once more the handle rattles. Bang! The door quakes with the force of his punch or kick, and he is gone, stamping down the stairs.

I tremble in my nest of blankets, tremble as violently as my poor door has done under his onslaught. What a fool I've been. How he tricked me with his lies, while all the time he was bedding her. I can't even cry for the fury that fills my heart.

There's no sleep to be found, no rest from this. Morning comes and Mr Banville must be washed and fed and read to. I'm sick with tiredness, sick with hatred, but none of that is his fault. He sips at the walnut drink I make him, smiles his lopsided smile as I pick up Great Expectations. The words quiver as I quiver inside, but somehow I read it, although afterwards I cannot remember a single thing that happened in those pages.

Mr Banville sleeps and still I sit there. The fire is out now, and the room grows chilly. I creep into the corridor. Voices *filter from Imogen's room. I stumble at the sound of Harry's voice; my head grows faint. My hand clutches at the wall. I must not think of him. He's nothing to me now. Nothing.*

In church on Sunday there is no escape, nowhere to hide from his relentless, piercing stare. I leave before the final blessing, and race back to the house.

Feet pound the earth, closer, closer behind me. 'Maud, wait.'

His legs are longer than mine.

'Please.'

I stop, focus on the ground at my feet. Perhaps I'm mistaken. Please God, let me be mistaken.

His footsteps slow, falter. 'I don't understand.' His breath comes in short gasps.

I must get away, or his voice will snare me. I will look into his eyes and I'll be lost.

'What's changed?' he says.

I walk away.

'Come to the marsh.'

'No.'

He catches my arm. 'Why?' His fingertips are raw and inflamed. A drop of blood oozes from his fingernail. 'What's wrong with you?'

'With me?' I try to laugh but it gets stuck in my throat. 'There's nothing wrong with me. I'm not the one sleeping with my father's wife.'

He recoils as if I've slapped him.

'Tell me I'm wrong,' I say. 'Go on. Tell me it's not true.'

He won't even look at me. He pulls out his silver cigarette case with trembling hands and opens it. Its contents spill over the ground.

'Tell me.' Please say it. Say it's not true, that I am mistaken.

He bends low, head bowed as he tries to pick up the broken, soggy cigarettes. His fingers search blindly, missing every one. 'Damn it,' he says. 'Damn.'

'Damn you,' I say, and walk away.

My brain is numb, empty. My legs take me to the kitchen, and there I sit, as every Sunday, waiting for dinner. When it comes, I move the meat around the plate, hide it under the cabbage. I can't even pretend to eat anything.

Price sits back, hands on his paunch and belches.

Mrs Price wipes her brow with her apron. 'Young Harry says he's going, then, back to London?'

Price nods. 'Aye.' He's watching me. 'Whores aplenty there.'

Good. Let them have him. Perhaps then he'll leave my dreams and let me be.

But no, my dreams are of him with Imogen in my bed. I open my bedroom door. Their heads turn to see me, and they laugh, giggle like children. Over and over, I dream the same dream, of their naked bodies, their laughing faces.

My life has become one of stale air and brooding silence, and waiting, endless waiting for him to go, and the dread of him going, and the strain of stopping myself from running to him, falling on my knees and begging him to stay. The strain of it all.

Fresh air. I will feel better then. Perhaps by the time I get back, he'll be gone, and I'll forget him. I walk across the fields behind the house, and up to a ridge of hawthorns. They're everywhere, these spiky trees, but here they're bent almost double by the prevailing winds. Price says these stone walls are the remains of a Roman villa, that a massacre took place on this field, that it's a field of blood. I don't believe him. How would he know, anyway? He only knows one book – the Bible – and there's nothing about a massacre at Hawthorn Ridge in there.

The sky is pure azure and the sun warm. I trudge over the fields, talking aloud to myself, listing the plants I see – hogweed, yarrow, herb Robert – plants I have gathered here many times. My interest in them, my interest in anything, has vanished. Still, I list them aloud because it stops me thinking.

From up here, I can see the village and beyond it, all the way to the sea. No one moves in the landscape, as if the whole place is deserted. The church bell tolls the hour – three o'clock.

Despite the sun, the wind is chilly on the exposed ridge. I walk on to a shallow dip in the field. A blasted oak is split clean in two, one section lying flat on the ground. I sit on it, but it's bumpy and uncomfortable, so I sit instead on the mossy roots, determined to sketch the village.

The pencil rests on the paper. I stare at Ashton House, at the church and the trees beyond. I stare and wonder if he's there now, perhaps with some other girl. He can have his pick, after all. I imagine not one girl in the village would refuse him.

Disturbed nights and long, tense days have left me weary. I lean back against the trunk and close my eyes. I'm so tired of it all – of thinking of Harry and her together, of hearing that cry of his, or imagining it.

My thoughts drift to him constantly. He's leaving, and it's for the best. Then I'll forget, and all will be well. I'll put my mistake behind me, and never, ever trust a man again.

I lie down, my head on the mossy pillow, and for the first time in days, I fall asleep.

'I don't love her.'

I sit up with a start, eyes stinging in the bright sunshine. He's lying on his back next to me. I think him a vision, a figment of my imagination. How real his face is, every tiny detail, each black hair on his head, each black eyelash, each pore of his skin.

He lights a cigarette, pulls on it, and lets the smoke out in a long, slow stream. It curls lazily up towards the sky. Fascinated, I watch the smoke crawl between his lips, fold and sway with his breath. Those lips were mine once, or I thought they were. That skin around them, with its shadow, its slight stubble – that was mine, too.

'Did you hear me?' he says.

'Yes.' I shift my gaze to the gnarled roots of the tree digging their way into the soft earth, or out of it, like arms from some long-buried corpse.

'I've tried to stop it many times,' he says.

The bark of the tree is criss-crossed by deep fissures and coated in moss that looks like velvet – beautiful, deep green velvet. I stroke it, bury my fingers in the softness.

'How long . . . ?' I wave a hand in the air because something is stopping my tongue.

'Since I was fourteen.'

Is he nervous? No, his hand, the one that holds the cigarette with its long end of ash that surely at any moment will fall and disintegrate on top of him, that hand is steady.

My hands, in contrast, shake so violently that I have to pin them to the ground, holding them under my legs.

He stares up at the sky. How blue his eyes are in this light, like jewels. 'That mausoleum where you and I first met,' he says, 'is where my mother is buried. Buried and forgotten.' Now his hand shakes, now the ash falls from the cigarette. 'They wouldn't allow her in the churchyard.' He sits up and rests his elbows on his knees, head bowed, hiding his face. 'She died when I was away at school. By the time I came home for the summer, she was long buried and forgotten.'

'No one thought to tell you?'

He shakes his head, glances at me. 'I was a child.' His lip curls. 'It was none of my concern.'

I press down on my hands to stop them reaching for him. I long to hold him, to pretend all is as it was, but that mouth has deceived me all summer; those eyes, too. He must think me a fool if he plans to deceive me again.

'I arrived to find the servants I'd known all my life gone,' he says, 'ousted by those vile Prices.'

'But your father – surely he . . .'

'My father?' He takes a deep breath, looks up at the sky. 'I despised him and told him so. He would not speak of my mother, would not allow her name to be mentioned. It was as if she'd never existed. I thought he'd forgotten her. I was

wrong, but . . .' He rubs his eyes. 'He hid from me after that, hid in his laboratory and left me to the gentle ministrations of his new wife.' His mouth twists in a bitter smile. 'On my first night home, she came to my bed.' He stubs the cigarette out on the grass. It goes out with a small hiss.

'Couldn't you stop her?'

'I thought she meant to comfort me.' He turns his head away with a harsh laugh.

Can it be true? I think of the way he looked at Imogen on the terrace as she flung her head back – that hungry, unholy look, the same one he used with me, the same hunger, the same desire – and I can't believe him. I daren't believe him.

'You're a grown man now,' I say. 'Are you telling me you can't stop her?'

'I will. I'm going to.'

'You're still bedding her?' Say no. Please say no.

He hesitates. 'No,' he says, too late.

'Liar.' Tears prick at my eyes. My throat stings. If he doesn't go soon, I'll break down, and I mustn't do that. I dig my nails into the moss.

'Please.' He catches my arm. 'I can't bear my life without you.'

I daren't look at him. I daren't, so I stare at his ragged fingertips. 'I've heard you – you and her – together.'

He turns his face away. A flush rises up his throat.

A picture comes into my head of Mr Banville bursting out of the morning room, and Harry's ashen face. I catch my breath.

'Your father found out, didn't he? That's why he . . .'

He jumps to his feet, looks as if he's about to take a step, but doesn't. He just stands there, his face averted, staring intently at the horizon, as if there's someone there. There's no one, nothing to be seen but grass and sky.

'Go to London, Harry,' I say.

He swallows, nods. 'You'll take good care of him? My father?'

'Of course.'

He nods once more, then turns and stumbles downhill, back towards the house in a clumsy half-walk, half-run. He's crying. I know he's crying and I long to call him back, but I'm too afraid, afraid of this broken boy-man, afraid he'll destroy me along with himself.

Pipes creak, footsteps pass my door, someone shouts out in the ward next door. I'm back in the asylum and must write – write what I remember before it disappears. I wipe my eyes, sit by the window in the moonlight and write the facts as if they happened to someone else, as if they are nothing to do with me. It's easier that way. My tears won't spoil the paper. By the time I finish, weariness has overtaken me. Too tired to move the table, I wedge the notebook into the gap under the window. It's no easy task. Flakes of plaster fall off, but it fits – just. There will be time enough to move it in the morning, and it's almost hidden anyway. I climb into bed and fall straight into a dreamless sleep.

Keys jangle in the lock. I open my eyes to the pale light of early morning. The door creaks open. I don't turn to look. It will be Prune or Chins with breakfast – bread and milk, the same as every other morning.

'Hello, Mary.'

Womack. Womack here, now, so early? I sit up, blink. Is this a dream? Another nightmare? I slip my hand under the pillow. No pencil. Nothing, nothing but fabric.

'So –' Womack makes a half-hearted attempt at a smile '– how are your sessions with Doctor Dimmond going?'

I slip out of bed. It's safer to stand, easier to fight him off should the need arise.

'It says here your memory is returning.' He looks from my notes to me, and back again. 'Excellent news. What have you remembered?' His voice is as tight as his smile. 'Exactly?'

'Nothing,' I say. 'Nothing at all, as I told you before.'

A nerve twitches in his jaw. He nods. 'Really?' His eyes flicker as he scans the room.

My heart thumps so hard he must be able to hear it as he walks to the bed, lifts the mattress, and drops it again. 'I should like to see your notebook.'

'I don't have a notebook.' My voice is thin and high and not its usual self.

'In that case . . .' He bends forward, reaches under the bed, and holds the pencil in the air. 'What do you use this for?'

There's nothing I can do – nothing, except pray.

'You are under my care, Mary. I am responsible for your well-being.' Oh, he's looking at the window, a smile playing over his lips. The notebook is surely hidden in shadow. It is surely . . .

He stretches out his hand, slides a stubby finger and thumb into the space and pulls it out, my flowery notebook. 'What have we here?'

'It's mine.' How pathetic I sound.

He's opening my book, turning the pages, reading my secrets. His fingers slide over his moustache as he reads. 'What an inventive imagination you have.' He's reading about me and Harry and what we did – what we did at the marsh – and his face wrinkles in disgust.

'Filth,' he says. 'Nothing but filth.' And on he reads until he reaches the words I wrote only hours ago. He frowns, peers closely at the page, turns one page, then another, then back again. Twice, three times he reads. His face pales. 'These are foul lies.' His lip curls in disgust. 'What wretched poison runs in your veins?' He steps closer. 'Admit these are lies, these depraved stories, or I will have you . . .'

I hold his gaze, see fear and rage in those bloodshot eyes. I shake my head. 'But they're true.'

He slams the notebook shut and turns for the door. He's leaving, leaving with my notebook. If he opens that door, I'll never get it back, and all those memories will be gone. He will never let me remember again, not ever. My feet make no sound on the floorboards – one pace, two and there. I jump on to his back, cling on to him. My arm closes about his throat. His hands tear at my arm, but I have him. I have him. 'Drop the book,' I hiss in his ear. He reaches for my face, catches at my hair, but I have had my hair torn out before. It didn't stop me then and it won't now. 'Drop it.'

The book clatters to the floor, and yet I can't let go. I dare not.

The door crashes open and all is shouting, shouting. Hands pull at my middle. An arm clamps around my neck, pulling, pulling, and Womack slips from my grasp. Slam, my back hits the floor, knocks the wind from my lungs, and the two monsters have me, have my arms, my shoulders.

Womack rubs at his throat, bends to retrieve my notebook.

'Give it back,' I shout. 'Give it.'

He shakes his head. He is pale now, deathly pale, save for his red throat. 'Your mania has returned, Mary. You are delusional, psychotic.' And he's gone, taking with him the book that holds my life.

CHAPTER 23

It's pitch dark. There's no window, no glimmer of light. My room smells different – of damp and cold stone and wet earth. They've buried me alive. There's no air. The more I try to breathe, the less air there is. Oh God. Oh God. Blood pounds in my ears, in my throat. 'Help me.' I scream it. 'I'm not dead. I'm still alive.'

My words echo, bounce back at me. I slow my breathing, try to think. If I'm in a coffin, then my breath will come back to me, hit my face. It doesn't. No coffin, then, but something larger. I scream, try to guess how big this prison is, how close the walls.

I can't move my arms. They're folded across my body and something's stopping me from unfolding them, but I can move my legs. I lift one, waiting to hit some barrier, but there isn't one. I stretch it to the right, hit something – a wall. To the left there's nothing, empty space, and below, too. It's a ledge I'm on, flat on my back, and I don't know how far I'll fall if I roll off. This place smells like a cave – a cave with stale urine and human waste.

Then I realise. It's a nightmare. I realise and laugh. I'll wake any minute to find Diamond's gentle face and daylight and to me that seems as close to heaven as I can hope to get. There's more air now I've realised. I can breathe, even though the air still smells, and I try not to think about the fall to my left, should I move. Nightmares always end. All I have to do is wait.

So I wait, and breathe, and try to forget about the thing holding my arms, and the dark, and the scuttling noises that speak of rats. They could eat my eyes and I have no arms to defend myself. The thought sets my pulse racing again, so I breathe slowly. They can't hurt me. They're not real. They're not real – those sounds, those creatures.

I wait but it doesn't end. There's no light, no Diamond. Now my breathing has settled, other sounds reach me – whispers and, further away, screams and manic laughter. I am in the asylum, then. My thoughts turn to Womack.

'Two grams,' he shouts. 'Two grams, *now*.' And his face, crimson and sweating, and those eyes – those eyes, and the brown stuff – again. On and on, and all the time I vomit, he watches me, watches me, and smiles.

Perhaps it didn't happen. Perhaps it was a dream. But no, my stomach hurts every time I move. No dream then, no nightmare.

He thinks he can destroy me with his potions and punishments, have me on my knees pleading for my life. Never. I will never give him that satisfaction.

At least I can't hear the bell down here, at least there's that. Although . . . yes, there it is, quieter, but still there, and growing louder. Someone's ringing it, ringing it and bringing it closer. They're trying to drive me mad.

I hum a tune to shut it out. 'She's only a bird in a gilded cage . . .'

There's light at last, a strip of it, and a figure. The strip widens. Two figures silhouetted and then blinding light. I blink away tears, my eyes stinging. It's a cell I'm in – a square room and the figures are attendants – the man-like ones. So it's real then, this place of nightmares.

A smell of food, boiled cabbage or some such fills the room. The grey-haired one holds a bowl in her hand. I won't eat it. I'd rather die. I'll spit it out.

The other one holds my head and tries to open my mouth. I clamp my teeth together. She presses thumb and forefinger either side of my jaw and presses where it hinges together. She's too strong for me, or I'm too weak, because my mouth opens despite my efforts. The grey one pours some slop in. I spit it out. It hits her apron and her chin.

She wipes it off, flips me on to my stomach, smacking my face against the ledge. They're lifting my skirts.

A sharp pain in my right buttock.

They roll me on to my back, and I think, *here we go*. Now they'll start, when I can't defend myself, but they don't. They take the bowl and the light and leave me in the dark. As if the dark can frighten me.

'This is nothing,' I shout. 'You don't even know true darkness, not until you've been in the marsh on a moonless night. This is nothing.'

It's hard to believe I won so easily. I'm giddy with victory, or hunger, or both. I can't move my arms because it's a straitdress, one with long sleeves, tied behind my back. They're still there, my arms. Nothing's happened to them. The room doesn't scare me, either, now I've seen it. It's just a cell in the basement, with a floor and walls and a door and nothing nightmarish about it. I have been in one before, although not for a long time, and never in a straitdress.

Diamond will come and get me soon. I know he will. There's no need to panic now. It's just a matter of time. My head grows woozy.

I drift, weightless, through green rooms, peer into shadows where figures writhe, legs entwined, and grunt and sigh and whisper and cry out. The slow glide across floors, the distorted sounds, feels as if I'm underwater. Faces loom – pale, anxious, or angry, and teeth rotten and putrid breath. I wake sweating, my ears plugged, my screams silenced.

Before me lies a wide, flat saltmarsh stretching to the horizon. Gulls scream overhead in an eerie night sky. It's cold. So cold.

I can't remember how I got here or how to get back. No coat. No coat and no shoes. Icy water washes over my toes.

Where are the hawthorns? The crows? The ravens?

This is not my marsh.

There's no telling how long I've been dreaming. It could be days, for all I know. I can't think or move, can barely open my eyes.

I can't remember why I was so cross now, or what I was cross about. It's the madness, I expect. They think locking me in here will break my will, but they're wrong. I'll die before they break me. I'll starve before they do.

I laugh. It sounds strange in that cell, echoing off the damp walls, as if there are dozens of me, all laughing. Hordes of laughing mouths.

The door has opened without my noticing. I squint into the bright light. My heart jumps. It's Diamond, come to rescue me. Why does he stand there like that? Why doesn't he speak, rush in, release me from this dress that's a trap, a prison?

He turns his head, and my hope turns to dread because this man has a moustache, a hated moustache. Bright light fills the room. He hasn't come alone. The coward knows better than that. Even with my arms tied, I could damage him, *would* damage him and he knows it, so he's brought his guards, the trusty bullies. One holds a bowl. It's the same smell, the same slop.

Womack's carrying a coiled tube with a funnel at one end.

She places the bowl carefully on the floor. If I leap off the ledge now, I can escape.

My legs are so heavy. I try to slide them off so at least I can stand, but nothing works properly. It's as if I'm made of solid rock. Never mind. If he comes close enough, I'll find a way. I don't know how, but I will.

The mousy attendant moves to the end of the ledge where my feet are. I'm so busy watching her, I miss the other one getting behind me. She grips my head between her hands, pressing her palms to my temple.

No. No, he's coming. I can't move. He raises one leg, places his knee on the ledge, just beside me. So close, touching my shoulder. Before I can move away, he swings his other leg over me, straddles my chest. His weight presses down on me. I can't breathe.

He brings the tube up to my face. I want to scream but daren't open my mouth. I know what he's going to do. I'm not stupid. I keep my mouth clamped shut and wait for the finger and thumb where the upper and lower jaw join.

Why is he smiling? Why? Why doesn't he prise my mouth open like the attendant did?

No, no, not up my nose. Oh God! Oh God! I open my mouth. Better that, but he's not interested. He wants to hurt me and it does. The pain is so intense, my eyes fill with tears. There's no stopping them. They pour from my eyes, trickle into my ears.

The tube is in. It's down my throat and I'm retching, retching. On and on, he keeps pushing in more and more tube.

Thank God. He's stopped. He's waving his hand and I think maybe it's over.

But no, the attendant hands him the bowl. He pours the contents into the funnel and there's nothing I can do to stop him. I hate him. I hate him.

He's finished. The bowl's empty. He hands it to the attendant, clambers off me, and brushes his trousers down, face screwed up as if I've contaminated him.

'I hate you.' I want to shout it, but I have no voice, and it stays inside my head. 'I hope you burn in hell.'

He doesn't look into my eyes. Perhaps he knows what he'll see there. His eyes are on the tube as the attendants pull it out. It's feet long, almost as long as my entire body, and the whole time, it stings.

As the last of it comes out, I vomit. I vomit it all up, all over my prison dress and the ledge, and my hair.

The mousy-haired one tuts. 'It's too late to get a clean dress now.' Her voice is fat with satisfaction. 'You'll have to sleep in that.'

Womack watches and smiles. He wants to see me cry. Sobs build in my chest but I won't let them out. I won't. Not with him watching me. Not ever.

He tries to hold on to his smug smile, but he can't because I'm staring at him and he's still scared. I hold on to that. I hold on to it, cling to it and vow revenge.

Later, I wake – or think I do – but it could be a dream.

Womack's face is so close to mine, his moustache tickles my skin. 'I'm going to stop your unnatural fantasies,' he says. 'I'm going to cure you.' His smile is evil, evil, and now it's me who's scared. When I scream, there's no one there. The door is shut and it's completely dark.

CHAPTER 24

A long-legged spider crawls slowly to the corner above my bed, cradling a clutch of creamy eggs on her underside. She sits and watches me as I watch her. Silence, thick and heavy, makes me think I'm still asleep and dreaming.

The chair's been moved. It's by the window instead of where it should be. I don't remember coming back to this room, or them taking off that stinking dress with the long sleeves.

The door opens and Diamond comes in. His face is flushed, his nostrils white-edged. He's been arguing with Womack again, I bet. About me.

The jolly attendant with prominent teeth, the one who plays the piano, closes the door.

'This is Mrs Tucker,' Diamond says. I never think of them as having normal names, or even of them being normal people with lives and families.

He pulls the chair to its proper position. We're attuned, Diamond and I, about things like that. We understand the importance of place, of things being where they should be. He sits. Tucker stands beside him.

'Mrs Tucker is trustworthy,' Diamond says, 'so anything you say in front of her will be confidential.'

Tucker smiles.

'I know why you were angry with Doctor Womack,' Diamond says.

I expect he does. We're alike, me and Diamond. Like two peas.

'But violence will never make things better.'

He's wrong, of course, but I don't tell him that. If I'd been violent perhaps people would have treated me with respect instead of contempt. Perhaps Price would have been afraid to cross me, Imogen too. Maybe I wouldn't have ended up here, maybe I'd be safe.

'It's good for you to cry,' Diamond says.

I wipe my eyes, and my hand is wet. It's a surprise because I have no sensation of crying or even of being sad. It's Diamond's fault. If he wasn't kind to me, I wouldn't cry. I must tell him to stop it, this being kind. It's no good for me.

'Doctor Womack says it's filth,' I say, 'the things I wrote.'

'It's the truth, and that's what I asked you to write.'

'He says he's going to stop my unnatural fantasies. He says he has a new treatment.'

Diamond frowns. 'New treatment?'

'That's what he said.' I don't tell him it might have been a dream. He'll think I've made it all up, everything I've written. He'll think it's all lies. It isn't. And now Womack wants to steal those bits of my life away again, just when I've found them.

Something splashes on to my hand. I'm crying again.

'You're tired,' Diamond says, 'exhausted after your ordeal. I'm sorry you had to endure such . . .' His jaw clenches. 'Such barbaric treatment. I had thought those methods consigned to history, but it seems I was wrong. Rest now, and we will have tea once you are recovered.'

Tea. How I long for tea now, when there is none.

They are almost at my door, and suddenly I can't bear to see them go.

'It was Womack,' I say. 'The doctor at Ashton House. It was him.'

They turn back. Diamond frowns, sits back on the chair. 'When did you realise this?'

'When . . .' I can't say it was that vision of him with Mr Banville in my room. Even I know visions aren't real. 'I can't remember precisely when.'

Diamond purses his lips. 'I know you are angry with him.'

'You think I'm lying?' I say. 'You say you believe me, but you think I'm a liar, just as he does.'

'No.' He sits forward, clasps his hands together. 'Not lying, but mistaken. I believe you see him there, truly I do, but it simply means the doctor bore a superficial resemblance to our medical superintendent – hair, perhaps, eyes.'

'Both,' I say.

'This is not uncommon,' Diamond says. 'We attach some-one we see in the present day to our memories.' He doesn't care about Womack, then. No, he won't even entertain the thought that it could be him. My memory is false, and I am mistaken, and now they really are leaving, leaving me alone with my madness.

I wake on Thursday to find the world blanketed by snow. Fields and hedges are all one, all white. Trees stand like skeletons, with icing on their branches.

What have I gained by all this remembering? For here I am in this same room, looking out of this same window, with the same hollow emptiness inside me that was there at the beginning.

Perhaps today the healing will start.

'Expect you'll be glad when this nonsense is done with, eh?' says Prune as we go down the stairs to Diamond's room. 'Then you can get back to normal.'

'Yes,' I say. How glad I will be to miss tea, and warmth, and being treated like a sane person. Glad to miss Diamond and his crinkly eyes, and the way he listens to me when I speak, and doesn't interrupt or laugh or mock or sneer. Oh yes, I will be glad indeed.

Prune opens the door and there is Diamond, standing by the fire. I'm so happy to see him that my heart flutters about like a caged bird.

'Oh!' Prune's eyes widen as she sees her usual seat is already occupied.

'Mrs Tucker will be assisting me in Maud's hypnosis sessions from now on,' Diamond says, with a brief smile.

Prune dithers.

'Thank you,' Diamond says. 'You may go now.' He waves a brisk hand, and she hurries out, shutting the door behind her.

He turns to me. 'I thought we would sit by the fire and read through your notes.'

Tucker fidgets under my gaze.

'Go through all that you've remembered,' Diamond says.

Why is she so uncomfortable? Perhaps she's a spy sent by Womack, after all.

'Maud?' Diamond says. 'Are you willing to do that?'

'I don't know.' She meets my gaze and doesn't look away.

'Mrs Tucker and I have worked together before,' Diamond says. 'I can assure you that anything you say in here, anything I read, will go no further.'

I could say no and go straight back to my room, but steam curls from the spout of the teapot, and the fire is so welcoming, and I may never see Diamond again.

'Very well,' I say.

Diamond pulls my chair up to the fire. The three of us sit in a semicircle so that I needn't look at either of them, not if I don't wish to. The tea is hot and sweet, the fire low and glowing red. A longing for my childhood home takes me by surprise; the kitchen fire with ovens around it, the smell of baking bread. There was happiness then, and love. All gone now. My life is changed for ever, as I am changed.

We drink tea, while Diamond tells Tucker all my secrets.

'Maud was betrayed by a lover,' Diamond says.

Tucker watches me.

'I suspected the young man in question had ill-treated her in some way, and so it transpired.'

I want to protest, but he has the facts there, on his notes.

'One would think it the cause of her sickness.' He turns the pages of his notebook. 'Indeed, I thought so myself. However . . .' He looks up at Tucker, eyebrows raised.

'There is no sign of madness?' Tucker says.

Diamond smiles. 'Precisely.' He taps his desk with his pen. 'That attendant, Maud, the one you call Chins?'

Tucker coughs into her handkerchief.

'She said Doctor Womack brought you here. Do you recall anything about that?'

It feels like a trick question. 'No,' I say, although there *is* something, some memory of a cart – of lying in the back of it, and rain on my face. 'It was raining,' I say, 'when I came.'

His eyes narrow. 'What can have happened between Harry leaving and your admittance here?'

I don't attempt an answer. Inside my head is a maelstrom. There's no sense to be made of it.

My gaze drifts to the window. The snow is so beautiful and light – so bright that it stings my eyes – and silent, silent with an unearthly, muffled hush.

'I know it was deathly quiet,' I say.

'Deathly quiet?' Tucker says.

'That house, without him.'

Diamond waves the ring in front of my eyes. The clock ticks a warning, but it's too late. I'm already there.

A hush lies over the house. It holds its breath as I hold mine, listening, listening for Harry, lost without him.

Only the clock is unaffected. It ticks on as if nothing has changed.

Empty silence, day after day. Oh, there's noise enough – Imogen's clumsy piano, Price and his prophecies of doom, Imogen and the doctor at play in the drawing room, the sitting room.

Their noise bounces off the silence, the emptiness where Harry should be.

Almost everywhere reminds me of him – the marsh, the ridge, the grounds. Every thought leads to him, every breath of wind. In the morning, I wonder where he's waking, whether it's in the arms of some foolish girl like me, or different, perhaps older, like Imogen, and I think of us, of how we were together, how I thought it meant something to him, how I thought he loved me. Humiliation brings me out in a sweat. Hatred and jealousy churn my stomach. The smell of Mrs Price's cooking grows worse by the day, so that I can barely swallow a mouthful of any meal. I am sick often, and always weary, always weary, but never able to sleep.

I rise after another sleepless night and go to Mr Banville's room. Today we are to begin Great Expectations *for the third time. 'You will tell me,' I say, 'when you tire of this book, Mr Banville, won't you?'*

He nods. He is so like Harry – a broken, weary, aged Harry.

I tip lily of the valley elixir into a spoon, hold it to his lips, but they are shut fast.

'It's good for you.'

He shakes his head. 'No more.' The words are indistinct, clumsily formed, but they're words.

I jump to my feet. 'You spoke.'

His eyes sparkle with laughter.

I laugh too, clasping my hands together. He will recover, and I will be an assistant again, and this time it will be different. I'm so sure he will trust me that my mind leaps ahead of itself, imagining us working together, making discoveries together, imagining my name alongside his on academic papers, and I will forget Harry and all will be right again. It must be so. Please let it be so.

I don't mean to tell the Prices – after all, they're the last people I would choose – but at dinner, I cannot keep it to myself.

'Mr Banville spoke this morning,' I say, as Mrs Price takes her seat.

Two pairs of cold eyes fix on mine.

'It means he's getting better,' I say.

The pendulum swings, back, forth – tick, tock, and still they stare.

'For God's sake.' My voice is high, brittle. 'It's good news, isn't it?'

Nothing – not even a blink.

'Well, isn't it?'

Price turns to his wife. 'Didn't I tell you?'

'Aye.' She nods, sighs. 'Aye, right enough.'

'Tell her what?' I say.

They slurp at their meal, but my appetite has gone. I stand, push my chair back. It grates on the flagstones.

'You're both mad,' I say, but I feel sick inside. They know something I don't, and I hate it. Halfway down the hall, I realise Price is behind me, and the hairs on the back of my neck rise.

I turn to face him. 'I'm going for a walk.'

He leans against the wall, shotgun in hand, and fixes me with a dead stare. 'The wages of sin is what's comin' to you. Ye shall die in your sins.'

'No doubt I shall,' I say, 'but so will you.' I lift my coat from the hook in the atrium, open the front door, step outside and slam the door, shutting him inside.

The day is dull and grey. I pull on my coat and walk as fast as I am able. The cool wind against my face helps, calms me. They're stupid, that's all, harmless. Their cryptic words mean nothing.

I walk to the ruined chapel. All is silent, still and empty. And there sits her gravestone, his mother.

Eugenie Banville. Wife of Edward Banville, Esquire, of Ashton House. Departed this life the 3rd day of February, the year of Our Lord 1893, aged 31.

So that, at least, was true, that they would not allow her in the churchyard.

I turn back to the house and imagine him coming back from school as a young man – no, still a child – and looking for his mother, only to fall into the clutches of that witch. Poor Harry. Poor, bereft Harry.

I go to the hollow, to the dead oak, and sit and wait. The ground is dry, so I lie down, close my eyes, and pretend to sleep. Maybe today – a day of miracles, after all – maybe today I'll wake to find him there next to me, just like before, but this time I'll let him explain. This time I'll listen.

The air chills. I open my eyes and I'm alone. Perhaps it's for the best. I could never forget hearing that cry, no matter what the explanation, and what reasonable explanation could there be? I must concentrate on Mr Banville. He's all that matters now. Once he's well, I'll have my work to distract me and I'll be able to think of Harry without this pain. It will be a silly mistake I made when I was young, one I can scarcely remember.

CHAPTER 25

The church clock strikes five. I've been away too long and missed Mr Banville's teatime. I hurry back to the house. All is uproar in the yard. Price is struggling to shackle the mare to the cart. She's frisky, rearing up and snorting.

Mrs Price stands at the top of the steps.

'What's happened?' I say.

Price doesn't hear, or chooses to ignore me.

''Tis the master,' Mrs Price says, with a sniff. 'He's taken a turn.'

My heart jolts. 'Taken a turn?' I lift my skirts and bound up the steps. The bedroom door stands wide open. Mr Banville lies on his back, staring up at the ceiling with bloodshot eyes, unblinking.

Another attack, that's all. I run to the side of his bed and pull the covers up to his chin. 'You're cold.' I rub his chilled hand between my two. 'No wonder you're ill.'

A strange rash of tiny purple dots speckles his face and neck. 'You have caught some disease,' I say. It surely explains the bluish tinge to his lips, and his nose. 'It must be an ague of some kind.'

I add coal to the fire and poke the ashes until it glows. 'There! It will soon be warm, and your colour will return.'

His eyes are so dull, the light quite gone from them.

'And we'll read our book.' I pick up Great Expectations *and open it where we last left off. 'It was a rimy morning, and . . .' The words blur. Something hard sits in my throat. I cough. '. . . a rimy morning and . . .' Tears spill from my eyes and on to the page.*

The fire burns, the room warms, the clock ticks. Imogen's playing the piano in her room. She must know what's happened, and yet on she plays. The pendulum swings back and forth, back and forth, and yet no colour comes to Mr Banville's cheeks. How still he lies. So horribly still.

What a noise the carriage makes as it trundles up to the house, comes to a halt beneath the window.

'The doctor is come,' I say. Perhaps, just this once, he will be of some use.

Here they come at last, the doctor and Imogen, clattering up the stairs. Too late. Too late. He is gone.

They burst in. Oh, such grief as never was. How she wails, that faithless wife, sobbing over his body as if her heart will break, while he, that doctor, stands, hat in hand, head bowed.

'He was getting better,' I say.

Imogen straightens up. 'Nonsense. He was deteriorating every day.'

For a moment, I can't speak. She has not visited her husband's room, not once. I say nothing – a coward. She holds my future in her hands, after all.

The doctor leans over Mr Banville, frowning.

'He spoke,' I say, 'only this morning. He spoke, just before dinner time.'

Imogen looks up at me. No red-rimmed eyes, no teary lashes. The doctor's pale eyes meet mine and away, back to Mr Banville. 'That's impossible,' he says, but there's uncertainty in his voice.

Imogen hears it, too, because she casts an anxious look at him. 'I found him,' she whines. 'It was most upsetting.'

She came to his room then, after all this time. She came to his room too late.

The doctor is pale, distracted, examining the rash. He straightens up, catches my eye and looks away. 'The death is not unexpected,' he says.

'It is.' I want to spit at him, at the pair of them. 'It is unexpected. His words were slurred, but . . .' My throat closes up. Tears prick my eyes. How excited he'd been. How excited we'd both been, and now, with no warning, he's gone. 'This.' I point out the tiny purple dots. 'What caused this rash?'

The doctor clears his throat, flashes a look at Imogen. 'This often happens after death.'

I've never seen such a rash on a body, never. He's lying, but I know better than to contradict him this time.

I pace to the window. This cannot be. It can't. Price. Would he dare commit such a crime as to murder his own employer? Perhaps. Perhaps Harry was right and Price is truly evil. I must take care, must guard my tongue.

Imogen's eyes meet mine. Her mouth opens.

I know what she's about to say and speak quickly to stop her. 'Your husband's research is almost ready to send to the Royal Society,' I lie. 'It was his last wish to have his work recognised.'

She frowns.

'I believe there will be monies to come, also.' I know no such thing, of course, but it will give me time to find another position, at least.

'Oh,' she says. 'Oh, well, in that case, perhaps, before you leave –' a tight smile '– you could see to that.'

'Of course.' I stand, bob a curtsey. As I reach the door, I take a last look at poor Mr Banville. The doctor slips his hand around Imogen's waist and kisses her neck. 'You must not distress yourself, my darling,' he murmurs, 'not in these early months.'

Early months?

Perhaps I gasp, because they both turn their heads.

'My husband was surprisingly virile,' Imogen says, with a complacent smile, 'even at the last.'

We both know that's a lie. We both know it, and yet there they stand, so blatant, while Mr Banville lies dead beside them. No doubt my face shows my disgust, because her smile fades, turns to a sneer.

'See to your work,' she snaps. 'The sooner you're gone, the happier I will be.'

'And I too,' I whisper as I leave the room. 'And I too.'

Fury is all I feel until I reach the steps to the laboratory. Only there do I pause. The child cannot be Mr Banville's, but why should I think it the doctor's? I run up the steps, my stomach churning. Dear God, don't let it be Harry's. Not his. Let it be that doctor's, anyone's but his. I step inside, the breath quite gone from my lungs, but even here, where I have felt so safe, so content, there is no escape.

Well, it's nothing to me, not now. I have my own life to think of, my own future. The only good person in this family is gone now, lying dead in his bed. There is nothing left for me here. I will leave these poisonous devils and make a new life for myself, with decent people. I have experience now, and knowledge, and didn't my father say the world was changing, that women would have opportunities they had been denied for too long? Then I will prove him right.

The drawer in Mr Banville's desk slides open. The sight of his tiny, cramped handwriting makes me catch my breath, makes my eyes swim. 'You taught me well, Mr Banville,' I whisper. 'I will for ever be grateful to you.' I can hardly bear to touch anything, but I must. How long can I keep Imogen at bay? Weeks, perhaps, at best. I must find another position. I pull a sheet of writing paper out, and my eye is drawn to the paper beneath it.

'Noxious' is the heading, and underneath:

Hemlock. Conium maculatum. *Paralysis. Respiratory collapse.*

Henbane. Hyoscyamus niger. *Coma. Paralysis.*

Lily of the valley. Convallaria majalis. *Cardiac disturbance. Cardiac failure.*

Lily of the valley. I stare at the words, at the heavy line he's drawn under each one. Did I kill him with my elixir? My head buzzes. I sit down, bend forwards, head between my knees until the nausea subsides. No, he was improving.

He spoke. Surely it . . . There they are, those words: cardiac disturbance; cardiac failure. That rash, those tiny pinpricks, they must be from . . . Oh, I can't bear it. My only friend, my only hope, and I killed him. I stand, and swoon. The room spins. Everyone I care for dies. I am cursed, after all. Price was right.

The clock strikes seven. A new dread confronts me. If Price should mention my potions, I'll be done for. Worse, if they find the elixir, I will hang. I hurry to the cupboard, take the bottle to the sink, and pour every drop of it away and all the time I sob. 'I'm sorry. I'm so, so sorry.'

What have I done? What horror. It's not Harry who should fear damnation. It's me. Damned and damned again.

Voices. The hairs on the back of my neck rise. Voices in here? I hold my breath, turn my head, but it's not the laboratory I see. It's Diamond's room and there, standing in the doorway, Womack. My heart thumps as if it has leapt into my throat. Womack, chest thrust out.

'You're conducting a hypnosis session?' he says.

Diamond remains seated as if everything is normal. 'Yes?' he says.

I inch backwards on the chair. All will be well. Womack has no tube or funnel. There's no smell of cabbage, and Diamond is here, and Tucker, although she has retreated to the wall. Even so, there is no need to fret.

'Despite your best efforts,' Diamond says, 'Maud is well enough to continue.'

Light from the window hits Womack's face. Such a strange pallor, a waxy, grey sheen, like a dead man. 'Hypnosis is not suitable for this patient.'

Diamond's eyes widen. 'Not *suitable*? Hypnosis? But your brutal purges and force-feeding *are*?'

Womack's scalp pulls back. He holds out my flowery notebook and shakes it. 'Filth – the imaginings of a depraved mind.'

'Memories,' Diamond says. 'Which is exactly—'

Womack talks over him. 'Her psychosis erupted into violence only days ago.'

'Yes,' Diamond says, 'because you took her notebook.'

Womack's laugh crackles. 'Violence. Psychosis. I will not tolerate it. Do you understand?' He takes a folded sheet of paper from his pocket and throws it at Diamond. 'The hypnosis is to cease, by order of the committee of visitors.'

Diamond's face pales as he unfolds the paper and reads it. A vein throbs in his temple. 'And what of my other patients? Am I to continue with their treatment, or merely blindly follow the tried and tested – not to mention ineffective – methods already in use?'

Womack stares at Diamond for a long moment. A drop of sweat runs from his hair down the side of his face and trickles in front of his left ear. He wipes it away with the back of his hand. 'You may continue with your other patients.' He pulls a grubby handkerchief from his pocket and wipes his brow. 'In Mary's case, however, the hypnosis has caused harm rather than good. I forbid it, do you hear? I absolutely forbid it.' He turns on his heel, flings the door open.

'You brought Maud here, I believe,' Diamond says.

Womack turns back, blinks.

'Perhaps I've been misinformed.'

Womack stares at me. 'I did have Mary brought here, yes.'

'From her employer, I presume?'

'No.' Womack's jaw tightens. 'I was called by the vicar of a parish some miles west of here. Mary was psychotic, hallucinating. She disrupted a service and frightened the parishioners.'

Did I? There was a church, yes – a church and faces, and discordant music.

'By the time I arrived she was raving, soaking wet, having apparently tried to drown herself in the river – a habit of hers.'

No, no, I would never do that. There was water, though, and the dress clinging to my legs, and pondweed. Did I truly try to kill myself? Is that why I'm cursed?

'I think you'll find I followed the correct procedure.' Womack's lip curls. 'She's taking you for a fool, man. Can't you see it? She's making up stories for you, and you're stupid enough to believe them.' He strides out into the corridor, leaving the door open.

All is silent after he's gone. Tucker gets to her feet and shuts the door with a small click.

Diamond's eyes focus on me. 'Is it true? About the church?'

I shrug. 'There was a church. That's all I remember.'

'What drove you to such distress, I wonder?' He taps the desk – tap, tap, tap. He reads through my notes and looks up. 'The attendants say you hear clocks and bells. Is that true?'

'Yes,' I say, and add quickly, 'I know they're not real,' in case he thinks me deluded.

'Can you think where you might have heard such a clock?'

'There are clocks everywhere.'

'Indeed.' He's waiting.

'There was one at my home, in the hallway. I remember it ticking that morning, the morning I found my ... my ...' I swallow, clasp my hands together until the knuckles stand out white. 'My brothers.'

'And the bell?' Diamond says. 'What kind of bell do you hear?'

I hear it now, that ominous knell. 'It's slow,' I say, 'and deep.'

'Ah!' He sits back, as if all is solved. 'Funereal, would you say?'

'Perhaps.' There it is, that one, low note. Bong, bong, bong.

Diamond scribbles something into the margin of his notebook. 'You feel yourself responsible for your employer's death ...'

I stare at my feet.

'It was not your doing, Maud.' His voice is soft now, and quiet. 'The rash and blue-tinged extremities you describe suggest suffocation rather than poisoning.'

'So it wasn't my lily of the valley?' I'm almost scared to believe it, scared to hope that Diamond is right.

'You say he'd begun to recover his speech?'

'Yes. Just a word or two.'

'Then I imagine, had he fully recovered, it would have proved ... awkward for some of the occupants of Ashton House?'

Imogen, of course. Had Mr Banville recovered, she would have lost everything.

'Guilt is destructive, Maud, and, in this case, misplaced. You blamed yourself for your mother's death, your brothers', and your employer's. It's no wonder you hear bells. It is this guilt that has made you ill. You must free yourself from it.'

It sounds so easy. Free myself from it, just like that, after all these years.

'As soon as you do, you'll feel unburdened.'

Tucker nods. 'It's true, Maud. You will.'

'You'll find the relief that we have been striving for,' Diamond says.

'Yes,' I say, 'I'm sure I will.'

CHAPTER 26

Winter persists. The snow remains pristine. Ice forms beautiful patterns on my window. Icicles hang both inside and out. I stand with blankets wrapped around me. These dresses do not keep out the chill, though they are worse when wet, far worse. Worse when caked in mud and pondweed and trailing in the marsh. Oh, they are far worse then.

I'm innocent, Diamond says. The deaths that haunt me are none of my doing. I believe it as much as I'm able. Even so, something rotten still sits in the dark corners of my memory, seeping its poison. It does not lessen with each new dawn. It's unchanging, constant, like a nagging toothache.

The sun crosses the sky, barely rising above the horizon. Trees cast long shadows across the fields. They stretch towards me like tentacles.

'Cheer up,' Prune says. 'It's Christmas Day tomorrow. Plum pud. How about that? And chapel, too.'

Plum pudding will likely be a lump of tasteless brown stodge, but chapel – chapel means a trip outside, a walk across the snowy grass, and, if luck is on my side, a few moments of freedom. Or more. If it's Prune who takes me, she may let me wander the grounds and pretend I'm free. Perhaps I can get to the river this year. Oh, to get to the river and see that swollen rush of water, to smell the rushes, the weeds, the ice. Perhaps I can dip my feet in the shallows, feel the freezing water running over my toes. Oh, what a joy that would be.

My hopes of escape are dashed before I even leave my room, because Prune is not alone. She and Chins are to escort me. I'll have to run, then, free myself as soon as they loosen their hold, for I have nothing to lose. Womack won't allow me outside, so I must take my chance, I must fight for it.

We step through the door after the other lunatics, the ones trusted to walk alone. Down the steps. Down the steps and on to the path and . . . I twist my body, but oh, they're expecting it.

'We're wise to your games, Mary,' Chins says.

They clamp my arms so tightly, press their bodies so closely to my sides, that it's impossible to do anything other than walk with them like some strange, six-legged creature. Inside the chapel, they sit either side of me, clutching my arms, and still don't let go when the door is closed and lunatics sitting either side of us, and there's no chance of escape. They don't even loosen their grip, but press so hard that my fingers tingle and grow numb and I must flex them like he did – Price.

The chaplain stands at the pulpit. His voice is quiet, and the lunatics are talking, anyway. Even the attendants are whispering. I pity him, standing up there in his robes, preaching to this congregation of misfits, not one of whom is listening.

After chapel, there's mutton dinner, then plum pudding and custard. The pudding is stodgy and sweet, as expected, and sticks to my teeth and the roof of my mouth. The chatter is deafening. How excited they all are.

An old woman with wild eyes and even wilder hair stands talking to the wall, rapping on it with her knuckles. She steps back, smiles like a girl, coy and shy. She's tiny, this woman, all skin and bone.

'Sit down,' the attendant shouts. 'Sit down and drink your milk.'

Perhaps she's deaf, the old woman. She's still at the wall, leaning close, whispering. She giggles, covers her mouth with her hand.

'Hettie, sit down.'

The woman waves a hand, frowns, presses her ear to the wall. 'I'm awfully sorry,' she says, in a voice like the queen, 'I didn't catch that. The bloody attendant was shouting.'

I don't know why the lunatics are laughing. They're every bit as mad as her – every bit.

'Drink your milk, Hettie.'

'It's Henrietta,' she says. 'Lady Broughton to you.'

'Lady Broughton?' They shriek, the attendants – shrill, piercing. Oh, how the lunatics giggle as Chins and a male attendant drag her to the bench. There's no need for them to be so rough, not when she's so small, like a tiny, starveling bird.

She pushes them away and there's fear in her bright eyes, fear and confusion, and still they're laughing – the lunatics, the attendants – laughing as she picks up her tin cup, that tin cup of milk, and smacks it into her forehead. Crack! Milk splatters over the lunatics, their hair, their faces, their dresses. They jump up, shrieking and laughing still.

Crack! Hettie smacks that cup into her forehead, and again, and again. She'll knock herself senseless.

'Someone stop her.' The laughter's too loud, and my words lost, and the attendants watching, arms folded, as the woman's forehead reddens, and the milk spatters, until her skin splits and blood and milk mingle.

'Stop it.' I stand up.

Smack, smack, smack.

'Stop her.' I run to the woman and snatch the cup from her hand. It's slippery with blood. I drop it. Blood and milk, on my hand, on my dress. Blood and milk.

I turn for the door. It's so far away, and my stomach lurches as I lurch. Air. I just need some air. I shake my hand behind me but I can still feel the slime on my skin. One shudder follows another, and another, and then I'm outside in the corridor and someone has my elbow.

'Calm yourself.' It's Tucker. She puts an arm around me. 'Breathe now, Maud. All is well.'

'No, no, it's not.' I hold out my milky, bloodied hand. 'It's not.'

'We'll wash that off. It will wash off. You'll see.'

Her calm voice soothes me, so that the shudders grow further apart. 'It's the milk,' I say. 'The milk and the blood.'

'I know.' She takes me to the wash house, runs the tap and holds my hand under it, washing off the filth with the gentlest of touches, as a mother might her child. 'Why does it upset you so?' She says it without looking at me, her eyes focused on my hands.

Another shudder runs through me. My eyes sting so I turn my head away, but the tears spill out just the same.

'Let's get you back to your room, shall we?' I can tell by the cheerful tone of her voice that she knows I'm crying. She knows but is pretending not to.

Something, some sorrow or loss, or fathomless grief wells inside me until I feel I may burst with it. I daren't breathe in case it explodes. As soon as we get to my room, I run to the window and stare out.

'Rest now,' she says.

I nod. Go, for pity's sake, go.

The door closes. I wait, breathe, and . . . and nothing. No great wave of sadness breaks forth, no wailing, no heartbreak or torrent of tears. There's nothing. I stare at the copse. They're not my trees. They're probably not even hawthorns. There's no marsh beyond them, no lovers with limbs entwined, no festering bodies. It's simply a group of trees standing at the edge of a field, like a million others, and more. Perhaps there never was a marsh. Perhaps there never was.

A key turns in the lock. I slide the pencil down my sleeve until its tip rests in the palm of my hand. But it's only Tucker, and she has brought Diamond with her. I slump on to the bed.

'Mrs Tucker tells me you were a little distressed.' Diamond pulls up the chair and sits. Tucker stands beside him and hands him my notes. His sharp eyes watch me. 'How are you feeling now?'

'Perfectly fine,' I say. My eyes flash to Tucker and away.

'You were upset by the milk?' He looks to Tucker.

'And blood,' she says.

'Ah! Why did that upset you, Maud? Do you know?'

'No.' Why am I lying? I do know, somewhere in the back of my mind. I know, but I can't bear to go there. 'It's too dark.' I don't mean to say it aloud, but it comes out.

Diamond frowns. 'Too dark?'

'The thing.' I wave my hand. 'The thing that happened. It's too dark. I don't want to remember it.' There. I've said it. Now they'll leave me, and I can get back to normal – normal madness, my familiar, comfortable madness.

Diamond glances up at Tucker. 'What think you, Mrs Tucker?'

'Oh!' A flush suffuses her face. 'I, er . . .' Her eyes flit from me to Diamond and back again. 'I would imagine, from Maud's reaction –' she swallows, clears her throat '– that there could be something, some past upset, yet to be uncovered?'

Diamond nods. 'Precisely.'

'No.' How my heart thunders. 'No, there's nothing – nothing hidden. Nothing.'

'Of course, we're not permitted to use hypnosis,' he mutters, tapping the notes with his pen. 'There's a possibility, but it's rather cold there, that's the problem – uncomfortably cold.' He stares into space. 'We will need blankets and so on, and I shall need an attendant.' He smiles at Tucker. 'Would you be willing, Mrs Tucker?'

'Yes, doctor.'

At last he looks at me. 'If you tell anyone, Maud, I will lose my position.'

'Tell them what?'

He lowers his voice. 'We are to continue our sessions in secret.'

'Who would I tell?' I say. 'No one believes anything I say.'

'We do,' Diamond says. 'We believe every word.'

My gaze drifts to the window, to the bright sky and the dark, livid clouds gathering on the horizon. They are there for me, those clouds. They're coming, and there's no stopping them.

Tucker comes after dinner the next day, that time in the afternoon when the asylum drifts into doziness.

She leads me downstairs, holding her finger to her lips as we pass the lunatics' ward. We don't go to Diamond's office this time, but down another flight of stairs, underground – a dungeon. It's the same place, the place where Womack imprisoned me. It still smells of cabbage. I pull back.

'Don't fret,' Tucker says. 'No one's going to hurt you.' She grips my arm, not so tightly that it hurts, but enough to tell me she's not going to let go.

We walk through a corridor with rooms leading off it. Some of the doors are open. As we pass with our lantern, shelves of cardboard boxes, one on top of another, flash into view. Further along, the doors are closed. These are different, with small, barred windows, and great, heavy bolts on the outside.

The cabbage smell is stronger here. I can almost taste it.

I stop. 'I want to go back.'

'Nothing bad will happen. I give you my word.' Her word – how much is that worth, I wonder?

'Here we are.' The door facing us has no window. The bolts are there, though, three of them, solid metal, thickly painted white. The paint is worn in places, chipped, or raised in bubbles with the tops knocked off, leaving sharp edges like barnacles.

She knocks on the door. It opens and my pulse settles. She didn't lie. There's no Womack, no cabbage slop. There's only Diamond, smiling, in a small, damp room. A lamp's glow gives a sense of warmth even though there is none. Our breaths form puffs of mist that spread and waft away towards the ceiling. Like smoke from a cigarette, from a mouth with perfect lips . . .

Diamond's voice makes me jump. 'It's not what I would choose.' He glances at Mrs Tucker. 'Did you have any problems?'

'No, doctor.'

'Excellent.' He leads me to a chair. I sit, and Tucker covers me with a blanket. She tucks it in, around my shoulders, behind my arms, around my legs, so it's almost like the straitdress, but not quite. Still, my arms are pinned at my sides, and the edge of the scratchy wool blanket presses against my throat. I try to still the rising panic. All is well. Diamond is here. I must be safe. I must be.

The blanket warms me, but Diamond and Tucker have no such luxury. Goose pimples stand up on their skin.

'Why are you doing this?' I say. 'Why suffer this cold, just to hear my dreams?'

'My curiosity is insatiable,' Diamond says. 'Insatiable. It's landed me in a few scrapes in the past, and now my colleague has aroused it again.' He raises his eyebrows. 'Once intrigued, I'm a terrier. I cannot let go until the truth is revealed. Besides, if this hypnosis works, it could revolutionise the treatment of insanity.'

'And if it doesn't?'

'It will.' He sits next to me, notebook and pen in hand.

Tucker leans forwards. 'You'll be famous, doctor.'

He blushes. 'I hardly think . . .'

'You will.' Her eyes are fiery. 'It's wonderful, what you're doing for these poor souls – truly wonderful.'

He clears his throat. 'Thank you.'

Tucker sits back, her face blotched with purple as Diamond waves the ring.

I close my eyes, but open them again immediately; afraid they'll sneak away while I'm not looking, lock me in and leave me to moulder.

'Don't be afraid.' Diamond looks right into my eyes. 'I promise we'll look after you.'

How these men make promises they cannot keep. His quiet voice counts and with each number, I fall further into the past.

'You are in the laboratory,' Diamond says, 'after Mr Banville's death. Do you see it?'

Yes, yes, I see it, see my hand gripping the pen, forming the letters, copying Mr Banville's hand as closely as I can.

It's dark before I manage to write a reference that will have any chance of success. I must leave here as soon as possible for somewhere far away, somewhere no one will know me. I fold the letter, slip it into an envelope and sit back, my back aching. This dress has grown uncomfortably tight from all my alterations, all my sewing and mending and . . .

I catch my breath, choke on saliva. When was my last monthly blood? When was it? I can't recall.

I stand, pace the laboratory. When was it? Two months? Three? Breathe. It will come. It's the upset, that's all, the shock of seeing Harry with her, the despair of being without him. That is all. Those tender breasts that hurt when touched – they are yearning for Harry, nothing more.

Back and forth I pace. The pendulum swings. The clock ticks.

It cannot be. It cannot, and yet my skirts, they are painfully tight around my waist and have been for weeks, despite my lack of appetite. The buttons on my bodice strain to hold together.

No, no. Oh, no. Please God. Not now that he is gone, and Mr Banville, too, and my enemies are all about me.

The clock ticks. The sun rises and sets, rises and sets, and I sit at that desk with no plan, no idea how to save myself from disgrace. Everywhere I turn, every new idea is thwarted by this seed that grows inside me. Tears spring easily and often, for I can see no future, no escape from ruin. There is one mercy.

Imogen is confined to bed, so will not have noticed yet. The doctor insists she rest, for the sake of her child. Mrs Price clatters up and down the stairs all day, trays laden with morsels of this and that, delicacies that must have been brought by the doctor. Neither of them casts even a glance in my direction, but my condition will soon become too obvious to miss and then I will be for the workhouse.

I sit at that desk day after day and now it is only one day before Mr Banville's funeral and Harry will be here.

'A fleeting visit,' Imogen says.

Fleeting. I must tell him about my condition, somehow, but how? My stomach churns with hatred and love, hope and despair.

I write a letter several times and every time I baulk at telling him, instead asking polite questions about his health, or commenting on the weather. I can't say it, can't write the words. Sometimes, despite my changing body, I'm still able to convince myself it's nothing, merely wind or indigestion. If I write the words it will be true, a fact, and all I see before me is shame and destitution.

It's late, already past midnight, and I'm so tired my head keeps drooping on to my chest.

Once more I try.

My dear Harry,

Forgive my writing to you, but I am sorry to tell you that I am with child. I don't know what to do. Already my stomach swells. I fear that Imogen will dismiss me and I have nowhere to go.

If you have any affection for me, please intercede for me with your step-mother.

I hope you will read this and remember how you liked me once. Please help me, for soon someone will notice and I shall have to leave. And I'm frightened. I'm so frightened.

Ever yours,
Maud

I seal it in an envelope and sleep with it under my pillow. There is hope yet.

CHAPTER 27

At first light, I tiptoe to Harry's room and slip my letter under the door. I'll go to the laboratory and watch for his arrival from the window. Price is in the hallway, busy with the clock. He's absorbed in adjusting the weights for the pendulum. For once I'm spared a biblical tirade.

The laboratory is peaceful. No one will disturb me here. I'm hopeful, and afraid of that hope. One more chance, just one, and I will never send Harry away again. I shan't think of what he did, for there's more than my pride to consider now.

I stand at the window, my gaze fixed on the gates, watching for the coach. I'll tell him I love him, how I cannot bear life without him. Perhaps he loves me still. God, please make him love me still. The seconds drag by – on and on – and still no sign of him. No, wait. There – there, a carriage. It turns into the yard and everything inside me lurches. It slows to a halt outside the front door, and there he is. Oh, I'd forgotten how beautiful he is. My heart faints at the sight of him. Oh, please God, let him remember me.

I rush to my room and wait – and wait. Perhaps he's reading my letter right now. Perhaps he'll be pleased. After all, he said he couldn't bear to live without me. Yes, he said it and yet here he is, living perfectly well without me. I can't keep still, thoughts rushing through my mind one after the other. Has he found a new love? Does he tell her he can't live without her? Is he holding my letter now, overwhelmed with love for me, or sniggering with Imogen about a stupid servant girl who fell for his charms?

Back and forth, I pace the floor, listening for his footsteps on the stair. Back and forth, my hands knitted together. The clock ticks. This delay means nothing. He will need to see Imogen first, of course, and probably the vicar, and he can hardly come rushing to me on such a day. I must be patient.

At the first toll of the bell, I hurry across to the church. Hope and fear swamp me, but he's not there. The church is almost empty, save for the Prices, a few villagers whose curiosity has overcome their fear, and a group of middle-aged gentlemen, scientists perhaps, colleagues of Mr Banville's. I sit in my usual pew. He will know where to look for me. I would not have him miss me, not for the world.

Mr Banville's coffin stands in front of the altar, where it's been all night. Poor Mr Banville.

Someone's snivelling at the back of the church. It's her, Imogen, dressed in her widow's weeds, face veiled but not enough to hide her beauty. If anything, the veil accentuates it. The physician is close behind, but where is Harry? I stare as others come in, and there – there he is, walking with that long, loping stride of his. His head is lowered. Surely, he'll look at me. He can't walk past me, not knowing . . .

He's level with me now. Turn your head, my love. Turn and look at me. His stride falters, just as it did the day I sent him away, and he is past, without a glance. Does he know I'm here? Does he even remember me? I long to call his name, but dare not. Instead, I gaze at the back of his neck, at the soft patch of skin between his collar and his hair. I've kissed that skin many times, can smell it now, taste it.

He sits next to Imogen. She is sandwiched between her two lovers. Poor Mr Banville.

In no time, it seems, the coffin is carried out, Imogen and Harry following on behind. Not once does he look up, not once.

The congregation spills out into the windy churchyard.

Imogen looks dramatic, tragic, among the gravestones. How the gentlemen cluster around her like flies around dung. With her beloved husband not yet underground, they clamour for her bed.

Harry stands apart, eyes downcast, and fidgets, picks at his fingers, his poor fingers. I'd forgotten how I love those hands, that mouth, those eyes. Why did I tell him to go? Better to have shared him with Imogen than this – better anything than this.

I step towards him, but he turns away. Of course, he must be at the graveside, he of all people. He didn't see me. Not once did he raise his eyes. He couldn't have noticed my approach. His heart is full of grief for his father, after all. I shouldn't expect him to talk to me here in front of everyone. I'll go to the marsh and wait there. He will come. He will come if he loves me. Please, please love me.

*

It's dusk. Plump bats swoop low over the water, darting this way and that. A song thrush sings close by, warbles, clicks, repeating, repeating, then silence.

The last light dies. A chill mist rises from the water, and still I wait. Why doesn't he come? Why?

All night I wait. The sky lightens. Birds sing. I go back to the house, a glimmer of hope flickering. Perhaps he came to my room. Perhaps he's there now, sitting on my bed, waiting for me. I run up the stairs, afraid my heart will give out at the hope, the dread.

Empty. My room is empty.

Perhaps he didn't see my letter. Perhaps it hides, sits under a rug unseen, unread. I run to his room and knock. Silence.

'Harry,' I whisper.

Perhaps he sleeps still, exhausted by his travelling, and by grief. I turn the handle on his door and push it open. The room is empty, the bed a tangle of blankets and sheets. There is no rug. No rug and no letter, so he must have seen it, must have read it. He has read it. He knows.

I stare at the floor where my letter lay. All is lost – all is lost for me and my little one.

The room sways, sounds grow muffled. I stagger to the door. Oh, I will die of it, this pain.

My legs can scarcely hold me as I stumble down the stairs. How weak they are, trembling and giving way.

Mrs Price is stacking plates in the kitchen. They crash together, hurting my ears. I try to sneak past her, but a faint comes upon me and I must sit.

She turns her head. 'What now?'

'Nothing.' I lay my head on the table. 'I'm faint, nothing more.'

She grunts, turns back to her work. I can't stay here. He could come in and see me. The bell rings.

'Missus wants you,' Mrs Price says.

'Not now. Later, perhaps.'

She stares. 'No, you must go now. She telled me. After breakfast, you're to go to her room.'

I pull myself to my feet. Is he with her, standing there, smoking? Is their plan to mock me, to sneer at me, at my foolishness? I can't bear it. I cannot, and yet my feet take me there, one step at a time. It feels like a walk to the scaffold. Make me strong, Lord. Help me – oh, help me. I'm there already, and there is the door, and I must knock. I raise my hand. Oh, how it trembles.

I turn away. Where, then, can I go? Where can I be safe? There is nowhere. Harry is my only hope.

I raise my hand, take a deep breath and knock.

'Come.'

I push the door open.

'Ah! There you are.'

He's not here. There's only Imogen, standing at the window, one hand on her stomach. She smiles.

She never smiles at me, never.

'Is something wrong?' I say.

'No, no. Quite the opposite.'

Her smile makes me nervous. There's something triumphant about it. She looks out of the window. 'Ah, here he is. Come.'

She beckons me, takes my hand, and draws me to the window. Her cloying perfume sticks in my throat. Please, please don't let it be him.

She slips her arm through mine as if we're friends or sisters.

It is. It's Harry – of course it's him, pacing up and down, head bowed. My chest tightens. He used to be mine, that beautiful man. And now?

Imogen squeezes my arm. 'He is rather lovely, isn't he?'

'Yes,' I say, for what is the point in pretence now? 'Yes, he is.'

She looks at me out of the corner of her eye. 'He tells me you and he have been – close.'

I step back and meet her steady gaze. 'He told you?'

'Oh, yes.' She pulls my arm back, clamps it to her side. 'He tells me everything. Everything.'

He's told her. Then why has he not spoken to me?

'Especially when he's in an awkward situation.'

Awkward?

'He's soft-hearted, you know. He always finds it difficult to end these dalliances.'

Dalliance – that word.

'Such a bad boy.' She says it with pride, with affection. 'But so handsome, it's no wonder you girls can't resist him.'

Girls. Plural.

'He has quite a penchant for serving-maids, the naughty thing.'

Shut up. I can't think. I can't . . .

'Oh, my dear.' Her brow creases in concern. 'You've gone quite pale.'

'I'm perfectly well.' I try to withdraw my arm, but she holds it fast.

'The last one was quite taken in by him.'

She's lying. She must be, and yet there's that hunger of his, the way he looked at her throat.

'Needless to say, she ended up in an unfortunate condition.' Her lip curls. 'She thought he loved her.' A small laugh. 'Oh, yes, he's quite the actor, our Harry.'

Is he? Was it all an act, then? 'Where is she now?' I have to ask. 'Where's the girl?'

Her eyebrows shoot up. 'Why, the workhouse, of course.' As if it's nothing, of no consequence. Her eyes widen. 'Oh no. I do hope you're not . . .'

My face has betrayed me. I try to think of a way to deny it, but it's too late – far too late. She knows already, has probably known for a while. She's playing with me as a cat does a mouse.

He's still there, Harry, still pacing up and down. I pull my arm free of hers. 'I must speak with him.'

'No.' She catches at my arm, but I'm stronger, and wrench it away. He will not ignore our child. I won't let him.

Carriage wheels crunch in the yard. He's leaving. I pull the door open and run. 'Harry!'

Imogen shouts behind me, but I'm flying down the stairs. 'Harry.' Almost there – almost. One more step, and just the hallway, and . . .

Price. Price stands with his back to the front door, shotgun in hand, but he won't stop me.

'Move.'

The coachman's voice filters through the door.

'Harry,' I shout.

The coachman whistles, and Price smirks. The coach door slams. The horse snorts.

'Get out of my way, idiot.' I reach out to grab his arm, but there's something in his eyes, something that stops me. My arm drops to my side as he raises the gun, oh so slowly, and points it at my face. It's inches from me. I could shout now, and perhaps Harry would hear me, but that black, round hole of death stares back at me, and I dare not. Price will use it, I do not doubt that, and I am a coward.

Carriage wheels crunch on the drive. That awful sound, taking him away, taking him away from me, and I can do nothing to stop it.

'Calm yourself,' Imogen snaps. 'You'll harm the child.'

My laugh catches in the back of my throat.

'We wouldn't have you go to the workhouse,' she says, 'not when you were so kind to my dear husband.'

Perhaps pregnancy has softened her. After all, she and I are in the same condition. 'You will let me stay here?' How quickly hope rises. How quickly it's extinguished.

'No, no. Good heavens, that would be no good at all.' Her laugh is high, brittle. 'I do know of somewhere you can go until your confinement, however.' Her eyes are wide, glittering and hard. 'It's the perfect place for you.'

'Come back, Maud,' Diamond says, and I'm glad to leave – so glad to leave her there and to open my eyes to the cold cellar.

Diamond rubs his hands together. 'You were right, Mrs Tucker. There was indeed more to discover.'

I try not to think about the memory, but Price's gun keeps flashing into my mind. That gun and the fear that went with it, and something else, some unfathomable dread that I dare not think of.

'I suggest we warm ourselves by the fire in my office,' Diamond says, 'and have a cup of tea.'

'And how we need it.' Tucker blows on her hands, on her blue-tinged fingers.

Despite the blanket, my feet and fingers are numb with cold, but she and Diamond look worse.

It's a slow journey back to Diamond's room. They're no quicker than me, now, their movements slowed by the chill. No one touches me. No one grabs my arm, no one restrains me. I could run, escape, but there's warmth in Diamond's room and, anyway, where would I run to? Into the abyss, that's where – right to the edge of it, and tip myself in and fall and fall, and fall for ever into icy black nothingness.

Diamond shivers, even as we sit close to a roaring fire. 'We will need more blankets for our next visit, I believe.'

'And warmers for our feet,' Tucker says. We all smile and nod and, for a moment or two, I don't feel separate, a species apart. I feel human and real, just like them.

Diamond fixes me with those warm brown eyes of his. 'Do you remember what happened to your baby, Maud?'

'No.'

'But you do remember you were with child?'

'No,' I say, too loudly.

Diamond pinches his nose between thumb and forefinger. 'We will have to find out what happened. You must know that.'

I watch the fire, watch the flames fold and stretch, flicker and sway, and I will not think of anything else, anything but those flames.

He sighs. 'Then we will leave it for today.'

Tucker stands to take me back to my room. 'We wouldn't want you to miss your supper.'

Miss that hard biscuit and cup of milk?

'Perhaps, next time, we will uncover the truth,' Diamond says.

'Yes, I expect we will,' I say, 'next time.'

'We're almost there.'

'Yes,' I say. 'I expect we are.' But I have no intention of remembering any more. No, I will not go into that darkness.

CHAPTER 28

A week or so after our visit to the cellar, Tucker and Diamond come to my room in the early afternoon. The sight of them sets me trembling. I have managed to keep my memories at bay for the most part, except at night when darkness closes in. Then I see Price's gun, see my hands fly to my stomach to shield what lies within it.

During the day, the knowledge that there is worse to come sits in the corner of my mind, in the shadows, a lurking, sick poison, but I can look at the sky and pretend all will be well. Now they are here, though, the foreboding comes flooding back.

'How is your mood now?' Diamond peers at me.

'My mood is good,' I say. 'I am relieved and unburdened.' I will not have them take me back there, not again.

'Do you remember our last session?' he says.

'Yes, of course.' I smile, for I must show them that I am well now, cured, and that there is no need for any more hypnosis. 'We had blankets and afterwards tea in your room, if I remember rightly.'

He casts a sideways look at Tucker and away. 'And the hypnosis – do you remember what you recalled?'

'Not in any detail.' Snow is falling, large flakes floating down, dancing in the breeze. 'Price had a gun pointed at my face,' I say, 'and Harry left.'

Diamond nods. 'I'm afraid we must endure the cellar once more. We don't have the luxury of time but must go now, while the asylum is quiet.'

My pulse races. 'I have remembered enough.'

'We don't know how long we'll be able to continue, Maud,' Tucker says, 'and there are still questions that must be answered.'

'I don't need them answered,' I say. 'I am perfectly well now.'

Their eyes meet. Diamond sighs. 'One more session. One more, I promise.'

'Come on.' Tucker takes my arm. 'Just once more.'

Terror courses through me. I pull back. 'I can't.' And now the tears come, spilling down my face.

Her eyes widen. 'What is it?'

'I don't know,' I shout. Shudders run through me. 'I just know it's horrific.'

'Shush now.' Tucker strokes my arm. 'Shush. You're safe with us.'

Safe? They don't see those sinister black clouds waiting. They don't know what secrets they hold.

'We're almost there, Maud.' Tucker's voice is comforting, but her grip is firm. 'Truly, we are almost there.'

I have no choice. She will lead me there whether I want to go or not.

The cellar seems even colder than before, but we all wear hats this time, and have stone hot-water bottles at our feet. We wrap blankets around ourselves from head to toe.

'I'm afraid,' I say, and the room goes silent. 'At what is to come. I think it's my grave. I think it will kill me.'

'No.' Diamond shakes his head. 'It's not your grave, nor will it kill you. It may feel like that now, but you're here. You survived.'

'Yes, I survived.' My laugh turns into a hiccough. 'I survived like this – as a feeble-minded lunatic.'

He sits back and watches me.

'You've been sick,' he says, after a long pause, 'in the same way that any of us may be sick. You lost yourself for a while, that's all. You are definitely not feeble-minded. Neither, I venture, are you any longer a lunatic.'

Oh, Diamond, how I wish I could believe you. No longer a lunatic? With these thoughts?

He waves that shiny ring.

'One.'

I'm sliding away, slipping into the past faster and faster and I can't stop.

'Two.'

Back I go, into the waiting darkness.

'Where does Imogen send you,' Diamond says, 'for your confinement?'

Confinement? Oh, yes – yes. Now I remember.

*

Price is taking me to my room. He struts behind me, waving the gun about. He thinks himself powerful, but without that gun he is nothing – less than nothing. I long to tell him so. If it weren't for the tiny person living inside me, I would. I would fight him and risk the consequences, but something infinitely precious is relying on me to keep it safe.

I'm to stay in my room until he comes back to transport me to this 'perfect place'. My possessions are meagre, and my trunk is only half full. In my bag, I pack a change of clothes for when I get to my new home. Imogen says she'll send the trunk on once I'm settled. I will have new clothes where I'm going, she says, and medical care should I need it. The frocks, slips, underwear ruined by Harry, I place in a bag to be thrown out. I remember every missing button, every torn seam. And each one hurts, each one causes a sharp, stabbing pain in my chest.

I'm as unimportant as these clothes – something to be used and thrown away.

I dress in the only reasonably respectable frock I have left – the green silk.

It grows dark outside, the lamp is low, and still Price doesn't come. I lay my head on the pillow and fall instantly into a dreamless sleep, only to be woken by the sound of my door opening. Price, at last.

'Is it time to go?' I say.

He steps inside, shutting the door behind him.

My pulse quickens. 'I'm ready.' I jump to my feet, bend to pick up my bag. 'Could you possibly help with my bag?'

His tongue flicks out, licks his lips.

'Could you?' My mouth's so dry, the words are hard to form. There must be a reason why he's shut the door, a perfectly innocent reason, and I'm trying to think what it could be. 'Could you possibly carry . . . ?'

'Think yourself clever, don't you?' His eyes are flat, empty.

'No, of course I don't.'

'Think yerself better 'n me?'

'Not at all.' At least he doesn't have the gun. At least there's that. I glance about for a weapon, but everything is packed away – everything. But I'm strong. I can . . .

'You called me an idiot.' He takes a step towards me, pokes a finger in my face. 'No one does that – no one.'

He seems taller, close up, and wiry. I raise my hands. 'If I've offended you, Mr Price, I'm truly sorry, but now we need to go.'

He's so close now I can smell his breath. I step back. The bedframe digs into my calves.

'Mr Price . . .'

'I seen you. Lifting them skirts to run across the road, layin' on the grass there for any man to see.' His eyes blaze. His face is rigid with disgust. 'The devil is in me now,' he says. 'And that's your doing, and now I must rid myself of him.'

He pulls his belt from his trousers. 'For thou hast trusted in thy wickedness,' he says, his voice deep and portentous. 'Thou hast said, None seeth me.'

'Stop it.' How my voice shakes and quivers.

'I been watching you – you and him, fornicating.'

He unbuttons his hose with filthy hands. I can smell him, sweet and dirty. My stomach heaves.

He's so close now, touching me. His fingers dig into my shoulder and I freeze. Something smacks into the side of my head and the world goes dark.

A noise wakes me. For a moment, I think I'm in my room – but no. This room is larger than mine, and bare, except for the bed I'm lying on and a table in the corner. It's dark, a strange half-light, so that I pinch myself, thinking it a dream. A woman stands by the table, her back to me – a woman I don't know, dressed in blue with a long white apron, and white headdress. A nun, perhaps.

'Who are you?' I say.

She continues with whatever she's doing.

I look about me. 'Where am I?'

There's one deep-set window, the glass filthy and cracked. Not that it makes any difference, as it's boarded up on the outside. A few, narrow slivers of brightness filter through the gaps.

I sit up and wetness leaks from me. That smell. Price. I retch, and retch again. That vile, Bible-spouting hypocrite has left his mark on me, in me.

'He attacked me,' I say. 'Price attacked me. He . . .'

The woman turns and the disgust on her face silences me. 'That's enough o' your stories.' Her voice is deep, with a strong West Country accent. She's a big woman, twice my size, with small eyes, too close together. ''Tis lucky he found you.'

'Lucky?' My laugh catches in my throat.

'Cavortin' in the woods with men from the village? In your condition?'

'What?'

'They'd 'a' left you for dead.' Her mouth is one tight, grim line. 'Comin' from miles around they was.'

'That's not true.'

She sniffs. 'You can thank that gent for saving you and that babby o' yourn.'

'He's lying,' I say, but my voice is quiet. She's already decided who to believe, and it's not me.

She hands me a plate on which sits a lump of bread, and a dried-up chunk of cheese. Then she brings me a cup of milk from the table. After this she leaves. A sound I don't recognise follows, and another. Bolts – she's sliding bolts across the door. I jump off the bed, run to the door, and pull, and push. Nothing.

'Let me out,' I shout. 'You can't leave me here.'

Silence. I look back at the bare, dilapidated room. Is this the place Imogen intended, or has Price disobeyed her? At the thought of him, bile rises at the back of my throat. Harry was right about him. He's not harmless. He's evil.

'Let me out!' I scream, and kick the door, until I hear footsteps and bolts being pulled back.

The door opens, but it's the same nurse. She blocks my way.

I imitate Imogen's haughty tone. 'Let me out this minute.'

She pushes me back inside and shuts the door behind her. 'Drink this.' She hands me a cup of brown liquid.

It smells strange, bitter. 'What is it?'

'A tonic – to make the babby strong.' She takes the cup and holds it to my lips, her other hand on the back of my head. 'Drink it.'

It's bitter and sweet and slides down the back of my throat. She ignores my shudder and holds it there until every drop is gone. The room grows dark, her large face fuzzy and indistinct. And I must sleep.

CHAPTER 29

The sound of bolts being drawn wakes me. I jump off the bed and stand behind the door, back pressed to the wall. I have no weapon but if I can catch her unawares, perhaps I can overpower her from behind. She won't be expecting me to be awake. The door inches open. I hold my breath. Just come in. Just . . .

The door slams into my face, and she's there, the nun–nurse. Her hand grips my wrist and twists. Pain shoots to my shoulder and I cannot but fall to my knees.

'You be needing more medicine,' she says. 'I'll be askin' doctor.'

Not a nun, then. Perhaps she will have pity on me, even so. Perhaps a tender heart hides beneath that uniform. I sob. 'Please, let me go.'

Let me go so I can knock you aside and run.

'Into bed.' She hauls me to my feet, drags me across the room, and pushes me on to the bed. No tender heart, then – no heart at all. Back to the table she goes. There's something – some linen folded on top.

She holds up a dress. It looks grey, but everything does in this light. 'You're to wear this.'

'Why?'

'Your dress, 'tis filthy.'

'But my bag.' I look about me. 'Where have they put my bag?'

'Off with that dress now.' She stands towering over me. I do as she says. She's right. It's filthy and smells of Price and I'm glad to be rid of it, even for this rough, ugly wool shift. She watches me, her face twisted with bitterness, distaste or both.

I slip the wool shift over my head. 'You can't think it right that I'm kept a prisoner.' Something flutters in my stomach. It's as if there's a butterfly trapped in there. I place my hand over it. 'I felt something.'

'Tis the babe quickening,' she says. 'You're further along than doctor thought then. T'will be kicking soon.'

'What happens then, when it's born? What happens then?'

'Not fer me to say.' She sniffs. 'I do my job is all.' And I must be satisfied with that, because she doesn't speak again, although I bombard her with questions.

Three times a day, she brings me food worthy of Mrs Price – slop for the most part, with stale bread, and always a cup of milk. I wear the same scratchy dress day and night. Only when it's filthy does she bring me another. Every night, I drink the brown tonic.

I don't ever remember going to sleep. Each morning, she examines my continuously-growing bump, feeling and probing with large hands that are surprisingly gentle.

'Why am I being kept here?' I say. 'Mrs Banville said I would be looked after.'

'You have food and drink, and a bed to sleep on, and medicine to make the baby strong.'

I look about me. 'Yes, but what of daylight and fresh air? What of freedom? I'm a prisoner here.'

''Tis for the good of the child. You should be grateful.' Her mouth clamps shut.

I sleep, and wake to the same room, the same nurse every day. I mark each one on the wall with my fingernail, counting them by the narrow light that squeezes through the gaps between the boards and travels across the floor like a sundial. One week passes, then another. Then I lose track of what day it is and forget to mark the wall. How will I know now how long I've been here?

'I was a scientist once,' I say, but the nurse is not here to listen. 'I was a scientist and I cut up plants with a scalpel and knew their Latin names.'

Weeks turn into months. My world is still and silent. I am grown used to living in shadows. Sometimes, I list all the plants I know, say their names aloud, but the list grows shorter day by day, and the Latin names are gone completely. 'I'll remember them once I'm free,' I say. 'And I will teach you all about them.'

The babe hears. It kicks and pushes against me, as tired of its prison as I am of mine. I wrap my arms around my bump. 'I love you,' I say. 'I love you.' I hope it hears me. I hope it knows.

I've become so large that I can no longer see my swollen feet. It can't be long now before I see my child. Oh, what a

*wonder it will be. Everything else will be forgotten. There will
be only joy.*

*I walk back and forth across the room, as I do every day, to
keep my limbs moving, to stop them seizing up. I'm halfway
to the boarded-up window when water spills down my legs.
On and on it pours out of me, warm and smelling of the sea.
I can't stop it, cannot stem the tide. I shout and shout until
my throat is sore, but no one comes. It floods the floor. I sit
on the chamber pot – sit there until the bolts slide back and
light pours in.*

'Something's happened,' I shout.

She takes one look at the floor. 'Ah, waters are broken.'

'Waters?'

'Waters around the babe. Your pains'll start soon.'

'And what will happen then?'

'I'll deliver the child.'

*Soon the babe will be here. I will hold it in my arms, see it
for the first time. 'And then? Will we leave this place?'*

Her mouth shuts tight.

'Where will we go?'

*She doesn't answer, but we will surely go somewhere. No
decent person would allow a child to grow up in such a place,
so I must not fret. I must think of what is to come within hours.
A new person. A miracle.*

*All day I wait for the pains to begin. Nothing happens. The
nurse makes me walk about the room, round and round, then
has me jump up and down, and still there are no pains. No
kicks, either.*

'The baby's quiet,' I say. 'It must be asleep.' I stroke my round stomach. 'If it's a girl, I'm going to call her Violet. If it's a boy, I'll name him Jonathan, after my brother.'

She says nothing, just hurries away, and comes back with a bottle of clear oil.

'This'll get 'em started.' She pours some into a spoon. 'Baby needs to come out soon.'

My heart lurches. 'Is something wrong?'

She doesn't answer, but I take the oil willingly, even though I gag as it goes down. It's for my baby and that's all that matters.

The pains start slowly – tightening, griping pains, building then dying away. They strengthen, get closer together, so that no sooner has one finished and I can breathe, than another begins to build.

A wave of pain intensifies, takes my breath away. I wait for it to subside, but before it fades away, another begins. The room blurs. The nurse's voice sounds far away, muffled.

Stillness, blessed stillness, and the pain is gone. There's a clock somewhere, a pendulum swinging back and forth. Tick, tock. Tick, tock. I slip into a dream, take a step into the shade of the trees and . . .

No. No. Pain builds, rises. I sleep or pass out. There's no respite, none, just pain, unconsciousness, pain. Someone cries, moans, screams and all the time the clock ticks.

I open my eyes. There's a man. 'It's essential this child is born as soon as possible.' He's sweating. His hands shake. His head is lowered. I can see little of his face, but I'm sure I know him.

His outline blurs, vanishes into pain.

Hands press on me, on my stomach, between my legs. Cold metal, inside me – hurting.

I'm going to die. He's killing me. He's actually . . .

She's praying, the nurse, her two hands pressed together, lips moving. Pray for me. Oh, pray for me.

For one blissful second the pain eases, and I see him clearly, and I know him – the family doctor. Sweat trickles down his forehead. 'It's essential that we save this child,' he says, 'at all costs.' He braces his feet against the bed and pulls. The sinews in his neck stand out as he pulls my insides from me. And suddenly, it comes out, slithers like an eel, grey and coated in slime and blood, and it's so small, so small.

'Is that my baby?'

'The cord.' The doctor's panicky voice makes my chest tighten.

There's something around its neck, a thick, grey rope, and now the nurse is in the way and I can't see. Their movements are quick, urgent.

'What's wrong?' Babies cry, but not this one, not mine. 'Why doesn't it cry?'

The doctor snatches the tiny grey body to his chest and steps towards the door.

'Can I hold my baby?' I say.

'It's dead.' He goes out, shuts the door behind him.

'Dead? How? How can my baby be dead?'

The nurse has her back to me. She throws blood-soaked rags into a metal bucket on the floor, and I think maybe I'm the one who's dead, or invisible.

'Where has he taken my baby?'

She drops bloodied instruments into the same bucket. They clink as they hit the sides.

The doctor will come back in a moment, saying he made a mistake, that my baby's alive, after all. I watch the door and wait. I'll stretch out my hands and he'll lay my precious child in my arms.

I watch and wait, but the door doesn't open.

The nurse washes me, stitches me.

'Can I hold my baby, just once?'

She turns away, slams something into the bucket. Bloody water splashes on to the floor.

'Please,' I say.

She looks away, folds bloodstained cloths.

'But what will happen to it? Where will they take it?'

She bustles about, moving things here and there, avoiding my gaze.

'He's not taking my baby.' I swing my legs over the side of the bed and sit up. Blood floods between my legs like a river gushing. I run to the door. 'Bring it back.' I pull at it. 'Bring my baby back.'

My legs fold, and I fall to my knees. My hands cradle my bereft, empty middle where once those tiny feet kicked, where knees and elbows pushed, pushed under my skin. 'Bring it back. Please, bring it back.'

The clock counts the seconds – tick, tock. The pendulum swings, and I watch the door.

I watch the door, but it doesn't open. It never opens.

*

'Maud.' Diamond wipes my face with a clean handkerchief. 'You're safe now.'

Safe? Of course, I'm safe, for there is Diamond, there Tucker.

Diamond's face is ashen, his eyes watery as if he's been crying. I don't ask him what's wrong. Men don't like to cry. They're ashamed. I don't like to cry, either. It makes me weak and I hate that.

I won't think of . . . of . . . of . . . I won't think of it, not yet. I won't think of anything, anything at all.

We walk back to Diamond's room in silence. Tucker dabs at her eyes with her apron. 'It's the cold,' she says when she sees me looking, but she's still at it when we're in the warm and sitting around the fire – dabbing, swallowing and taking deep breaths. I wish she wouldn't. It makes it harder for me to keep the memories away.

Diamond pats her shoulder. 'Today we have a special cake, as well as tea,' he says, in a chirpy tone. 'I had a feeling we might need it.'

It's sponge with apricot and cream – real cream. I eat it quickly. 'I haven't had real cream for years.' My voice is chirpy, too – and strained, and far too high. 'Since I don't remember when.'

He lifts another slice on to my plate, then sits and reads through my notes, frowning as he does so.

'I'm surprised no mention is made of such a distressing event in these notes.'

Distressing event. He means the cellar, and what happened there. My mind shies away, as if stung.

I think about the fire instead – the orange glow, the dark hollows that look like strange, imaginary worlds. Is hell like that? A dark hole surrounded by flickering flames and glowing coals?

'The birth must surely have played some part in the illness that followed.'

Birth. That word. What pain comes with it, like touching a splinter deep in my soul. Tears spring into my eyes. I let them fall on to my bodice, soaking the wool.

'Poor mite,' Diamond says.

Tucker nods. 'Yes, indeed.'

Poor mite. Poor, poor mite. Poor slithery, grey mite. My baby. My poor baby.

The fire glows – red and auburn and orange.

Silence, save for the crackling coals. How dangerous silence can be, with nothing to distract my thoughts from that lost little life.

I cough, wipe my eyes. 'Will I be well now?' I say it loudly to fill the empty space. 'Now that I've remembered what happened?'

'Not yet, but we're very close,' Diamond says.

Very close. Almost there. So many times I have heard these words, and yet still it is not finished.

Diamond pours the tea, stirs in the sugar. The spoon slows, stops, and still he stands there, as if frozen. 'Do you remember?' he says.

'No.' I almost drop my plate, just managing to save the cake, and I laugh because I do remember. I do. I laugh and laugh, and the more they stare at me, the louder I laugh until I fear I'll be sick.

'Come now.' Tucker envelopes me in her arms and squeezes me. I breathe in the clean, starched smell of her and it's the first time I've felt loved for such a long time. It makes me cry, so that the laughs change to sobs and I can't stop.

CHAPTER 30

I lie in bed, eyes open, staring into the darkness. This room is like that other, although that had no patch of night sky – no stars, no small glimmers of light, of hope. That one had blood streaking the floor and spattered on the wall in a fine spray of brown. I knew it for what it was by the smell, the smell of rusty iron. I can smell it now.

Was it my blood? I think it was. And yet here I am, alive and breathing and all of a piece with no scars to speak of, so where did it come from?

The memory comes back with a sickening thud.

Over and over I forget, then I remember. Each time the earth crumbles beneath my feet, the sky falls in on my head, a huge, dark cavern of blackness opens up in front of me, a yawning abyss, waiting to swallow me whole.

Breakfast comes as it always does, every morning. My room is the same as ever. Everything is normal, so that now *it*, the thing, the thing I remembered with Tucker and Diamond, feels melodramatic and unreal. This is reality, this dry biscuit and tepid milk, this sky. Nothing has changed, so I need not think of the other.

The hands on the clock turn. Tucker comes in the afternoon. She sits on the chair and watches the snow and neither of us speaks. It's a comfort, the presence of another living, breathing human being, another heartbeat in the room.

A thaw sets in after weeks of cold. Icicles crack and fall, snow slides off the roof and falls in great clumps past my window, and the countryside turns brown and grey.

Tucker tells me I'm no longer permitted to be Diamond's patient but must be Womack's. There are no visits to that warm room, no hot tea, no cake. Rarely do I leave my room these days. Womack says reading novels causes melancholy and mania, so there can be no *Great Expectations* for me, and I have no desire to read the scriptures. I wouldn't want to come across one of Price's favourite verses by mistake, so I sit and stare at nothing. I don't think I dribble. I hope not, anyway. Even the maniac has stopped running up and down the stairs. I miss her in a funny way. There was comfort in the rhythm, in the madness.

Tucker sits with me sometimes, in silence for the most part. We don't speak of what happened, but only of the changing weather and the sky and other harmless, safe subjects.

This morning is bright – a day of watery sunlight and mist over the river. I open my window and breathe. The air smells of spring. Soon all the country will be bursting into life, while I stagnate in this room.

There are noises in the corridor, footsteps and voices. The pretty one and Prune.

'There are some visitors for you,' Pretty says.

'Visitors?' My brothers are come at last? No, no, I'm forgetting.

'They're from the committee. Doctor Dimmond wants you to meet them.'

We walk in single file along the corridor, down the stairs. Perhaps the visitors have come to take me to Newgate. My heart falters. Perhaps they've come to take me to the scaffold. I cling on to the stair rail. No, no, Diamond says I'm innocent, and I am to believe him. Perhaps the visitors are going to release me, then. And what shall I wear? I have no clothes of my own, no coat. I haven't had a coat since . . .

I smooth down my skirts. I am recovered. I am sane, as sane as anyone else – a new person, a new me. It will be fine as long as Womack's not there, staring at me, or any man with a moustache – and most of them have them, after all – or any man with a voice like Price's, or with white fingers or dirty fingernails.

We walk down the corridor with its pale green arches and patterned windows, past Diamond's room and on towards Womack's. My heart is jumping about all over the place.

If I run now . . . I turn to check how far I have to go, but Pretty is right behind me. She smiles as if she's my friend, and yet I seem to remember her chopping at my hair when I first came here, when I was cold, so cold. She was not my friend then.

The door opens, and there is Diamond. My heart lifts at the sight of him, so that I have to stop myself from running to him as I would to my father. He looks older, and tired, though it's been scarcely two months since last I saw him. His eyes still crinkle when he smiles.

'Hello, Maud,' he says, and my eyes fill with tears.

I look at the ceiling, take a deep breath. Now I can look at him, now I can smile.

'Good morning, doctor,' I say.

Womack is sitting behind his desk, bolt upright, not slouched in an armchair as usual. The room smells of his pipe. There are other people, too, three shadowy figures, sitting on chairs against the wall. One is older, corpulent, with greying sideburns, the other two are younger and identical, like twins, with the same neat moustaches, the same sideburns.

'Gentlemen,' Diamond says, 'may I introduce Maud.'

'Mary,' Womack mutters.

Diamond blinks, continues. 'For the last two months I have been prevented from seeing my patient.'

'*My* patient,' Womack says.

The elder of the three men speaks. 'The complainant must be heard, sir.'

Womack grunts.

'Thank you.' Diamond takes a breath. 'I have been prevented from seeing Maud, who is vital to the success of my study. Her history, her sickness, make her the ideal subject. I have been commissioned to undertake this research and yet Doctor Womack has consistently undermined, interrupted and otherwise interfered in Maud's treatment.'

'Thus speaks the man whose foolhardy experiment caused the patient to become violent.' Womack's gaze alights on me for a moment. He sighs, turns to the visitors. 'She grew agitated, heard bells where there were none.'

It's ringing now, the bell.

'Heard clocks were there were none.'

The grandfather clock behind him ticks away the seconds. Back and forth the pendulum swings.

'When the patient became violent,' Womack throws his hands in the air, 'I was compelled to intervene.'

He and Diamond lock eyes. The stare goes on and on and on, as if they've forgotten about the visitors, who fidget and cough and clear their throats.

'Doctor Dimmond,' the older man says, at last. 'Please continue.'

Diamond bows. 'Doctor Womack did indeed intervene, by administering a tartar emetic, by the use of mechanical restraint, force-feeding and isolation of over twenty-four hours – methods that are surely seen as barbarous in these enlightened times.'

'Is this true?' It's one of the twins, and he's asking me – asking me.

My mouth dries, my tongue sticks to the roof of it, and the pendulum swings back and forth – tick, tock, tick, tock.

'It is.' Womack hauls himself to his feet. 'And with very good reason.' His pallid face glistens in the light. 'Gentlemen, with your permission, I shall call the relevant attendants to tell you in their own words what happened on that unfortunate occasion.' He rubs his hands together as if it's cold. 'In the meantime, may I suggest we have tea?' He rings the bell and Chins appears, so quickly that she must have been listening, her ear pressed to the door, as I did once or twice at Ashton House.

'Tea for these gentlemen, please,' Womack says, 'and tell Pedrick and Stokes they are to come immediately.' He turns to the gentlemen. 'We'll soon lay this matter to rest.'

There are nods all round, and chatter, and all seem relaxed except for Diamond, who sits amongst them, but somehow alone. He and I – we are excluded. I feel it and wonder if he does, too. He raises his eyes and meets my gaze. Yes, he feels it. We are embattled, he and I, and both equally afraid of what is to come.

First to come, of course, is the tea. Chins and Prune bustle in with laden trays on which there are five cups, a teapot, a jug of milk, and a plate of biscuits.

They pour the tea and hand a cup to each of the gentlemen, serving Diamond last. He stands, strides over to me and hands me the cup. 'I suspect you need this rather more than I,' he says. I try to take it, but my hands tremble so that it spills into the saucer. I can't even say thank you, not with my tongue stuck to the roof of my mouth. I shake my head.

'All will be well, Maud,' he murmurs.

I knit my fingers together tightly and press them until they hurt. My tongue loosens, and my breath comes back. What's the worst they can do? Nothing I have not experienced before. I'm more afraid for Diamond, that his kindness to me will result in his downfall.

Womack regales the gentlemen with stories as they drink – amusing anecdotes, mad letters some patients have written, his lip curling in mockery. And they laugh. Oh, how they laugh.

A spasm of disgust ripples over Diamond's face. 'I have lived and worked all my life with the insane,' he says, loudly, silencing the laughter. 'I was born in a madhouse that my father ran. There, the patients were treated with respect. No one mocked them. My father would not have it and I, sirs, am offended by your laughter. As for you, Doctor Womack – you, sir, should know better.'

A stunned silence fills the room.

Oh, Diamond! What have you done? You have made enemies of them, mortal enemies. It's a dangerous game, making enemies. I should know. It's a game I have played myself – and lost.

Voices echo in the corridor outside, footsteps growing closer. Womack flings open the door, and there are the two burly attendants. I shrink back into the chair, try to make myself invisible as my pulse hammers on the inside of my skull.

Womack ushers them in and shuts the door. They stand awkwardly in the middle of the room like oversized children.

'Mrs Stokes,' Womack says, 'tell these gentlemen what transpired on the afternoon of the twenty-seventh of November.'

'Yes, sir.' Stokes is not the one I remember. No, it's not her.

'We accompanied . . .' Stokes says.

The older visitor pipes up. 'When you say we?'

'Myself and Pedrick here, sir.' She points at her companion, the one with grey hair.

'I see.' He nods. 'Go on.'

'The patient – this patient.' She points at me. 'Her was agitated, I'd say, sir. She struck Doctor Womack with force, sir. She give me a good clump 'n' all.'

'And then?'

'Well, then we restrained her, for her own good, like.' She licks her lips, glances at Womack, who nods. 'Doctor prescribed a tartar emetic, but even that weren't enough. She's a proper fighter, is 'er.' She looks to Pedrick.

'We had no choice then, sir,' Pedrick says. That voice – that accent and those eyes, so close together. It's definitely her. She's the nurse from that cursed place. She shoots a sideways glance at me. Yes, it is her, and she knows. She knows the truth of it all.

'Her was hell bent on killin' us all, and, and . . .' Stokes glances at Womack and blinks. 'And p'rhaps herself, sirs. Yes, was hell bent on doin' herself a mischief, she was, so doctor had us put her in a straitdress.'

'All noted in the register of mechanical restraint,' Womack says.

'Yes – yes, all noted in . . .' Stokes swallows. 'And then, 'cause her weren't settling, we took 'er down to solitary.'

'And the force-feeding?' Diamond says.

'Her refused her food, doctor.'

I did. I spat it out – spat out that slop and thought myself clever, thought I had won.

'You say you administered a tartar emetic.' Diamond says it as if it's an aside, unimportant.

The attendants glance at each other. Pedrick nods. 'We did, doctor, yes.'

'And how many grains did you use – just out of interest?'

Another glance. 'Two.' Her voice is so quiet, it's hard to hear.

'Two grains.' Diamond nods. 'Thank you.'

Womack runs a finger around his collar. His eyes reflect the burning coals, and for an instant, it's as if hell itself lives inside him. Perhaps it does.

'You may go back to work,' he says.

The attendants escape into the corridor. Womack closes the door after them and turns to the room, smiles. 'I hope that will . . .'

'You used it as a punishment,' Diamond says. 'That emetic – tartar of antimony – is a poison, two grains a potentially lethal dose for a patient such as Maud, with so slight a frame.'

'It's a perfectly safe dose.'

'Safe?' A flush suffuses Diamond's face. 'These barbaric so-called treatments were nothing short of revenge, a punish-ment for the patient having struck you.'

Womack doesn't even look at him. He addresses himself to the gentlemen instead. 'These are all treatments I have used for many years. They have proved to be beneficial. Indeed, several of my patients have made a full recovery under this very regime.'

'Which patients?' Diamond says. 'Where are they?'

Sweat glistens on Womack's forehead. For a moment, he hesitates, before his gaze alights on me, and he smiles. 'Why, gentlemen, I need no more proof of the efficacy of my cure than the patient you see sitting before you.' He waves a hand in my direction.

I look about me, but there are no other patients, only me.

'Here she sits, both sane and calm – cured, I suggest, by the very treatment my colleague seeks to prohibit.'

He takes a step towards me. I shrink back, but there's nowhere to go. I'm trapped in this chair.

Womack's voice booms. 'You see, gentlemen –' he grips my shoulder, digs his fingers into the flesh '– how my treatment has transformed this erstwhile lunatic.'

'It was Diamond,' I say. 'It was the hypnosis.' Does he hear me? No one else seems to.

'Bravo,' one of the twins says. 'So this patient is to be released.'

Womack swallows, clears his throat. 'I . . . by that I meant . . .' Too late, Doctor Womack. Too late. 'There is still some way to go before she will be ready for release.'

'Nonsense,' the older man says. 'Our asylums are hugely overcrowded, as we all know. Why, even now they are building yet another hospital on your doorstep, are they not?'

Womack stares.

'They are indeed,' Diamond says.

The older man turns to him. 'Is it true that you applied for the post of medical superintendent here, some seven or eight years ago?'

'Yes, I—'

'And the post was given to Doctor Womack here in your stead?'

'That's right, but I fail to see. . .'

The visitor talks over him. 'Then I think we can assume that your criticism of your colleague is rooted in nothing more than envy.'

Diamond's face reddens. 'It is concern for this hospital's inmates and disquiet at the methods used by my colleague that have forced me to bring this to your attention, nothing more.'

'Methods that have cured patients, it seems.' He holds out a hand to Womack. 'We will trouble you no longer, sir. Thank you for your time.' He turns to Diamond. 'Perhaps we can repair to your office, Doctor Dimmond?'

'Of course.' How dejected he looks as he walks away – a smaller man, broken. Poor Diamond.

Pretty leads me back to my room. 'Womack didn't cure me,' I say. 'It was Diamond and the hypnosis.'

She appears not to hear me but heads for the stairs.

'Will you tell them for me?' I say. 'The visitors? I can't have them thinking—'

She stops and jerks me around to face her. 'Do you know what would happen to me if I told them?'

I shake my head.

She peers down the empty corridor and lowers her voice. 'I would lose my job, and my home, too, so you must forget it. There is nothing to be done.'

Nothing to be done, not against Womack. It won't always be so, though. One day his sins will find him out, just as mine have found me.

Darkness falls. Chins brings my medication, and I must go to bed. I lie in the dark and wonder at all that has happened. Were it not for the emptiness inside me, the hollow pain of loss, I could pretend it was all a dream, an invention. But this emptiness is real and vicious, and nothing will ever fill it. My baby's gone, Mr Banville is gone, my brothers and father are gone – everyone. All dead. I lost them all, and the aching loss grows with every breath I take.

How I wish I could bury that memory again, smooth it over until it disappears, vanishes, as if it never existed.

Sleep steals across me. As I sink into oblivion, I realise that not everyone is dead. No, there is still Harry. Somewhere, there is Harry.

CHAPTER 31

My dreams are of the marsh. Ravens stalk the bank, peering into the dark water and pulling at the pondweed. They find something white and fleshy. Pecking at it, they drag it free of the water. It's a body, the tiny body of a baby.

'Maud.' Tucker is kneeling by my bed like a nun. 'This can't wait.' She turns her head.

Diamond is here, too, standing in the moonlight. 'You may be released very soon,' he whispers. 'This is our last opportunity to uncover the truth.'

I sit up. 'Isn't it enough that I've lost everything? I don't want to know any more.'

'Come now, Maud.' Tucker sits next to me on the bed. She places her arm around my shoulder. 'You've been so brave, and we're so nearly finished.'

'Once more, and I promise it will be over.' Diamond pulls up the chair and sits. 'There's no need for the cellar. You can stay here, just as you are.'

That ring is in front of my face. How bright it is, the spark of moonlight – so bright in the darkness. Every instinct screams at me not to close my eyes, not to go there, but I must – just once more, and Tucker is here, holding me close, and I am safe. Yes, I am safe with these two.

I wake to the same dark room, with the same narrow strip of light across the floor, but something is different. That smell, like rusted metal.

I sit up. My baby. Where is it? I clutch at my middle. 'Where are you?'

No kicks. Nothing.

So, the baby is born? Then where have I put it? It's so dark in here, it could be anywhere. I hold my breath and listen for another breath, a small, tiny breath. Nothing.

The bolts slide back and the nurse comes in. She must have taken it, but here she is, coming through the door with empty hands.

'What have you done with my baby?' I say.

She frowns.

'My baby. I can't find it.'

'There is no baby,' she says. 'The cord were round her neck. Did strangle her.'

I see it, that grey rope around that precious neck. 'She was a girl?'

The nurse pours some medicine into a beaker and holds it to my lips. ''Tis best to forget it now.'

'Forget my baby? I'll never forget her,' I say as sleep washes over me.

The door is locked, the room dark. If I could see the sky, see daylight, maybe I'd be able to think. Instead, I sleep the sleep of oblivion, punctured by sudden, sharp nightmares that wake me in a sweat.

She's back, the nurse, with food and medicine. She washes me, checks between my legs, tuts, then binds my breasts. 'This is to stop the milk,' she says.

It doesn't work. The milk keeps coming, soaking the binding. Every time she unwraps it, milk shoots over her, over the floor, everywhere. There's so much of it. Wasted – all wasted.

A cry comes from far away. 'Is that my baby crying?'

"Tis a cat.'

It cries again, a longer cry this time, and less like a baby. She is right, then. Just an old tom after the mice. She binds me tighter than ever so that I can scarcely breathe. 'Them'll move you tomorrow.'

'Move me where?'

She doesn't answer.

'But what of my baby?'

She stares. "Tis dead. You know that. You saw her, remember? A grey and lifeless thing she was.'

Yes. Yes, of course. My baby is gone, dead. My little Violet. All gone, as if there had never been a seed inside me that grew arms, and elbows and feet. All gone, as if she had never been at all, as if Harry had never kissed me, never held me, never loved me.

'Let's have none of that,' the nurse says, and I realise I'm crying. She holds the back of her hand to my forehead. "Tis the fever.'

'*I keep forgetting she's dead,*' I say, through my tears. '*I keep forgetting.*'

She hands me a cup of the bitter, brown liquid. '*Drink that and you'll feel better.*'

'*Yes,*' I say, and I drink it. I drink it and sleep.

I wake in the dead of night to that sound, that grating from the door. It's the bolts being slid across, but slowly, quietly. The nurse never comes at night. Has Harry come for me at last? Oh, please, let it be him. Perhaps he has our baby. Yes, he must have her. He's the father, after all. She will be cradled in his arms, safe and sound, and he'll hand her to me, and we'll be happy, the three of us. My heart jumps at the thought of it.

The door inches open. Why does he take so long? Why so hesitant? I hold my breath, peer into the darkness. Is it him? Is it?

No – too short. But it is a man.

I should stand. I should, but I'm so weary.

'*This is my room,*' I say. He has made a mistake and will go now, go to his own room. He doesn't hear and steps inside and closes the door behind him. Something about that stealthy movement, that slow, deliberate gait, chills my bones.

'*Get out!*'

He's coming towards me, towards my bed, and I know that walk. I know it.

'*Can't have you talkin' now, can we?*' he says, and I remember what he did to me.

Blood pounds in my temple. Let this be another nightmare. Please, let it be.

'Can't have you telling my missus.'

'I won't,' I say. 'I won't say a word, I promise.'

He laughs, but he's forgotten his gun. He's forgotten it. He thinks me unable to defend myself, thinks childbirth has rendered me helpless, but he's wrong. He's so wrong.

I lie back on the pillow, hold a hand to my brow. 'I'm so weak,' I say. 'Please help me.'

Come closer. Come on. Come and see how helpless I am. That's right. Closer now.

He stands over me.

Closer now. Let me see those eyes so cold, like a dead fish – so cold and full of hate.

He bends over me, and there they are, black holes into his soul, wet and yielding. Wet and yielding as my fingers jab into them, hard.

God, how he screams – enough to wake the dead. And he is gone. Like magic, he's gone to the floor, arms flailing.

I stumble to the door, while he squeals like a stuck pig – squealing, squealing. On and on. I'm through the door and down the steps in an instant.

I know this place. I'm in the yard. The yard at Ashton House. All these months I've been above the barn. That barn that sits only yards from the house. All these months.

A crashing noise comes from above. Price is on his feet. He won't be long. Not long enough.

The marsh. There's nowhere else to go. There is only the marsh.

I run, my breasts and belly heavy. I run across the yard, across the road, past the church. The trees are so far away, and hazy now, shrouded in fog. No, not fog, because I blink and it goes, then comes back again, and it's so hard to see.

My foot catches on a stone and I'm falling, my hands scraping along the stony ground, burning. I'm so tired, I long to crawl behind a gravestone and sleep, but no. He would find me, smell me out and kill me. The marsh – the marsh and safety – lies only yards away. If I can just reach it. I clutch at a gravestone and pull myself to my feet. The road behind is clear, silent, the churchyard, too. Perhaps he'll never come. Perhaps I've blinded him. But no – there, something moves beside the church.

I stagger on and on, into the trees and across the stream, and on further, deeper into the marsh than I have ever been.

A vast, barren wasteland opens out before me. Mudflats stretch to the horizon, glimmering in sudden unearthly moonlight. A full moon appears between the clouds, round and buttery and so bright, like daylight, and there's nowhere to hide.

This is not my marsh. No, this is not the marsh I know.

I turn back to the trees, and it's not so far. There ahead lies the stream – our stream, mine and Harry's. Now I know where to place each foot, where I have placed them so many times, with him. Hawthorns gather around me, my protectors. Oh, guard me. Guard me from him, that devil. I will go to the willow, to the darkness.

The ground shifts beneath my feet, the world tilts. The marsh doesn't know me any more. It thinks me a stranger and wants me gone.

'It's me,' I say. 'It's only me.'

The trees sigh and whisper, and now they know me, welcome me. The marsh holds me in its arms, as a mother holds her baby.

I watch the trees and wait. It's so cold, and I am hungry, and so, so tired. I crouch among the hawthorns. My eyes grow heavy, but I dare not let them close. My teeth chatter and will not be still.

Movement – a figure slipping through the trees, creeping, a malign shadow, a spirit of darkness. My heart falters. It's him. That silent, stealthy gait belongs only to him.

He stands, silhouetted, a branch, thick and heavy in his hand.

I try to still my breathing, covering my mouth with my hand. He can't reach me here, and anyway, I am hidden, by these dense, thorny trees.

His voice echoes around the marsh. 'I know you're here.' He smacks the branch into the palm of his left hand, turns this way and that. 'Your sort always end up in the marsh.'

His search is slow and methodical. He's in no hurry. 'I'm going to find you,' he snarls. 'May as well come out now, make it quicker.'

He sees me and freezes, a predator spotting its prey.

He can't get to me unless he knows every dip and hollow, every hidden threat this marsh holds.

He's splashing through the shallows, smacking the branch into the palm of his hand with every step. He knows this marsh, knows it as well as I do, but the river's rising – the full moon, a spring tide.

I turn to look for a hiding place. All is water, nothing but water.

He slips, curses and rights himself. Take him. Take him, not me. He slides and stumbles, but he's close now, so close I can see that cavern of a mouth of his, smell his breath. Too close.

I turn and step into the unknown, into the darkness, praying the marsh will be merciful. So slippery, this mud, and still he comes. On and on, the water to my knees now. I stop, listen. Silence. Perhaps he is drowned. Yes, yes, for he cannot see well, no, not with his eyes so damaged.

Something catches at my hair, catches and pulls. I fall back, and it's dragging me, he's dragging me through the water, and on to land, to dry ground, tearing my hair from the roots. He's dragging me back towards the willow, over earth and rocks. I scrabble for a footing, but he's too strong, too fast.

As suddenly as it started, it stops. The marsh has swallowed him, as I knew it would. My marsh, my saviour. All is quiet and still, silent save for my ragged breathing and the gentle trickle of the stream, water lapping against the bank, as it did in those days, those summer days with Harry when sunlight filtered through the trees and we lay in each other's arms.

A flash of moonlight. Price. Price standing over me, his face gleeful.

I kick him between his straddled legs, and again as he teeters, but he's still on his feet, and roaring.

The branch lies where he dropped it. He sees it and dives for it, but I'm closer. My fingers close around it and I'm upright. This is my one chance to survive. If I don't stop him, he will kill me. I swing it, whack it into the side of his head. The impact jars my elbow and my shoulder but it must hurt him. It must.

He staggers backwards, hands clutching his head.

Again, I swipe at him. A glancing blow. Not enough. Still he comes, bent double and wild-eyed, and laughing. A madman. I raise the branch, bring it down on his head and he falls. The branch slips from my hand, but all is well. I have him now. I step forward, but no. He lifts himself from the water, this creature of nightmares, and comes, crawling on his knees now, swaying, cursing. Blood runs down his forehead. He rubs at his eyes, blinks, reaches for me, but he misses. He can't see, not well enough.

The mud slips away under my feet. My back hits the marsh, the water. He's pushing me down, pushing and pushing. My chest aches. He's sitting on me and I can't breathe. My fingers scrabble in the mud, desperate for something. They clutch at a stone. Yes, yes, and sharp enough.

My free hand clutches at his jacket. One chance. I raise my head, take a breath, and swing my arm with all the strength I have. The stone smashes into his temple, and he's gone.

I sit up, suck air into my parched lungs. But he's not done. He's on all fours, trying to get to his feet, swaying from side to

side. With all the strength I have left, I kick him on to his back
and climb on top of him.

I have the branch. My fingers close around it and I lift it
high. He raises his head from the water, and there's fear in
those black eyes. Fear as the branch comes down across his
neck, and then those eyes are under water. I push, and push,
while he kicks and bucks, but he's weaker now, too weak to
throw me off. He's screaming, that filthy mouth wide open, but
there's no air down there. There is only water.

Everything stops. The water grows still.

It's a trick. I'm too clever to fall for that – as clever as any
man. I press on and on. If I move, he'll jump up. I keep kneeling on him while the water rises.

I wait, watch and wait.

Staring eyes gaze up at the night sky. His filthy mouth
screams silently – on and on and on.

The water is still and Price motionless within it. I must
move or lie for all eternity with the one I hate above all others.

I scramble off him and wade backwards into the shadow of
the willow. He must be dead by now, but I daren't take my eyes
from the tip of his shoe where it pokes out of the water. As long
as I can see that, I'm safe.

No, I'm not safe, not yet. He's there for anyone to see. They'll
find him, and then what of me? Am I to hang for this devil?

All about me is water, but to my left is an overhang, and
beneath it, dark, deep water. I heave and roll Price towards
it, up to my thighs in the marsh. My arms ache. I can't do it. I
cannot. Despite the freezing water, I'm sweating – sweating at

the horror of what I've done, sweating with fear at the thought of the hangman's noose. I straighten up and stretch my back. One more push, just one, and now the ground slopes away, and he rolls easily, slips into the hollow. It's as if it's made for him, so beautifully does he fit. I push his body further in with my feet, wedging him into place, then I pile on stones and branches to hide him. He is utterly concealed. No one will ever find him. I drag my skirts through the water, through the mud and clamber on to dry land. Every part of me aches. I'm so tired that the world is blurred. Where there should be one tree, there are two, and they will not stay still, but quiver and sway.

I blink and turn my eyes to the shimmering water. 'Ye shall die in your sins,' I say.

And I laugh.

CHAPTER 32

The night is cold and blue, like my mind. I sit and rest my head against the rough bark of the willow. My eyes close and I drift into hell.

Trees rustle, twigs snap. Rainbow colours flicker and flash, glide across the water. Footsteps come closer. I peer into the trees. Strange trees that sway and hiss and whisper secrets.

'Harry?' It comes out as a croak. 'Harry?'

It's him. It's my love. He turns his head. No, it's the doctor. He holds something in his arms, something wrapped in a blanket, and the blanket trails in the weed. I shout at him. 'Doctor.'

He smiles, and his teeth are black and rotten. Price's teeth.

It's my baby he holds in his arms. She cries. She recognises my voice, so I call her name, 'Violet'. The doctor turns towards the wood and they vanish. My scream echoes. I hold my breath in case Price comes up out of the water to investigate. Price and the doctor together would be too much. I hold my breath and listen. The doctor's hiding in among those trees, keeping very still. He doesn't know I can hear my baby breathing. He doesn't know I can sense her. We're attuned, my child and I – the same flesh. She's nearby, so close. My heart swells with joy. I knew she wasn't dead, I knew it. I get to my feet. She cries, frightened in the dark and cold, frightened of the doctor and his pale eyes, and the eerie flashing lights. There, that's him just ahead, hiding with his back to me. I see my baby's face, her eyes, staring into mine.

She's just out of reach, just beyond my fingertips. The doctor moves away silently, like a ghost, vanishing in the mist as I draw near. He reappears behind me, only to vanish again as I reach out. Again he appears, and disappears, reappears and disappears, so that I must turn and turn until I am dizzy.

'Violet.' I stumble and trip, reach out to save myself.

Her cries grow louder. She knows me, she knows me.

I tread lightly now, careful where I lay my feet. I must be as silent as he is. I must catch him unawares. There! I see him between the trees. He holds my baby out in front of him. He lays her on the cold earth. No, he lays her on the marsh, in the weed, and the water rises over her little limbs, and he turns his head and laughs. A loud, roaring laugh that goes on and on until it's a roar of fury. No, it's me who roars.

He slips away into the trees and he's gone. But where's my baby? There's the weed, there, where he laid her, and the water. 'No!' I wade into it. It's deep and boggy and thick with weed which catches at my legs and pulls me. Mud sucks at my feet, at my dress, tugging me, dragging me under. I bend forward, feel for her under the water, down, down into the soil beneath, but she's not there. I cry, and search and cry, and then I hear him laughing. He's standing on the path to the church and she's in his arms again, dripping water, trailing weed. Her hair is curled and black and wet, and her eyes are Harry's eyes – muddy blue and green and grey and beautiful. I reach for her, though she's far from me. My fingertips touch the soft fabric of her shawl.

Church bells wake me. It's daylight. I'm cold and stiff and my head aches when I sit up. My skin tingles all over, hurts when I move. Bells echo in my head, pound against my skull. It must be Sunday. Perhaps Harry will be in church, and I can tell him about the doctor, and Price and what he did, and he will search for our baby and bring her to me. I hold on to the willow and haul myself to my feet. The hem of my dress drags in the marsh. The heavy wool cloth chafes against my skin, clinging to my legs. Cold. So cold.

I hobble towards the church as fast as I'm able. My skirts catch at my feet, tripping me again and again. I stumble and fall face down in the marsh. I'm so tired. Perhaps I should let it take me, the marsh. It would be so easy. I don't need to do anything except breathe that water, and it will all be over – everything – and I can rest. I stand, brush at my dress, at the mud and grass and pondweed. The dress is so drab and grey, the mud barely shows, and he won't mind, anyway. He never minds pondweed in my hair, or mud on my dress. He never minds as he tears the buttons, as he kisses my breasts and lifts my skirts.

Those bells – they go on and on and on. They're giving me a headache. If only they'd stop. My feet catch in brambles and twisted roots. *They slide in the mud. Every step trips me, as if the marsh itself is trying to stop me. No, not the marsh, the dress. There's no ridding myself of it, though, not now, not with the bells calling me. Run, trip, run, trip and I'm out of the trees.*

Sunshine. I wasn't expecting that, not when it's so cold.

The churchyard is empty – of the living, at least. I stamp my feet. They're numb. All I feel is a jarring as they hit the ground. Perhaps he's there already, sitting with his legs outstretched, that arrogant, bored look on his face, just like that time, the time I saw into his soul.

The bells stop. Silence for a moment, then birdsong, and then, from inside the church, the organ wheezes out a tune, some maudlin melody or other.

Now. Now, I must go. I cross the churchyard, push the door ajar, and step inside.

The organ's so loud it hurts my ears. A cold blast of air follows me in. Dead leaves blow past my feet. My toes are so blue, so muddy. How dirty my fingernails, their tips tinged blue and purple.

Everyone stares at me. Of course, they would. I've been away for such a while, and I'm not dressed for church, with no shoes and this dress so filthy.

'Harry?' I hold my hands to cover my still-swollen belly. My wet dress is heavy and clings to my legs as I walk. 'Where is Harry?'

He should be here, waiting for me. I look about me. Strange faces, pale and hollow-eyed, stare back. The doctor's not here, either. 'Where's that doctor?' I shout over the music. 'Where has he put my baby? My Violet?'

The music stops, sudden and jarring, the notes discord-ant. Shouts ring out around me, angry roars, but I am louder. 'Where is he?'

Running feet pound behind me, closer and closer, trampling the memorial stones that pave the aisle.

The priest – white-lipped, pinched nostrils – says something, his words lost in the melee. Someone catches at my hair, my shoulders. An arm tightens around my waist and I'm falling, tipping backwards and there's no way to save myself. The last thing I see is the vaulted wooden roof.

Rain patters on to my face and wakes me with a start. For a moment, I think I'm at the marsh, but no, I'm in the back of a cart as it lurches along the road. Every jolt, every pothole in the road sends a sickening pain up my neck from my shoulder to the top of my head. Price is talking to the horse. No, it can't be Price. Price is . . .

Then who? All I see is a dark shadow, a spectre. I can't see him. Why can't I see him? My eyes hurt when I blink, but they don't clear. All around me is blurred and shadowy.

The horse slows to a walk, then stops. Rough hands drag me from the cart, manhandle me towards a building. It's as blurred as everything else, but even so, I can tell it's not Ashton House. The steps are different – wider and broader. There's a light ahead, and two shadowy people without faces or edges. 'Where are we?'

Rain patters on my head. I blink, blink again, but can't clear my eyes. The shadowy figures come towards us and take my arms, almost lifting me from the ground. A stabbing pain shoots through my skull.

'Thank you.' It's a woman speaking, the one on my right. 'We'll take her from here.' They lead me towards the light.

I stumble and trip on the steps. 'Is this a hospital?'

'That's right,' the woman says.

'Is it because I can't see?' I turn towards her, can just make out the shape of her face – square and large. 'Something's happened to my eyes.'

'You've had a knock on the head,' she says. 'That's all. Size of an apple, that bump.'

Inside smells of carbolic. All's well, then. It's a hospital, that's all – for my eyes.

The door slams behind us.

'Hello, Mary.' It's a man's voice. I turn to see him, but he's just a blur.

'My name's Maud.'

'She has a history of violence,' he says.

'Violence? No, you have the wrong person.'

'Above all, she must be kept calm,' he says.

'Yes, doctor.'

'You have the wrong person. I must go back – back to the marsh.'

'Sulphonal three times a day,' he says. 'Paraldehyde at night. Chloral as needed.'

The nurses' voices chime in unison, 'Yes, doctor.'

'*You don't understand. I have to go back there now.*' Their grip is so tight on my arms, it's giving me pins and needles in my hands.

'*When you're well again, Mary. Then you can . . .*'

'*My name's not Mary.*' I try to free myself.

'*Delusions,*' he says. '*Acute mania. Paranoia. Sexual excess.*'

'*What?*' My blood chills. '*What did he say?*'

'*Do not concern yourself, Mary.*' His voice is calm, gentle, sympathetic. '*You will have the very latest scientific treatment here. You will recover.*'

'*There's nothing wrong with me.*'

They drag me away from him. I kick at their shins. '*There's nothing wrong with me.*' I can't get at them. My heels keep missing their target, hitting the air. My chest is so tight, I can't get the words out. '*For God's sake, why won't you listen?*'

The doctor shouts over me. '*Wet wrap. Six hours.*'

'*I just banged my head.*'

They drag me up the stairs. I can't get a purchase on the steps to fight. '*I just banged my head.*' My arms are being pulled from their sockets. '*I'm not Mary. You have the wrong person.*' Twisting my body achieves nothing; it just causes more pain. '*I just banged my head.*' No reaction – none. They continue dragging me.

I roar, at the top of my voice, '*There's nothing wrong with me.*'

They take me to a large, bare room containing nothing but a bath and a narrow bed. At least my sight is returning, enough to see the multiple chins that lie beneath that square face.

'I can see now,' I say, 'so I should like to go home, please.'

Perhaps I just think it instead of saying it because they don't appear to hear me. They sit me on a chair.

One of the women picks shears from a tray. She's younger than the one with chins, and pretty. She lifts a handful of my hair and cuts it. Then they're both at it, hacking at it, pulling it. The scissors are cold against my scalp.

'Lice,' Chins says.

Lice? Me?

They take my frock off, take everything off. Chins shoves my clothes into a bag, her nose wrinkled, arms outstretched as if she's afraid she'll catch something. 'Filthy.'

'What happened to your baby, Mary?' the pretty one says.

'My name's Maud.'

'Course it is.' Chins rolls her eyes.

The pretty one catches my eye. She looks away, but I think she believes me. I think she knows.

'Make sure to tell doctor she's given birth,' Chins says, 'and recently, too.'

The pretty one nods. 'Do you know where your baby is, Mary?'

'I don't know.'

Why are they looking at each other like that, as if they pity me? It makes me feel ill, makes my eyes sting. I look away, at the bag of clothes, my clothes. That dress was indeed filthy and stinking and stiff with blood and milk and mud, so it's no great loss. I never liked it anyway, with that scratchy wool and the way it soaked up the water.

The pretty one helps me into the bath. 'You'll feel much better once you're clean, eh?'

'Yes.'

The water is lukewarm and within seconds I'm shivering. The two of them scrub me with carbolic soap until my skin is red and tingling. They lift me out.

'There's something in the marsh,' I say. 'It's under the water, in the cold.'

'Is that right?' Chins says. 'And what is it?'

What is it? 'I don't know.' And now I'm crying.

They dry me with scratchy towels and, at last, warmth makes my skin glow, although my head feels strange. The room tilts away from me.

'Oops!' Chins catches me. 'Come on now. Don't be silly.'

They dip long sheets into the bath water, wring them, and start wrapping them around my body. Round and round they wind them, turning me until my whole body is swaddled, and only my head free.

'Can you tell someone?' I say. 'Tell them to go to the marsh?'

'Of course we will.' The pair of them lower me on to a narrow bed. They're careful, cradling my head.

'Tell them there's something in the water, under the water, in the pondweed and the mud, in the dark.'

Chins sews stitches into the sheets, trussing me up like a spider does its prey. 'We'll make sure to tell them, won't we?'

The pretty attendant nods.

I breathe. 'It's cold there, in the marsh at night.'

'Yes, I'm sure it is,' Chins says.

'It's not safe.' My words echo from the high ceiling. Tears run down my face. 'I'm cold,' I say. 'That's why I can't remember what it is.'

'Cold is calming. Doctor only wants what's best for you.'

The pretty one's sweeping my poor hair into a pile. 'There's no lice in this,' she says. 'Nothing at all – not even a nit.'

'If doctor says there's lice, then there's lice.'

The pretty one lowers her eyes. 'Of course.'

'You will tell them, won't you?' My teeth chatter, so the words sound strange. 'It's important.'

'Course it is.'

'It is,' I say, but I'm not sure it's true. I'm not sure of anything any more.

A ringing bell wakes me. On and on and on it rings.

I open my eyes to a long room full of beds – thirty, forty, perhaps even fifty of them, and women lying or sitting or standing – old and young and all ages in between. They're dressing themselves in clothes that are folded at the ends of their beds. I sit up. I too have a pile of folded clothes on my bed, so I copy them. I pull on the dull, grey woollen dress. It's the same dress I had before, but this one is clean.

A nurse comes through the door. 'Come on.' She claps her hands. 'Come on.'

We stand in line. I'm last because my bed is furthest away from the door, and because the others know what they're doing, and I don't. I'm dizzy and my head hurts. I lift my hands. My hair. It's gone – all of it. All that's left is stubble.

No one else has a bald head. I step either side of the line and check. They're all normal. It's only me.

My gaze drifts to the back of the woman directly in front of me.

There's something embroidered on to the back of her dress. At first, I think it's just a pattern, but when I blink I see it's writing – three words:

Angelton Lunatic Asylum.

CHAPTER 33

My bed is nearest the small, grubby window, the ward's opening on to the world. The glass is covered by a white-painted metal grille. Out there are gardens, with trees and flat lawns and flowers. I push at the window and it opens a little, enough to let some air through. I close my eyes and breathe, smell peaty earth, green wood, brackish water.

A hand touches my arm. It's the pretty one. 'I've been calling you, Mary,' she says. 'Have you gone deaf this morning?'

'My name's not Mary.'

She tuts. 'You're to see the doctor now, so come along.'

I hurry beside her. 'The doctor must have realised there's been a mistake,' I say.

She doesn't reply, but I'm certain it's the truth. I'll be free of this place before the day is out, and I'll go back to the marsh and find . . . and find whatever it was.

The pretty one takes me downstairs. The name 'Doctor Womack' is written on the door in gold lettering. Inside it's warm and comfortable, like a sitting room, a fire blazing in the grate. A grandfather clock stands in the corner. Back and forth the pendulum swings. Tick. Tock. Tick. Tock.

The doctor's sitting at a desk, writing, his head bent low over his work. He has dark hair and a waxed moustache. I stand before him, hands clasped in front of me, and stare at the pattern on the Persian rug – swirls and flowers, and bright colours. I wait. He's still writing.

His pen is made of mother-of-pearl. The nib is gold and makes a scratching noise as he forms the letters.

I shift from one leg to the other. 'Am I free to go now, doctor?' I say. 'Have you told them to let me go?'

He raises his eyes – washed-out, palest blue – and spends several long seconds looking at me. He stares at my body, his gaze lingering on the two dark wet patches on my dress where my breasts still leak. I fold my arms across my chest and press hard.

He consults his notes. 'How are you, Mary?'

'I am as you see me.' I can't say I'm well. That would be a lie, what with the blood still coming, and the pains, and the nightmares and the milk. 'But I must return to the marsh. There's something I have to save.'

He nods, writes something on his notes. Scratch, scratch, gold nib on paper.

There's a patch of pink, wrinkled skin on the top of his head. I've seen it before, that skin, like a baby's. I see him, see his sweating face, as he pulled something out of me, something grey.

'It's you,' I say.

Pen on paper, scratch, scratch, scratch.

I remember. Now I remember. 'You put my baby in the marsh, on the pondweed, in the water – my baby.'

He frowns. 'Your baby? No Mary, you are mistaken.'

He did. I see him lay her on the marsh, see her frightened eyes, her black hair, and the water rising. I know it's him. But wait. I must be careful. If I anger him, I'll never get her back. 'Is she here?' I say. 'Did you bring her here?'

Gold nib on paper – scratch, scratch, scratch.

Pitiful wailing fills the air. 'There,' I say. 'Do you hear her? She's just the other side of the . . .' I step towards the door. No, now the cries are behind me. I turn, turn again. The cries – they come from everywhere. Milk spurts, soaks my bodice. 'She's hungry.' Oh, I can't bear to hear it. I fall on my knees. Tears burst from my eyes. 'Please bring her to me.'

He sighs. 'We were told your child was stillborn. It never lived, therefore it cannot cry.'

'Never lived?' I take a breath. 'She lived. She lived in here.' I lay a hand on my middle. 'She kicked and moved and lived in here.' Tiny elbows and feet and knees pushing against my womb, so alive, so alive.

His lip curls. 'You're bleeding on my rug.'

I hold on to the desk and haul myself to my feet. Blood, yes. There's blood on the rug. My blood. Blood from when he tore that living child from me. 'You killed her.' I whisper it. 'You killed my baby.'

His hand stops moving. With slow, deliberate movements, he picks up the pen lid and clicks it into place. 'You'll have to clean up that mess.'

Three paces and I'm beside him, looking down on that pink skin. 'You killed my baby.'

He lays the pen on the desk and turns his head with peculiar slowness. His eyes swivel. He holds my gaze. 'You're excitable.' His voice shakes, as well it might. 'A dose of chloral will . . .'

'You murdered her.'

His lips move. Noise hits my ears, but it means nothing. I throw myself at him, but I'm too slow. He's on his feet before I get there. Hands circle my neck, pressing, pressing, and his face, red and sweaty, pulsating, as it was before.

The room blurs. All I can see is that throbbing white lump in his neck, bobbing. My hands reach for it. I press my thumbs into the lump and press and press and press.

His grip loosens. His knees buckle, and still I press. He's a dead weight. He slips from my grasp, falls as if the bones have gone from inside him. He drops like a stone, and I'm flying backwards. My head hits something sharp. Shouts fill the air. Hands clutch at me, lift me in the air. They're dragging me away, dragging me from him.

'He killed my baby,' I scream. 'He killed her.'

'Come back, Maud.' Diamond is white-faced, Tucker too. They stare at each other.

'They might not be true,' I say. 'These things I remember. They might be inventions.'

Diamond glances at Tucker. She shakes her head, just once, one tiny shake.

Diamond's voice is soft, gentle. 'Do you remember what happened after that attack?'

'He made me scrub the rug and the floor beneath, and I couldn't get it out.' A shudder runs through me, followed by another, and another. 'The blood. No matter how hard I scrubbed, it wouldn't come out.'

'And afterwards?'

'He sent me for a shower bath. Fifteen minutes, he said, and then a purge and I nearly died.'

'And then?' He's not interested in the shower bath, nor the brown stuff. He's not interested in the blood. 'Maud?'

'Then I woke in my room.'

'And you've been there ever since?'

'Yes.'

All is silent save for the sound of our breathing.

'Is it finished now?' I say.

'Yes. Yes, I suppose it is.'

'I was happier before,' I say, 'before I knew what I'd lost. You should have left me as I was.'

'Perhaps.' He rubs his eyes. 'And yet you are cured, so the treatment works. The question is, at what cost.'

'Maud will be able to resume her life,' Tucker says breathlessly. 'She can become a scientist again.'

'Yes,' Diamond says, with enthusiasm, and I nod, and Tucker smiles, and not one of us believes it.

'You've done well, Maud,' Diamond says. 'There is nothing to fear now. It's over.'

Over for Diamond, perhaps, and for Tucker, but it will never be over for me.

CHAPTER 34

Diamond's room the next day looks very different. It's lifeless now, cold and grey – as cold and grey as my own. No fire blazes in the grate, no lights glimmer.

He's aged since we first met. How careworn he looks now. A light has gone from his eyes, as if his hopes have been brought to nought, as my hopes were, so long ago.

The door closes behind me with a small click and we are alone.

I sit in my chair, take comfort from the smooth arms, the solid wood. At least this is the same, unchanging, reliable.

'Now.' Diamond's smile is broad and unconvincing. 'It's time to take your photograph again.'

He loops a curtain over two hooks in the wall and positions a chair in front of it.

'Am I truly cured, then?' I say.

'You seem quite recovered to me.' He brings his camera and the three-legged contraption out from behind a cabinet.

I go and sit on the chair in front of the curtain while he fixes everything together. I fold my hands in my lap and keep quite still, looking directly into the camera. He thinks I'm cured and therefore I must behave as if I am.

Diamond disappears under the black cloth. This time I don't jump when the camera explodes.

'You look very different to that first day,' he says. 'You are quite transformed.'

'Will they let me go?'

He rubs his hand over his eyes. 'My colleague has little choice, having pronounced you recovered in the presence of the visitors.'

'He looked horrified when he realised.' I feel my mouth stretching into a smile.

'Yes.' Diamond's eyes crinkle. 'Yes, he did.'

Womack won't let me go. He'll find a way to keep me here. Of that, I am certain.

The door swings open, and there he is, the man himself. 'You're leaving us, I hear, Dimmond.' He shoots a triumphant look in my direction.

'No,' Diamond says. 'I have no intention of abandoning my patients.'

'I see.' Womack steps forward and closes the door with slow, careful movements.

'I'd like you to go.' Diamond's voice is surprisingly strong.

'I'm sure you would. And why, I wonder, would that be?'

'I beg your pardon?'

Womack sits in the armchair, spreads his legs. 'Have you or have you not conducted hypnosis sessions without an attendant present, including in the patient's own room?'

Diamond frowns. 'On occasion, yes. Why?'

'With this –' Womack waves the pipe in my direction '– this lunatic here?'

'This patient, yes.' Diamond's frown deepens. 'But not for some time, and then only . . .'

'Not with any other patients?'

'No, although I fail to see how that's relevant.'

'And your motivation for that was?' Womack raises one sardonic eyebrow.

'Motivation?' Diamond glances at me. 'To maintain confidentiality, of course.'

'Is that so?' Womack smirks. 'Not in order to assault the patient whilst she was rendered insensible?'

A flush suffuses Diamond's throat, rises, then drains away to leave his whole visage a ghastly grey. 'How dare you, sir.' His lips are white, like a dead man's. 'How dare you? I should never countenance such a thing.'

'We only have your word for that.'

Diamond clears his throat. 'My word, yes, as a doctor and a gentleman.' His Adam's apple bobs as he swallows, again and again.

'You have *my* word, too,' I say. 'Had anything untoward occurred, I would have known it.'

Womack turns his head slowly, oh so slowly. 'The imbecile awakes.' His eyes threaten violence, sending my pulse skittering. 'Your word, Mary –' his lip curls '– means nothing. Less than nothing. You would have been insensible, as you so often are.' He turns to Diamond. 'Should you attempt to remain in your post, Doctor Dimmond, I will have no choice but to report my concerns to the commissioners. Should you leave of your own volition, however, I shall be content to take the matter no further.'

Diamond nods, with a small, bitter laugh. 'Get out. Get out of my office.'

'With pleasure.' Womack bows, and is gone, leaving the door open behind him. His jaunty whistle echoes in the corridor.

How Diamond trembles. His gait is unsteady as he walks across the room. 'I hope you know nothing untoward happened,' he says.

'I would never believe anything Womack said,' I say. 'He killed my baby.'

Diamond takes down the curtain, folds it. 'He was employed here at the time, Maud. I've checked.'

'But I saw him.' I see his face at the end of that bed, pulling and pulling, and the sinews standing out on his neck, and the sweat running.

'As you saw Imogen play piano in the gallery?' Diamond watches me. 'Are you certain it was him? Absolutely certain, beyond doubt?'

'Yes,' I say. But am I? Am I truly? Wasn't I equally certain it was Imogen playing the piano when it couldn't have been?

Diamond rubs a hand across his forehead, leaving a dusty streak. 'He may not be the most pleasant colleague I've worked with, but kidnap? Holding you prisoner?' He shakes his head. 'No one would believe it.'

He's right, of course. Even if it's true, no one will ever believe my word over Womack's. 'And my baby's not in the marsh – and never was in the marsh?'

'No, Maud, truly.' He holds my gaze. 'Those nightmares we have when feverish are particularly vivid. You were very sick, almost on the point of death. They will feel real for you, but you must believe me, they're not.'

'Then what happened to her?'

'I thought you understood. The child *was* stillborn.' He fetches the register from his desk. And there, written in neat handwriting: 'Lovell, Mary. Stillbirth'.

I can't drag my eyes from the words. 'Then where is her grave?'

His face is drawn and grey. 'I'm afraid I don't know. Still-born children. . .' His sad eyes meet mine. 'Their graves are unmarked. There will be no record.'

So, it is as if she never lived, just as Womack said. I clasp my hands together until the knuckles are white, and breathe.

'And Price?'

Diamond turns back to the camera. 'The same. A hallu-cination.'

So that vile creature still lives. 'I didn't *kill* him?'

'No.' The word is clipped. He is busy, packing away the camera, covering it with a cloth.

Let him be wrong. Please let him be wrong. 'Are you sure?'

'Yes.' He's fussing with the cloth, folding it this way and that, then unfolding it, only to fold it again exactly as it was.

'I dream of him often,' I say. 'Of his hands.' A shudder runs through me. 'I can still see him there, under the water.'

'It's not real.' The words snap out of his mouth. He straightens up and wipes his brow again, adding another streak of dust to the first. 'Do not mention it again, to anyone, not ever.' He stops fiddling with the camera, takes a breath and finally looks at me. 'Promise me.'

I nod.

'It's time to look to the future, Maud,' he says. 'The past is behind you and you must leave it there. It will do no good to cling to it. Ahead lies a new life of freedom. You must think of that.'

Freedom? With Price living and breathing? I shall never be safe. Never.

CHAPTER 35

They've stopped my medication. No more draughts, no more purges or injections. Perhaps they've given up hope of ever curing me and don't want to waste their medicines on a hopeless case. They still lock my door. I know because I check every time they leave.

The world is brighter – too bright for my eyes. Sounds are jagged and loud, and sharp. Even the sound of my sleeve brushing against my side makes my fingertips hurt. I'm not used to it, all this sensation, and long for the old numbness, where edges are dulled and the world's spin doesn't make me dizzy.

Keys rattle in my door. I jump to my feet and press my back against the wall, but it's only Pretty.

'Come on,' she says in an odd, cheery voice. 'Doctor's waiting.'

My heart does a little flip. At last.

She doesn't hold my arm on the way downstairs. I'm no longer a threat, it seems.

'You believed me, didn't you?' I say. 'When I first came here and said my name was Maud and not Mary?'

She smiles a wan smile but doesn't meet my gaze. Perhaps she's forgotten. It was long ago, after all, and she must have bathed many a new patient since then, and cropped many a head.

We walk past Diamond's door.

'Wait.' I step back. 'I don't want to see Womack.'

'You do this time.'

I don't believe her, but I'm curious all the same. And besides, I have no choice. She pushes Womack's door open. He's not in his armchair, but behind his desk. Prune sits with a cardboard box on her knee. She's smiling – the first smile I've ever seen on her face. It changes her completely, makes her look almost pretty. Womack's smiling, too, as if they have a secret. *His* smile makes me shudder.

'What?' I say.

Prune holds the box out to me. 'These are yours,' she says. 'Your possessions.'

'Mine?' I stare at it. 'I've never seen it before.'

'It's the box they gave us when you were first admitted.'

'Oh.' I wonder why they're giving it to me now, when it's far too late for it to be of any use. The box is not large and weighs very little in my hands. Is this all there is then, of my past? I daren't open it, afraid that the smell will take me back there, bring back all the horror. 'I'll look later,' I say, 'when I'm back in my room.' When I'm alone, and away from your curious eyes.

'It means you're officially sane,' Womack says, his fake smile wavering, looking more and more like a sneer. 'You are recovered, Mary.' He pushes the register across the table and tries the smile again.

It takes me a moment to find my name on the list, my wrong name, and to follow the line across the page until the last column where someone has written: 'Recovered 2nd April 1907'.

'So, I'm to be free?' I look out of the window, at the trees swaying in the breeze, at the grey, lowering clouds.

'Indeed. It will take a few days to organise everything, but yes, on Monday next you will be a free woman.'

A free woman – free to go where I will, with no one watching my movements, no one holding my arm. With no one at all.

'There are conditions,' Womack says. 'Should you cause any trouble, commit any crime, you can be brought back here in an instant.'

I look into his eyes and see the fear, and I smile.

In my room, I stand on tiptoes at the window and peer out at the copse in the distance. Tomorrow I will be out there. How I've longed to be free, but now it's a reality, I'm less certain. The world is strange to me now, and this small prison of a room so familiar, so safe.

Sleep eludes me. My mind conjures pictures of untold dangers, of horrors and men with white fingers and dirty fingernails. What a coward I've become. Price saw to that, and Imogen, and Womack. Hatred festers in my stomach so that I tremble. Pins and needles prick at my hands and feet as I toss and turn. I won't let them win. I will not.

Prune comes to get me after breakfast. 'Are you ready?' Her gaze drifts to my cardboard box.

'You haven't dressed.' She clicks her tongue. 'You can't go out into the world like that.' She picks up the box. 'You haven't even opened it.' She takes the lid off, pulls out my old green frock.

'Come on,' she says. 'On with it. Quickly now.'

It doesn't smell as I feared – not of the past, nor of Price, but of cardboard with a hint of mildew.

I pull off my scratchy wool dress and put on my own. It's clean now but faded and too large for me, the fabric hanging off my skinny arms, my shrunken shoulders.

'You'll have to alter that when you get home,' Prune says.

'Yes,' I say. 'Yes, I shall do that.' In my imaginary needle-work room, next to a blazing fire, with a spaniel by my feet, and a full stomach, and perhaps a servant, or even two, to attend to my needs. 'Yes, I'll do that.'

The leather of the shoes has hardened, so that it rubs against my toes and heels as we go downstairs. Prune turns neither left nor right, but straight on to the front door where Tucker is waiting, smiling. Diamond isn't here to say good-bye. I have things I wish to say to him, but it's not to be.

Tucker and I walk to the gates.

'Doctor Dimmond is to open his own private asylum,' she says, her cheeks bright pink, 'and I am to go with him.'

'Oh, I'm glad.' I hold her hand and squeeze it. 'I'm so glad.'

I look back at the grey building, at the familiar windows with their white-painted grilles, so pretty from the outside.

Womack is in there somewhere, and Chins, Prune, Pretty and the two monsters – people I dislike or hate for the most part, and yet it's all I have known for five years. It's familiar and safe, while in front of me lies the unknown.

Tucker takes a slip of paper from her pocket and hands it to me. On it is written an address in Wiltshire. 'He wanted you to have this.' She hands me a pencil, sharp and pointed. 'He said you may need it.'

'Thank you.' I slip it into my bag.

'Where will you go?' she says.

'Back to my village.' I stare at the horizon, as if that's where I'm going. 'My father had many friends there. They will not let me starve.'

Her worried frown disappears. 'Do write and send us your address once you're settled, or we will worry.'

I stare at the paper. 'Would you ask Diamond – would you ask him to find Harry and tell him . . . ?' I stare at the trees and swallow the ache in my throat. 'Tell him what they did?'

'Of course,' she says.

'He must know, about the . . .'

'I know.' She hugs me.

If I don't go now, I'll cry and make a spectacle of myself. I turn away and step out of the gates into a new life.

'We will find him, Maud,' Tucker calls after me. 'We will find him.'

I am free. I can cross the road and no one will stop me. No one will chase me into the marsh. No one is trying to kill me.

The countryside is springing to life everywhere I look. Acidic green leaves burst from plump buds, pale yellow primroses dot the verges. The air is sweet and fresh and all around me, birds are singing. Blackbirds, song thrushes, dunnocks.

My heart lifts. I am free, truly free to go where I will. I wonder where other recovered patients go. To the coast, perhaps, to find a ship to take them across the sea to foreign lands. Perhaps they go to America or Australia, where no one knows them, where they can start again. Not me. No, I cannot start again, not until this is finished. I take the coins from my pocket, count them and laugh. No one would offer me passage with these small pennies, anyway. Besides, I already know where I must go. Back to Ashton House.

I enter the first inn I come to. It's a ramshackle old place of dust and spilt ale, and old, dry wood. There are no other women inside. I buy a pie and a glass of ale and sit in the darkest corner, but men's eyes follow me, even so. My skin prickles. Is this to be my life now? Hiding in dark corners? The smell of the pie makes my mouth water so much that I fear I'll be sick, but I cannot eat with these men, their silent stares raising the hairs on the back of my neck. I drink the ale and wrap the pie in a napkin. Better to be outside in the cold than in here with these lechers. Perhaps they know where I've come from and think me an easy target. My fingers grip the pencil in my pocket as I leave, but no one follows me.

Outside, I can relax. I stand in watery sunshine, my back to the wall. The pie is steak and kidney, in a thick, rich gravy. I can't remember when I last tasted such food. I try to make it last, nibbling a small piece at a time, but I am starved of such goodness and eat it all. As I lick the last crumbs from my fingers, a stagecoach arrives. How naïve I was when I last travelled in such a thing. Not any more. No one will ever catch me off-guard again.

The journey's longer than I expect. It's mid-afternoon before the carriage turns a bend in the road, and there's the church, just as it was that first day.

The gates of Ashton House look as unwelcoming as ever, but I won't enter them just yet. Instead, I hurry through the churchyard, remembering hot, sultry days and nights when the whole marsh, the house, even the church was feverish. How different it is now, as if evil has been expunged from the place. It's so calm and peaceful. Birds sing, butterflies flit here and there. Even the hawthorns are pretty, their innocent white flowers disguising those cruel thorns. All is harmonious and beautiful, and it frightens me. Surely death should linger here if nowhere else, unless Diamond is right, and my memory wrong. And then? What am I to do then? Confront Price? A violent tremor runs through me. He must be here. He must be, or all is lost.

Ah, the bank where Harry first sat with me all those years ago. There it was that we first made love, that spot where the sweet violets grow. The stream meanders through the trees, and there ahead stands the willow. How rough that bark was against my back as he . . .

Not now. Later I can remember, but not yet. I walk into the darkness beyond. A step further into the shadows. It's dark here, though the afternoon is bright. It takes a moment or two for my eyes to adjust to the gloom. Was it here? I crouch, peer into the water. Closer, closer I go until my nose touches the water.

Pondweed and stones and fallen branches, that's all. I straighten up. Not here, then. Not here. I try to stem the rising panic. He must be here. He must be. Perhaps I ventured further. Yes, I remember now. I went further than I'd ever been before, into the unknown, while he chased me. I pick my way, stepping across the deepest water, from one clump of dry land to another, checking every pool as I go. This landscape beyond the willow is alien to me, as if I have never been here. Again and again, I peer into the water but there's nothing. The marsh seems so big, bigger than I remember, and with so many pools and ditches and hollows. A sob catches in my throat.

On and on I go, and each time the dread doubles, trebles, until my insides quiver and I fear I may faint. My skirts trail in the water. Pondweed snatches at my shoes, tangles in the laces, and still I go, this way and that, checking every body of water, every ditch and hollow. I go on until the sun is low in the sky and the light fading fast.

So, Diamond was right. It was nothing but a hallucination. And now? Can I go to the house knowing Price is there waiting for me, flexing those white fingers? No. No, I can't. Tearful, I turn back. All is lost, after all, for I am too cowardly to face that devil. I'm watching my feet, so don't see it until I'm upon it – the mound where he dragged me by the hair.

I run, splashing and slipping and sliding and so afraid. The water's muddy now, stirred up by my frantic search, and yet this *is* the place. I step on to the dry ground and, after all these years of trying to forget, I try to remember, try to put myself back there.

He's here. I can smell him. I step into the shallows and listen. Yes, he's here. I sense him watching me, so close. 'Where are you?' I bend, stare into the water, into the blue and green and black. 'Where?' I breathe in the smell, turn my head towards it.

There, the hollow and my wall of stones and wood. All is green now, and slippery as I pull it apart, rock by rock, stone by stone.

There. There he lies with that filthy mouth open in a never-ending scream. Gone are his eyes, eaten away. Black, empty sockets stare up at me. I laugh. I throw my head back, close my eyes and laugh and laugh. 'Their eyes shall consume away in their holes.'

He's still here, where I left him, where he belongs. He's not coming after me, not ever.

'Thou art altogether become filthy,' I say. 'Thou hast died in thy sin.'

CHAPTER 36

The house stands much as before, dark and sinister in the twilight. Dead crows no longer hang from the trees. With no Price to slaughter them, the birds are free to fly, to live. How they must mourn him.

The house truly misses him if the dilapidated state of it is anything to go by. Smashed roof slates lie scattered about the yard, paint peels from the window frames, a smell of decay hangs about the place. It's as if fifty years have passed, not five. Price's trusty shotgun still leans against the stable wall, but there's no mare, and the gun is rusted and useless. The roof of the barn – the barn that was my prison – has fallen in. From here I see the boarded-up window. I won't think of what happened there.

Ivy covers even more of the building than before. Purple wisteria flowers hang like ripe fruits, masking the ugly, grey limestone. A pair of ravens circle overhead. Perhaps they're the same ones I knew. Perhaps they remember me. Perhaps Harry will be here. The clattering of my heart takes over my body. My hands beat in time to its pulse.

I climb the steps to the front door and push. It swings open.

'Hello?' The vestibule is as cluttered and dusty as ever it was. The furs are eaten away by moths, revealing bare patches of leather. 'Hello?' I shout. The clock chimes the quarter-hour. Quarter past what? I step into the hallway. The smell of damp and decay is stronger here than outside.

'Harry?' I shout.

'Why do you call for Harry?' A girl no older than four or five stands half hidden in shadow, peering from the morning room. I fear she'll notice my old, tattered clothes, muddy from the marsh, but as she comes into the light, I see hers are not much better.

'Hello,' I say.

'There's no Harry here.'

'No?' My gaze takes in the hallway and stairs. Empty – deserted. 'Then where is he?'

She shrugs. 'Happen you're come to the wrong place.'

'No.'

This is the right place. This very spot is where I stood that evening and listened, and heard him, and heard him with her. Fierce pain tears through my innards and takes my breath away. I clutch at my middle.

The child steps back. I'm frightening her with my swooning.

'Come here, child,' I say.

She comes closer but stops beyond arm's reach. Solemn, dark eyes stare at me. They're Harry's eyes, the colour of a river in spate. She is his then, not Womack's.

She glances at the stairs. 'You'd best go now,' she says. 'We don't like strangers here.'

'I'm not a stranger. I'm a friend of your mama's.'

She frowns. She doesn't believe me, clever girl. You can see Imogen in her; the imperious way she lifts her chin, the way her dark hair hangs loose about her shoulders, and yet I can't hate her. She's Harry's.

'You're very like your father,' I say. 'I should like to see him.'

She frowns. 'He's dead, long since.'

My heart falters. Dead? No, no, of course she has been told the lie. She speaks of Mr Banville, not Harry. Relief swamps me. 'I mean your brother, Harry.'

She scratches at her matted hair. 'There's no Harry hereabouts, nor never has been. No brother, neither. 'Tis only me.'

The lamps flicker and make me jump. Is that Price? There in the shadows, watching me with cold eyes? No, Price is dead – dead under the water. Haven't I just seen him? And there are my sodden feet, with pondweed that trails from my shoes.

The child taps her foot and sighs.

'Be a dear and ask Mrs Price for tea and cake. Would you do that?'

'There's no cake.'

'Just tea, then.' A window rattles somewhere, and I jump again, so violently it hurts to my fingertips. 'Where's your mama?'

'In her sitting room.' She points at the stairs, then sidles past me, eyes wary. Only when she's out of reach does she turn her back and skip towards the kitchen.

I tread the stairs, careful to make no sound. The door opens at my touch and there she is, draped across the velvet chaise as of old.

She squints. 'Where've you been, you—?'

'Remember me?'

Her hand flies to her throat. She makes a choking sound.

'Do not fear.' The smile comes easily, as if I am born to this play-acting. 'I come only to see Harry and collect my trunk.'

She opens her mouth. Her face is flushed, her lips blue. I stand in front of her, close enough to reach her should I choose to.

'Are you not pleased to see me looking so well?' I say.

She nods, eyes wide.

'I shall never forget your kindness.' I say it with a sad smile. 'But did you know that devil Price disobeyed you?'

She shakes her head.

'He took me *not* to that perfect place you'd arranged out of the goodness of your heart, but to a room above your own barn, just across the yard from this house.'

For a long moment, her face is frozen.

'He kept me prisoner there, and then – you will scarcely believe it – then, when I escaped, he had me taken to an asylum, a lunatic asylum.'

Her expression flits from confusion to horror, fear to bafflement. I mustn't laugh. No, it would not do to laugh.

'Where is he, that wicked servant?' I look about me, as if expecting him to be lurking in the shadows.

'He . . .' She coughs, clears her throat. 'He disappeared.'

'Ah, afraid you would find out.' I hold her gaze and nod, and she does the same, hers a frantic, exaggerated series of nods. I fear for that fragile neck, I really do.

'Here.' I pick up her silver flask, open it and sniff. The bitter, acrid smell of laudanum. 'Have a drink for your nerves –' I hold the flask to her lips '– for that is not an end to Price's betrayal.' Her hands flutter as she drinks. Glug, glug, glug, down it goes. Drink, dear lady, drink your sin away if you're able. Her white throat bobs as she swallows. I could press my thumbs into that throat if I were that way inclined.

I lean close to her, whisper in her ear. 'There's something else.' I take the flask away and step back. 'He murdered your husband.'

She chokes, sits up, coughs and sprays the foul liquid all about her.

'Perhaps even now he's in Newgate, paying for his crime.'

She covers her mouth with her hand.

'The doctor must have known.' I frown, put a finger to my lips. 'Yes, he must have, for that rash – you remember that rash? The tiny pinpricks?'

She shakes her head.

'He was smothered, you see, your beloved husband, while I was taking my walk. Smothered by Price – or someone else.'

Horror fills those wide eyes.

'There are those who suspect you yourself of taking part,' I say. 'Some even believe you to be the *instigator* of that heinous crime.'

She's shaking her head so that I fear it may fall off her body altogether.

'I told them no. No, I said, Mrs Banville's love for her husband was pure and true. She was utterly devoted to him and would never sanction such a crime.' I smile. 'I'm sure you wouldn't want me to tell them I was mistaken.'

Her mouth drops open. I haven't enjoyed myself this much for many years.

Sudden dread comes from nowhere, clutches at my innards, tightens and twists, until it takes the breath from my lungs. I walk to the window and breathe once, twice. 'Where's Harry?' My gaze drifts to the church, to the copse of trees beyond. I turn to face her. 'Where is he?'

Her lips stand out, a garish purple in contrast to her pallid skin.

'The child is very like him,' I say, 'very like him, and yet doesn't know him. Why is that?' I'm afraid of the answer – so afraid that my body shakes from head to toe. 'Where is he?'

'He's gone.'

'Gone?'

Footsteps sound on the stair, accompanied by a hacking cough. I recognise that cough, know the sound well. I heard it often enough in the asylum – consumption, phthisis.

'Where did he go?' I step closer. 'I'll write to him, tell him how his father died.'

She sits up. 'You cannot.' Ah, she is recovering. There is that imperious note in her voice.

'I can – and I shall.'

'Oh, for goodness' sake,' she says. 'You can't write to him because he's dead.'

The room spins. I stumble, trip on my skirt and steady myself. Dead? No. No, it cannot be.

The door opens and there is Mrs Price, with her mouth hanging open, and the teapot sliding across the tray, and steam, and clashing crockery, and all the time, all the time, he is dead. And still they breathe, and I breathe, while he . . . he . . .

'The tea will go cold,' Imogen snaps.

Tea, as if everything is normal, as if Harry isn't dead. She destroyed him, polluted his life, and ruined mine, and all she is concerned about is tea.

Mrs Price coughs and coughs.

A face peers around the door. Harry's face, but smaller, much smaller, and all that's left of him. But there *is* some small part of him living and breathing, at least.

'Cordelia,' Imogen snaps. 'Go to your room.'

The child vanishes.

Cordelia? Harry would have hated the name. And the girl doesn't even know of him, her own father.

Mrs Price pours tea, a splash of golden liquid on porcelain, sugar – one, two – chink of spoon against cup, chink, chink.

And still he's dead. 'How did he die?' I say.

Imogen shrugs. 'Some pestilence or other. From that foul marsh, I imagine.'

Pestilence from the marsh? From *our* marsh? Where Price lies? Am I to blame, then? Oh, I can't. No, I can't bear it, can't be in this room a moment longer.

I stand. 'I'm unwell and will have to impose on your hospitality tonight.'

Imogen's expression of absolute horror would only minutes ago have delighted me, but not now.

Mrs Price's eyes are as flat and cold as ever. 'You're not staying 'ere, missy.'

'Only one night, Mrs Price.' A smile is impossible. 'I'll be gone tomorrow. I'm sure your sweet mistress –' I turn to Imogen '– would allow me that one night, since I have travelled so far.' I hold Imogen's gaze. 'Unless she would like me to write . . .'

'No, no,' Imogen says. 'You may stay one night – one only.'

Mrs Price opens her mouth, shuts it again, and turns on her heel.

I hurry out of the room after her. 'Is it true – about Harry?'

'Many a poor soul fallen foul o' that marsh,' she says. 'Many a poor soul.' She's heading for the stairs. No doubt she expects me to sleep in that damp attic room, but I'm no servant now, nor ever will be again.

'I'll sleep in Harry's room.'

'You'll do no such thing.'

I grip her arm and pull her to face me. 'Your husband – your filthy husband did unspeakable things to me. I should think nothing of killing you.' I snap my fingers. 'Nothing.'

What little colour she has drains from her face. 'Where is he?'

I shrug. 'I don't know. What I *do* know is he murdered Mr Banville.'

'No.' She looks away.

'Look at me.' I shake her arm. 'Why don't you ask what he did to me? You must be curious, surely.'

She twists herself free and turns back, hurrying towards Harry's room.

'Perhaps you already know,' I say.

I can't see her face, but I hear it, a small sob, and my anger evaporates. What a life to be wed to that monster, and to finally be free of him, only to suffer the slow death of consumption. She has her punishment, poor woman, and with no help from me.

CHAPTER 37

Tick, tock, the pendulum swings. Tick, tock. On and on and on. I pace back and forth across Harry's room, keeping my gaze fixed on my feet, moving to the rhythm of the clock. Is this retribution? An eye for an eye? Harry for Price?

I run my hand over the cold marble of the washstand, and imagine Harry standing in this very spot, combing his hair, pulling that cigarette case from his pocket. I see him looking from this window across the field, up to the ridge of hawthorns, along to the blasted oak. He must have seen me that day, that day he came and begged me to love him still, and I would not.

This bed. Did Harry think of me here? Did he dream of me? This bed knows him better than I do, better than anyone. It's the bed where she came to him, after all – came and took his soul. Did he cry on this pillow when I told him to go? Me, so heartless and cold. I knew he was broken, and I made him go. Why? Why didn't I call him back as he stumbled down that hill? If only I had.

I climb under the covers and lay my head on the pillow. The bed smells of him. The whole room smells of him, as if he were here only minutes ago, has just left for a walk, or for dinner, or to meet Imogen.

My head aches from weeping and I drift into sleep. Ah, here he is, back from wherever he's been, bringing the cold air with him. He crosses the room, leaving wet footprints on the boards. He's soaked, his hair plastered to his head, dripping. He stands at the window, silhouetted against the night sky, and unbuttons his shirt. It's muddy and stained and as wet as the rest of him. It falls to the floor. Moonlight glimmers on his bare skin. How beautiful he is – so, so beautiful.

He climbs into bed next to me. His skin is ice cold, damp from the marsh. It smells of pondweed. I rest my cheek against his chest and listen to his heartbeat, strong and steady like the pendulum. Tick, tock. Tick, tock.

'I love you,' I say.

He turns his head. I lift my face to kiss him, but his mouth is gaping, full of black, rotting teeth, stinking of rotting wood and putrefying flesh. He laughs.

The covers are too tight, trapping me like the straitdress. I tear at them. At last they come free and I'm out of the bed, halfway to the door. I blink, look back. There's no one there, only a tangled heap of blankets. I watch for movement, for some rise and fall.

Nothing. There's nothing. It's a nightmare, that's all.

The room is empty, empty save for me and my madness.

I wake just before dawn. The grey light brings no relief, merely a renewal of the horror.

My dress is filthy, caked in mud. I must find my bag. All is quiet as I hurry through the house. The dark, narrow stairs up to my old room are just the same. It's as if the past five years have never been. I followed Price up these same stairs on that first night. The wall is the same to my touch, clammy and cold. The same steps creak. I can almost catch sight of myself as I was in those heady days when I would run up here, bursting with joy and love.

The door stands ajar. No one's been here – no one, not since that night. The imprint of my body is still visible on the covers where Price . . . I shudder, look away. There's my trunk, and my bag, the bag I packed when I thought I was going to safety, poor, naïve fool that I was.

I snatch it up, hurry back to Harry's room and dress with clumsy hands. That woman in the mirror – can she be me? Can that haunted face be mine? Those shadowed eyes? That thin, wasted body in a threadbare frock meant for someone plumper, healthier, younger? How altered I am in so few years – a different woman, bearing no relation to the original.

An envelope lies on the hall table, waiting for the postman. The name written on it means nothing to me. I pick it up all the same and slip it into my pocket.

The morning is overcast, the air chilly. I run across the road to the churchyard. My heart falters as I walk through the gates, as if preparing to give out altogether should I find him. The graves closest to the building are old and grand, with railings around and stone angels watching over their dead. Does Harry have an angel, some celestial being to watch over him?

There are fresh graves – two of them, one not even covered with grass yet. The names are written on small wooden crosses, and neither is him. I am lost already and can't remember which stones I have examined and which I have not. I start again, working methodically this time through the rows of graves. So many names. So many dead, and with each name I read, my spirits lift. Twice now I have circled the church. There's not a single stone that I have not studied. He's not here. He's not here because he's not dead. Elation swells, overwhelms me.

She lied. How stupid of me to believe a single word that came out of that treacherous mouth. She means to trick me, to keep me away from him, but I'm not so easily fooled.

The churchyard looks different when I turn back, so that I'm no longer sure I've checked every grave. That patch of ground where the churchyard ends. There are grave-shaped mounds there, unmarked. Paupers' graves perhaps. And there's one, there beneath the yew.

I step closer. There's no stone, no cross, no marker of any kind, so it can't be him, and yet it is. I know it is.

'Harry?' I whisper it, but he hears. He hears and stirs beneath the sod. His heartbeat pulses through the earth, steady as a pendulum.

There is no gravestone, no comforting words of peace and love. No 'beloved son' or 'beloved lover'. Nothing, not a mark to show he was ever here. No angel guards his soul, watches over him as he sleeps. No matter, I am here now. I will watch over him.

I sit with him, sit beside that grassy mound and tell him of Price and what he did, of Womack and the asylum. I tell him of the child he has with Imogen, how something good and wonderful has come from that horror after all. I tell him about the child that never was – our child, mine and his. And I cry. I sob and tell him how lonely I am, how I wish I'd saved him, how I wish he could save me.

Sunlight catches the top of the trees like flames of fire. I wipe my face with my hands. How long have I been sitting here? I can't tell, but I'm chilled to the marrow. As I walk back through the churchyard, I pull the letter from my pocket and open the envelope. Inside is a short letter: 'Please come and remove a lunatic from Ashton House with all speed.'

Oh no, Imogen. Not so easy. I won't leave Harry now. As a tick to a dog, I will cling to this place. I'm a very different creature to that poor, foolish girl she packed off to that asylum. I have the measure of her now and she has no idea what I'm capable of, no idea at all.

Rich green yew needles glisten, tempting me, but no, I can't hate her enough for that – not for yew. Ivy berries will suffice for now. I slip them into my pocket.

Mrs Price is carrying Imogen's tray up the stairs as I come through the door. She's watching her feet and doesn't see me until I'm upon her. A paroxysm of coughing follows. I take the tray from her hands.

'I'll see to this, Mrs Price. You go and take some honey for that cough.'

She's too breathless to argue, poor woman. As soon as she's out of sight, I take the ivy berries from my pocket and squeeze their pulp into Imogen's flask.

'You will not part me from him again,' I say. 'Not ever.'

A rattling snore vibrates around Imogen's bedroom. He kissed that mouth. That neck, too. And yet she sleeps, knowing he's dead. How can she? How can she sleep when, if it weren't for her, he would still be alive? Those poor fingers would never have been bitten. He wouldn't have been afraid, would never have gone to London. Price would never have come here, would never have seen me, would never have . . . All because of her. Even Mr Banville would still be here, teaching me about plants, and we would be happy – me and Harry and Mr Banville. We would be happy, the three of us, if it weren't for her.

My fingers itch to do mischief to that slender throat, but I must not. No, I will not hang for her sake.

The child is in the kitchen, shovelling porridge into her mouth. She glances up. No smile, but no fear, either. I sit opposite her.

'You're very like your father,' I say.

She chews her porridge, assessing me with dark eyes. 'I'm not to talk to you.' A huge lump of porridge disappears into her mouth.

'Why?'

She swallows, picks up another spoonful. 'Mama says you're mad.'

'Does she?' I keep my hands still and smile, while she chews the next mouthful. 'Do I *look* mad?'

She plays with her spoon, a frown creasing her brow. 'No,' she says at last. 'You look sad.'

'Yes, yes, I am. I think perhaps a walk will help,' I say. 'Fresh air is always cheering.'

She frowns, squints up at the window. ''Tis going to rain.'

'I like the rain.'

She smiles. 'So do I.'

As I reach the door, I hear her running after me. 'Can I come?' She's breathless, excited.

I should say no.

'I can show you where the bluebells grow,' she says.

Oh, she's a pretty thing, unspoiled as yet by life, despite having such a toxic mother.

'You'll need your coat and hat,' I say. 'It's chilly.'

She points to the pile of coats hanging from the hooks, and there's one small, grey woollen coat with frayed cuffs. I help her on with it. How small her hands are as they push through the sleeves. Tiny, soft hands.

Watery sunlight suggests the child is right about the rain. Slate-grey clouds sit on the horizon, their edges a sickly, jaundiced yellow. Amongst the long-unused boots and rusty shotguns in the vestibule, we find several moth-eaten umbrellas. I shake two of them. Spiders, disturbed from their homes, scuttle to safety. The child tries to catch them in cupped hands, laughing, but they are too quick for her.

What a picture we must make as we traipse over the road in our ragged, old-fashioned clothes and our broken umbrellas. Like wild things from underground, long buried and only now brought to the surface.

The child skips ahead. The trees, the sun, the silvery raindrops – everything is so picturesque and pretty, as if death has never visited this place, nor darkness, nor sin and murder, as if he doesn't lie there, cold in his grave.

She leads me through fields, down a narrow path into the woods. Rain pitter-patters on the leaves. She skips on ahead, dark hair swishing from side to side, then stops, pointing ahead. 'There they are.'

A carpet of blue stretches beneath the trees all the way to the horizon. Hundreds and thousands of them, arching heads of darkest, purplish blue, and the smell, so heavenly. A gust of wind ripples through them, bending the heads still further.

Something's wrong. That smell. It's the stench of Price's mouldering bones. We're close to the marsh – too close.

'Come back,' I shout, for the child is running towards it. Oh, I would not have her drowned in the marsh – no, I would not, not all there is left of him. 'Come back.'

She runs to me, hair flying. If only Harry could see her now, see those flushed cheeks and sparkling eyes. If only.

The sky darkens; the rain grows heavy as we walk back to the house.

Mrs Price is running about the yard like a clucking hen. She stops, wide-eyed when she sees us. 'Where've you been?' She grabs the child's arm and pulls her to her side.

'We've been for a walk,' I say. 'She was perfectly safe.'

'Don't you come near her.' She succumbs to a bout of coughing.

I step close to her, whisper in her ear. 'Your cough is a danger to the child, Mrs Price, whereas *I* am not.'

''Tis just a cough.' She knows it isn't. I can see it in her eyes. Nevertheless, she takes the child away.

It's midday before I see her again. Mrs Price slams my bowl on to the kitchen table, so that slop spills over the edge. It spreads like blood, sits glistening on the surface before sinking into the wood. She takes a tray from the room. Perhaps she eats with Imogen now, in the dining room. That's good. I don't like the dining room, anyway, and I like the company of Imogen and Mrs Price even less.

I lift my spoon. Brown liquid shimmers, a sheen of grease over the top. Oxtail soup. I force it into my mouth and swallow.

The child wrinkles her nose. 'Don't you like it?'

'Not really.'

She laughs.

To eat is impossible. Again and again, I lift my spoon, and put it back into the bowl untasted. 'I fear I've caught a chill,' I say.

'Can I eat your'n then?' the child says.

'Yours, not your'n, and yes, you may have it if you say please.'

'Please?'

I push my bowl across the table. How thin she is, with scarcely any flesh on her bones. They're not caring for her.

They're not caring for all that is left of him. 'We shall have to feed you up,' I say, 'like a goose for Christmas.'

Her laugh is the most beautiful sound, like the song of an angel.

Mrs Price appears in the doorway, flushed and out of breath. ''Tis the mistress.'

'What of her?'

'Sick,' Mrs Price says. 'Everywhere, it is – all over the coverlet.'

I glimpse the child's face, recognise the fear in it, and am ashamed to be the cause of it. 'Do not fear, little one,' I say. 'It's but a passing ague, I'm sure.'

I know it to be true, of course. The ivy berries won't kill her. Nevertheless, there's a dreadful, nauseating mess to clear up. Mrs Price is quite unable to do it, so I must. I won't use ivy again.

Mrs Price bends to pick up a clean blanket and is racked by another coughing spasm.

'Has the doctor treated you for that cough, Mrs Price?'

'Haven't seen hide nor hair o' him since last autumn,' Mrs Price says. 'He come shouting, accusing mistress of . . .' Her mouth shuts. 'Since then, he never come back. And the mistress so upset. 'Twas an awful shock to her, poor lady.'

'I can imagine. Poor lady indeed.'

I must be certain that I am not mistaken. After all, many men have moustaches and thinning hair on top – many, many men. 'Would you know the doctor's name, Mrs Price?'

'Womack, he's called. Doctor Womack.'

So I wasn't inventing my past then. I haven't falsely accused an innocent man. The very opposite. My memories are real, and he, Womack, is the liar, the lunatic.

'Perhaps if I write to him,' I say, 'and tell him of your illness, he'll relent. We're friends now, Doctor Womack and I.' Come, treacherous, murdering doctor, and I will be waiting for you.

'Mistress wouldn't have him in the house. She said as much when he left. Accused her of dreadful sins, he did.' She shakes her head, shudders.

Oh, he will come in time, and I will wait, like a spider in her web.

CHAPTER 38

That night, I wait to dream of Harry again, to see him come in from the marsh, to watch him there in front of the window, his skin glistening. Never has a nightmare been so longed for, but he doesn't come. I drift off to sleep, but only moments later, cries wake me. They come from outside, from the marsh. Someone's crying, crying as if their heart will break.

My skin creeps. It's the madness, that's all – just the madness. I cover my head with the blankets and hum 'Daisy Bell', but still the cries echo inside my head. I push the covers off, hold my breath and listen hard. My heart jumps. Is that Harry? Is that him crying in the dark night?

I leap out of bed, run to the door, down the stairs and outside. The moon is full, the world grey and black and silver. My breath forms a mist as I run. A chill wind cuts through the thin fabric of my nightdress as I cross the road. I should have stopped to put on a coat – or shoes, at least.

All is silent now. I stop. The cries must have come from inside the house, or perhaps I dreamt them or invented them. Didn't they say I do that – invent things?

I turn to look back at the house. I should go back. I'm normal now, recovered, and need to stop hearing sounds that don't exist. But Harry's out there in the cold graveyard all alone. How can I leave him there?

The grass is wet with dew, and cold against the soles of my feet. My nightdress soaks up the moisture as I run so it clings to my ankles, slowing me down. Harry's grave shifts and settles in the moonlight. I go to him, feel him stir, fretting beneath that black earth.

How cold he must be, down there in the damp, dark earth, how lonely. I lie on top of his grave and talk to him of the past. I tell him how I loved him and love him still – words that should have been said long ago.

The first blackbird bursts into song as my eyes close.

A hand touches my shoulder.

I sit up, blinking in the pale morning light.

The child stands before me. 'I thought you dead,' she says, her eyes huge in that small face.

'I'm well.' I get to my feet, brush mud and grass from my nightdress, but it makes it look worse. My bare feet are muddy and the toes blue. 'I'm perfectly fine. I just fell asleep.'

She nods, frowns. Of course, she frowns. What she sees before her is a madwoman in her nightdress with no shoes or slippers.

'You weren't in your bed,' she says, 'and 'tis breakfast time.'

She came to look for me. 'How did you know where to find me?'

She bites her lip. 'I see'd you yesterday.'

'You followed me?'

She grins. Oh, she is like her father. He too followed me. How I wish he followed me still.

'Are you not afeared to be here?' she says.

'Of course not.'

She widens her eyes. 'Mama says evil lies buried beneath this ground, ghosts run amok in the darkness and drag children to their doom.'

She's waiting – waiting for me to say something. 'Are you afraid?' I say, at last.

'No.' She laughs. 'I thought to frighten you.'

'Nothing frightens me.' And yet there are ghosts here, of that I am certain. A shiver runs down my spine.

The child sees it. Her eyes narrow. 'Are you never frightened, then?'

'No,' I say.

'Nor me neither.'

The grass is heavy with silvery dew as we walk back together.

'Why did you go away?' the child says.

'Go away?' The cold confuses me, makes me unsteady.

'You said you went away for a long time.'

'Oh, that.' The trees shimmer. The world shimmers. 'I was sick, very sick.'

'Not mad?'

'No.'

She's silent for a moment. 'And now? Are you well now?'

'Yes,' I say. 'Yes, I'm quite well.' My nerves are twitching from the cold, from the ghosts, the memories. The ground shifts under my feet, slides, tilts this way and that. He is dead. How can I live? How can I? My head aches. I haven't eaten, that's all it is. I'll have some food, and all will be well, except that he will still be dead, just as everyone I have ever loved is dead. Tomorrow again he will be dead, and the next day, and the next, for ever.

The child slips her small hand into mine. 'I'm glad you are come,' she says. 'Mama and Mrs Price are always tired.' She looks up at me with his eyes. So, Harry is not dead after all, not altogether. He lives in her.

Imogen is sicker than I had envisaged. Perhaps the laudanum has reacted with the ivy. I must try other herbs. There are many to choose from, after all, ready to use, sitting on those shelves, waiting.

The laboratory is as I left it, but with layers of dust – five years' worth. Does Mr Banville haunt this place? Perhaps. I set about cleaning until every surface sparkles and all the time I feel that if I turn quickly, I will catch him sitting at his desk. I'll see the tremor in his hand, the fear in his eyes. Tears take me by surprise. I'm turned soft, it seems, by this place. No matter. There's no one to see my weakness except Mr Banville's ghost.

Every surface is clean now except for the shelf with the yellow jars. I should be able to face them after all this time. Their pleading eyes beg me to set them free, but I can't, I dare not. They will have to go, or else I will build a wall and trap them inside. Even then their frantic pleas will reach me. Their despair will be muted not at all by bricks and mortar.

Ah, there are the potions I made for Mr Banville, all except the traitorous lily of the valley. That's done now. I mustn't think of it. And it didn't kill him. Diamond said so, and he should know.

The one I'm searching for is behind the others, hidden at the back of the shelf. *Digitalis* – foxglove.

'What are you doing?' The child stands at the door, as I did myself all those years ago.

'Come in.' I slip the vial up my sleeve. 'There's nothing to fear.' Except the souls in jars trapped by your grandfather, perhaps.

She wanders about, peering into cabinets, asking questions. She approaches the shelf of yellow jars.

'If you like –' I say it brightly, to distract her '– I can teach you about plants – about science. Would you like that?'

She frowns. 'I suppose so.'

'You're an heiress, you know. All this . . .' I wave an arm. 'This house, the grounds, all will be yours, but you must study and improve your mind.'

Her eyes darken, grow shiny. 'Will I have to go away?'

'No.' I beckon her. 'Not if you don't want to, and certainly not until you're grown.'

Her smile is uncertain, but she comes.

'This is a microscope.' I move it to face her. 'I can teach you to use it, so you can see tiny, tiny cells.'

She nods.

I lift her up until she can look through the eyepiece.

'You're clever,' I whisper into her soft hair. 'Every bit as clever as any man – every bit. Do not forget it.'

Mrs Price is waiting in the kitchen when we get back. 'Where've you been now?'

'Learning about science,' the child says, with a toss of her head.

'You can sit and drink your milk.' Mrs Price turns to me, lowers her voice. 'You must leave today.'

'With Imogen so poorly, and you with that cough?' I say. 'I'll stay a day or two longer, I think, to help you, Mrs Price.'

She is about to protest when another bout of coughing takes over. I don't wait for her to recover, but hurry through the hallway and up the stairs to Imogen's sitting room. The door swings open without a sound. She lies asleep, her head tilted back, mouth hanging open. Would Harry love her now? Would he look at that neck, his eyes glittering with insatiable hunger?

I pour some of the foxglove infusion into her flask, then wander to the window and look out on to the grey, empty yard. 'Remember how we stood and watched him from this window,' I say, 'you and I, that day? That cursed day?' The chaise creaks as she stirs. 'How handsome he was. How beautiful.' I see him standing there below, so alive. I turn to face her. 'You promised to help me. Do you remember?'

She groans, rolls her eyes. She thinks it nothing – all gone, forgotten. But oh no.

'He didn't know, did he – Harry? He didn't see my letter.' Price, adjusting the clock in the hallway, pretending not to see me. 'Price gave it to you. You knew of my condition and didn't tell Harry.'

'*Tell* him?' Her voice is shrill. 'Why would I tell him? You think I'd let him waste his life on someone like you?'

'Why? Why did you hate me so?'

She chokes, splutters. 'Why do you think? You stole him, took him from me – you, a mere servant.' Her lip curls. 'Oh, he still came to my bed, all right, when I led him. Men are simple creatures – their bodies react even if they don't wish them to, but it was not *my* name he whispered in the dark, not *my* name he cried out in his dreams.'

He did love me, then. At least there's that. 'You left me trapped there in the dark all those months. How could you?'

She sits up. 'You were fed, weren't you?' She fixes me with her icy stare, as imperious as ever she was. 'You had medical care. Not many employers would be so compassionate. It cost me dear, feeding you, so greedy. Most would have simply sent you to the workhouse.'

That word no longer chills me as it once did, no longer stifles my thoughts with dread. No, a strange calm has descended, settled my racing heart. In its place is something, some suspicion as yet unformed.

'Then why didn't you? Why did you keep me here?'

She stares.

'Why?' I take a step towards her, and another as she blinks furiously. 'You meant to steal my baby, didn't you?'

She's shaking her head. I snatch at her shoulders and stare into her eyes. 'You meant to steal my baby. Why?'

The colour drains from her face, her lips, leaving a deathly pallor. I release her and step back.

'Have you any idea what it's like,' she hisses, 'to try and try for years and then to find that, yes, you have conceived a child? Can you imagine the joy?'

What new trick is this? What new game?

'Can you?' Hatred twists her features, making her ugly. Her lip twitches as she speaks, so that the words tumble over each other. 'Only for that short-lived joy to die in bloodied sheets?' A sob catches in her throat. 'And then to find out that *you*, some common slut, had what should have been mine?'

Her eyes widen. She shuts her mouth, but too late. Far too late.

All is still, silent, save for the crackling of the fire, the tick tock of the clock.

'You stole my baby.' My child lives, my little one, my Violet. My knees tremble. Perhaps I make a sound, because her voice softens, quietens.

'You're utterly unfit to be a mother. You must see that.'

A sweet voice drifts from the hallway, drawing closer. My child, my lost baby. How did I not know? Ah, but perhaps I did. My heart knew from first sight of her.

Imogen sits up, straightens her back. 'Do not tell her.'

I turn to the door. I'm all of a tremble. She's not dead, my baby, my grey, slithering eel, but is grown and beautiful, and so, so alive.

'Tell her, then,' Imogen hisses. 'You think she'll believe a madwoman she barely knows over the mother she's known all her life?'

She's right, of course. She won't believe me at first, but in time . . .

'You would destroy her happiness?' Imogen says.

Can I? Can I tell her the truth? I don't have time to decide because the child bursts through the door, hair windswept, rosy-cheeked, coat buttons awry, Mrs Price following on, out of breath.

'There's a hedgehog,' says the child, *my* child, pointing at the window, 'outside.'

'You're not to go out in the dark,' Imogen says.

'I'm not scared of the dark.' She tosses her head. 'I'm not a baby.'

'You were,' I say, 'not so long ago – such a small, beautiful baby.' Oh, I must turn away, look at the ceiling, swallow. 'I think the name Violet would suit you better than Cordelia.' I say it with a smile, but my heart is thumping wildly. 'What do you think?'

She nods. 'It's a pretty name.' She twirls, arms outstretched. 'Violet, Cordelia, Violet.'

'You'll make yourself sick,' Imogen says.

'Cordelia, Violet, Cordelia . . .'

'She has your madness,' Imogen says, under her breath.

How joyful she is, how innocent. I can't do it, can't shatter her world. She stops, swoons this way and that, laughing. 'I'm Violet,' she says, breathlessly, 'just Violet.'

'It's bedtime,' Imogen snaps. 'Take her away, Mrs Price. You know she wearies me.'

The child's laughter dies. 'Sorry, Mama.'

I want to shout out, don't call *her* Mama. I'm your mama – me. They stole you from me. They told me you were dead. The words choke me, pushing to burst out of my mouth.

Mrs Price takes her hand and steers her from the room, and I must let her go, for now.

'Goodnight, Violet,' I say.

She looks over her shoulder and smiles. 'Goodnight.'

As soon as the house is quiet that night, I go to Harry. The ground is still wet from the rain, but I sit anyway, beside his grave.

'Our child lives,' I say. 'Our precious little girl lives.' My breath is all but gone. I can't stop these tears.

How I love her. My heart clamours in my chest for love of her. Our baby who was dead is alive, and wonderful, and glorious, and I can't lose her again. No, they will not take her from me, not again, not ever.

CHAPTER 39

Day by day, Mrs Price's condition worsens. Her coughing spasms exhaust her, leaving her flushed and sweating. Dark shadows surround her eyes, while the eyes themselves seem to be aflame.

Every day, there's another letter – not on the tray, but hidden close by, in one place or another. Every day, I find them and tear them into pieces.

'The tapestries must go,' I tell Imogen. 'The mildew is bad for Mrs Price's chest. Nor is it good for the child.'

I live in dread of my precious girl catching the sickness. Her slightest cough makes me tremble.

Imogen is in no state to argue. She can barely open her eyes. Oh, blessed foxglove, you serve me well.

I stand on a ladder and pull. The corner of the first tapestry comes away from the wall, revealing blotches of mould and green-black slime. Another pull and it tears, sending clouds of mouldy dust into the air. I close my eyes and hold my breath for as long as I'm able, but even then, the dust chokes me and makes my eyes itch. I clatter down the ladder, run to the front door and open it. I stick my head outside and breathe, once, twice.

'What are you doing?' Her little face peeps from the morning-room door.

'Go inside and shut the door.' I say it too sharply, so that her mouth turns down and she disappears.

Later, once all the tapestries are gone, and the dust swept away, I go to the library and find *Great Expectations*. The child is still in the morning room, drawing in condensation on the window with her finger.

'Shall I read you a story?' I say.

She's wary now, but nods, and once she's sitting on my lap, she settles.

'You mustn't go near Mrs Price when she coughs,' I say.

'Why not?'

'Because it could make you ill, too.'

'But it makes me sad.' Her sweet mouth turns down.

'I know.' I hold her to me, kiss the top of her head. 'I know, my love.'

I open the book. 'My father's family name being Pirrip . . .'

I read until she sleeps, and then I cry. I cry because I've found her, my Violet. I cry until my shuddering breaths wake her.

'What's the matter?' she says.

'I thought I'd lost everything.'

'But you're home now.' She wraps her arms around me and squeezes me so tightly, it makes me laugh.

I wipe my tears away, and think how she's the only person, the only one in the whole world, that I can trust.

The herbals recommend various remedies for Mrs Price's cough – borage and rosemary and cabbage – but so far nothing has helped.

To hear her struggling to breathe distresses Violet and makes her lovely eyes brim with tears.

'Let's go outside,' I say. 'There is much to do out there, and I fancy you may make a good gardener.'

She smiles. 'But I'm only little.'

'You're the perfect size to be a gardener's assistant.'

She runs to the back door, Mrs Price and her cough forgotten for the moment.

The old vegetable garden is overgrown with weeds now that Price isn't there to tend it. The child chatters and sings as we pull up the worst of them. I teach her 'Daisy Bell', and we both sing it as we work. I can't remember being so happy. If ever I was, it was long ago, and forgotten.

The next dry day we dig over the black earth, then search the outbuildings for seeds. We find battered paper envelopes, the writing on them faded to nothing. We sow them anyway. 'It's an adventure,' I say. 'Each plant will be a surprise.'

She sprinkles seeds here and there, frowning in concentration. How beautiful she is, her cheeks touched by the sun. How like her father. How Harry would have loved her.

'In springtime, we'll grow violets,' I say. 'Sweet violets, and dog violets, and heartsease. They're the best of flowers – the most beautiful flowers in all creation.' She's not listening, but runs hither and thither, sprinkling seeds at random. We'll never know the weeds from the good plants but no matter. It makes her happy, and me with her.

The following day, it rains. Relentless drizzle. Violet stands by the window, staring at the sodden earth.

'The plants need a drink,' I tell her. 'They'll grow all the better for it.'

She nods, looks back at the window and sighs.

'Shall we read more of our story?'

She sits on my lap, and I open *Great Expectations*. 'Has your mama taught you to read?'

She shakes her head. 'She says I give her a headache.'

'Does she now?' She stole my child, then tired of her? 'Well, no matter,' I say. 'I'll teach you, and one day, you'll be able to read this yourself.'

She lays her head on my chest. 'Not now.'

'No.' I stroke her head. 'Not now, but one day. I'll teach you all manner of things, show you great wonders, as your grandfather did me.'

Her head is heavy with tiredness. I have barely started reading when she falls asleep.

One day I will tell her the truth about her birth. I will tell her of Harry, how beautiful he was, how fragile, and how I loved him, but not yet. Not until she is ready. I kiss her soft hair. 'I love you,' I whisper. 'I love you more than my life.'

How the garden is transformed. It's only two weeks since the first weed was pulled, the first seeds sown, and already green shoots push through the earth in a higgledy-piggledy pattern. Violet is as wild as her father, a being of the woods and fields, forever muddy and holding some small creature in her hand to show me – a shiny beetle, a spider or caterpillar, and once a slow-worm. She's a child of nature, but not of the marsh. No, never the marsh, please God. Not with Price waiting, his white fingers flexing, ready to catch her ankle, to drag her under.

Summer comes early. It's unseasonably warm for May. One still, sultry day follows another and never a breath of wind or drop of rain. Every day, the child waters the young plants with her watering can, singing 'Daisy Bell' as she goes, oblivious to the oppressive atmosphere.

The marsh simmers. The stench of rotting leaves and wood, of decomposing flesh, suffuses the air. The foul miasma cloaks everything. It's inescapable. It catches at the back of my throat.

Inside the house is little better; it seeps in here, too, between the windows and the walls, under the doors.

Slipping foxglove into Imogen's flask has worked well so far, but she is slow to drink it now. She becomes quite hysterical at times. However, my time in the asylum was not wasted. I have learned well the efficacy of applied pressure to the hinge of the jaw. Its effect is quite miraculous.

How drowsy she is today. She can barely open her eyes when I come in. I pull the curtains open. Brilliant sunlight streams in.

She groans.

'Come now,' I say. 'It's time for your medicine.' I sit her up, cradle her head in the crook of my arm, and tip the syrupy elixir into her greedy mouth. She would drink it all, but I take it away. 'Too much will harm you,' I say.

She nods, as gentle as a lamb.

Poor Mrs Price. Her ample frame shrinks by the day. Grey skin circles her sunken eyes. She had no part in their scheming, had no more power than I did, after all. I try new medicines – mugwort, sundew, rue – and yet she gets worse rather than better. Marshmallow tea with valerian calms the coughing spasms and helps her sleep.

Light hurts her eyes, so that she can't bear the daylight. She keeps to her room, the curtains drawn. She lives in darkness, as I have lived in darkness.

I sit beside her and feed her beef tea. As I stand, she catches my arm.

'You're good to the child,' she says, 'and to me.'

'I've no quarrel with you, Mrs Price. You're not responsible for the actions of your husband, or for those of your mistress.'

She grips my hand, squeezes it. 'Harry did write to you, many letters.'

'He wrote to me?'

She nods. 'Mistress told him you were to wed another.'

'And he believed it?

'No, not at first. He come back to look for you, and when he found you gone . . .' Her eyes fill with tears. 'They found him in the marsh.'

I step back. She's wrong. She must be. 'Harry knew that marsh, knew it well.'

She nods, her lip quivering.

'Imogen said he died of a pestilence.'

Mrs Price shakes her head. I see the truth in her eyes and turn away.

Harry. Poor, broken Harry. I look to the sky, but there is no comfort to be found there, not with those menacing purple clouds tinged with sulphurous yellow. I should have guessed when I saw the grave. That dismal grave, with no stone, no angel, no mark. Unconsecrated.

Harry, both killed and damned by Imogen's lies.

CHAPTER 40

I wander to the marsh naming each plant I see until I find what I'm looking for. Tall spikes of sinister purple blooms stand brooding beside the stream. Dusky monkshood, cowled hoods like lowered eyelids hiding malign intent. I slip my gloves on and cut three flower spikes.

Once the house is asleep that night, I tiptoe to the kitchen and arrange them in a vase. They are beautiful in a toxic way, just like Imogen. It's fitting that they should find their home so close to her bed. Oh, Imogen, your sins have found you out. There are many ways to die, and not all of them as merciful as foxglove.

The weather is beautiful today – warm but not hot, with a gentle, soothing breeze. It persists day after day. After break-fast, I've taken to sitting in the garden. In the warm sunshine it's quite heavenly. I should write to Diamond and tell him how well I am, how my life has been transformed. How pleased he would be.

Mrs Price shows some improvement. She is able to bear the daylight now and will take a little food. I begin to hope she may recover and am glad for the child's sake. The lawn is a blaze of colour now, vibrant with dandelions and daisies and red clover, full of joy, just like my Violet.

Here she comes now, with something in her hand – a drawing, perhaps.

'What's that you have, my love?' I say.

She holds it out to me. 'A letter.'

I take it. 'To me?'

'No.'

There's been no post, surely. I'd have heard his cart on the road from here, heard his cheerful whistle.

'Then . . ?' I turn the envelope over in my hand. It's addressed to Womack at the asylum. The sight of his name chills my blood. She would use my child, then, to get rid of me. I place it on my knee to hide my shaking hands.

Violet skips around in a circle. 'Mama wants me to give it to the postman, but I don't know when he's coming.'

'Of course you don't.' I force a smile.

'She said I could have a cake if I did.'

'Did she now?' I keep my tone light. 'That's very kind.' I pretend to think for a moment, then catch her eye. 'What if *I* give it to him, and we keep it our secret? That way you still get the cake.'

'Yes.' She jumps up and down, clapping her hands.

'Your mama took a letter of mine a long time ago,' I say. 'The least I can do is return the favour.'

The letter stays in my pocket until after supper, and after I've dosed both Imogen and Mrs Price with their medication.

Both are quiet and biddable, and so much easier to care for these days. They are silent, too, for the most part.

I sit on my bed, unseal the envelope and smooth the letter out on my knees. Imogen's writing is shaky and almost illegible in places, the address veering downwards.

'Dearest Charles,' it begins.

So, Womack's name is Charles, then. It's hard to imagine him having a Christian name, hard to believe he was once a child, with parents who loved him – at least initially, until he grew into a monster. I turn back to the letter.

Please, my love, come quickly. That girl Maud has escaped the asylum and is at this very moment living here as if she has every right.

Do not fear for the child as she is happy and well cared for, but both myself and my housekeeper grow increasingly weak with every passing day. I fear this madwoman means to kill us.

Please do come and take her away. Whatever you may have heard about myself and Harry, you must know it is not true. Would you truly believe the word of a lunatic over that of your lifelong sweetheart? My heart belongs only to you, my love, as it ever has. You must know it.

Do not let the ravings of a madwoman stand between us, I beg you.

Your true love,

Imogen

I tear the letter twice and throw it on the fire. Yellow flames lick at the paper. It curls, grows dark, until nothing but grey ash is left.

'For thou hast trusted in thy wickedness,' I whisper. 'Thou hast said, none seeth me, but the day of thy watchmen cometh.' My mouth stretches in a broad smile. 'The day of thy watchmen is here.'

Acknowledgements

This book would never have seen the light of day without my brilliant (and very patient) agent, Victoria Hobbs, and my fantastic editor, the wonderful Rosa Schierenberg. Thank you both so much for all your hard work, encouragement, insight and support. Thanks to all at A M Heath and to the team at Welbeck, especially Alexandra Allden, the cover designer, whose fabulous artwork made my hair stand on end.

Particular thanks to Diane Paul at Glanrhyd Hospital for being such an informative guide, taking me on a tour of the old Angelton Asylum building and giving me some real insight into how patients would have lived. Also to staff at the Glamorgan Archives in Cardiff, who went out of their way to help me in my research, for which I am hugely grateful.

Thank you to Georgie, Ally, Grace, Debs and Gail for reading and giving feedback on multiple versions of this story. I don't know what I'd do without you. Thanks to my writer friends for being there with advice, support and general wonderfulness, particularly Kevin Thorne, Kerry Fisher, Fiona Mitchell, Louise Jensen, Jane Isaac, Ian Patrick, Debra Brown, Tina De'ath, Lucille Grant, Ruby Speechley, Maddie

Please, Jane Ayres, Kirsten Hesketh, Susanna Bavin, Christina Banach and Amanda Reynolds.

Thank you to Chris, Joe, Steve, and my whole extended family for being so loving and supportive. Finally, thank you to my parents for encouraging my interests, no matter how bizarre they must have seemed, and for giving me the confidence to always be myself.

Author Bio

Karen Coles was born in Taplow, Berkshire to rather nomadic parents. Countryside walks with her father instilled in her a lifelong love of nature, particularly wild plants, insects and amphibians.

Karen studied Fine Art and Aesthetics at Cardiff and is a painter and sculptor. As a child she was a voracious reader of fairy tales, myths and legends, and this led to a fascination with dark, Gothic literature.

She now lives in Wales, not far from a town that once had three Victorian asylums. Their history inspired the writing of her first novel, *The Asylum*.